To thea one a
Any!
xoxo
CC

THE SKYLIGHT
ROOM

CHARLIE CARILLO

Charlie Carillo

This book is dedicated to my parents, with special thanks to Catherine Allen and the real Clare Owen.

CHAPTER ONE

She's a onetime super model, the kind whose face graces billboards and magazine covers for two or three years before her time runs out, as it must for everyone who rides on their looks.

But she has more than just looks. She has vision. She doesn't sit back and enjoy the money she's made, enough for ten everyday people to live comfortably upon. She takes what would have been fleeting fame and pushes it to the next level, making herself a brand name.

And it works. Fragrances, a clothing line, Facebook and Instagram accounts with countless friends and followers who are really more like disciples...it all clicks, and to top it off she marries a star baseball player for the New York Yankees in a ceremony at St. Patrick's Cathedral, presided over by the Cardinal himself.

Not bad for a kid from a tiny town in Germany that nobody ever heard of, and you can just keep your green card jokes to yourself - this girl was already an American citizen, courtesy of her first marriage to a man who suddenly lost interest in his wife, as well as everyone else from the opposite sex.

That was back in Los Angeles, a city she's grown to hate. Life is so much more *real* in New York, a city she loves, and who wouldn't, with a Central Park West penthouse that turns the park into your own back yard?

But she wants more. She's sick of apartment living, elevators and doormen and annoying co-op board meetings with those endless rules and regulations. She wants a house in Greenwich Village, her *own* house, where you call your own shots.

Mostly, she needs it for the reality show she's dreamed up - "Beauty and the Ballplayer," and their two adorable children. The co-op board on Central Park West is forbidding such a show, for all the trouble it would cause their neighbors.

So the search for a house is on. Her assistants do the legwork, taking her to one house after another, but she's not happy with what she sees. Too dark, too narrow, too close to Seventh Avenue traffic...the ass-kissing realtors are startled by the way she abruptly walks out of a house tour, the moment she sees a detail she hates.

She's that way, like a spoiled child, a creature of impulses. And there's always someone to attend to those impulses.

The Village prices are the highest on Manhattan island, even higher than she expected. When she *does* make a bid, it's always well below the asking price - six million dollars lower, in the case of a brownstone on Charles Street with a $12 million price tag.

The real estate agent actually laughs out loud. "That's *half* the asking price!" he says. "I can't go back to the seller with that offer!"

Without looking back she reaches back for her bottle of spring water, which her assistant nestles into her hand. She takes a sip and passes the bottle back without breaking her gaze at the realtor.

"Why not?"

"It's ridiculous. Insulting, really."

She's not used to this. People, including her husbands, past and present, know it's never a good idea to contradict her, or - even worse - laugh at her. She didn't get where she is by hearing "no," except from her dietician - no sugars, no carbs, no desserts, if she wants to maintain the figure that made her rich and famous.

So she's always feeling hungry, which does nothing to improve her temperament, especially now that she's crowding forty.

She takes a step toward the realtor. She's half a head taller than him, so she's gazing down like an avenging angel as she says, "Tell the seller the offer is coming from Hannah Schmitt."

She speaks her own name as if it's somebody else's, as if its announcement should be followed by a rumble of thunder. Again, the realtor laughs.

"You think he'll part with six mill just to sell to a former super model? Never happen, my dear. I'm sorry, but *nobody's* name is worth six million."

Her eyes narrow to cobalt-blue slits. That word "former" has not gone down well.

"You won't present my offer?"

"Again, I'm sorry. No."

She breezes out of the house, her assistant running to catch up with her, and by five o'clock that afternoon the realtor has been fired.

So her search goes on in the Village, pushing westward toward the river, the onetime badlands for S&M sex clubs. But times have changed. The clubs are gone, and giant glass high-rises for the rich have sprung up along the West Side Highway. Floor to ceiling river views, but that's not what she wants.

She wants a *house*, a place with *history!* Why is it so hard to find the right house?

And suddenly there it is, a block from the river on a crooked cobblestone street. It's like the doll house she wanted but never got as a child - a red brick four-story house, fronted by a sagging New York City stoop and a robust ailanthus tree. It looks as if it's made of candy, and what delights her most is that it's topped off with a multi-paned skylight, its copper framework gone green with the years.

It's love at first sight. She wants it even before she has a chance to look inside. It's been a rooming house for as long as anyone can remember - one tenant to a floor, hotplates instead of ovens. The asking price is millions less than the other houses she's seen, but there are reasons for that.

It needs a ton of work - the mortar between the bricks is crumbling to dust, the boiler is wheezy and feeble, the floorboards are loose, the wiring is ancient...in short, it's what contractors call a "tote-reno," short for total renovation.

Then there's the matter of its residents, five senior citizens who've been there forever. They'll have to be paid off to leave, and that's always a tricky business, but Hannah is prepared to be generous. When you're rich and you really want something, you get it.

So she gets the seller to knock half a million off the price, completes the purchase and starts haggling with the tenants. It takes months, but four of them go for the buyout and leave town for gentler places to live out the time they've got left - upstate New York, Florida, the Carolinas.

The fifth tenant, the one in the skylight room, is another story.

CHAPTER TWO

She's the type of woman you spot now and then if you live in Greenwich Village, old and bone-thin, with a slight hunch to the shoulders that comes with the burden of all those years. She's got a face like an old wallet, wrinkled as a walnut, but her bright green eyes are ageless and her stride is surprisingly brisk as she ducks into the corner grocery shop for an onion, or a head of cabbage - never more than one or two items, always fruits or vegetables, nothing that involves more than a few coins in the exchange, and they go into a small knapsack she slings over her shoulder like a hunter's game bag.

She lives alone. That's obvious from her shopping habits, and as you watch her leave the store you wonder if the battered Nikes on her feet were new when she got them, or something she found on top of a trash can lid outside the home of a runner who'd grown tired of them and left them for someone less fortunate to find.

A widow? Probably not. You've seen those old widows trudging down Bleecker Street, Italian women all in black, wide-hipped from rampant childbirth as they drag their shopping carts behind them, laden with cans of crushed tomatoes and boxes of pasta to cook for their children and grandchildren.

This woman doesn't fit that bill. She never looks tired, her hips are narrow and she just keeps going, unlike the Italian widows slowing down and dying off one by one, waked and mourned by loved ones at the Nucciarone Funeral Parlor on Bleecker as their jubilant landlords slap a coat of paint on those apartment walls, liberated at last from the stranglehold of rent control.

You don't see her for a while - a month, two months - and you figure that's it, the green-eyed old lady is gone, too, but then comes springtime and she pops up like a crocus, making her way down Bleecker, knapsack on her back. Same bright eyes, same strong stride, same battered Nikes...What does she do all winter? Hibernate? Burrow into a hole in Washington Square Park and emerge when the last of the snow melts?

She seems indestructible. You'd gladly switch life spans with her, even though she's got to be well past eighty. There's something funny about her, beyond the obvious stuff, and at last you realize what it is:

She's always on the move. She never wanders, never dawdles, never stops for small talk, as so many elderly people do. This is the kind of person who makes every day count.

But how? Where's she off to in such a hurry? What's she got going that's so important?

Or is she just half-crazy, the way anyone would be after so many years on her own in New York City?

You'd love to stop her and have a chat, but you suspect she'd ignore you and keep going. Which is probably what would happen. She will remain a mystery to you and everyone else, until the day that Clare Owen, age eighty-nine, does something that puts her in a spotlight she never craved.

She turns down an offer from Hannah Schmitt, refusing to leave the skylight room, or even allow Hannah inside for a peek.

CHAPTER THREE

Tom Becker is a longtime tabloid newspaper reporter who lives by an unspoken credo:

Avoid the general public, at all costs.

In his youth he'd been the ultimate street reporter, a boots-by-the-bedside gunner eager to race off anywhere, any time for a breaking news story.

But it doesn't last. He gains weight, he slows down, and people are so goddam *predictable!* The things they say, the things they do! When the chance comes for a spot on the rewrite bank, he jumps at it.

For years it seems a perfect fit, because Becker can knock out a breaking news story faster than anybody, and he never has to leave his chair. Take the information on the phone from street reporters, mix it with whatever the wires are saying and make it *sing!*

His prose is clean and lively, and if it sometimes seems as if he's taking the First Amendment out for a little joy ride, well, that's what a tabloid is all about, isn't it? Pushing it as far as you can.

Then trouble sets in. Second-source phone calls he can't be bothered to make, blind quotes that seem too good to be true. One day it blows up in his face when he invents not only a quote, but a name to go with it, and that's a problem when the person you've invented happens to be a real person who never said that inflammatory thing that's been attributed to him.

So Becker - lucky to still have a job! - is banished by that reckless coincidence to Page Six, with the idea that a lively imagination can't do too much damage on the gossip page. At sixty-two, never married, no kids, he seems to have reached his final stop on the tabloid express train, fielding phone calls from flacks trying to get free publicity for their clients.

He is depressed. His career is in a deep rut, from which there seems to be no escape.

Until he gets a phone call from Josephine Rodriguez.

For two years, Josephine has kept Hannah Schmitt's penthouse spotlessly clean - scrubbing, vacuuming, polishing. Never a sick day, no task ever shirked.

Then one day Henry's World Series ring goes missing. Henry is reluctant to accuse Josephine, but Hannah is not. She waits for Henry to leave the house before confronting Josephine while she's cleaning the bathtub with a sponge.

"Please stop scrubbing, Josephine."

Puzzled, the cleaning lady obeys, rising with a groan from her knees.

Hannah puts her hands on her hips, which are not quite as narrow as they once were. "Henry's ring is missing."

Josephine is breathing hard. Not because she's guilty, but because she's never gotten this look from Hannah before. It's the kind of look that makes you feel as if you're about to be swallowed whole.

"I don't know nothin' about that," Josephine says, so softly that she can barely hear her own words.

Hannah spreads her hands. "You're the only one with access to our bedroom."

"I didn't touch it."

"Are you sure?"

"Of course I'm sure."

Hannah forces a tight little smile. "The thing is, you can't sell it."

"That's right. Because I ain't *got* it."

"If you try to sell Henry Rivers' World Series ring on E-bay, you'll get caught. Simple as that."

"Don't tell *me*, Mizz Schmitt. Tell whoever took it."

"I believe that's what I'm doing right now."

There it is - a flat-out accusation. Josephine has been called a thief. She struggles to stay calm.

"This ain't right, Mizz Schmitt."

"All right, then, let's do it this way." She clasps her hands together, to indicate unity. "Bring the ring back tomorrow, and put it on the bureau next to the lamp, where Henry leaves it."

Hannah points to the exact spot where the ring always is when it's not on Henry's hand. "Okay? Do that, and we'll all carry on like nothing happened."

Josephine squeezes the sponge, dripping suds on the floor. "I can't do that."

"Did you sell it already?"

"I can't do it 'cause I didn't *take* it! I swear on my life!"

"Oh, come *on,* Josephine! The ring is gone! I don't have it, Henry doesn't have it. The only person who could possibly - "

"If you're gonna fire my ass, bitch, just *do* it."

Hannah gasps. Josephine's gaze is level, steady and unafraid. Hannah points to the door with a shaky hand.

"You're fired, effective immediately."

"Fine." Josephine hurls the soapy sponge at Hannah's chest. "And you *still* ain't gettin' that fuckin' ring back, 'cause I didn't take it."

Josephine leaves. Hannah moves to the bed and sits down, trembling. She's having trouble believing that someone who was making just twelve dollars an hour, a *servant,* can upset her so badly.

When she gets home to Brooklyn Josephine phones Page Six. Becker answers and is immediately put off by the Hispanic accent, until she says, "Got somethin' to tell you 'bout Hannah Schmitt."

Becker sets down his half-eaten Big Mac and sits up straight.

"The super model?"

"Huh. Used to be, yeah."

"I'm listening."

"She's tryin' to kick an old lady outta this building she just bought."

"What old lady?"

"I don't know. Some old lady, been livin' in this building down the Village. Hannah paid off all the other tenants, but the old lady won't go. Been there forever."

"How do you know all this?"

"I was Hannah's cleanin' lady."

"Was?"

"She fired my ass."

"Why would she do that?"

"No reason. Look, that's what I wanted to tell you, that's all I know. Do your job, check it out, I gotta go."

"Whoa, *whoa,* I don't even know your name!" Becker says, but he's talking to a dead line.

He hangs up the phone, picks up his Big Mac. If he's going to pursue this thing, it's going to take some digging, and his shovel has gone rusty. He could just let it die, and hope the cleaning lady doesn't call the rival papers.

But then again, it may be a way out of his rut. Hannah Schmitt has always had a rep as a bitch, and bitches are what gossip is all about. Plus, she's married to baseball legend Henry Rivers, so it's a two-for-one deal. Maybe a page lead. Maybe more than that.

Maybe his ticket back to the rewrite bank.

He gulps down the rest of the Big Mac in two bites and starts typing. This story calls for a "teaser," to get things rolling. Becker is excited. For the first time in a long while, he's really excited about something.

CHAPTER FOUR

Hannah Schmitt is livid. It's in the lower left corner of Page Six, under the headline **FAR FROM MODEL BEHAVIOR:**

What onetime super model is having trouble evicting a longtime tenant from a vintage $6 million house she's bought in Greenwich Village? The way we hear it, all the residents accepted payouts to leave - except for a woman who occupies the skylight room. "The old lady won't go," says a source close to this story. "She's been there forever." Stay tuned.

She shakes the newspaper at her husband's head.

"How could this happen, Henry?"

"You're asking *me?*"

"It's got to have come from Josephine."

"You don't know that for sure."

"I fired her for stealing your ring. Reason enough, don't you think?"

Henry sighs. "At least they didn't name you."

"Everybody will know it's me."

Maybe not, Henry wants to say, but he doesn't dare. Hannah seems to be the only person in the world who doesn't realize she's not as famous as she used to be.

And neither is he. But at least he knows it.

"It'll blow over," he says, rising to kiss her cheek. "Try to relax."

She tolerates the kiss. "If 'Beauty and the Ballplayer' is going to happen, we need everything to go smoothly, Henry."

He hates the reality show idea, hoping it will die a natural death, but he's willing to play along, even though the last thing he needs right now is to be followed around by a camera crew.

"I'm off," he says, kissing his wife on the forehead and heading for the elevator. "Fuck Page Six, honey, nobody takes it seriously."

Once inside the elevator he digs into his jacket pocket for his World Series ring. He'd been lucky to recover it from the Warwick Hotel, thanks to an honest cleaning lady who found it tangled in the sheets of the bed where he'd had a noontime romp two days earlier with a female reporter from ESPN. A curious, giggly young woman who wanted to try on the ring, which fell from her skinny finger in the throes of passion.

Henry regrets what he's done, and he's sorry Josephine got canned for no reason, but what's his next move? Hannah will want to know where he found it, and what's he supposed to say? It's the first time he's ever cheated on her, and he feels lousy about it, but Hannah hasn't been there for him lately, obsessed as she is by the reality show.

So Henry decides to stash the ring somewhere, and live with the lie that it was stolen. It won't be the first lie he's lived with.

Henry Rivers was an exciting, stylish, exceedingly quotable man for the sixteen years he played center field for the New York Yankees. At six-feet-four and 225 pounds, he had both power and speed, crowding the plate with a fearlessness that was legendary throughout the American League.

He's also a native New Yorker, born and raised in the projects of the South Bronx by a Puerto Rican mother who scrubbed floors at night and an African-American construction worker who died in a scaffold collapse when Henry was seven.

"Stay strong," the dad used to tell little Henry, and the boy listened.

Hit him with a fastball on the shoulder, and he barely flinches as he tosses his bat aside and trots to first base. And when he swings and connects, the ball leaves the park on an arc that some believe would bring rain.

It's after socking a home run in Boston that measures nearly six hundred feet that Henry speaks words that make everyone sit up and listen.

"I'm a blue-eyed black man," he says. "There's nothing I can't do."

Then he tilts his gaze skyward. "Move over, Joe and Mickey, Henry's got it covered."

He's referring to Joe DiMaggio and Mickey Mantle, his legendary predecessors in center field.

But his post-baseball life is troubled. Despite 563 lifetime home runs, he knows he probably won't be elected to the Baseball Hall of Fame in Cooperstown, as rumors of steroid usage taint the last few years of his career.

And his first wife files for divorce, citing his rampant sex life on the road. He's at loose ends, drinking too much, carousing more than ever.

Then it happens, the thing that will turn his life around.

He sees Hannah Schmitt on the cover of the Sports Illustrated swimsuit issue, and asks his agent to contact her agent for a date.

There is no shame in this process. It's how the rich and famous get to know each other. The agents confer, a date is arranged, and from that night, Henry and Hannah are never apart.

They click. It's electric, it's wild, it's the kind of love story people love to read, watch, and devour.

Five months later they are married at St. Patrick's Cathedral, and then it's on to the Plaza Hotel - five hundred guests, an ocean of Dom Perignon, and an outdoor corral to keep the herd of paparazzi in place. They sell exclusive indoor photo rights to People Magazine for $600,000, which pretty much covers the wedding expenses.

The truly rich rarely pay for anything.

And now they are a "brand," H & H, Hannah and Henry, the little girl from that forgettable village in Germany and the poor boy from the Bronx. Something happens with branding - the sum of their qualities adds up to even more than their individual attributes, and business booms. Scents, clothing, swimwear, even vitamins...people want to be just like H & H, and the products jump off the shelves.

So it all rolls on smoothly for a few years, until their brand starts to lose steam, and that little old lady in the skylight room refuses to budge.

CHAPTER FIVE

The Sunny Time Rest Home overlooks the Bronx River Parkway and, in the distance, Yankee Stadium. Breakfast has just been served - poached eggs, stewed prunes and whole wheat toast - but 94-year-old Carmine Rotolo barely touches his meal. He sits in his wheelchair in the solarium, a blanket over his bony knees, a Yankee cap on his head, the New York Post on his lap. He's been crying all morning, but silently, in a way that has the attendants concerned.

They've never seen him cry before. A longtime widower who landed here after a series of small strokes, Carmine won't tell them what's wrong, and he doesn't want to speak with anyone in his family. The only phone call he makes is to a man he hasn't spoken with in nearly seventy years.

His words are both blunt and brief: *I need to see you.*

An hour later, Jonathan Kaplan shows up at the rest home, astonished by the sight of his old friend in a wheelchair. At 91, Kaplan remains tall, rangy and mobile, with the same mutton chop sideburns he's always worn, now gone snow-white. He hates being here, hates knowing that he's been an incredibly lucky man, health-wise, and that it's only a matter of time before his body betrays him and he winds up in a place like this.

Unless he dies suddenly, which is how he hopes it'll happen.

He can only hope that it doesn't happen today, as he offers his hand to Carmine, who takes it in a surprisingly strong grip.

"My God, Carmine. Trying to break my hand?"

Carmine makes a scoffing noise. "Is that the best you've got, after all these years?"

"Give me time. I'm still shocked that you called."

"I'm shocked that your phone number hasn't changed."

"You know me. I dig in, I stay put."

Carmine muffles a cough with his hand. "You look pretty good for an ancient radical lawyer. How many wives did you wind up with?"

"Three. Three exes."

"Beat me by two."

"I heard about your wife. I'm sorry. Cancer, was it?"

Carmine's eyes fill with tears. He wipes them with the back of his hand, and hesitates before saying, "I never *really* loved her, Jonathan. Not the way you should love a wife. Maybe she knew it. Maybe that's what made her sick, that good, good woman."

Kaplan is astonished. Is this why Carmine called him? A confession to an old friend, before it's too late?

"Come on, Carm," he says. "How can you say that?"

Carmine looks him dead in the eye. "Did you love *your* wives, Jonathan?"

"Of course I did, at the time."

"At the time. Christ! What I mean is, did you *really* love them?"

"Yes."

Carmine's eyes widen. "As much as you loved *her?*"

Kaplan feels his belly tighten. A light sweat breaks out on the back of his neck. "Why do you bring her up?"

"She's the reason we haven't spoken in sixty years!"

"Closer to seventy, but what's that got to do with anything?"

"Have you seen today's Post?"

"I don't read that rag, if I can help it."

Carmine slaps the Post into Kaplan's hands. It's turned to Page Six, and Carmine points with a crooked finger.

"Right there. *Read.*"

Kaplan's hands are trembling. "Oh my God."

"How about that?"

"Think it's her?"

"Who else could it be? In a skylight room?"

"She's *alive!*"

"Yeah, and she's right where we left her."

"I was sure she was dead."

"You and everybody else in the Village."

Now they're both crying. Carmine takes a Kleenex from a package in his pocket and passes it to Kaplan.

"You gotta help her, Jonathan."

"Of course I will."

"Make it one o' your damn crusades."

"Whatever it takes."

Carmine wipes his eyes, looks into the distance and sighs. "I can still see her. The way she looked the first time she came into Reggio's, right off the fuckin' bus."

CHAPTER SIX

A crisp afternoon in October of 1950, the kind of day that makes Carmine Rotolo think about bringing the outdoor tables inside at Caffe Reggio's on MacDougal Street.

But he's reluctant to do that. Maybe one more week. It's so nice to have people outside, especially when they're all smoking. Bearded musicians, somber women and tortured poets, puffing away. Village folk, the scruffy and unshaven, bonding over their espressos and their Lucky Strikes.

It reminds him of Paris. He'd helped liberate Paris at the end World War II, and one of his favorite things about his brief time in the City of Light was all those outdoor cafes, and all those pretty girls sitting at them, happy that the war was over.

And here comes a pretty girl right now, in blue jeans and a denim jacket. Not a downtown girl, that's for sure - she's too chubby-cheeked, too well-fed for that. An out-of-towner? Must be. These days, they're pouring into the Village from all over.

She's got a canvas sack slung over her shoulder, and she stops and stands in front of Reggio's with a look of awe on her face, as if she can't believe she's here. Like Dorothy in "The Wizard Of Oz," when the tornado whisks her from her dreary black-and-white existence and drops her into a world of color.

Carmine stares into the biggest, greenest eyes he's ever seen. He knows he's being rude, but he can't help it. He feels as if he could fall into those eyes and drown.

"Hello," the girl says, shattering his stare.

Carmine clears his throat. "Inside or out?" he asks.

"I'm sorry?"

"Would you like to sit inside, or out?"

The girl seems to think its a trick question. "I don't know."

"You don't *know?*"

She tosses her head with a natural nobility, like a race horse in the winner's circle. "Look," she says, "can I have a job?"

She says it plainly, abruptly, as if Carmine has been wasting her time. He can't help chuckling. "You want to work here?"

"Yes."

"Why?"

"I read about it in a magazine. It seems like a cool place."

15

Carmine studies her, head to toe. Shoulder-length hair the color of honey, a flawless complexion and those eyes, those *eyes!* She could be a runaway, or a young wife on the lam from an abusive husband. He's seen that type before, but there's a strange sense of calm to this girl, as if she expects everything to work out, for no good reason.

He points at the canvas sack. "What've you got there?"

"My stuff. I just got here."

"Where are you staying?"

"Nowhere, yet."

Carmine is stunned. "You just got to New York, and you don't have a place to stay?"

"Figured I'd take care of a job first."

How can she be so relaxed, with no job, and no place to stay?

"Where are you from?"

She scowls at the question. "Does it matter? What matters is, I'm here now."

"But *why* are you here?"

She cannot tell him. It would be embarrassing to say it's because she saw a movie called "Portrait of Jenny" when it came out two years ago, and it changed her life. She saw Joseph Cotten and Jennifer Jones falling in love in New York City, and the beautiful skylight studio in Greenwich Village where Cotten painted her portrait, and she thought: *I want to be there.*

But he'd probably laugh at her, so instead she smiles and spreads her arms, to indicate the perfectly obvious.

"This is where everything's happening, isn't it?"

Carmine can't deny that. He's a Brooklyn boy, a mere borough away, but even he knows that the Village is a whole other world. Whenever he climbs the subway steps at West Fourth Street he feels the electricity of the neighborhood, like something that rises right up through the sidewalk and through the soles of your shoes.

It's all happening here. This girl has just gotten here, but she knows it, too.

Carmine can't hide a smile as he asks, "How old are you?"

"Twenty."

"Let's try it again. How old are you?"

She rolls those remarkable green eyes. "Nineteen, next month."

"Ever worked in a cafe?"

She shrugs. "Do diners count?"

"Depends. What was the coffee like in the diners?"

"Awful."

"The coffee here is good. In fact, it's great. So are the pastries. We take real pride in our products."

The girl giggles. Carmine feels himself blush.

"What's so funny?"

"Are you the owner?"

"Manager."

"You talk like an owner."

"It's my uncle's place."

"Well, am I hired, or not?"

"What happens if I don't give you a job?"

"I'll ask someplace else. This is my first choice, though. I wanted to start with my first choice."

It's a crazy situation. Carmine has all the waitresses he needs, and he knows nothing about this girl. But her confidence borders on arrogance, and he's gripped by a sudden fear, a crazy one - the fear that if he *doesn't* hire her, he might never see her again. He cannot let that happen.

"Okay," he says, "you start tomorrow morning. Nine o'clock."

Her eyes gleam. "What do I wear?"

"What you've got on is fine. Casual, but clean."

"Got it."

She turns to leave.

"Whoa, *whoa*. Where are you going?"

"Have to find a place to stay."

"Sit tight."

Carmine beckons for a dark-haired, smoky-eyed waitress to come over. "This is Marie," he says. "Marie, say hello to....what's your name, honey?"

"Clare."

"Clare. She's our new waitress."

Marie's eyes narrow. "Since when?"

"Since five minutes ago. Marie just lost her room mate, didn't you, Marie?"

Marie nods. "Skipped out in the middle o' the night. Still owes me for September."

"Clare needs a place. She's good people. What do you think?"

"I think it's amazing you think she's good people, when you didn't even know her name."

Carmine laughs. "Come on. You know my instincts never let

17

me down."

Marie folds her arms, giving Clare a head-to-foot once-over. "You got fifteen bucks for the first month?"

Clare pays up. Marie tucks the money into her pocket. "Okay, roomie," she says. "I'm off in an hour, I'll take you home then."

"Perfect," Carmine says, guiding Clare inside. "Meanwhile, let's get some food into this girl. Not bad, huh? A job *and* a home, all in ten minutes? Is this a great city, or what?"

Clare can't even speak. She's so happy she's afraid the whole thing is going to burst like a soap bubble. This is exactly how she dreamed it would be, if she ever made it to Greenwich Village.

And then she does something Carmine will never forget, something he thinks about when he awakens each day at the Sunny Time Rest Home.

She drops her canvas sack, wraps her arms around him and kisses him. Not a thanks-for-helping-me-out kiss. The real deal, a hot-breathed tongue-tangler.

A promise of things to come.

CHAPTER SEVEN

It's been years since Jonathan Kaplan has ventured this far west in the Village. He's astonished by the giant glass boxes that have sprung up on the riverfront, and the thick shadows they throw. Midtown shadows, the type that aren't supposed to happen in Greenwich Village.

Who let these monstrosities go up, right in my own neighborhood? Why wasn't anyone there to stop this?

Oh, how you had to watch those real estate rascals! Once they find a loophole in the zoning laws, it's all over. They tear into it like hyenas, and the new buildings spring up like mushrooms after the rain. In years gone by Kaplan would have been on the front lines to keep it from happening, bullhorn and subpoenas in hand.

But it's harder to fight as you get older. It's harder to do everything. This five-block walk from his house on Charles Street is taking a toll on his knees, and his heart pounds as he reaches that red brick house on the cobblestone street.

It has the look of an abandoned building, ready for the wrecking ball. The windows and sills are filthy, filmed in dust from nearby construction projects. He climbs the stoop to find there are no doorbells. He hadn't expected to find any. There were none the last time he was here, nearly seventy years ago.

There's no lock on the front door, either. He takes a deep breath, goes inside and begins the climb to the skylight room.

It's not easy. The carpeting on the steps is shot to hell, filthy on the sides, worn down to fiber in the middle. No windows in the stairwell, so he's climbing by the feeble light provided by circular fluorescent bulbs in the ceilings known as landlord halos. Some of them are flickering. They make a faint buzzing sound.

The climb is making him dizzy. How can Clare do this, day after day, at her age? At last he gets to the top door. He stops to catch his breath, squeezes his hands together to stop the trembling.

Then he knocks, for the first time since 1950.

A shuffling sound, then the door opens just wide enough for Kaplan to see the face of an old woman beneath a crown of short, silvery hair.

There is no mistaking those green eyes gazing straight into his.

"Yes?" she demands.

His knees ache, and he can feel his heartbeat in his throat. "Oh my God, Clare, it's really you."

She squints to study his face, and a faint smile tickles her lips. "Jonathan?"

"Uh-huh."

"Well. You're looking pretty good."

Her voice is eerily calm, as if she expected him to show up. Kaplan is breathing hard. He fears he might faint.

"Jesus, Clare, you're still *here!*"

She chuckles. "So are you, it appears."

"I mean *here* here, in the skylight room."

"I'm guessing you saw the item on Page Six."

Kaplan is stunned. "You saw that?"

"Yes, I read the papers."

"You do?"

"Jesus, Jonathan, I'm not a hermit."

"I live five blocks from here. How is it possible I've never seen you on the street?"

"Guess our paths just never crossed."

"How is that *possible?*"

"It's Greenwich Village, Jonathan. Sometimes you bump into someone three days in a row, then not for another ten years."

"Okay, but sixty, *seventy* years? Everybody assumed you were dead, or gone."

"Where would I have gone, Jonathan?"

He shrugs. "Florida, maybe?"

"Thanks, but no thanks. I wouldn't want to go face-down in the early bird special. And while we're on the subject, *you're* still here, too."

"Yeah. Couple of old beatniks, you and me." He wipes his forehead with a handkerchief, still breathing hard from the climb.

Which is what lucky guys called a trip to the skylight room, back in the day. *The climb.*

Jonathan can't help smiling at the memory.

"What's funny, Jonathan?"

"These stairs almost killed me when I was young. They're no easier now that I'm ninety-one."

"That's not what you're smiling at."

He's nailed, and he knows it. No use trying to bullshit this woman.

"I was thinking about how badly I wanted to get you to bed, without even knowing you. That's kind of insulting, isn't it?"

Clare shakes her head. "I couldn't wait to get *you* into bed, without knowing you, so don't feel bad. We all had fun, didn't we? Wasn't that what it was all about, back then? Being young, and making the most of it?"

Kaplan rubs the left side of his chest. "This kind of excitement is hell on my pacemaker."

"You'll live."

"May I come in?"

He obviously wants a better look at her face, which is ghostly in the light from above, and at her life, on the other side of the door. Clare shakes her head.

"Sorry," she says, as if the skylight room is off limits for reasons beyond her control. She tightens her grip on the doorknob. "Why are you here, Jonathan?"

He spreads his hands. "To keep you from being thrown out."

"Nobody can throw me out. I have a lease."

"Clare, this woman has money and power. This can get ugly, trust me. The peace-and-love sixties are long over."

Clare smiles. "Still the crusader, eh, Jonathan?"

"You're all alone in this building, and it's not safe. Not even a lock on the front door!"

She jiggles the doorknob. "For the record, there's no lock on this door, either."

"Oh for God's *sake,* Clare! Take my card. I'm right on Charles Street. I'm here for you. Call me if you change your mind."

She accepts the card without looking at it. "I don't have a phone."

"Well, bang on my door. Let me help you. We're worried about you."

"*We?*"

"Carmine called me. Remember Carmine?"

Her face softens. "Of course I remember Carmine. How is he?"

"Withering away in a nursing home."

"You two are back on speaking terms?"

"We figured seven decades is long enough for a grudge."

Clare shakes her head. "So silly, the two of you."

"He was crazy about you, Clare. He never got over you."

"You did."

"I'm not sure about that."

Her eyes seem to shine, perhaps with fresh tears, but it's impossible to tell in this light. "Well," she says, "we never really get over anybody, do we?"

He doesn't answer. He takes a deep breath, like a boy working up the courage to approach a pretty girl. "What do you say you let me take you out to dinner?"

Clare shakes her head. "You're sweet, Jonathan."

"Is that a 'yes?' "

"No. But thank you. Take care."

She touches his cheek, then pushes the door closed. Kaplan just stands there for a minute, as if this whole thing has been a dream. Then he begins his slow, achy descent to the street.

CHAPTER EIGHT

Sometimes, a tiny flame on the gossip page can burst into a bonfire. The Post is getting phone calls and e-mails from dozens of readers, wanting to know where the building is, and who the old lady is.

It's enough to interest the editors up front. They give Becker the green light to saddle up the story and see how far it can go.

He writes a follow-up officially revealing Hannah Schmitt as the owner of the building. He learns the name of the skylight tenant, but nothing more about her. A young reporter is sent to the building to bang on the door to the skylight room, and he gets up those stairs just as Jonathan Kaplan did, but there is no answer to his repeated knocks. He tries again two hours later and again two hours after that, but there is still no answer.

"It's a spooky building," he says with a shiver when he returns to the newsroom. "Couldn't wait to get out of there."

Becker doesn't want to hear this. He realizes it's going to take more than words to keep this story alive.

What it calls for is a photo spread - pictures of the old lady from the skylight room, to make it real to the readers.

What it calls for is Paul Frisch.

There are always problems when Frisch is sent to cover a standard press conference - his framing is off, and the shots are sometimes slightly out of focus. This is because he has no interest in people who agree to be photographed.

He craves prey, so the Clare Owen assignment is right in his wheelhouse.

He sits outside the house at six in the morning aboard his low-slung Sting Ray bicycle, in a black t-shirt and jeans, a light knapsack on his back, a cup of black coffee in hand, looking bored and blank. Frisch is tall and bony, graying slightly at the temples, blue-eyed and boyish at forty. You might take him for a man who's just lost his job, and isn't the least bit worried about it.

The camera in his right hand is as small as a deck of cards. Technology has made it possible for him to get whatever he needs from that one little camera, and he's found it's easiest to get around on a bicycle when you're chasing someone, especially in Greenwich

Village, with all those crooked one-way streets.

The Post is paying him for photos of the mysterious old lady going about her day. It's an all-day assignment, which suits Frisch fine. He's got a five-gallon bladder and he never gets bored or drowsy while on stakeout. The joke in the office is that he can sit still for so long that pigeons mistake him for a statue and land on his shoulders. The tires on his bike are pumped up just right, his legs are strong, and he is well rested.

He is ready.

And now, at five minutes to seven, the door to the building opens and here comes Clare Owen, making her way down the stoop. Slowly, almost casually, Frisch gets off his bike, crouches behind a parked car and squeezes off his first shot.

The hunt is under way.

Frisch returns to the newsroom that night. He downloads his pictures into Becker's computer, and Frisch's narrative is a monotone, as thorough and dispassionate as an accountant reeling off numbers.

"Okay, here she is leaving the house. Lots of energy. I was surprised by that. How old is this broad?"

"Nobody knows."

"Well, she moves like a teenager."

"It's all those years of climbing the stairs," Becker says. "Makes 'em tough. She'd be dead if she lived in an elevator building. Holy shit, is that her in the water?"

"Yeah. Doin' laps at the Carmine Street pool. She must have swum twenty laps. Un-fuckin'-believable. Then she's off to that library on Sixth Avenue and Tenth, readin' the papers. She read all of 'em - Post, News, Times."

Becker studies the shots of Clare reading newspapers on sticks. "She didn't notice you following her?"

"No, man, I changed my shirt and put on a baseball cap before I went in the library."

"You're a genius."

"Hey, it works."

"Where the hell is she *now?*"

"Soup kitchen, basement at St. Joseph's on Sixth Avenue. Lunch time."

"Jesus, she's eating in a soup kitchen?"

"Look closer. She's serving lunch. See the ladle in her hand?"

"Holy shit, she's a *volunteer?*"

"Looks like it to me."

"Don't tell me you ate there."

"I've had worse lunches."

"Yeah, but you can't bill them for this one...Holy Christ, what is *this?*"

Becker is stunned by Frisch's last set of photographs. Clare is sitting cross-legged at the end of the Christopher Street pier, reading a book as the river glows orange with the setting sun.

One shot is especially beautiful, an artistic shot, the kind of thing Frisch will land by chance, once in a great while. The way it's angled, Clare looks as if she has a halo.

"Jesus," Becker says, "this one's a killer."

"Yeah," Frisch agrees. "Anyway, she read her book on the pier until it got dark, then she went home."

Frisch doesn't seem affected by what he's captured in these final shots. Becker, to his own surprise, is fighting back tears.

"So," Becker says, when he's able to compose himself, "what's the sense you got of her?"

Frisch shrugs. "She's an old lady in good shape. Probably crazy."

"Oh, that's so good, Paul. Very perceptive."

"Whaddaya want from me?"

"An *opinion,* or maybe an observation or two. Did she talk to anyone?"

"Nothing I could hear."

"What about in the soup kitchen? Didn't she say anything to you?"

" 'Enjoy your lunch.' That was it."

"Jesus Christ, man, you followed her around for twelve hours, you've got to have *some* idea of what she's all about!"

Frisch helps himself to a pretzel from a bag on Becker's desk. "She's a fuckin' saint," he says, crunching down on the pretzel.

Becker's nostrils widen. He feels a warm tingle across his shoulders. Frisch is right. This is the way to play it. She even has a damn halo!

"The Saint of Greenwich Village," Becker says.

Frisch makes a face. "Too biblical."

"Saint faces eviction?"

"Depressing."

"Holy shit, what's wrong with me? I'm leaving the villain out!" Becker spreads his hands. "Supermodel to Saint - Get out of my house!"

"Not bad," Frisch says. "I'd read that story." He steals one last pretzel before patting Becker's shoulder and leaving.

Becker reviews the photos, lingering on that last set, on the pier.

And what he could never have imagined is that the last time Clare Owen had her picture taken it was on this very same pier, in 1951, by Richard Avedon.

CHAPTER NINE

It happens after Clare has been working at Reggio's for a little less than a year. Those extra pounds she'd been carrying are gone. She is now reed-thin, a result of working and walking and leafy green meals, instead of red meat and deep-fried foods. There's also the appetite-suppressing effect that comes with excitement, the thrill of being young and healthy in the most vibrant neighborhood in the world.

It's her face that's changed the most. Her cheekbones have appeared, and it's as if they've been quarried from rock. Her eyes seem even bigger.

She is stunning, far and away the most beautiful waitress in Greenwich Village, and a true drawing card. Word gets around: *Have you seen the green-eyed girl at Reggio's?* People drop in just for a look at Clare. As soon as she sets a cappuccino in front of Richard Avedon, he knows he must photograph her.

So here they are walking to the end of the Christopher Street pier on a cool, cloudy morning, Clare and Avedon and a makeup artist named Francisco. Clare is wearing blue jeans, sandals and a navy blue t-shirt. Avedon can't help chuckling as he watches her go.

"That's not a New York City walk," he says. "You walk as if the sidewalk is a hot beach, and you're rushing to reach the water."

"Is that a bad thing?"

"I think it's great. Where'd you grow up?"

How many times has she been asked this, since coming to New York? Why does everybody want to know? She's always ducked and dodged the question, but somehow, Avedon seems entitled to an answer.

"Pittsburgh," she says softly. "Land of the steel mills."

"Ah! No wonder you walk like that. Had to step lively when they poured that hot metal."

"I had to step lively to avoid the advances of those mill workers."

"Oh-ho. A randy bunch, I should imagine."

She hates being reminded of those nights in the back seats of cars, their bare backs greasy and pocked with acne from the poisonous air of the mills, the beer on their breaths, the lies that rolled so easily off their tongues....it literally makes her shudder.

Avedon notices. "Looks like I stirred up a bad memory."

Clare blushes, amazed at this man's perceptivity. "All they wanted was a wife to fill up with babies. Make more little mill workers."

"I can't see you as a mill worker's wife."

"*Anybody's* wife," Clare says. "That's not for me."

Avedon smiles. He doesn't believe her, but he plays along. She's just young, strong and selfish. Like every model he's ever photographed, in their early days.

"Well anyway," he says, "for what it's worth, Pittsburgh has left you with a wonderfully distinctive walk."

"I just like to get where I'm going, that's all."

"Slow down a little, before Francisco has a heart attack."

Francisco is chubby, short-legged and gay. He's all puffed out when they reach the end of the pier and needs a moment to catch his breath before breaking out his makeup kit, which looks like a miniature suitcase.

Francisco is proud of himself. He's a regular at Reggio's, the one who told Avedon he had to come and see this girl. If she hits it big, she'll be Francisco's discovery.

He's fascinated by Clare's complexion, dusting her face ever so lightly with his makeup brush.

"Your skin is *amazing,*" he says. "What do you wash with?"

Clare shrugs. "Whatever's on sale."

Francisco rolls his eyes. "Unbelievable. Richard, have you seen this skin? Have you *seen* it?"

"I've seen it," Avedon calmly replies.

"These eyes, these cheekbones...have you *ever?*"

Avedon smiles but does not reply. He knows he's got himself an emerald in the rough, here, but he also knows how easily things can go wrong. Drink, drugs, bad boyfriends....anything can happen to dash the fragile dream.

The three of them are alone at the end of the pier, save for the occasional seagull. The air is clear, the river is smooth and thanks to the clouds there are no shadows. Perfectly even light for Avedon.

Suddenly Clare is dizzy, as everything that's going on hits her like a fist. One day she's a waitress living from payday to payday, tip to tip, and suddenly she's on the brink of something that could land her on the pages of Harper's Bazaar. She feels it in the knees, a sudden weakness that forces her to sit down on a rusty mooring.

Avedon, fiddling around with his equipment, does not notice, but Francisco rushes over and squats in front of her.

"Are you okay, sweetheart?"

Clare forces a smile. "Just a little dizzy."

"Would you like some coffee? I brought a thermos."

"No, thank you. I'll be okay. I just..."

She can't finish the thought, but Francisco can.

"Beauty is a burden," he says. "If you didn't know that already, honey, you're about to find out."

The dizziness passes. Clare gets to her feet. Avedon guides her to a spot he likes, lifts his camera to his face, squints through the viewfinder and smiles.

It's as good as he'd hoped it would be.

He instructs her through a variety of poses - arms folded, hands on hips, head back, head forward. Francisco dips in to fix her hair, but only when bidden.

Avedon shoots the whole roll, sets the camera down and picks up another. He's had nothing to say during the shoot. Clare can't take the suspense.

"Am I doing okay?" she asks. Avedon loads film into the second camera, then does a strange thing. He pats it, as if it's a faithful hound.

"The camera likes you, Clare," he says. "I knew *I* liked you, but it's always a relief to get a second opinion."

Avedon continues shooting. A light wind picks up, enough to blow her hair around. Avedon waves off Francisco, choosing to smooth it back himself. He cocks his head this way and that while fixing her hair, like a man deciding whether or not to say what's on his mind.

Then he says it.

"Put yourself back there, Clare."

She's puzzled. "Where?"

"Where you came from. Pittsburgh."

"Hot steel a-pourin'!" Francisco giggles helpfully.

Clare's eyes narrow. Then they widen with a look that could be surprise, or horror. Total vulnerability.

Avedon snaps away. He struggles to hide his glee.

He has found The Look.

They wrap it up in an hour and a half. Avedon is in the middle of another project, and will need a week or so to develop and print the film, which is fine by Clare. She has no telephone, so the best place to reach her is at Reggio's.

She leaves Avedon and Francisco to pack up their gear and walks alone down the pier, those long strides bringing her to the street in no time.

"She's a wild thing, Richard," Francisco whispers, though they are alone out there.

Avedon, who hates gossip, can't resist asking. "How do you mean?"

Francisco purses his lips and winks, like a true-blue bitch. "The way *I've* heard it, she's cut quite a swath with the boys since she's been here. I mean, even by Greenwich Village terms, this girl stands out." He giggles. "A true adventurer."

Avedon shoulders his camera bag. "Keep that to yourself," he says, knowing Francisco will not obey.

CHAPTER TEN

When the Post goes big on a story, they go nuts. Clare's tale is a two-page photo spread in the middle of the paper, under the headline:

SUPER MODEL TO SAINT: GET OUT OF MY HOUSE!

By TOM BECKER

She's the elderly woman who refuses to budge from the place she has called home for nearly seventy years - despite pressure from onetime super model Hannah Schmitt.

Super-stubborn Clare Owen has reportedly turned down repeated buyout offers from Schmitt to leave the skylight room in a long-neglected building on West 12th Street.

Schmitt, who shelled out six million bucks for the building, plans to totally renovate it for herself, baseball legend hubby Henry Rivers and their two children - but it can't happen while Owen is in residence.

Repeated attempts to interview Owen, exact age unknown, have been ignored - so Post lensman Paul Frisch was sent to follow her around on a typical day in her life.

The remarkably frisky octogenarian pops out early in the morning for a brisk swim at a public pool, and then it's off to her local library, where she reads all the daily papers.

From there it's a quick trek to the soup kitchen at St. Joseph's Church on Sixth Avenue, where - get this - *she serves the needy!*

"She told me to enjoy my lunch," said Frisch, who posed as a homeless man to gain access to the soup kitchen.

"As far as I'm concerned, she's a saint."

But this saint may need more than prayers, if she hopes to stay put in the skylight room....

The story goes on to include a rant from a Legal Aid lawyer saying Clare "cannot be kicked out like a bum," a real estate expert's take on the uphill climb Hannah Schmitt faces to get her way, and a few

31

spirited if useless opinions from elderly rights activists.

It's a huge hit. Becker is back on the rewrite bank, savoring his success the day the story runs. He's just taken a bite from his souvlaki when his phone rings.

Tucking the mouthful into his cheek, he picks up the phone and all but sings, "Becker here."

"I'm no saint."

The voice seems to come from another time, gentle and tough at the same time, and it freezes him. He swallows the gob of souvlaki, like a snake swallowing a mouse.

"Are you there?" Clare demands. She's standing at a decrepit pay phone on Sixth Avenue, across the street from the Waverly movie theater. It's the first phone call she's made in many years, not counting the one she had to make to get the number for the Post from information. She can't believe a local call costs half a buck.

Becker clears his throat. He can hear noise from the West Fourth Street basketball courts behind Clare, balls bouncing and lots of shouting, so he knows she's outside somewhere, in the weather.

So he says - feeling stupid, even before he opens his mouth - "Are you getting wet?"

"What the hell kind of a question is *that?*"

"I mean, because it's raining."

"It stopped."

"Oh. See, I don't have a window. It was raining when I got to work."

"A little rain never killed anyone. Now what's this saint nonsense all about?"

Becker feels his face go hot. "Well, it's just, you know, all the good you do."

He's relieved to hear her laugh. "It's all so *simple* to you people, isn't it? Good or bad, black or white. Heroes and villains. No gray areas."

"So you believe in gray areas?"

"Life is one big gray area, young man."

"I'm not so young, Miss Owen."

"It's Clare."

"Clare, I was only trying to help - "

"Oh, please, *save* it. You were trying to sell newspapers. Don't you understand how insulting it is to be called a saint?"

"Well, no. I think it sounds like the ultimate compliment."

"Wrong. It deprives me of my humanity. I don't have wings, and I don't have a halo. I'm just an old woman trying to get by, and the last thing I need is to be thought of as some mindless do-gooder because I spend a little time serving stew."

Becker lets it sink in. "Well, what is it you've done that a saint *wouldn't* do?"

Clare laughs out loud. "Clever. You know something, Becker? You're pretty good."

"I'm serious. I'd really like to know."

"I'll bet you would."

"The whole city would like to know. And I could make it worth your while."

"Excuse me?"

"We could pay you for your story. Exclusively, of course."

"Oh, Mr. Becker, you're *such* an asshole."

Clare hangs up the phone so gently that Becker needs a second or two to realize she is gone. He takes another bite of his souvlaki, but suddenly his appetite is gone. He goes outside and lights up a cigarette, leaning against the building as he smokes it down to the filter.

He's been called an asshole many times, but this is the first time it's ever bothered him.

CHAPTER ELEVEN

When celebrities in New York City reproduce one of the things they don't count on is the enforced socializing they'll have to do with regular people, for the sake of their children.

Hannah Schmitt and Henry Rivers are no exceptions. On this particular Saturday Desmond has a morning Little League game in Central Park, and Greta has an afternoon birthday party.

The easiest thing to do is have the nanny handle both events, but if 'Beauty and the Ballplayer' is to have any credibility it won't hurt for Henry and Hannah to attend events like these, before any cameras are rolling, to show the world what regular people they really are.

That's how Hannah convinced Henry to come to the ball game. They won't hide, even if Henry's upcoming eligibility for the Baseball Hall of Fame has stirred up his steroid past, and Hannah is the evil witch who wants to throw a little old lady out on the street.

"We have to brave it out," Hannah says to Henry. "It's the only way."

So they sit together in an upper corner of the bleachers, far from the other parents. Nobody approaches them - everybody is too cool for that - but everybody knows they're there, and when Hannah sees people whispering to each other she knows they're not talking about the ball game.

The kids are too young to know about Henry's glory days, but their dads remember all those home runs, his World Series triumphs, and of course the steroids scandal. Henry, five years retired, twenty pounds over his playing weight, looking lumpy in a black H & H warmup suit and sunglasses, looks about as happy as a man awaiting a colonoscopy.

But Hannah is another story. She sits smiling with perfect posture in a navy blue H & H warmup suit, her hair in a pony tail and one of Henry's old Yankee caps on her head. No sunglasses. She wants to look people right in the eye, if they're brave enough to approach her, but nobody does.

Hannah figures it's Henry's fault, the way he sits there scowling. They start conversing out the sides of their mouths, like a prison yard conversation.

"Pull up your sleeves," Hannah says, doing the same to her

sleeves. This way, their his 'n' her tattoos will be visible - DESMOND in blue script on their right forearms, GRETA in red script on their left forearms. Grumbling, Henry does as he's told.

"Cheer up," Hannah says. "Be willing to mingle a little."

"No way, baby."

"Henry. You look like you're ready to bite somebody's head off."

"I'm just sittin' here."

"That's my point."

"Hannah, I *hate* this shit."

"Oh, that's the spirit."

"Why are we here? My parents never came to see me play when I was a kid."

"Your father was dead by then, wasn't he?"

"Damn, woman, you got a sweet way of puttin' things, did you know that?"

"What I mean is, Desmond is lucky, compared to you. You're here to see him play!"

Henry shrugs, sighs. "These kids should just be havin' fun, at their age. Don't need their fathers out here, organizin' every move they make."

Henry has a point. Desmond's team has a manager, a coach, an assistant coach, and a safety officer - a man who makes sure the kids wear helmets and remain behind the dugout fence, in case there's a foul ball or someone flings a bat. They're all the dads of the kids on the team, and the most important job is the pot-bellied dad doing the pitching. He's actually an ally to the batter, doing his best to hit the bats of these seven-year-olds, lobbing the ball over home plate, or at least trying to. Henry shakes his head as he watches the man take pre-game practice pitches.

"Look at this guy," Henry says. "Can't pitch for shit."

"Why don't you get out there and pitch?"

"Yeah, right."

"Be a great photo op, Henry. Everybody would love it, and we could use the good will."

"God damn it, Hannah!"

"Shhh! What the hell is *wrong* with you?"

Henry takes off his sunglasses, turns to face Hannah and looks her in the eye.

"Desmond can't play," he whispers. "Got no hand-eye

coordination. You watch, they're gonna stick him in right field, where he can't do much damage."

Sure enough, Desmond Rivers trots out to right field at the start of the game, a too-big cap on his head, a half-buttoned "Pirates" shirt flapping untucked around his waist, a leather baseball glove that nearly reaches to the elbow of his skinny arm. He is the image of his father, dark skin and blue eyes. Hannah cheers. Henry hangs his head.

The first two innings pass painlessly, except for a fly ball to right field that jolts Desmond from the reverie he's been enjoying, his back to home plate as he watches the jagged flight of a white butterfly. The kid who hit the ball has the speed to leg out a home run by the time Desmond tears his attention from the butterfly to locate the ball, pick it up and drop it twice before the frantic second baseman - who has run all the way to right field - grabs the ball from Desmond and makes the useless throw to home plate, amid much jeering.

Hannah watches the disaster stoically but Henry is moaning.

"Jesus, Hannah, let's get out of here."

She's shocked. "We can't abandon our son!"

"We can pick him up after the game."

"Henry, we are *staying.*"

The dreaded third inning begins, the one in which Desmond is batting for the first time. Helmet clapped over his ears, he stands there holding the smallest bat he can find, knees quaking as the pot-bellied dad pitcher does his best to aim for the bat.

But it's hopeless. Desmond's first two swings are nowhere near the ball. He looks like he's waving at a pesky gnat. On the third pitch he actually swings after the ball lands in the catcher's mitt. Strike three.

"Jesus," Henry says, "I can't be*lieve* he's my son."

"Henry, for God's sake!"

"Seriously, Hannah. How can he be this bad, if he's mine?"

"Are you doubting that he's yours? *Look* at him!"

"I'm just sayin.' "

Hannah's heart is breaking. Has she just been accused of infidelity, because their son is a bad ballplayer? If they were at home having this conversation she could tear into Henry, but it's got to be all smiles out here, in the Central Park sunshine of a perfect day, in the midst of hundreds of witnesses.

Then it happens.

As Desmond trudges back to his dugout, a fat man sitting in the opposing team's bleachers stands up, cups his hands around his mouth and yells: "Ask your Daddy for a 'roid!"

Slang for steroid.

A few suppressed chuckles and scattered "oohs" fill the air, the sound of self-proclaimed liberals who find something funny but want their objection to its tastelessness read into the record.

Henry gets to his feet and removes his sunglasses. He stares at the fat man, and if a hard look could dissolve a human being, the fat man would be a puddle. He didn't know that Henry was in attendance, and it's too late to run, so he sits back down and hopes Henry will do the same.

Which he does. Best way to handle a heckler - stare him down, and say nothing. He's done it thousands of times over as many ball games.

But Hannah gets to her feet and, ignoring Henry's objections, makes her way to the opposing team's bleachers. She stands directly in front of the fat man, smiling broadly as she addresses his sweaty and rapidly reddening face.

"Which one is your boy?" she asks, oh so softly. The fat man swallows and points.

"Number seven," he says.

Hannah looks at the boy, who's playing first base. He's the kid whose fly ball to right field jolted Desmond from his butterfly reverie.

"Hey!" Hannah says. "He hit a home run, didn't he?"

"Uh-huh."

"You must be proud."

He nods, wipes his brow. "I am."

"Well, I just wanted to say hello. My husband wanted to come here and break your fucking legs, but I talked him out of it."

Her gentle tone makes it all the more horrifying. She pats the fat man's cheek, wipes the sweat on the sleeve of his shirt and returns to Henry.

"Jesus, Hannah, what the hell was *that?*"

"He says he's sorry. You didn't want to do it, so I did it."

"Did what?"

"Defended Desmond's honor."

She grips the front of Henry's shirt, as if to pull him close for a kiss, but when their lips are an inch apart she says, "I am so pissed off at you, I could kill you."

"Come off it."

"In case you have any doubts, let me assure you - Desmond *is* your son. And there is more to life than hitting a baseball."

"Oh yeah. There's watchin' butterflies in the outfield."

"Kiss me, you asshole."

She kisses Henry, her antennae having sensed the nearness of a classic paparazzo - an unshaven young man whose appearance is just a notch above homeless. Sure enough, the kissing shot will appear on the Daily News gossip page the following day, under a headline saying BLEACHER BUSS!, and no one looking at this picture would believe that it preceded a cold war between Hannah and Henry that has him sleeping on the couch for the rest of the weekend.

Henry gets up and leaves while that enraged kiss is still moist on his lips. Hannah stays for the rest of the game, which the Pirates win despite Desmond's dreadful play - two more strikeouts, and a fly ball to right field that nearly hits him on the head.

But Hannah cheers for the Pirates all the way, and gives Desmond a huge hug in front of everybody before they begin walking home.

"Where's Daddy?" Desmond asks when they are away from the crowd.

"He had to leave early."

The boy kicks a pebble. "I embarrassed him."

"No, of course not!"

"I suck at baseball."

"Desmond. You do not *suck.*"

"Yes I do."

"Maybe you're not the best player on the team, but that's not a big deal."

"It ain't?"

"*Isn't.* No, it isn't."

"It is to Dad."

"He just wants you to be happy," she says, hoping she can get away with a bullshit line like that, suspecting she probably can't. Desmond is smart. He's sensitive. She's got to go another way.

"May I tell you a secret, just between you and me?"

The boy grins at the prospect of something juicy. "Shoot."

"Don't tell Daddy, but I don't like baseball. I think it's *boring.* It takes too long, and nothing *happens!* All they do is spit and scratch their butts."

Desmond giggles. "I think it's boring, too."

"Would you like to know my favorite part of the game? It was when you watched that butterfly."

The boy's eyes widen in wonder. "You saw that?"

"Oh yeah. I thought it was beautiful, the way it floated around."

"Yeah! They never fly straight!"

"It would be boring if they did, wouldn't it?"

"Yeah! Boring like baseball!"

"Would you like to quit the team, sweetheart?"

"Can I?"

"Of course. You shouldn't do things you don't want to do."

"You mean, like, homework?"

"No, you *must* do your homework. But your own time is yours, and it's precious. I know just how you feel." She hesitates. "I was quite a good swimmer when I was a little girl in Germany, but I hated it."

Desmond knows from his mother's conspiratorial tone that he's hearing something special. "No kiddin'?"

"Oh, my God! Back and forth in the pool, day after day, looking down at that blue line on the bottom. It made me crazy. Then one day I swam straight into the wall. Look." She puts a finger to her nose. "See how it bends, a little to the left? I broke my nose on that wall."

Desmond studies his mother's nose, as if seeing it for the first time. It's the tiniest of flaws, and possibly the one thing that lifted her from the model population and made her famous when she was young, the way the gap between Lauren Hutton's two front teeth made her stand out from the crowd in the Seventies. It takes away from Hannah's perfection but increases her humanity.

"Wow," Desmond says. "Musta hurt."

"And how. No more swimming for me, I can tell you that."

"Your mom let you quit?"

"Well, she didn't mind, but my father was my swimming coach. He wasn't too happy about it." Hannah smiles. "But I was. And I want you to be happy too, Desmond. Okay?" She pulls him close. "No more baseball for you, young man."

Desmond leaps in the air and squeals with delight. Then it hits him.

"Won't Daddy be mad?"

"I seriously doubt it. But if he is, I'll handle it."

He stops walking and studies his mother from under the bill of the Pirates baseball cap he is wearing for the last time.

"Can I ask you something, Mom?"

"Anything, my darling boy."

"What's a 'roid'?"

Greta's birthday bash is a drop-off at a party mill on Columbus Avenue, three to five p.m. Hannah has no idea of where Henry is, and he's not answering his phone. She makes the drop-off a quick one, rather than lingering with the other moms, women her age who hated her for her impossibly lean body in her heyday but now rejoice at the appearance of a slightly sagging chin.

It's the kind of party where the kids come out sugar-crazy, full of pizza and Hawaiian Punch and ice cream, and when Hannah returns at five to pick up Greta she's greeted at the door to the party room by a woman named Marjorie, mother of the birthday girl, an annoyingly upbeat Upper West Side type whose capped-tooth smile belies the words that accompany it.

"I'm afraid we've had a bit of a situation with Greta."

On the Upper West Side "situation" is a synonym for "trouble," but nothing to worry about, except that these people worry about *everything*, especially when it involves a child making contact with another child, which is what happened with Greta and a boy named Toby, Marjorie explains.

Hannah can feel her blood pressure rising. Celebrities are lightning rods for lawsuits, and every other parent in this crowd is a lawyer.

"What exactly happened?"

"Well, it seems Toby reached out to stroke Greta's hair, and she pushed him away."

Hannah waits for more, but there isn't any.

"That's it?"

"Well, Toby is an especially sensitive boy, and it seems he's afraid of Greta now. He spent the entire party hiding in a corner."

"Maybe he didn't stroke her hair. Maybe he pulled it."

"Ohhh, he wouldn't do *that.*"

"Did you see it happen?"

Marjorie erases the air with her hands. "In any case, we'd like to clear it up, for everyone's sake."

Hannah looks over Marjorie's shoulder, like a person on line at a hot nightclub trying to get a peek inside.

"May I see my daughter, please?"

"We thought we'd bring Greta and Toby out together, so she could apologize. Would that be all right?"

Hannah agrees to it with a nod. Marjorie goes into the party and returns with the children, each carrying a red gift bag filled with candy treats and the kind of tiny toys that clog the hoses of vacuum cleaners.

Toby is a small child with a head shaped like a light bulb and big brown eyes, and Hannah instantly know that "sensitive" is an Upper West Side synonym for "probably gay."

Greta tugs at the waist of her party dress, a tomboy eager to change clothes. She's light-skinned and blonde, but that blonde hair is kinky, and it worries Hannah to think that one day, her daughter may want to have it straightened to pass for white.

Marjorie, hands on the backs of both children, turns to Hannah with her biggest smile yet.

"Would you like to take it from here?"

"Where's Toby's mother?"

"She's not here yet, but I think we can handle it."

She winks at Hannah, the go-ahead sign. Hannah squats in front of Greta, so that they are nose to nose.

"Greta, tell Toby you're sorry you pushed him."

"Sor-*ree,*" Greta sing-songs.

"And Toby, tell Greta you're sorry."

"Hold on," an alarmed Marjorie says, like an orchestra conductor addressing a rogue trumpet player. "What's *this?*"

Ignoring Marjorie, Hannah looks Toby right in the eye. "We mustn't touch people's hair," she says. "It's not nice."

Toby rubs his nose. "It's funny hair," he says.

"No, it is *not.*"

"It sure feels funny."

"It's beautiful hair. Now, apologize, please."

Toby studies his shoes. "Sorry," he mumbles.

"That's okay," Greta says.

Hannah takes her by the hand and heads for the door, followed by Marjorie, who catches Hannah by the elbow.

"That really wasn't right, Miss Schmitt," she hisses. "Ideally,

Toby's mother should have handled his apology."

"Then she should have been here on time to pick up the little hair-grabber."

Marjorie is stunned, but only momentarily. "Well," she says, a wicked gleam in her eye, "if it were up to you, I guess shy boys like Toby wouldn't stand a chance, would they? You'd just *evict* them from the party at the first sign of trouble."

The impulse to belt Marjorie in the mouth is so overwhelming that Hannah's free hand actually clenches into a fist. It takes every ounce of her will to say nothing, turn and leave with Greta, cringing at the sound of Marjorie's sickly sweet voice behind their backs.

"Bye-*bye,* Greta! Thank you for *com*-ing!"

On the walk home Hannah's head is pounding as Greta swings her gift bag back and forth.

"Sweetheart, you're going to break that bag."

"I don't *care.*"

"Wasn't it a good party, except for Toby?"

"No."

"What's wrong, baby?"

The child's eyes glisten. "I *hate* my hair, Mommy. Can we cut it all off?"

"Oh, no! Your hair is special!"

"No, it isn't. It's *ugly.*"

Hannah's heart is breaking, but she forges ahead. "Let me ask you something, Greta - does anybody else have hair like yours?"

"No."

"Well, that's why it's special. That's why Toby touched it. It's like spun gold, baby. See? Toby wanted to see what it was like to touch gold."

Greta is smiling. "Gold is good, right?"

"Oh, my goodness, yes!"

"Is gold the best thing in the world?"

"No, baby. *You* are."

Greta squeals with delight and skips ahead in her patent leather party shoes, chanting: "My hair is made of gold, my hair is made of *gold!*"

Hannah watches her go, trying to decide whether or not Henry needs to know about this incident. She's thinking she won't tell him. She realizes that when it comes to the kids, she and Henry are almost always at odds. It's a scary thought, now that the kids are old enough to know what's going on. How easy those early years were, with endless diapers and three a.m. feedings handled by nannies!

Now their children are walking, talking people who want answers from their parents, but whose answers? Hers, or Henry's?

Henry has little to say at the dinner table that night. Hannah has no idea of where he's been since he bolted from the baseball game, and he doesn't even ask Greta about her birthday party. Hannah tells herself he's preoccupied by the upcoming vote for the Baseball Hall of Fame, and leaves him alone.

That night she lies in bed staring at the ceiling while Henry, asleep on the living room couch, snores loudly enough to rattle the windows. She wonders what has happened to her life, and if everything is spinning out of control.

No! This is not how she handles things. The thing to do is to forge ahead, and focus on her work. Work heals everything, as far as Hannah is concerned, and the job ahead is crystal-clear:

Do whatever it takes to get the old lady out of the skylight room.

With that final thought, she is able to fall asleep.

CHAPTER TWELVE

Sudden celebrity does not change the life of Clare Owen. She does not alter the well-worn orbits of her life, continuing to live it as she has for so long - swimming pool, soup kitchen, library, pier. When people recognize her and urge her to hang in there, she smiles. When a local news crew tags along with Clare as she walks home from the pier, an eager young reporter peppering her with endless questions, she smiles.

The reporter grows desperate. He's getting nothing from the skylight woman. He thinks of one final question as Clare reaches the stoop of her home.

"What would you like to say to Hannah Schmitt?" the desperate reporter asks.

Clare smiles, and goes inside.

The media attention dies down, for a simple reason, something Clare seems to know instinctively.

Smiles are boring.

But way uptown, things are getting interesting with Hannah Schmitt and Henry Rivers.

They no longer live together. They've had an explosive fight over the reality show and have separated in the lucky way the rich are able to separate - he's gone to the summer house in Bridgehampton, simple as that. Didn't even have to pack. Full set of clothes out there, so he just walks out of the penthouse while Hannah is still screaming at him, gets in his SUV and goes.

No hurling of pots and pans, no division of property, no lawyers. Not yet.

But if they don't patch it up soon, word will get around, and Henry is sure to be sighted chatting up an attractive woman at the Candy Kitchen, and who's going to believe she's just a friend?

So it's Hannah and the kids back in the city, where damage control is in full throttle with her publicist, Max Marshall. The kids are in bed, and it's Max's job to find a way to make the super model who wants to throw an old lady out on the street seem sympathetic.

"I *am* sympathetic" Hannah says, pouring Chardonnay with a heavy hand for the two of them. "My God, I offered her a hundred thousand dollars!"

Max sips his wine. "I know, Hannah," he begins gently, "but no matter what you offer, you're still a diva evicting a saint."

Hannah laughs. "A *saint?* Because she works in a soup kitchen, she's a *saint? Even she* says that's bullshit! Look!"

She holds up a recent New York Post to show him Becker's story under the headline SKYLIGHT WOMAN DECLARES: I'M NO SAINT!

"I saw it," Max sighs. "But don't you see how this makes it even *worse* for you? When you call someone a saint, that's one thing. When the person denies being a saint, it makes her even more saintly."

Hannah rolls her eyes. "Is that how it works?"

"Trust me. No true saint ever thought of herself as a saint."

"What about *me?* I'm a good person! I run four charities! Do you know how much they raise each year?"

"I sure do, but when people hear about a celebrity with a charity, all they think is 'tax deduction.'"

Hannah takes a long swallow of wine. "What about Thanksgiving? Every Thanksgiving for the past seven years, I'm serving meals to the homeless!"

"That's nice, but it's a photo op. One hour a year, if we're being totally honest. Looks like the old lady has been doing it every day since the Earth cooled. Leaves a slightly deeper impression."

Max's sarcasm has always irritated Hannah. He sees her nostrils flare. This is never good.

"So," she says, "everything the old lady does is good and pure, and everything I do is bullshit."

"We both know that's not true. But the public doesn't."

"What the fuck am I supposed to do, Max?"

"First off, do not panic."

"Jesus, the best way to get someone like me to panic is to tell me not to panic!"

"Second, where's Henry?"

Hannah tops up her wine glass, as Max covers his glass with his hand.

"He's at the Long Island house."

"Are you two separating? I'm starting to hear things."

"Just taking a little time apart."

"What the hell does *that* mean?"

Hannah sips her wine. "He doesn't want to do the reality show."

"Oh Christ."

"He'll come around. I know him."

"If you're not on the same page with this thing - "

"We are. We will be."

"Is he screwing around?"

"Of course not."

"Don't 'of course not' me, Hannah. Now I have to ask you something you won't like."

"I haven't liked anything you've asked me tonight."

Max leans closer. "Is this crazy reality show really worth it?"

Hannah's eyes, always cool, turn cold. "It isn't crazy."

"Okay, sorry, wrong adjective. I'll start again - is the show worth it? The upheaval in your lives, turning your kids into inadvertent celebrities - "

"My kids are totally on board with it."

Bullshit, Max thinks, but he leaves it alone. "Okay, then, how about the rest of it? The house, the old lady, this mess we've got on our hands?"

Hannah looks for a moment as if she's about to strike Max. Instead, she gulps more wine. "The H & H brand is down thirty per cent," she says flatly. "So you see we need a jump-start for the business, Max. This isn't my ego speaking. We're in real trouble. The show will save us, and we need the house to do the show. Simple as that."

Remarkable, Max is thinking. Most people fall apart on alcohol. This woman becomes even more focused. She's rich, and she wants to get richer.

"Okay, then." He sets down his wine glass and brings his hands together in a loud, now-hear-this clap. "First of all, get Henry back here, and get back on track with him. That's vital."

"He'll be back in a day or two. He's cooling off."

"I hope you're right."

"Meanwhile, I can sweeten the offer to the old lady. Go to a hundred and twenty-five."

"Bad, bad idea."

"Why?"

"Because it's not about money for the old lady. You offer her more, you won't seem generous, you'll seem aggressive."

"So what do I do? Nothing?"

"How about this? You offer her a place to live. A little apartment in an elevator building."

Hannah rolls her eyes. "So we're talking a million dollars, minimum, if she stays in the Village."

"You're not *buying* it for her, you're *renting* it. Say, three grand a month."

"For as long as she lives."

"Right. How long can *that* be? Jesus, she's gotta be eighty-eight, eighty-nine. If she drops dead in a year you're only out thirty-six grand."

Hannah can't hide her smile. This is what she's paying him for. "I'll think about it, Max."

"Good. Now, I have another idea, and it may sound a little crazy, but hear me out." He sips his wine. "What I'm thinking is, you do some volunteer work at a senior citizens rest home."

"Oh my *God,* Max. Another photo op, like the Thanksgiving dinners? Who's *that* going to fool?"

"This is different. It's a paparazzo job."

He winks, a gesture Hannah happens to despise.

"You've lost me, Max."

He can barely hide his glee. "We catch you doing something you've kept secret from the world."

Max get to his feet. He's really excited, now. "I handle publicity for a rest home in Queens. I do it pro bono, so they'll play along with us. Okay! So, you put on your dowdiest clothes - "

"I don't have any dowdy clothes."

"We'll get you some. No makeup, hair pulled straight back. Bad lighting, so bad that people are going to wonder if it's really you, pushing an old man in his wheelchair."

All Hannah can do is listen, slack-jawed. Max thunders ahead.

"I send one of my guys in with a camera, and you go nuts. You flip him the bird, you scream at him. Honey, if that's not a page one photograph, I don't know what is. See how it works? We catch you doing something good. That's almost as good as catching someone doing something bad!"

"Holy shit, Max." She finishes her wine and stands up. "A fake ambush, huh?"

"Well, I like to think of it as a scambush."

"That is by far the stupidest idea I've ever heard."

"I know it sounds that way at first, but all I ask is that you give it time, let it sink in. Believe me, it's worked before."

"Who? When?"

"I'm sorry, I'm sworn to secrecy." He makes a locking motion on his lips, then holds her by the shoulders and gives them a squeeze.

"One more thing, Hannah, and it's delicate."

He releases her shoulders and looks left and right before asking, "Is the old lady Jewish?"

Hannah is stunned. "How the hell should *I* know?"

"Owen doesn't sound like a Jewish name, but you never know. The last thing we need is a German torturing an old Jew."

Hannah can't believe what she's just heard. She pokes Max's chest with a steely finger. "Nobody's being *tortured*. Offering someone a better place to live is not torture. And by the way, I'm American, as American as you are."

Max holds his hands up, palms out. "Honey, I'm sorry, but green card or no green card, you can't suddenly decide not to be German. Your accent is there. And if the old lady turns out to be Jewish, well, shit, we're lookin' at Auschwitz on the Hudson."

Hannah sets her wine glass down and points to the door. "Get out of my house, Max," she says through tight teeth. "You're fired."

CHAPTER THIRTEEN

If there's one thing wrong with young Clare's Greenwich Village experience, it's the room mate deal. She'd love to have a place of her own, but that's going to take a lot more money than what she's making at Reggio's. And now that Marie is getting married, Clare has to find another place to live.

Just like that, it's another waitress to the rescue - Julie, who's been at Reggio's for six years.

"Listen," she says to Clare one day, out of the blue, "what are you gonna do when Marie gets married?"

"I don't know. Find someone who needs a room mate, I guess."

"Want to take over my place?"

"You're *leaving?*"

"Already did. Moved to Astoria with my boyfriend. Going to work in his diner, starting next week. I've had it with the Village."

Clare can't imagine anyone having enough of the Village, but she's glad Julie wants to split and flip burgers for a Greek in Queens. A chance for her own apartment! What an opportunity!

But what's the catch?

Clare hesitates before asking, "Where's your place?"

"Twelfth Street, near the river. Sixteen bucks a month."

Clare is staggered. A Greenwich Village apartment, for just a dollar more than she's paying to share Marie's flat!

"Sounds perfect."

"Don't get too excited until you see it, honey. We'll head straight over after work."

The farther west they walk, the less genteel the neighborhood becomes. The riverfront is full of longshoreman bars, with boisterous drunks prowling the streets every payday.

"It's not exactly Greenwich Village proper," Julie says as they near her building. "It's a rooming house."

"What's a rooming house?"

"A place where you live in one room, with a hot plate."

"Oh."

Julie laughs. "See that? You learn something new every day." She stops and gestures at the building. "This is it. Ready for the climb?"

"The climb?"

Julie leads the way up the stoop and through the front door. "Top floor, I'm afraid. I'll tell you right now, I'm not gonna miss all these stairs. I thank God I moved to an elevator building!"

Julie grips the banister, puffing as she climbs. The stairs don't bother Clare at all. She's so excited she could run all the way up, but she doesn't. She savors the climb.

Odors and sounds, as they ascend: baked beans, someone playing scales on a saxophone, an argument over spilled wine.

"You might as well know, this building attracts weirdos," Julie says. "Solo types, you know? Take my advice, you'll be better off keeping to yourself."

"If I take the place."

"Yeah, right, *if* you take it." *And take over the last six months of my lease so I don't get screwed,* Julie thinks.

At last they reach the top floor. Julie grips the doorknob and turns to Clare with a wicked smile.

"Okay, so that's disadvantage number one, a million goddam stairs. Ready for disadvantage number two?"

Julie pushes the door open. "No lock on the door! Do you believe that? It literally fell off. Landlord's too cheap to fix it. You might have to shell out for a locksmith, if you take this place...."

But Clare barely hears whatever Julie says after that, because she is dazzled by the pink light of the springtime sunset that fills this tiny, empty room. Clare steps inside and stares up in wonder at twelve rectangular panes of glass, threaded with wire to keep them strong through all weathers.

"It's a skylight," Clare breathes. "Just like the painter's studio in Portrait of Jenny."

Julie cocks her head. "What's that?"

"A movie."

"Never saw it. Anyway, get ready for disadvantage number three - no shower. You have a sink and a toilet, but when you want to take a shower, you've got to go to the local gym. A pain in the ass, I know, but that's why it's only sixteen bucks a month." She folds her arms across her chest. "Interested?"

"Yes," Clare says, "This place is mine."

She says it with total possession, like a real estate baron. Julie can't help laughing. "You're not *buying* it, Clare, you're *renting* it! Believe me, you'll get sick of it before long. All those stairs, and you'll feel the walls closing in on you."

"I doubt that."

"Trust me, you'll be okay here for a year, maybe two, until you get married, or whatever. I'll talk to my landlord tomorrow, have him transfer the lease to you. And do yourself a favor, buy a good lock for this door."

It's advice Clare Owen ignores on that day and all subsequent days, nearly seventy years' worth.

Hannah Schmitt hires builders to begin exterior work on the house. Scaffolding goes up, and the dusty mortar between the bricks is dug out and replaced. This "pointing" of the bricks is a slow, tedious process, which is just as well, because the interior work can't begin in earnest until the old lady is out.

Up until now, all offers made to Clare have gone through Hannah's lawyers. She never met the four tenants she bought out, and she never expected to meet the final holdout, but it suddenly occurs to her that what's been missing from this process is the personal touch.

If you're asking someone to leave their lifelong home, the least you can do is to meet the person you're kicking out.

So enough with those high-priced buffers! It's time for Hannah Schmitt to climb those stairs and deal with the skylight woman face-to-face.

She waits until sunset of a spring evening, after the workmen have left. A light breeze is blowing, making the mesh curtains hanging from the scaffolding bellow and flap, like sails on a boat.

How crazy is it, that the front door has no lock? Hannah goes right in for the first time since the purchase was completed and begins the climb to the top.

She's confident, but also frightened. She's not used to doing things alone. Normally there's a personal assistant in her shadow, but she knows this is a job that must be done one-on-one.

She knocks on the door gently, the way someone reluctant to disturb anyone might. It opens as it did for Jonathan Kaplan, six inches, and then Hannah Schmitt is looking into those eyes that have dazzled everyone who's ever seen them.

"Hello, Clare. I'm Hannah Schmitt."

Clare's eyes widen, then narrow. Hannah thinks she's smiling, but it's hard to know if this is really a smile, or just her natural face at rest.

"I recognized you immediately," Clare says.

"I thought maybe we could talk."

"I turned down your offer."

"I have a new offer."

"Send it to me in the mail."

"I'd rather do it in person, if that's all right with you."

"In other words, you want to come in."

"I'd like that, yes."

Clare thinks it over for a long moment before opening the door wide.

Hannah doesn't immediately step inside. She stands at the door saddle and looks up at the skylight, its panes gone golden with the sunset. Blue-gray clouds tumble past like a herd of weightless elephants.

It is an amazing sight. She is, for one of the few times in her life, speechless.

"Wow," she says at last.

"This is the best time to see the skylight room," Clare says. "Late sunset, heading into night. Saw it for the first time myself on an evening like this."

The old lady watches as Hannah steps inside, gazing up at the skylight. She's breathing hard. Her mind races with the things she can do with this room, and how great it will look on television.

Clare knows exactly how she's feeling, and what she's thinking. She turns her head to hide a grin.

"Sit down," she says. "I'll make tea."

The word "basic" doesn't begin to describe conditions in the skylight room. There's a hot plate on a tiny wooden table, beside a small sink. A narrow mattress lies flat on the pine-plank floor, the kind that can give you splinters, and a goose-neck lamp stands at the head of the mattress. A battered two-drawer bureau holds all of Clare's clothing, except for what's hanging on the lone radiator to dry. It's obvious to Hannah that she washes her clothes in the sink, wringing them out by hand.

No chairs, no TV, no radio, no phone. It's hard to imagine the last time the windowless gray walls, devoid of pictures or photographs, might have tasted paint.

And one more "no" - no old lady smells. The air in here has a faint sweetness, like roses from a long-gone bouquet.

From a small shelf over the sink Clare takes a box of teabags and heats water in a kettle on the hot plate. Hannah sits on the worn red rug in the middle of the floor.

How big could this room be? Two hundred square feet, tops? It's like the crow's nest of an ancient whaling ship!

"Must get hot up here in summertime," Hannah says.

"I manage."

"But you're sealed shut!"

"No." Clare points to a handle beside one of the skylight panes. "That pane opens."

"Where's your bathroom?"

Clare points to a short door. Hannah opens it and is shocked to see that it's nothing but a toilet bowl in a windowless room, barely bigger than a closet.

"No tub? No shower?"

Clare shrugs.

"My God, how do you stay clean?"

"There's a good strong shower at the Carmine Street gym."

Hannah is stunned. "You go to the gym every time you want to take a shower?"

Clare smiles. "Since 1950."

"Oh my God."

"But I swim first, as I'm sure you know from that foolish story in the Post."

"Why was it foolish?"

Clare won't say. Hannah sits back down. Clare hands her a cup of herbal tea and joins her on the floor, sipping from her own cup.

Hannah sees that Clare has used one teabag for both cups. No waste around here.

They're facing each other cross-legged, with the wary politeness of two college room mates meeting in their dorm room for the first time. Hannah is ready to get to business but to her surprise, Clare speaks first.

"Before you say anything, the answer is 'no.'"

Hannah's soul sinks. "Don't you want to hear me out?"

"Tell you the truth, I'd like to eat first. Have you eaten? I was making my dinner when you knocked. Nothing fancy, just what I have every Thursday night."

Clare gets up and returns with a plate containing four slices of

Italian bread, dribbled with olive oil. She shakes a bit of salt on the bread, straight from the box.

Hannah can't help chuckling. "That's dinner?"

"It was better when Zito's Bakery was around. Did you know Zito's, on Bleecker Street?"

"I really don't know the neighborhood yet."

"Well, Zito's is gone. Best bread in the world. But this isn't too bad. Try a slice."

"I don't eat bread."

Clare grins. "You were a model, right? Still maintaining your figure?"

"Not very successfully."

Clare takes a slice and bites into it with strong, even teeth. A drop of olive oil makes its way down her chin.

"Excuse me," Hannah says, "but is that *oil* on the bread?"

"It certainly is."

"Never heard of that combination."

"I learned it from Frank."

"Who's Frank?"

Clare wipes her chin with her fingertips and rubs the oil into her palms, like a lotion.

"Sinatra," she says. "I'm sure you've heard of him."

CHAPTER FOURTEEN

It's obvious he's been drinking hard when he enters Reggio's with a burly male companion who looks to be part bodyguard, part bulldog, all wise guy. The late night crowd tries to play it cool, but sidelong looks and murmurs are inevitable, and for the rest of their lives everyone there will tell stories about the night they saw Frank Sinatra in the Village.

They take a table in the corner, Sinatra wobbly on his feet, his companion ready to steady him if necessary, but when he moves to help settle him into a chair Sinatra waves him off, saying, "For Christ's sake, I'm fine."

He's breathing hard, right into Clare's face, reeking of Jack Daniel's. Though drunk, Sinatra is somehow impeccable in a navy-blue suit. He loosens his black tie and opens the top button of his snow-white shirt, though the collar is already loose around his reedy neck. He looks as if he's been sick, or sad, for a long time.

But his eyes shine like a pair of blue suns.

His companion sits down and holds up two thick fingers. "Coupla espressos, strong and hot, sweetheart."

Clare goes to get the coffees. The barista is all but quaking as he prepares the drinks. He sneaks looks at the table where Sinatra hangs his head, like a commuter who's fallen asleep on a train after a killer day at work. The barista sets the cups on a tray with the solemnity of a priest at the altar, whispering, "For God's sake, don't spill them!"

"Why would I do that?"

"Serving Sinatra? Are you kiddin' me?"

Clare is stunned. "That skinny guy is *Frank Sinatra?*"

"Oh, you little rube," the barista chuckles. "Serve them, already!"

Clare brings the drinks to the table and sets the saucers down flawlessly, pinkies extended. The goon drinks his in a gulp. Sinatra ignores his espresso. He stares at Clare, narrowing his eyes, as if to bring her into focus.

"Take off, Rocco," he says, without even looking at his companion. Rocco obeys, like a well-trained dog. Still in command mode, Sinatra points at the newly empty chair.

"Sit," he says.

Clare points to herself. "Me?"

"Yeah, you. What's your name, sweetheart?"

"Clare."

"You got some set of peepers, Clare. Come on, sit down."

She looks toward the kitchen, where the night manager nods his okay. She sits. Everything seems to have stopped. Nobody's moving. Everybody's watching Sinatra, who's watching Clare, who can't take her green eyes off his blue ones. The silence lingers until she breaks it.

"You should drink that while it's hot."

Sinatra lifts the cup and downs it in a gulp, just like Rocco. He coughs twice, reaches into his jacket, pulls out a pack of smokes, shakes one into his mouth and lights up.

"That can't be good for your voice," Clare says.

Sinatra grins, exhales smoke through his nostrils. "What would you know about my voice?"

"I hear you can carry a tune."

Sinatra chuckles. The little smart-ass! "You know my music?"

"Not much. I don't really listen to music."

"No? What do you listen to?"

"In here? Other people's bullshit, mostly."

Sinatra puts his head back and howls. "Clare," he says, "you're all right."

It sounds like a dismissal, so she gets to her feet. To her surprise, so does Sinatra.

"You hungry, Clare?"

The question shocks her. Before she can answer, Sinatra speaks again.

"You like bread?"

What a question! "Who doesn't like bread?"

Sinatra stands up. "Well, then, let's go."

"Where?"

But Sinatra already has Clare by the elbow. He drops a crumpled ten dollar bill on the table and guides her to the door.

"She's off duty now, right?" he asks the night manager, who nods and waves.

"Have a good night, Mr. Sinatra," he says, in a voice shrill with excitement.

And just like that they are out on MacDougal Street, Sinatra still holding her elbow as he leads Clare on a weary walk westward, followed by a black limo with Rocco at the wheel.

"Do you trust me?" Sinatra asks.

"I don't know you," Clare says. "But if you try anything, I can take care of myself."

"Ooh," says old Blue Eyes, "looks like I found me a live one."

It's one of those rare nights in the Village when the streets are nearly empty, so as they make their way up Bleecker there are no shouts of recognition. Anyone who spots Sinatra is likely to dismiss him as a skinny, round-shouldered man who's had too much to drink, being taken home by his lovely young daughter.

Sinatra stops at 259 Bleecker and knocks on the glass door of Zito's Bakery, a place Clare has never been. It seems like a crazy thing to do, as every shop on the street is dark at this hour, including Zito's, but suddenly a light goes on in the back of the shop and a fat bald-headed man in a sleeveless undershirt waddles to the front door, unlocks it and pushes it open.

"My man Louie!" Sinatra says.

Louie is not surprised to see him. "Get in, Frank, it's cold."

"This is my friend Clare."

"Come, come in, both o' yiz."

Louie leads them to the back of the shop and down a set of wooden stairs. The air grows warmer with each step, and when they reach the cellar they see a young man with muscular arms pulling a tray of golden bread loaves from a huge black oven. He greets Sinatra with a wordless salute.

"My man Vito!" Sinatra says.

"I thought *I* was your man," Louie says as he grabs one of the loaves, tossing it from hand to hand to keep from burning himself. He leads the way to a round wooden table in the corner, surrounded by three rickety chairs.

"Best bread in the city," Louie says with true pride.

"In the *world,*" Sinatra says.

Louie sets three plates on the table, along with a bottle of olive oil and a salt shaker. They all sit down.

"Okay," Louie says, and then he tears the loaf of bread in half with his bare hands, bringing the halves to his nose to inhale the steam rising from its fluffy white interior. He is swooning.

"Jesus, I never get tired of that," he says.

"Me neither," Sinatra says, taking the broken loaf from Louie and holding it under his own nose. "Ahhh," he moans, before turning to Clare and holding the halves under her nose. "Breathe, kiddo, this is what heaven smells like."

She thinks she's smelled bread before, but realizes she was wrong. This is beyond bread. It's almost a religious experience. She feels as if she might cry. Sinatra knows exactly what she's feeling.

"So wonderful that it makes you sad, right?"

That's it, exactly. Clare nods, blinking back tears. Louie takes the bread from Frank, lays it on the table and starts slicing it with a long shiny knife. The blade squashes the bread.

"Too fresh to cut," Louie says. "I oughta have a serrated blade."

"I'll get you one for Christmas," Sinatra says.

At last the bread is sliced. Louie sets the pieces flat on the plates, then begins anointing them with olive oil and a little salt.

Sinatra smiles at the bread, then turns to Clare with his arms spread wide, to indicate the mock grandeur of this shabby basement, with sooty brick walls and innumerable pipes criss-crossing the ceiling.

"So," he says, "do I take you to the best places, or what?"

She has to laugh. It's beyond surreal. One minute she's schlepping coffee to the bridge and tunnel crowds from Jersey and Queens, the next she's breaking bread - *literally!* - with Francis Albert Sinatra.

"What do you do, sweetheart?" Louie asks.

"I'm a waitress at Reggio's."

"Best goddam waitress in the city," Sinatra says.

Louie gestures at her with the knife. "You got some balls, bein' down here with us. Not the smartest thing you ever did."

She notices Vito staring at her, sweating hard. They're all staring at her. It dawns on her that nobody would hear her scream if these guys decided to take advantage of her. They could even kill her, and bury her right down in that basement.

But it's a magical night, and such things don't happen on magical nights in Greenwich Village in 1950.

"Well, it's an adventure," Clare says. "I do love adventures."

Louie sighs. "You got lucky this time, but watch out for adventures. Pretty little thing like you - "

"Enough!' Sinatra says. "Nobody's gonna hurt her, we're all good people, here. Can we *eat* now, for Christ's sake?"

"Yeah," Louie says. *"Mangiamo."*

They dig in. Clare has two slices, Sinatra has three, and Louie downs the rest of the loaf. Between gulps he fetches glasses and pours red wine for everyone from a gallon jug. Then he gestures at Sinatra with the bread knife.

"He's a big star, but he's got a peasant's appetite."

"I *was* a big star," Sinatra says. "I'm nothing now."

"Hey," Louie says, "knock that shit off."

"It's the truth. My fuckin' voice is gone."

"No, it ain't." Louie gives Sinatra's cheek a paternal slap. "You hear me? Eat better and stop with the whiskey." He holds up his wine glass. "Stick to the dago red, you'll live longer."

"Who wants to live longer?"

"Come on, Frank, you gotta get serious, before it's too late."

Silence. The men chew and swallow. Vito pulls another tray of bread from the oven and dumps the loaves into baskets.

"Well," Clare says, "I never knew bread and oil could taste so good."

"Only when it's *my* bread and oil, sweetheart," Louie says with a wink.

Vito carries the baskets upstairs. He's got the passionate look of the kind of person who does just one thing, but does it better than anyone in the world. Sinatra gestures at him.

"Maybe Vito could train me," he says. "I could be a baker."

"Hey! What did I say? Knock that shit off."

Louie seems truly angry. Sinatra sips his wine before bowing his head, chastened. His eyes close. He actually falls asleep, chin to his chest, snoring lightly.

"Shouldn't have given him the red on top of the whiskey," Louie says. "Jesus, when he gets goin' on the Jack Daniel's..."

Louie stands up, hoists Sinatra to his feet, wraps his arms around him and turns to Clare.

"Get him home, will you, honey?"

Home?

And just like that they're climbing the stairs, Clare following Louie and Sinatra, who dangles like a bony marionette from Louie's arms.

Upstairs, Vito is stacking warm loaves in the front window. Louie is still carrying Sinatra, who comes to life with a startling suddenness.

"Look!" he shouts. He's pointing at the clock on the wall, beside a framed illustration of the Virgin Mother. The big hand is on the nine, the little one is on the three.

Sinatra breaks free of Louie's grasp, stands in the middle of the floor, spreads his arms and breaks into song.

"It's quarter to three....there's no one in the place, except you and me..."

He falls into Clare's arms, nuzzling his cheek against hers, once again a marionette. She holds him up while Louie shoves two loaves into white paper sleeves with the Zito's logo. He smiles at Clare.

"One for you, one for him."

Sinatra's limo pulls up in front of the bakery and Rocco gets out, ready for whatever comes next. He's obviously done this kind of thing before, many times.

"Lean him against the wall for a second," Louie says to Clare.

She does so. Louie quickly hands the loaves to Clare, then catches Sinatra as he sinks toward the floor, hoists him over his shoulder and carries him outside. Rocco opens the back door and Louie slings him across the seat like a sack of flour.

"Okay," Louie says to Clare, "you better sit up front."

She clutches the loaves against her chest, warm as a pair of twin babies. "He doesn't need me," she says. "He's unconscious."

"Oh, no. He'll remember everything, believe me. If you're not there when he comes around - "

Louie is interrupted as a cop car roars down Bleecker Street, siren wailing. Then a gray cat strolls along, stopping to stare at Clare. Middle of the night life in the Village.

"Please don't ditch him," Louie says. "He's had a bad run with the broads lately."

"I'm not a broad."

"Of course you're not. You live around here? Take care of Frank this one time, you got free bread forever."

Clare laughs. Louie seems offended.

"I'm serious," he says, hand over his heart. "You see me behind the counter, you come in, *boom!* Free bread."

"Are you sure you'll recognize me if I come in a week from now?"

Louie chuckles. "Honey," he says, touching her cheek, "this is a one in a million face. Don't worry, I'll recognize you. Just get him home, that's all I ask."

She's startled by a sudden grip on her wrist. It's Sinatra, awake and sitting up in the back seat, trying to tug her inside.

"Don't leave me, Kate," he pleads.

"It's Clare."

"Right, Clare. Please, *please,* get in."

"Make up your mind, lady," Rocco growls from the driver's seat.

She looks around. Louie has gone back into the bakery. There's not a soul in sight, but the gray cat is still there, staring at her. He seems to be nodding. It's the nudge she needs.

With a sigh she succumbs to Sinatra's tugging and gets into the limo.

Hannah can barely believe the story she's hearing. She almost forgets why she's come to the skylight room. Clare calmly finishes the last of the olive oil bread.

"So what happened next?" Hannah asks.

"We went to Hoboken."

"Hoboken!"

"He wanted to show me the little house he grew up in. It later burned down, that house."

"So that was it? A tour of Hoboken?"

"Well, we came back to the city, to his suite at the Waldorf."

Hannah's blood is tingling. "So you slept with him."

"It was more like, I put him to bed."

"So nothing happened."

"I didn't say that."

"Something happened."

"Well, obviously. Two young, healthy people."

Hannah needs a minute to digest everything. At last she shakes her head and says, "You made love to *Frank Sinatra.*"

"It wasn't love, my dear, it was sex."

"Wow."

"Why are you surprised? Do you think your generation *invented* lust? Seems to me you've done all you could think of to destroy it."

Hannah can't help giggling. "Did you find him attractive?"

Clare shrugs. "There was something vulnerable about him, like a little boy lost. That was a bad period in his life."

"So?"

"So *what?*"

"So, how was he?"

"Surprisingly large, for such a skinny little man. Truth is, he was half asleep the whole way, and then he passed out. I'm sure you know how that happens."

"Only too well."

Clare laughs. "Oh, *men!* What can you do with them?"

"How was he in the morning?"

"Who?"

Hannah rolls her eyes. "Who are we talking about? Frank Sinatra!"

Clare shrugs. "Snoring, when I left."

"Did you leave him a note?"

"What for? I didn't want a relationship with him. I wanted to go home. I took my bread and left."

"That's pretty cold."

"Hey, I earned that loaf of bread. And I didn't steal his loaf, which should improve your opinion of me."

"So that was the last you ever saw of Frank Sinatra."

Clare smiles, the full extent of her answer.

"He never returned to Reggio's?"

"Not on my watch."

Hannah leans forward, then looks up at the skylight. It is dark. When did that happen, she wonders, and how long have I been here?

She points upward. "Look at that shiny star."

Clare looks up. "That's not a star, that's Venus."

"The planet?"

"Yes."

"You can see *Venus* from here?"

"As long as it isn't cloudy."

Hannah feels herself shiver, though it's far from cold. She stares like a child making a wish on a star.

"Anything else you want to know?" Clare asks.

Hannah needs a moment to return to Planet Earth. She switches to her no-nonsense tone. "In exchange for this room I'm offering you a one-bedroom apartment in an elevator building in the neighborhood of your choice. Free of charge, for the rest of your life."

"No, thank you."

"Don't you want to think about it?"

"I just did."

"Wouldn't you like a shower of your own?"

"There are twelve showers at the gym, and I can use any one I want."

"How about a bathtub? When's the last time you had a good,

hot soak?"

"Never cared for baths, my dear. Sitting in your own soup...no, thank you."

Hannah rises to leave. Clare gets up to open the door. "One other thing," Hannah says, stopping just outside the door. "Was that free bread offer you told me about for real?"

Clare smiles and nods. "Louie was good to his word. But it didn't last long."

"What happened?"

Hannah is surprised to see Clare's eyes misting up. "Louie died," she says. "A heart attack, right in that basement where we broke bread."

She sighs, wipes a tear from her eye. "This is the problem with talking about the old days. One way or another, it's going to make you sad. That's why I keep moving forward. Good night, Miss Schmitt. Watch your steps on that carpeting, it's pretty ragged."

"I'm going to re-carpet the stairs, once..."

She feels her face flush. Clare smiles.

"Once I'm out of here," she says.

"I didn't mean it that way."

"Sure you did. I understand. I'm an obstacle."

Hannah hesitates. "Could I visit you again?"

Clare can't help chuckling. "Why?"

"Just to talk."

"About what?"

"I don't know."

Clare cocks her head, as if to examine Hannah from a new angle. "You're a little bit lost, aren't you?"

Hannah says nothing, but her long, deep sigh says it all.

"Well," Clare says, "it's your building. Most of it, anyway. Guess I can't stop you from knocking on my door. Good night."

She closes the door. Hannah lingers a moment before starting slowly down the stairs.

Late that night Hannah makes a phone call to the Brooklyn home of Rico Cusumano, the builder she has hired to oversee the renovation, jolting him from his sleep to tell him to drop whatever he's doing and get the staircase carpeted as soon as possible.

He can't believe what he's hearing. "Miss Schmitt, that don't make sense," he whispers, so as not to wake his wife. "We're gonna be knockin' down walls next to that staircase!"

"I don't care. I want the stairs carpeted, immediately."

"But we'll be ruining it, with all we gotta do!"

"Just lay the carpet next."

"We should lay the carpet *last.*"

Her German accent, barely detectable most of the time, flares up when she's angry. "Am I speaking English, here? Let me try this again. Lay the carpet on the staircase *next.* Understood?"

Rico sighs. "You ain't gonna be happy when we gotta rip it all out again, and you're payin' for it twice."

"I don't care. Will you do as I say? Tomorrow?"

"Okay. Whatever you say."

"And replace the light bulbs in the staircase ceilings. Half of them are dead, the rest are flickering."

"Yes, ma'am."

She hangs up without another word. Rico settles back under the covers.

"Fuckin' crazy Kraut," he mumbles.

CHAPTER FIFTEEN

Jonathan Kaplan takes it upon himself to protect Clare from eviction, soon after the death of Carmine Rotolo at his Bronx nursing home. Kaplan tells himself he's honoring Carmine's dying wish, to keep the one true love of his life safe in the skylight room, for old times' sake.

So he breaks the law without a second thought, forging her signature on a document giving him the right of attorney for her affairs. Then he locates the management company for her building, which turns out to be a crumbling onetime gas station on Hudson Street.

He makes an appointment to meet with the manager and is welcomed into a dusty-windowed office that looks out onto a patch of macadam sprinkled with tall yellow weeds. The manager, Adam Weiss, has the fat, sleepy look of a man who's been doing his dull job for more years than he can count. He has a fleshy red nose, elongated ears and a comb-over to rival Kaplan's.

But he perks up at the sight of this legendary lion of a lawyer.

"The great Jonathan Kaplan, in my office!" he says, with a rare surge of energy.

Kaplan looks down at his shoes, an attempt to seem humble. "Not so great these days."

"What can I do you for?"

Kaplan gets right to business, requesting a copy of Clare's lease. Weiss gives Kaplan's phony document a glance before getting up and squatting to open the bottom drawer of a battered metal file cabinet. He roots around before pulling out a manila folder containing a lone sheet of paper, yellowed with age and flaking at the edges. He cradles it in his hands like a newborn baby.

"Don't even breathe on it, Jonathan, it'll crumble like a cookie."

It's the original lease for Clare Owen and the skylight room. Sixteen dollars a month, with minimal increases in the decades that followed.

Kaplan has a moment of apprehension. The signature he's forged on the right of attorney document looks nothing like Clare's faded fountain pen signature on the ancient document, but he's ready to defend it. A lot can happen to change a person's handwriting over almost seven decades.

His worries are groundless. Weiss doesn't seem to notice the difference, or maybe he's just dazzled by the presence of this famous rebel lawyer in his office. He carries the lease to a nearby copying machine and makes two copies for Kaplan, then sandwiches the original lease back in the manila folder before returning it to its tomb.

He hands the copies with a flourish to Kaplan, who folds them and slips them into his jacket pocket.

Weiss sits back down with the sigh of a man who's just run a marathon. "Anything else? Coffee?"

"I was wondering if we can we talk about Clare for a minute."

Weiss is suspicious. "What do you want from me?"

"Well, I assume you have contact with her one way or another, since the monthly rent comes to you."

"Yeah. She delivers it in person."

Kaplan tries not to appear stunned. "She actually comes here and hands you a check?"

Weiss hesitates, the hesitation of a man deciding how much of the truth to tell.

"No checks," he says. "Cash, first of every month, without fail. Unless the first falls on a Sunday, in which case she shows up on Saturday. We're open 'til noon on Saturdays." He chuckles. "Like clockwork, that woman. Never missed a month in all my time here. And it's the same deal with her only other bill, Con Edison. She told me she walks to their office on Irving Place every month and pays her electric bill in cash. Funny, huh?"

Kaplan gestures at a chair opposite Weiss's desk. "Is it okay if I sit?"

Without waiting for an answer he eases himself into the chair, like a man overwhelmed by life itself. He figures Weiss will relate to such anguish. He also knows he'll have to trade information to get information.

"I've been checking into Clare's affairs," he begins, "and I've been wondering about the source of her income."

"What do you mean?"

"Well, for instance, I know she doesn't collect Social Security."

Weiss keeps a poker face as he asks, "Why not?"

"Who knows? Some people exist under the radar. I mean, for all we know she was born in a log cabin, and never got a Social Security number."

"But she has to have worked, when she was young. Bosses always demand the Social Security number."

"Things were looser back then. Also, she was a waitress. Off-the-books, I'm sure."

Weiss rubs his chin. "If she's not getting the Double-S," he says, "she's not on Medicare, either."

"Probably not."

"Wow. At her age, no medical cover? Anything could happen!"

"She's living on the high wire, all right. She's been very, very lucky."

Weiss is relaxing, enjoying the sense that he and Kaplan are peers.

"I gotta tell you, Jon, she seems fine when she comes in here," he says. "Never says much, but she's polite enough, I guess."

Kaplan hunches slightly as he leans forward, trying to look both vulnerable and desperate.

"Could you tell me about that, Adam? I can see from your face there's something unusual about that monthly transaction."

Weiss reddens. "How do you mean, unusual?"

"Come on, what is it? You want to tell me, so just tell me."

It's checkmate for Jonathan Kaplan, as it has been for so many of his opponents in the past. You give them the vulnerable bullshit, and they tip their hands. Adam Weiss never even realizes there's a game going on, until this moment.

He leans back in his swivel chair, a posture of pure surrender. Then he says with a grin, plain and simply: "Old money."

Kaplan is surprised. "Old money? You mean she inherited it?"

"No, no, not *that* kind of old money." He unlocks a squat steel safe beside his desk and takes out a twenty dollar bill.

"This kind," he says, handing it over.

Kaplan examines the bill. It's a valid twenty, all right, with Andrew Jackson on its face and the words "In God We Trust" where they belong.

But it seems faded, as if someone left it in their pants when they did their laundry, a theory that quickly evaporates when he catches the date on the bill: 1951.

Kaplan is stunned into silence.

"How about that?" Weiss says. "Her rent is now thirty-eight dollars a month. Every month she comes in here with two of those twenties, and I give her two singles in return."

Kaplan feels dizzy. It's a good thing he's sitting. "What are you saying?"

Weiss jabs his forefinger on the desktop. "I'm saying that *all* the twenties she brings here are at least that old. Nothing minted after 1951. Mostly from 1950, and the late forties, even."

Kaplan's mouth goes dry. "Unbelievable," he murmurs.

"Exactly," says Weiss, taking back the bill and holding it up like a winning lottery ticket. "I mean, this is weird. You gonna tell me what it means, Jon?"

He cannot.

Jonathan Kaplan makes his way up Hudson Street in a daze. What is the deal with Clare's money? Where does it come from, and how the hell does it keep coming?

He's saddened by the sights along Hudson, once one of his favorite streets. Now it's Italian restaurants that are trying too hard, with those oh-so-cute bottles of olive oil and balsamic vinegar on each table, and exposed-brick breakfast joints, and family-friendly restaurants where every table includes a jar of crayons and the word "organic" appears on the menu, the awning and the waiters' t-shirts.

He hasn't walked this stretch in years, and when he looks north he remembers why. There on the corner of Hudson and West Eleventh stands the White Horse Tavern, looking as bold and noble now as it did back then.

His heart races at the sight of it. He hasn't been to the Horse since 1951, but if ever there was a day to return, this surely is it.

He crosses the street, goes inside and takes a deep breath, catching a sweetly sour mop-up odor of beer and Lestoil, not at all unpleasant. It's pretty much the way this joint smelled in its heyday.

It's early, so hardly anybody is here. There's a jukebox that never used to be there, but otherwise the cluttered decor is pretty much the same as he remembers it - lots of horses in paintings, sculptures and on clocks.

He takes a stool at the bar and asks if lunch is being served. The bearded young bartender says, "Food service starts in five minutes."

"Is it too early for a beer?"

The bartender smiles. "Never, as far as I'm concerned. What'll it be?"

"A draft. Surprise me."

It arrives in a tall glass. Kaplan tosses a twenty on the bar and gets thirteen dollars back.

"Beer was half a buck the last time I was here."

"Must have been a long time ago."

"Better believe it."

"How come you haven't been back?"

Kaplan takes a long swallow of beer. "Actually, I was kicked out for life," he says with a smile. "But I'm guessing sixty or seventy years is close enough to life, no?"

He hoists his glass. "Here's to my friend Carmine. We had our last drink together, right here."

CHAPTER SIXTEEN

Jonathan Kaplan and Carmine Rotolo arrive at the White Horse ten minutes before Clare Owen has agreed to meet them on an autumn evening in 1951.

The place is packed. They're lucky to find two empty stools at the bar and order draft Rheingolds. This meeting is Carmine's idea, and Kaplan thinks it's a bad one.

"I don't see why I have to be here," he says. "This is *your* game, buddy."

"It's not a game," Carmine says. "We've both dated her. We can't both go on dating her."

Why not?, Kaplan would like to ask, but he does not. And what Kaplan would also like to say is that we've both fucked her, but that would be a mistake. Carmine is basically a prude, a devout Catholic. For all Kaplan knows, he hasn't gone all the way with Clare.

Kaplan sips his beer and regards Carmine, who's all slicked up - shirt and tie, fresh haircut, and a barbershop shave. There's a bit of shaving cream on Carmine's left earlobe, which Kaplan doesn't tell him about.

"My point is this," Carmine says, jabbing a forefinger on the mahogany. "She's gotta choose."

"She's got other things on her mind, Carm. That hot-shot photographer took pictures of her, did you hear about that?"

"I heard, I heard."

"Could be she's on her way to something big."

"I don't care. She's *still* gotta choose."

Kaplan takes a long swallow of beer. Can his friend be this innocent? He wasn't working the night Sinatra showed up at Reggio's, but he must have heard about it. Kaplan belches with his mouth shut, through his nostrils. It's a technique he finds useful to clear his head.

"Well," he says, "I don't know much, but I know a girl like Clare isn't going to like an ultimatum."

"Hey, pal, you wanna split? Go ahead. Nobody's forcing you to stay."

"Too late," Kaplan says, jerking his chin toward the door.

Clare enters the White Horse in a classic Village getup - loose t-shirt, cutoff jeans and sandals. Her hair is freshly washed and combed back into a ponytail, revealing the perkiest of tiny ears.

Heads turn to regard her. She is unique. Even in Greenwich Village, she is unique. She might have just walked in off a beach in California, or Australia. A man looks at her, he wants her. It's just that simple.

She goes to the guys, kissing each on the cheek before ordering a glass of the house red. Carmine offers Clare his stool, but she wants to stand, so he sits back down, flushed in the face.

"What's up?" she asks cheerfully, with the over-politeness of someone who can't stay long.

Carmine is nervous. He's had a speech ready in his head, but suddenly he sneezes and the speech is gone, as if he's blown it away. He wipes his nose, sips his beer and looks miserable.

"Carmine is concerned about us," Kaplan says.

Clare is puzzled. "Us?"

"Yeah. You, me and Carmine."

Before she can respond Carmine finds his tongue and blurts, "It's me or Jonathan, Clare. You've gotta choose."

She sips her wine and tosses her ponytail. "No, I don't."

Carmine can't believe his ears. "Yes you do! Which one of us do you wanna be with?"

Clare shrugs. "Both."

The word hits Carmine like a bullet. Clare makes it worse by adding, "And what about anybody else I might want to be with?"

Carmine and Kaplan look at each other, then at Clare. Kaplan can't hide a tiny smile, while Carmine's soul is collapsing. He looks like a kid who's just found out Santa Claus doesn't exist.

"Clare," he whispers, a broken voice coming from a shattered soul. "My God."

She strokes Carmine's cheek, as a mother would to comfort a troubled child.

"I don't get it," he says. "How can you like *both* of us?"

"Why not? You're both good guys."

"Yeah, but..."

Carmine can't finish the thought. He turns to Kaplan. "Can she do this?"

Kaplan laughs. "Apparently she just did. We've got ourselves a true maverick, here. A free spirit!"

He toasts Clare with his beer glass. Clare finishes her wine, glances at the bar clock and says, "Gotta go."

"Where?" Carmine says. "You just got here."

"I'm meeting someone."

"Whoa, *whoa*. Someone else?"

"Yes."

Carmine slumps in the stool as his heart tumbles to his ankles. "Clare," he says, "we had something special."

"We still do. You're the first person I knew in New York. You gave me a break. I'll never forget that."

"Really? Feels like you forgot it already."

She looks him in the eye and says, in a dark voice he's never heard before: "Please don't ask me to apologize for who I am."

It's both a request and a demand. It chills Carmine.

"Who *are* you?" he asks in wonder.

She smiles. "I think you know." She reaches for his earlobe, giving it a gentle tug before holding up her forefinger to show him a dab of white.

"Shaving cream," she says with a giggle.

And with that she wipes it on his nose, kisses his forehead and is gone, fast as a jackrabbit.

Carmine is in agony. He lets his head fall until it thumps the mahogany. Kaplan rubs his shoulders like a corner man comforting a boxer after a brutal round.

"Easy, buddy," he says.

Carmine lifts his head and wipes the shaving cream off his nose. "Do you believe this shit?"

"Tell you the truth, its pretty much what I expected to happen."

Carmine regards Kaplan through bleary eyes. "Fuck's *that* mean?"

"She's a wild thing, Carm. You've got to accept that."

"Look at you, all cool and calm."

"What do you want me to do? Cry?"

"She's livin' a crazy life, man! Anything could happen to her! Don't you care at *all?*"

"She's living the life she wants to lead. You can be a little part of it, like we are, but if you go for the whole enchilada, you get nothing."

Carmine snorts. "Oh, very nice. Fuck her every once in a while, and be happy with that, huh?"

"Pretty much, amigo."

Carmine sits up straight. "So that's what you're gonna do?"

Kaplan shrugs. "Buddy boy, I just passed the bar exam, and if I know *anything* about love, it's this - there are no laws when it comes to matters of the heart. You've got to be grateful for whatever comes your way in this life."

Carmine glares at Kaplan. "Listen to the big philosopher! Know something, man? You disgust me."

"I think maybe it's Clare who disgusts you."

"Fuck you."

"Come on, Carm, have another drink. Let's celebrate, I just became a lawyer."

"Just what the world needs, another fucking lawyer."

"Good point. But I promise to try and do some good, along the way."

"Don't you get it?" Carmine pleads, shoving Kaplan's chest. "Don't you *get* it?"

With a quaking hand Carmine digs into his jacket pocket and pulls out a little blue box. It opens on a hinge, revealing a diamond ring.

"Oh, Jesus, Carmine."

"Yeah. How about that?"

"Put it away, people will think you're proposing to me."

Carmine shuts the box with a hard snap and pockets it. "You're such an asshole, Jonathan."

"Easy, buddy, I'm still your friend."

"You're no friend of mine."

"Calm down, man, you're out of control."

Like a snake striking Carmine is upon Kaplan, hands around his throat. They go down in a crash on the floor, chairs going with them, drinkers scattering. Screams all around as they roll on the floor, both half-drunk and too inept to gain any advantage.

They struggle to their feet, engaged in a sloppy mutual headlock, and with a sudden surge of strength Kaplan whirls Carmine around before flinging him toward the front window. It shatters as Carmine goes through it, landing on the sidewalk in a shower of broken glass.

He lies there moaning, bleeding from a gash on his head. A waitress rushes out to press a bar mop to the wound as a crowd gathers to gawk.

Kaplan stands there in disbelief, breathing hard until he is grabbed from behind by two men, each holding an elbow in an iron grasp. They hustle him outside and slam him against a parked car, then spin him around to make sure he sees their hard, handsome Irish faces.

The younger of the two takes his wallet from his pocket, pulls out the cash and starts counting.

"How much is there?" the older man asks.

"Eighty-seven."

"All right," says the older man, pocketing the bills. "That'll cover my new window."

The younger man tosses the wallet back to Kaplan. The older man jabs a finger in his face. "You ever come back here, I'll cut your balls off. Tell me you heard me."

"I heard you."

"Good. Get movin', before the fuckin' cops show up."

Kaplan does as he's told. An approaching siren wails as he looks back just once. He sees his former friend sitting up on the sidewalk, holding the bar mop to his forehead, waving off people who offer to help.

Kaplan stays away from the White Horse, and Carmine is never again seen at Reggio's.

The young bartender stares in awe at Kaplan. He points and says, "You actually threw your friend through that window?"

"Didn't mean to. I was just trying to get him off me."

"That's, like, incredible."

"Just one of those freak accidents."

"I'm guessing it ended your friendship."

Kaplan smiles. Do I tell this kid I went and saw Carmine just before he died? No, he decides.

"Yeah, that ended it," he says.

"Whatever happened to the girl you were both dating?"

"I don't know," Kaplan lies.

"Was she really that special?"

"Oh, yes." Kaplan is shocked to feel his eyes misting up. "It wasn't just because she was gorgeous. When she was with you, she was really *with* you. She wasn't thinking money, or security. She was thinking pleasure, pure pleasure. That was her finish line. She made love as if the world was going to end in fifteen minutes, and this was all that mattered."

He stops talking, embarrassed by his own candor. The bartender stares at him.

"Wow," he says, like a child seeing fireworks for the first time. "What a woman. Nobody around like that these days, man. You're lucky if they're not texting while they're humping."

Kaplan chuckles, hoists his glass. "Yes, Clare was a rare bird, for a girl in the '50s." He finishes the last of his beer. The bartender pulls him another draft.

"On the house, sir," he says. "Welcome back to the Horse. And by the way, the kitchen is now open."

He leaves the bartender a ten dollar tip and takes the fresh beer to a table in the dining area, near the big oil painting of Dylan Thomas, the Welsh poet who died after his famous final booze-fest at the Horse.

He looks at the chalkboard menu. He hasn't eaten bar food in years. A waitress with a half-shaved head and a series of rings along the rims of both ears shows up, asking for Kaplan's order in a flat, bored voice.

What the hell. He orders a cheeseburger and cottage fries. She brings it to him on a paper plate that quickly soaks through with grease.

Better on the plate than inside my arteries, Kaplan thinks, biting into the burger and soaking the fries in ketchup before diving into them.

He hasn't enjoyed a meal this much in years, but it's more than that. It's the thrill of the fight to come, the battle for justice. It's been a while since he's dug his dentures into a good crusade, and this will be a noble last hurrah for Jonathan Kaplan, with or without Clare's approval. Right where it all started, in Greenwich Village. Full circle.

He pats his jacket pocket, feeling the papery crinkle of Clare's lease. He'll make sure it stands up to all challenges. She's not going anywhere. Not on his watch!

He eats every morsel on his plate, then tells the waitress to bring him decaf coffee with skimmed milk.

"No!" he shouts as she's turning to leave. "Make it *real* coffee, with cream, and plenty of sugar!"

This is a day for it, a blow-out feast before digging in for the battle ahead!

The coffee is delicious. *Everything* is delicious. Full of beer and grease and coffee, Kaplan sits back and opens his belt a notch. The waitress asks if he wants anything else.

Kaplan smiles. "Well, my dear, you could answer a question for me."

She cocks her head. "Shoot."

"Do you actually think shaving half your head makes you attractive?"

She stops chewing her gum, the full extent of her response. Kaplan realizes he's gone too far.

"It's just that you're a pretty girl," he says, "and it seems to me you're determined to make sure the world doesn't know it."

She writes up Kaplan's tab, tears it off the pad, tosses it on the table and storms off.

"Forgive me!" he calls after her, getting to his feet. "It's none of my business. I tend to overstep boundaries, especially when it comes to wasted beauty!"

The tab comes to $24. Kaplan tosses two twenties on the table, bellows "Keep the change!" toward the kitchen and heads to the men's room.

"Pervert," the waitress mutters to herself.

In the bathroom Kaplan hurries to open his fly. Two beers and a cup of coffee have brought his bladder to the bursting point, and what a sweet relief it is to let it go!

He can't help chuckling as he remembers the old days, when the bottom of the urinal was filled with ice cubes, which melted under the flow. Now he's aiming at a pink urinal cake, which looks as if it could last years before dissolving completely.

But as his flow slows, a sudden pain hits him in the chest with the force of the night train. It travels the length of his left arm, and as he sinks to his knees right there at the urinal, hugging its porcelain sides, chin coming to rest on the wet pink cake, it dimly dawns on Jonathan Kaplan, maverick attorney at law, that this is not how he pictured the sudden death he'd always hoped for.

CHAPTER SEVENTEEN

It's a slow news day, so the obituaries in all the major papers have room to run. Kaplan, age 91, was a king, a rogue, a true defender of the little guy, a lover of the long shot and an unrepentant seeker of the spotlight.

His death at the White Horse is reported by all the papers, but only The Post reports that this champion of human rights died "hugging a urinal after a big greasy lunch."

The anonymous source for that detail is the waitress who brought Kaplan his final meal, still smarting over his crack about her half-shaved head.

What she never tells anyone is that during the chaos that comes with a corpse in a restaurant, she is able to rifle through Kaplan's pockets and relieve him of the remaining cash in his wallet, as well as those two copies of Clare Owen's ancient lease.

Which she crumples up and stuffs in the kitchen garbage can.

Clare Owen reads the obituaries in the library, fighting back a tear or two for her old friend. Could I be partly to blame, she wonders? He climbs all those stairs to the skylight room, then has a blow-out grease feast a few days later. A fatal one-two punch?

And beyond that, Jonathan's death at the White Horse brings back a memory she truly wishes she could bury, once and for all.

It's the morning after Carmine went through the window. Clare shows up for her shift at Reggio's, unaware of the havoc that ensued after she left the White Horse. The assistant manager, a short, sour-faced cousin of Carmine's named Gabriella, holds up a forbidding hand to stop Clare from coming inside.

"Before you start work," Gabriella says, "I'm sending you to Brooklyn."

Clare is baffled. "Brooklyn?"

Gabriella hands her a piece of paper with an address on it, and which subway to take.

"Why am I going to Brooklyn?"

"To see Carmine. You don't know what happened? He got into a fight with that Jew lawyer at the White Horse, after you left. Threw Carmine right through the window, believe it or not."

"Oh my God! Is he okay?"

"He's home. He's alive."

Gabriella points a stubby finger at Clare's quivering face. "They were fightin' over *you*," she hisses. "Yeah, that's right. Carmine was gonna pop the question. Not that you care, Clare."

Clare is stunned. She wonders if that last thing Gabriella said was planned, or an accidental rhyme. She suspects Gabriella has waited all her life for such an operatic opportunity.

"He was really going to propose to me?"

"You heard me. I helped him pick the ring. Take this and go, you're the only one he wants to see. Here."

She slaps a subway token onto Clare's palm.

"You be good to my cousin. He's the best man I've ever known, and he deserves better than you."

Clare lets those words sink in as she closes her hand around the token. "A lot better," she says to Gabriella, before turning and heading for the subway at West Fourth Street.

It's her first time to Brooklyn. The ride to Bay Ridge takes more than half an hour, and then she is walking these quiet streets with their carpet-sized lawns and knee-high hedges. A mailman points the way to the address she seeks, and moments later Clare taps on the door of a small brick house with a blue slate roof, nearly identical to the houses on either side of it as well as those across the street. Gulls drift overhead, and she can smell the nearby sea.

A chubby, graying woman in a black dress and a white apron opens the door, a sauce-stained spoon in hand. Clare can tell that the frown on her face is a perpetual thing. She squints at Clare, then widens her eyes.

"Oh," she all but growls, "you're the waitress, huh?"

Clare clears her throat. "Is Carmine home?"

"The waitress who broke my poor boy's heart."

"I'd like to see him, if that's okay."

"You didn't want to see him last night."

"May I see him now?"

Mrs. Rotolo looks her up and down. "You're nothin' special," she decides. "He's better off."

"You're right. I'm nothing special. May I see him?"

The old lady thinks about it. "Follow me," she says, gesturing with her spoon for Clare to enter. First stop is the kitchen, where

Mrs. Rotolo takes a moment to lower the flame under a frying pan full of meatballs. Then she turns each of the meatballs with expert flips of a fork, so they can brown on the other side. The smell of those meatballs is heavenly, as is the aroma off a steaming pot of red sauce, bubbling away.

"Do you cook?" she asks Clare.

Clare shrugs. "All I've got is a hot plate."

"Hmm."

It's a happy sound, relief that her son won't waste away to skin and bones by sharing his life with this girl. With waddling steps, Mrs. Rotolo leads the way up the carpeted stairs and bangs on a door.

"Carmine!"

"Leave me alone, Ma."

"You got a visitor. The *girl.*" Mrs. Rotolo turns the doorknob and opens it a crack. She holds up a crooked arthritic finger. "Be nice to him," she warns before heading downstairs.

Clare pushes the door open. Carmine is sitting on his bed in a sleeveless t-shirt and boxer shorts, a wide white bandage on his forehead. His legs and arms are hairy. His eyes are as red as a crocodile's, and he needs a shave. Clare realizes she has never seen him unshaven. She's never seen him in his underwear, either. All they've ever done is go to a few movies together, always ending the night on Clare's stoop with a kiss on the cheek. He has never been invited to the skylight room.

"Oh, *Carmine.*"

He manages a crooked smile as he points to the bandage. "Ten stitches. Lucky St. Vinnie's was around the corner, eh?"

"I'm so sorry this happened."

"Ahh, it's no big deal. Mild concussion."

"Did Jonathan really throw you through the window?"

Carmine shrugs. "Kind of a freak accident, really. So, how was your date?"

"Don't."

"Did you have a good time?"

"No."

This is the truth. The guy was a sculptor who spent the whole night complaining about the way his work was not appreciated. He wanted to show Clare his studio, but by that time she was sick of his whining, so she said good night and went home alone.

"You should've stayed at the White Horse," Carmine says. "Got pretty exciting. Cops, the ambulance."

"Was Jonathan arrested?"

"Nah, he took off."

"You could have pressed charges."

A funny smile tickles Carmine's lips. "This wasn't his fault, Clare."

She cannot stand his accusing gaze, so she looks around his bedroom and realizes it's like a little kid's room. A model plane dangles from the ceiling, a framed photo of Carmine in his Little League uniform hangs on the wall and the wallpaper is a pattern of red rocket ships and yellow stars on a silver background.

He's pushing thirty and he's lived in this room all his life, except for his time in the Army! A good Italian boy, looking after his widowed mother. Or maybe it's the other way around. A loop that could go 'round forever, unless he gets married, and Clare joins the loop, and moves in, and learns how to make meatballs....

Christ! Suddenly, it's hard to breathe. Clare goes to the window, which is halfway open, and takes a few deep breaths. The window looks out at the tiny back yard, with two strange objects that appear to be mummies wrapped in tar paper.

"What in the world are those things?"

"Fig trees. My old man planted 'em, ten years ago. Promised him I'd look after 'em. Gotta wrap 'em up before it gets cold, you know?"

"I didn't know that."

"I wanted to look after you too, Clare."

"Carmine."

He spreads his hands. "What, I'm not good enough? Remember how I got you a job, and a place to live?"

"I'll always be grateful to you."

"So? What's wrong with me?"

"Nothing."

"Must be something. My breath bad, or what?"

All she can do is stare at him. There's just no way he can understand that being a nice guy can be a disadvantage, like a hot dog with no mustard. You wouldn't want to eat a whole jar of mustard, but what's a hot dog without that little slash of sharpness?

How is she supposed to tell Carmine that she loves the thrill of new encounters? Exciting guys, writers and painters and musicians with their heads in the clouds and big, big dreams. Rascals? Sure, some of them, but at least they're not boring. And Carmine, bless his sweet soul, is *boring*.

He's looking at her with big puppy eyes, brimming with tears. His bare feet look heavy, like cobblestones with toes, and that's the problem. He's earthbound. There is no lift to Carmine, physically or spiritually, like there is to Jonathan, and all his big talk about changing the world.

So what if it's bullshit? What did Carmine ever change, besides the grounds in the espresso machine?

"Carmine," she says, "I'm just not the marrying type."

She can't bring herself to apologize, because that would be apologizing for her very nature. Carmine wipes his eyes with the heels of his hands.

"What about that kiss you gave me, on your first day?"

She was afraid he'd bring this up. "What about it?"

"I'd never been kissed like that before."

"I was excited! I had a job and a place to live, thanks to you. I was grateful."

"So it didn't really mean anything."

"It meant a lot. I was happy."

"So you kiss complete strangers when you're happy."

"No. I kissed *you.*"

He pats the mattress next to his thigh. "Sit down next to me, Clare, please."

She obeys. Carmine reaches behind his pillow and takes out a little blue box.

"Oh, Carmine, no."

"Do me a favor and just look at it. Please. You owe me that much."

Reluctantly, she holds out her hand. He sets it on her palm, and she stares at it as if it's a strange shell that's washed up on the beach, a shell that might contain a dangerous creature.

"Open it, already."

"I'd really rather not."

"Look, you're never gonna see me again, so please do this one thing for me."

"What do you mean?"

"I start my new job Monday at the Post Office."

Clare is stunned. "The *Post Office?!*"

"Yeah. Gonna need a pension some day, right? Can't stay at

Reggio's forever."

"Jesus, Carmine, you're going to sort mail for the rest of your life?"

"There's worse things. Come on, Clare. Open the goddam box."

She opens it and looks at the square stone on a gold band, wondering how many months of his salary went into this thing, and if he can get his money back, or if he'll keep it until he falls in love again, if he *ever* falls in love again.

And it's funny that she assumes these things, because he has never actually told her he loves her. His passion is just there, radiating from his soul, every time he's with her.

"So? Whaddaya think?"

"It's the most beautiful ring I've ever seen."

"But you don't want it."

"No."

She snaps the box shut and gives it back to him. Silently, his mouth a tight crooked line, he starts to weep. She takes him in her arms and plants gentle kisses on his cheeks, his chin, and his forehead, careful to avoid the bandage. He guides her mouth to his, and it's a different kiss than their first and only other one, gentle as a butterfly landing on a rose. Carmine is lost, but Clare knows what she's doing. She gestures at the bedroom door.

"Does it have a lock?"

It does.

She doesn't have her diaphragm, but Carmine has a condom, and it happens with the sweet sadness that always comes with something that's only going to happen once. Carmine doesn't kid himself. He knows what's what, here. Clare is doing this so he can get past her, and get on with his life. She doesn't want this good, sweet man to be mooning over her while he's with whatever woman becomes his wife. She doesn't want to be the shadow over his soul.

In the Army, Carmine remembers, guys had a term for this. A mercy screw.

They bury their faces on each other's shoulders until Carmine gets there. He whimpers as Clare pulls back, eyes down, and quickly gets dressed. Then she tucks him into bed and plants a light kiss on top of his head.

"Take care of yourself, Carmine."

She unlocks the door and goes downstairs. Mrs. Rotolo is at the stove, spooning red sauce over the meatballs. The whole visit took ten minutes, and most of it was the time spent talking.

"I'm going now, Mrs. Rotolo."

The old lady holds up an instructive forefinger. "Listen to me. Never put the meatballs in the sauce, or they suck it all up. You spoon a little sauce over them, like I'm doin' here."

Then she chuckles, a harsh chuckle. "Why'm I tellin' you this? You're never gonna make a sauce."

"Probably not," Clare agrees. "It was nice meeting you." With those words, she is gone.

"Putain," Mrs. Rotolo says, splashing more sauce over the meatballs. Whore.

Clare feels awful on the walk to the subway, wondering if what she's done will help Carmine, hoping it doesn't backfire. The neighborhood has come alive since she arrived, the sidewalks teeming with families - mothers pushing strollers, dads carrying kids on their shoulders, even a woman on a bench, nursing her newborn beneath the partial privacy of a pink blanket. Bay Ridge is like a breeding ground, and Clare feels abnormal in the midst of it, eager to board the train for that long ride back to West Fourth Street.

And it's amazing how it happens as soon as she climbs the steps to Sixth Avenue and sees the Village in full Saturday afternoon swing - street artists sketching, guitarists singing, rickety tables full of used books for sale, Chinese food delivery boys zig-zagging the wrong way on their bicycles, laughter from rooftop parties, and the occasional whiff of reefer.

She feels good. She feels normal.

She is home.

But she knows it'll never be the same at Reggio's, with their beloved manager gone. Gabriella will be a misery to work for.

She'll hang in there as long as she can, until the modeling thing happens. She's sure it will happen. It has to happen.

Reggio's is buzzing when Clare returns, with customers at every table. Gabriella pulls her aside.

"How's my cousin?"

"We talked. He's okay."

Gabriella doesn't believe it. She grins, not in a friendly way. "Don't make any plans tonight, Clare. Gonna need you to work a double."

CHAPTER EIGHTEEN

It's the lead item on Page Six: Hannah Schmitt and Henry Rivers are on the rocks.

It happens when Henry returns from Bridgehampton to pick up some things. He wants to go straight back to Long Island, but Hannah wants to talk. The kids are in bed, and they're out on their terrace overlooking Central Park, sipping Chardonnay.

After the obligatory chatter about the welfare of the children being the most important thing, Hannah gets to it.

"Henry," she says, "I'm having a lot of trouble with the old lady."

"Right. Because she doesn't want to go, and you're pushing her."

"To a better life."

"Yeah? Better for who?"

"Whom."

"Oh, look at this, I'm gettin' grammar lessons from a damn *German.*"

"Better for *her!* For God's sake, I've offered her an apartment anywhere she wants to go, elevator building, bath and shower, and she won't take it!"

Henry shakes his head. "You just don't get it."

"Oh really? Please enlighten me."

Henry gets up and walks to the rail for a better look at the park, and then his gaze turns skyward. "You never knew my mother," he says to the stars. "She was somethin' else."

Hannah is puzzled. "Why do you bring her up?"

Henry turns to look at Hannah. "When I signed my first big contract with the Yankees, I wanted to move her into a nice place. We'd lived in that damn project all those years. The greasy cookin' smells everywhere, the baby carriages in the hallways, the tiny rooms, all of us livin' on top of each other..."

He shakes his head to chase the memories before turning back to the rail. His eyes are brimming with tears he doesn't want his wife to see.

"But see, Mom wouldn't go. *Would not go.* By this time she's all alone in there, and the papers are runnin' stories about the bonus boy leavin' his mother in the ghetto, and didn't Henry Rivers *care?* I cared all right. *Begged* her to let me take her away."

He turns to Hannah, having blinked back the tears. "Know what she said? She said, 'Henry, I'm *home*. You all grew up here. If I leave now, what the hell did all those Christmases mean?'"

An ambulance roars down Central Park West, its siren piercing the night. When it fades to a whine Hannah gets up and joins Henry at the rail.

"You get it now, baby?" he asks. "You can't offer the old lady a home, because she's *already* home."

Hannah takes a gulp of wine. "Well, she can't stay."

"Why the fuck not?"

"It's too dangerous. She's alone in the building, and if she falls down those stairs, she'll sue us."

"Is that why you had the stairs carpeted?"

Hannah swallows.

"Yeah, I know about that," Henry says. "Rico called me. Wanted me to talk you out of that ridiculous demand. What a fuckin' waste."

"You didn't try to talk me out of it."

"I knew *that'd* be a waste. A waste o' my time."

"Well, it's cheaper than a personal injury lawsuit."

"No, that's not it. I know you, Hannah, and there's somethin' you're not tellin' me. This seems like an act of kindness on your part."

"Don't kid yourself, Henry."

"Come on. If she fell down those stairs she'd be dead, and your problem would be solved."

Your problem, not *our* problem. Hannah grits her teeth.

"No, she'd survive, Henry. She swims all those laps, she eats like a bird. She's tough, believe me." She hesitates before adding, "I've met her."

Henry is stunned. "When?"

"Dropped in on her the other day. Figured I didn't have anything to lose."

"Is she crazy?"

"Far from it."

"What's the skylight room like?"

Hannah hesitates. "It's small, but oh, my God, it's....special. The *light!*"

"Well, now you can see why she's determined to stay."

"I'm determined too, Henry. I'm not prepared to wait ten years

for what I want."

Henry forces a laugh. "No, of course not. You've never waited five minutes for anything you wanted."

"And what is *that* supposed to mean?"

"Means I'm sick of this, Hannah. I'm really, really sick of it."

"Of what?"

The word is right there, dying to be said, and then it is spoken out loud.

"You."

Hannah's jaw drops. She can't believe what she's just heard, but Henry does nothing to soften the blow. He lets his head fall and shuts his eyes with the weight of what's happening.

It's the worst kind of burden a husband can carry, the one he dreads unloading because it's going to send his life crashing upon the rocks. The burden of knowing he no longer loves his wife, and that the road to disentangle himself is going to be a long one, fraught with complicated, expensive bumps.

The first steps on that road happens when Henry begins a slow, heavy-shouldered walk to the door, much the way he'd walk to the Yankee dugout whenever he struck out.

"Get back here!" Hannah shrieks. "We're in the middle of this!"

Henry manages a faint smile for the good times gone by. "No, baby. We're at the end."

"Ex*cuse* me?"

"We're done. I'm gone."

"Henry!"

She jumps in front of him and puts her hands on his shoulders, those same rock-hard shoulders she remembers hanging from during their first time together, nine years and two children ago, when it was all wild and wonderful.

"Come back," she says, "and let's calm down."

"Oh, I'm calm, Hannah. Maybe for the first time in a long time, I'm calm, because I'm *out.*"

She lets her hands drop. "I don't believe this."

"Why not? Because it's not on camera? It can't be real unless it's being filmed, right, Hannah?"

"Henry!"

"That's the deal, isn't it? Want to call a camera crew, get them all over here, have a second 'take?'"

She rubs her hands together, like a penitent. "Why?" she

breathes.

Henry shrugs, as if the answer is obvious. "Because," he says, "you're a cunt."

Nobody has ever said this to her face. As he turns to leave he's followed by Hannah, pounding on his back with her fists. It hurts her hands more than it hurts his back, and then he pauses in the living room to pull a giant modern art painting off the wall.

"I'm taking the Pollock," he says. "You gave it to me for my birthday, the fuckin' thing is *mine.*"

Hannah his hyperventilating. That painting was delivered to the apartment by two guys who handled it as if it were made of eggshells.

"Henry! You're going to damage it!"

He makes a snorting sound. "I won four Gold Gloves, honey, it's in good hands."

And then he is gone, the painting under his arm, out the door and down the elevator to Central Park West, where the night air has never tasted so good.

A neighbor returning from a dog walk sees Henry heading out with the painting, and she's the one who calls Page Six.

Henry lays the painting flat in the trunk of his SUV with inches to spare on either side and begins the hundred mile drive to Bridgehampton. The H & H brand is as good as dead, and Henry forgot to pick up the personal items he wanted, and he didn't say goodbye to his kids, and there's plenty of ugliness ahead, but this night - oh, this *night!* The relief of the truth, however expensive it might be!

He's going to savor it the way he savored those 563 trips around the bases, the cheers of the crowd carrying him every step of the way.

CHAPTER NINETEEN

Clare isn't surprised when Hannah shows up at her door three days later at sunset. She makes tea and they sit as they did before on the floor, face to face, bathed in the rosy river light.

"Love the new carpet," Clare says. "And the light bulbs."

"Yes, well, we can't have you falling down the stairs."

"You shouldn't have done all that for me. I've negotiated that ragged rug for seventy years."

"It needed doing."

"You should have done it *last.*"

"So I'm told."

Clare takes a long sip of tea. "Okay," she says, "let's hear it."

Hannah clears her throat. "I'm willing to make it a two-bedroom apartment, with everything else I mentioned before."

"Why would I need two bedrooms?"

"Is that a 'no?' "

"It's a 'no.' But that's not why you're here."

"Why am I here?"

"I'm not sure. But I know there's a lot going on in your life. Maybe you just need a place to hide."

It's an interesting point. Because Clare doesn't have a TV she doesn't see Hannah's appearance on Good Morning America, but she reads about it in the papers.

Hannah was supposed to be promoting her new summer line of swimwear, but that was just a trick to get her on live TV to answer questions about the wreckage of her private life.

Are you and Henry finished? How are your kids holding up? And what about the octogenarian living in the six million dollar house you're trying to renovate?

Hannah hangs in there for a minute or two, explaining that she and Henry are taking a "breather," the kids are fine, and that she's currently in negotiations with the "octogenarian" in the skylight room.

But she turns a ho-hum interview into an Internet sensation when the anchorwoman suggests she's determined to kick the old lady out, no matter what dirty tricks it might take.

And then it's an executive producer's wet dream come true as Hannah stands up, rips off her microphone, declares "This fucking interview is *over!*" and storms off the set.

An f-bomb from a celebrity, on live TV. Doesn't get any better than that.

Paparazzi are staked out in front of Hannah's home on Central Park West and the gym she's known to use each day, hoping for repeat performances.

So in a funny way, Clare is right. Hannah needs a place to hide, and what better place than the skylight room? Who would think to look for her here?

She's actually relieved to be here. It's so...*peaceful.* She sips her tea and gazes through the skylight.

"It looks dusty," she says.

"Yes," Clare says. "That's from the work your men are doing on the bricks."

"Has the outside of the skylight ever been washed?"

"Only by the rain."

"Have you ever washed the inside?"

"Many times."

"How?"

"With a rag on a stick. This can't possibly be what you came here to talk about."

Hannah looks at Clare. "My life is falling apart," she says flatly.

Clare nods. "I read about your meltdown, and your husband taking off with that painting."

"Yes, well, it's not *really* his. It's a lesser-known Jackson Pollock, and I paid one-point-two million for it, and now some people are claiming it's a fake. A *fake!*" She chuckles. "Like I said, my life is falling apart."

Clare sets her teacup down. "I saw a picture of the painting in the Post, but it was very small." She cocks her head, like a curious sparrow. "Let me ask you something - in the middle of the canvas is there a bit of blue? Just the tiniest, *tiniest* bit of blue?"

Hannah is momentarily stunned. "How in the world would you know that?"

"Ah! So it *is* there!"

"It's the size of a dime," Hannah says, "but it's there, all right."

"Well, then, you've got nothing to worry about. It's the real deal."

"How can you say that?"

"Trust me."

"Clare, come *on*. How do you know about the blue dot?"

The old lady smiles. "I put it there," she says with a giggle that is absolutely girlish.

Hannah stares at Clare in disbelief. "You and Jackson Pollock?"

Clare nods, leans back against the wall and gazes at the sky. "He was up here a few times," she says dreamily. "He wasn't crazy about the skylight, though. Said it wasn't a true northern exposure. You know how fussy painters can be when it comes to their light."

Clare is surprised by how quiet Pollock is on the drive to Long Island. It must be because he isn't drunk. The times they've been together at the Cedar Tavern, she's never seen him sober. He was drunk and bold when he invited her out to his country house for the weekend, but now he seems shy and nervous, like a boy taking his date to the prom in Dad's car.

The house in East Hampton has the look of a woman's sudden absence - wilted flowers standing limply in vases of cloudy water, a sink full of dirty dishes, glasses and coffee cups perched precariously on window sills.

Pollock drops Clare's overnight bag right inside the front door and heads straight for the liquor. He pours two whiskeys and gulps half of his down before handing the other glass to Clare.

It's not yet noon. She's already sorry she accepted his invitation, but she is a long way from the skylight room. That's where she's in control, the perfect place to bring a lover like Jackson Pollock, who flees as soon as he's finished. He makes love like a puppy humping a stuffed animal, and then he is gone.

But now they're stuck together, a hundred miles from the city, and already Pollock is pouring himself another.

Clare takes a sip to calm herself. "Jackson," she says, "are you okay?"

He regards her with an embarrassed eye. "Driving makes me nervous," he says. "I'm a little shaky."

It occurs to her that he drives the way he paints - all over the place, unpredictably. It was a hair-raising trip and now they both need to unwind.

She sips more whiskey and takes in the house. It has the feel of a summer place, the kind of house not meant for winter. You just know how chilly and clammy a place like this can get in February.

Pollock finishes his second whiskey and sets his glass on top of a

Victrola.

"My morning limit," he says. "Come on, I'll show you the studio."

Clare follows him across a lawn of yellow grass to a weathered barn. Inside, the wood plank floor is spattered with paint. Ancient rusted garden tools hang from nails on the walls, like criminals who've been executed and left to rot. The air is ripe with smells of turpentine and linseed oil, and it tastes colder than the air in the house, as if by crossing the lawn they've voyaged to a distant northern climate.

Pollock's breaths are loud as he lays a canvas lain flat on the floor and paces around it. The canvas is as white as a snow drift, a virgin on the marital bed, absolutely untouched. He suddenly stops prowling and stands there staring at the canvas with his hands on his hips, like a man examining an exotic fish that's washed up on a beach.

Clare is shivering. She'd like to go back to the house for the sweater she's packed, but she's reluctant to leave Jackson. He needs her there. He needs *somebody* there.

It comes to her in a flash: he cannot stand being alone, this gifted, tortured man-child. Those times he'd fled from the skylight room he must have gone straight back to his wife, wherever they lived in the Village. Now she wasn't around. Now it was up to Clare to do the mothering.

Mothering, from a woman at least twenty years younger than him!

She goes to his side. They examine the blank canvas together for a few minutes before she dares to speak.

"Is anything wrong, Jackson?"

She wonders if he's heard her. The two whiskies have steadied his nerves without making him drunk. He's got an astonishing capacity. His voice is cool and clear as he declares, "I'm stuck."

"Stuck?"

"Can't get started. I look at it and *look* at it, but I can't get started."

His eyes suddenly brighten as he turns to Clare. "Would you start it for me?"

She doesn't understand. "Start it?"

"Make a mark, any mark."

He hands her a long paintbrush and gestures at a row of drippy paint cans on a long wooden table.

"Pick a color. Any color."

"Jackson, I'm not a painter."

"Would you please, *please* just get me started, for *fuck's sake!*"

He yells in a way that would get neighbors pounding the walls in Greenwich Village, but there's nobody around to hear it but Clare. Numb and frightened, she dips the brush into a can of sky-blue paint, wetting only the tip.

She paces around the canvas just as Pollock did, waiting for an impulse that does not come.

"Jackson. What do I do now?"

"Anything," he says. "Anything at all. Just do *something.*"

Clare squats at the edge of the canvas, brush in hand. She touches it ever so gently to the middle of the canvas, making a tiny blue dot.

She gets to her feet and hands the brush to Jackson, who stands transfixed by the mark she's made. Suddenly he lets out an animal cry of joy and plants a savage kiss on her forehead.

"Okay, okay," he says, his voice choked with excitement. "I've got it now, I've *got* it."

Clare watches in wonder as he prowls around the canvas with a cat-like grace, dripping and flinging paint from an artillery of brushes and cans. No bright colors - just grays and browns and blacks, respectfully avoiding the blue dot.

She sees that his motions are swift and sudden, but somehow far from random. A story is being told on that canvas, one only Pollock can tell.

The fury! The *passion!* Everything he's got is going into that work!

There's no other way to say it - the man is having a relationship with that canvas, both lustful and spiritual.

Pollock works steadily for an hour, oblivious to Clare's presence. It's just him and the canvas, and when at last he draws back for a look at his work and bumps into Clare he whirls as a man would to face an intruder, fists clenched.

"It's me!" Clare shrieks. Jackson drops his fists and shakes his head to clear it.

"Sorry," he says, shy as a schoolboy. "I get lost when I get going, you know?" He smiles. His eyes are heavy. He looks as if he's just given blood.

"Come on," he says, wiping his paint-smeared hands and

forearms with a rag, "let's get some lunch."

The meal consists of saltine crackers, tuna fish straight from the can and whiskey, whiskey, whiskey. Pollock's eyes are at half-mast. He seems happy, or maybe just a little less miserable than usual. Clare is glad that the whiskey bottle is finally empty, until he takes a new bottle and cracks the seal.

He pours for himself with a heavy hand and turns to fill Clare's glass. She covers it with her hand, but this doesn't stop him - he continues pouring onto the back of Clare's hand, ignoring the puddle forming on the wide plank floor.

Clare pulls her hand away. "Jackson, please!"

"Please *what?*"

Her heart is pounding. "Please don't waste good whiskey."

He laughs, an unkind sound. He squints and gazes into her eyes, like a man trying to figure out if he's being told the truth.

"What do you want?" he asks in a low, rumbly voice.

Clare is frightened and angry at the same time. "Nothing," she manages to say.

Pollock snorts. "Everybody who comes here wants something."

"You *invited* me, Jackson."

"What do you want?"

"I want you to stop drinking."

"Yeah? What else?"

"That's it. Put the bottle away."

"Anything you say, dear."

He hurls the bottle against the living room wall. It shatters in a hundred pieces, leaving a spidery wet stain. Like one of his paintings, Clare thinks as she gets to her feet.

"Goodbye, Jackson."

"Oh, sit down."

She turns and heads for the door, pausing to grab her overnight bag, and that's when he pounces.

She's never known such strength. He grabs her from behind and spins her to face him, gripping her upper arms so tightly that she can feel the pulse of her blood, struggling to get through.

Pollock presses his forehead to hers. "Don't leave," he begs, and she's astonished to see that he's crying, the tears trickling into the edges of his beard.

"Jackson, you're hurting me."

His grip grows impossibly tighter. "Please stay."

"Jackson - "

"*Stay!*"

He shoves her. Clare sees stars as her head knocks against the whiskey-soaked wall, and as he approaches to grab her again she launches her knee smack into his groin. Pollock lets out a sound like the howl of a dying wolf as he goes down, giving Clare the time she needs to grab her bag and flee.

She's out the door and halfway to the road when she looks over her shoulder, terrified that Pollock will follow, but it doesn't happen.

She stops running. She stands at the edge of his property and looks at the house, wondering if Jackson is okay.

No - it's more than that. She wonders if he's *alive*.

She walks back to the house and looks through the living room window. Pollock is lying on his side on the hardwood floor in the fetal position, eyes shut, fists under his chin, paint-spattered boots tucked behind his ass.

His broad shoulders heave with every breath. He's crying in his sleep.

Clare goes inside, finds a quilt on the back of a chair and drapes it over Jackson's body, tucking it in around his neck.

"Sleep, baby," she whispers, knowing he probably can't hear her. Then she heads to the main road to hitch a ride back to the city.

It's raining. She's soaked to the skin by the time she's picked up, but it's a lucky ride - the driver, a slim gray-haired man in a big blue Oldsmobile, is going all the way to Manhattan.

He introduces himself as "Bob" and gives her a towel to dry herself, saying he was out in Montauk to check on the progress of a summer home he's having built, a place for his wife and kids to spend the summer.

"That'll be nice for them," Clare says.

"Yeah," he says with a sigh. "Shame I won't be there much."

Here we go, Clare thinks, and sure enough it's the usual lonely guy spiel - too many hours at work, not enough time with the family, wife overwhelmed by the kids, blah blah blah. She's heard it a million times at Caffe Reggio and normally she can handle it but not today, not today...

She can feel his move coming on before he even knows he's going to make it. She'd like to get out of the car, but they're doing seventy on the Long Island Expressway and it's still raining like hell, and the chances of scoring another ride in this storm are nil, so she just lets it fly.

"Bob," she says, "I just gave Jackson Pollock a knee in the nuts to get away from him, which is why I was hitch-hiking in the first place, and I'm exhausted, so if it's okay with you I'm going to take a nap."

Bob is stunned. "You mean the artist, with those crazy drippy paintings?"

"That's him."

"Wow! Read about him in Life Magazine! He attacked you?"

"No, we just had a misunderstanding, that's all."

Bob grips the steering wheel and shakes his head. "Jesus."

Clare folds the towel into a pillow and sets it behind her head. "Okay with you if I take a nap?"

"Of course, of course!"

She rests her head and shuts her eyes. Of course she can't sleep, but at least Bob has stopped talking, and the next words he speaks come an hour and a half later.

"Where can I drop you?"

Clare opens her eyes and sits up. The rain has stopped, the sky has cleared and they're crossing the 59th Street Bridge. The sun is setting, giving the city that magical glow that can never be described the way it deserves to be described.

What a day! To the Hamptons and back, with a little bit of painting and domestic violence in between!

"Anywhere on First Avenue is fine," she says.

"I don't mind taking you to your door."

"That's okay, Bob. The rain stopped, I could use a little walk."

She's not about to tell Bob where she lives. She thanks him for the ride and the towel. He offers his hand for a farewell shake, and holds Clare's a little longer than necessary.

"You take care of yourself, Clare."

"I will."

He gives her his business card. "Call me if you need anything," he says before driving off.

Funny, how men like Bob word it. They don't say "if you need me." It's always "if you need anything," because things are a lot easier to give than selves.

She watches him go three blocks before turning a corner, then looks at the card. Bob is an importer of Italian delicacies, sun-dried tomatoes a specialty. Business must be good, if he's building in Montauk.

She drops the card through a sewer grate and heads for the subway and that long trip, crosstown and downtown.

Back in the skylight room, she strips down and is startled by the sight of her upper arms. Black and blue bruises, tapering tendrils. The marks of Jackson Pollock's fingers, like one of his paintings.

It's dark by the time Clare's story ends. Hannah would love another cup of tea but doesn't want to ask for it.

"Did you ever see him again?" she asks.

"Who, Bob?"

"Very funny. Pollock!"

"Once, months and months later. He came to Reggio's with a couple of guys who looked like art critics, or maybe they were dealers."

"Did you confront him?"

"Why would I do that? In those days you forgot about bad things, or pretended they didn't happen. You didn't talk about them in therapy for years and years and *years.*"

"So you served him coffee and didn't say a word."

"I asked him if he wanted strawberry shortcake. It was the specialty that night."

"Jesus, Clare."

"He had the cake. He had problems, too. Deep down he was a shy man, a gentle lover. I think his work made him crazy. That was the problem, on that trip to Long Island. I was competing with his work. He was never like that up here."

Up here, in the skylight room.

Hannah sighs. "He died in a drunken car crash, didn't he?"

"Yes. Took a young woman with him. It could have been me. I think about that, from time to time."

Hannah thinks about it, too. If it had been you, I'd have the skylight room to myself, without all this drama...

She's ashamed by this thought, and shakes her head as if to get rid of it. She feels pins and needles in her left foot as she stands up and says, "It's a definite 'no' on the two bedroom apartment, then?"

Clare shakes her head. "I'm sorry."

Hannah moves to the door, her left foot tingling. She fights an impulse to injure the old lady for all the problems she's causing, and then she surrenders to the impulse.

"Maybe Jackson Pollock didn't remember you at all," she says. "Maybe he blacked out on his nights up here, and on that trip the two of you took to Long Island."

"Oh, I thought of that. But on his way out of Reggio's that last night, he slipped me a twenty dollar tip."

"That's nice, but it doesn't prove he remembered you."

"True," Clare says. "But then he said, 'Thanks for covering me.' Imagine that? And I thought he was out cold on that floor."

CHAPTER TWENTY

The meeting happens in an ornate office building on Fifth Avenue, across the street from Tiffany's. Fred Schotter - tall, handsome, graying as gracefully as a movie star - greets Hannah with a gymnasium-muscled hug in the lobby and personally escorts her to a conference room on the twelfth floor, smiling all the way. His teeth are bleached so white that under fluorescent lights, they shine blue.

As executive producers go he's one of those hands-on guys, a believer in the personal touch, a birthday rememberer, an attender of important friends' childrens' graduations. He seems to hate delivering bad news but you have to wonder about that, considering how he does it so well, always making it seem like it isn't his idea, that he fought for you all the way, even as he's pulling the trigger that puts a bullet between your eyes.

In short, he can bullshit with the best of them, and if you can do that in TV management there are no limits to your career.

Hannah wonders why they're in the conference room, if it's just the two of them. Then she wonders why it's just the two of them. Then it hits her, from the friendly and pitying look on Fred's face, and the fact that there are no refreshments on the table. No coffee, no muffins, no strawberries dipped in chocolate...just a gleaming black table with nothing on it but a speakerphone.

She might as well be sitting over a trap door.

"What the fuck, Fred."

He spreads his hammy hands. "Hannah. I'm *so* sorry."

"You killed my show."

"I fought for it, believe you me."

"Not hard enough, apparently."

"Hannah, this situation with the old lady you're kicking out didn't help."

"Kicking out? You have no idea how *generous* I've been!"

Fred shrugs. "You know it, and I know it. But it can't help but play ugly in the media."

"Oh, the Post! That bastion of truth!"

Fred leans closer, holding her by the wrists, as her hands are balled into fists. "What about you and Henry?" he gently asks. "I assume you've seen today's story."

"Yes, yes."

"Your husband has his arm around another woman, in broad daylight."

"I saw it."

"A *younger* woman," he dares to whisper.

Hannah nods in agreement. "Young enough to put him in prison, I'd say."

Fred is stunned by this remark, but only momentarily. "Hannah, this is really bad. Your marriage is collapsing." He squints one eye, purses his lips. "Kinda defeats the purpose of a family reality show, don't you think?"

She breaks free of his grasp. *"Everybody's* marriage is collapsing! If anything, more people can relate to it this way!"

Fred sighs. "Not under your circumstances."

"Which are?"

Fred rubs his face with both hands, as if to erase a bad dream. "It'd be different," he says, "if we had some...*consistency* between you and Henry."

"What the hell does *that* mean?"

She's never seen Fred blush, until now. "Well, say, if you were both white. Or both black, for that matter. But a mixed marriage, falling apart on television? That's a fucking mess."

Fred drops "F" bombs so sparingly that when he does, people tend to listen. The room is air-conditioned, but Hannah feels sweat breaking out on her forehead. Fred offers her a handkerchief, which she pushes away.

"You bastards."

"Come on, Hannah, do you really want to put your kids through it? Just *imagine* how ugly it would get. Picture the viewers, choosing sides. 'Who do you like, the white woman or the black guy?' "

"You mean the bitch, or the *nig -*"

Hannah stops herself from speaking the second syllable. She is mortified. She can't believe she's spoken half of the "N" word, and she'd pay a million bucks to take that first syllable back, but it's too late, as she can tell from the shocked look on Fred's face.

"Oh my *God,* Fred, I didn't mean that."

"Of course you didn't. You're stressed out."

"I've never spoken that word in my life. I never even *think* it."

"I believe you, Hannah. The thing is, that's pretty much how it would shake out. Isn't this country divided enough, without a TV show making it worse?"

Hannah can't help laughing. "Oh, my God. Forgive me, Fred, I didn't realize we were in danger of starting another civil war."

"Hannah - "

"Fuck you, fuck the network, fuck the whole bunch of you."

She gets up to leave, stopping abruptly at the door. Her mind is racing, and when she speaks it's an idea that's barely formed when it leaves her mouth.

"What if Henry and I patch things up?"

Fred is still seated at that ridiculously long table. His eyebrows go up. "Any chance of that? Realistically?"

She swallows a sob. "No."

And with that word she's admitting to herself that her marriage, until now on life support, is truly dead. She's had to say it out loud to realize it.

But she's still a pro, and regains her composure in a matter of seconds. No point burning a bridge, however unlikely she'll ever again be crossing it.

"I'm sorry I lost my temper," she says. "You take care, Fred."

Fred is astonished. He can't believe that Hannah Schmitt has actually apologized.

"Hey, stay in touch," he says. "Maybe we can do something else, down the line."

"Sure," Hannah says. "A show about the way my life is falling apart. We'll call it 'Schmitt Happens.'"

Fred laughs, a real laugh. He's never thought of Hannah as a clever person.

"You see?" he says. "Your sense of humor will get you through this. And please let me know how you make out with that stubborn old lady in the skylight room."

Just as this disastrous meeting comes to a close, Tom Becker sits at an outdoor table at a downtown cafe, smoking a cigarette while waiting for the arrival of his date. He's never met this woman, never even spoken with her. They've arranged the meeting through a tantalizing exchange on Tinder, a system that couldn't be better for a guy like Becker.

It's an audition, this meeting for coffee. And if the first time turns out to be the last time, he's only out five or ten bucks, depending on whether or not the girl wants to split the tab.

100

Meeting in the late morning also relieves the pressure of sexual suspense, as Becker's shift starts at one p.m. If there's going to be sex, it'll have to happen next time. And if there is no next time, well, no big deal.

He finishes his cigarette and stamps it out under the table. Sometimes Tinder women are put off by smokers. You never know, and you don't want to kill your chances before she even gets here.

The trickiest part of the Tinder date is managing to recognize the person you're supposed to be meeting. The pictures people put up on their accounts often bear little resemblance to the ones you meet in the flesh. Women tend to be fatter, men fatter and balder. Becker's Tinder photo is more honest than most, only a few years out of date. His full head of hair was a little darker then, his face leaner.

He is the classic picture of an aging tabloid reporter - tie loose around the neck of a shirt that has never known the touch of an iron, comfortable-fit pants from The Gap, scuffed shoes, and basset hound eyes that have seen countless dawns break after lonely nights that didn't work out.

He's got a copy of the Post, and that's good, because his latest story about the H & H collapse is a doozy, with a Paul Frisch photograph of Henry Rivers with his arm around that younger woman, under the headline OH, HENRY! WHAT WOULD HANNAH SAY?

Becker loves it when a Tinder date coincides with a splashy story. Sometimes, it's just the nudge a girl needs. All he's hoping now is that Sheila Greene bears at least a remote resemblance to her photo.

And he is not disappointed.

They spot each other at the same instant, waving in mutual recognition as Sheila, looking exactly like her Tinder photograph, sits in the chair opposite Becker's.

She's a throwback, a latter-day hippie. A red scarf tied around the top of her head keeps her wild black hair under control, and beyond the edges of that scarf coils of hair cascade to her narrow shoulders like so many snakes. To Becker's delight she's wearing a loose sky-blue t-shirt with no evidence of a bra beneath it. Tight black jeans and sandals complete the picture of a fortune teller on a coffee break.

They shake hands formally, the way a loan officer in a bank greets a customer.

But who's the officer, and who's the customer? That's all part of the fun.

"Nice to meet you," Becker says. "Let's get it out of the way - I'm much older than you."

It breaks the tension. Sheila laughs, revealing beautiful white teeth, and Becker feels a jolt of recognition. That *laugh!* Where has he heard that laugh before? A short, sharp cackle, like something you'd hear from a startled hen.

"No big deal," Sheila says. "Are you worried about the age thing?"

"Not at all."

"I had a feeling you'd be an older man. Not *old*. I just mean, older than me."

"How old are you?"

"Twenty-nine."

"Everybody's older than you, dear. I'm sixty-two."

"Wow! Holy shit! Sorry, it's just...I mean, you don't look it."

"Watch out, or I'll hit you with my cane."

Again, that chicken-cackle laugh goes right through him, triggering a memory that isn't quite jelling. Becker worries when he can't remember things, fearing the onset of Alzheimer's.

But he doesn't worry for long. The prospect of easy sex nudges other worries aside. It's pretty clear this girl has Daddy issues, which should work to his advantage.

They order cappuccinos. Sheila, it turns out, is an actress, a poet and a psychic ("I feel things coming, like, the way goldfish sense when an earthquake is coming") and the rest of the time she's a telemarketer, selling magazine subscriptions over the phone.

The mention of magazines gives Becker the green light to bring up his career. He shows her the Post, and his big story on page five.

Sheila seems impressed. "Whoa!" she cries, pointing at the photo. "Isn't that guy married to the woman who wants to kick out the old lady?"

A surge of excitement reaches all the way to Becker's toes.

"As a matter of fact, I broke that story exclusively."

"Get *out!* How fucked up is *that?*"

"Pretty fucked up."

Sheila startles Becker by grasping his hand. A grim look has come to her face, a look that's almost scary. "You're doing a good thing," she says, with genuine passion. "I really dig that. I mean, that's what journalism is all about, protecting the weak, am I right?"

"Absolutely," Becker agrees, thinking, *Dig?* When's the last time I heard *that* word?

The crusading journalist image is fine, but it wears thin fast, and it's also depressing. Becker wants to make her laugh, so he shares a few choice tales about some of the craziest stories he's worked. He's good at this. He can spin a yarn, and soon Sheila is laughing her ass off.

A Tinder date starts out at second base, and once they're laughing you're on third, taking that long lead toward home plate. Suddenly Becker is sorry this is a coffee date, that his shift starts in less than an hour. This girl is a player. If he'd met her at night they'd be at his apartment by now, or at her place, wherever she lives. What a waste!

She's still holding his hand, laughing away. It's time to wind up the funny stuff and return to his serious side.

"Anyway," he says, "you're right about that old lady in the skylight room. She's just amazing. A true survivor. This city is hard on the poor, you know?"

"Ha! Tell me about it!"

Sheila pulls free from Becker's grasp and spreads her hands, which have silver rings on all ten fingers.

"My mother's in the same boat!" she cries. "She's had the same little basement apartment on Bank Street for thirty-two years, and now the landlord wants her out. Do you be*lieve* that shit? Never late with the rent, never asking for a paint job, and the plumbing? The pipe under the kitchen sink has been leaking into a bucket, like, *forever,* and if she asks for a repair..."

She can't even finish the sentence. "Landlords, man," she says. "Fuckers."

Becker is feeling dizzy from a distant rumble in his soul. He hesitates before asking, "Where on Bank?"

"Bank and Bleecker."

He does some quick arithmetic. "So you must have lived there, too."

Sheila rolls her eyes. "Still do. My cot's in the kitchen." She giggles. "All my life I've slept in the kitchen. Funny that I can't cook, right?"

Suddenly she brightens and leans across the table. "Doris is at work now, if you have time for a quickie. What time do you have to be at work?"

Doris. Her mother. She calls her mother by her first name. So did Becker, twenty-eight years ago, when he was humping single mother Doris Greene in that boxy little bedroom on Bank and Bleecker, while baby Sheila slept in a bassinet in the kitchen.

He remembers the drip, drip, drip of that leaky pipe under the sink. He remembers the way Doris chicken-cackled when she laughed. Only someone who came out of her could make that same sound.

And he remembers going with Doris and the baby to the Abingdon Square Park playground, and pushing little Sheila in the kiddie swing.

Becker and Doris only lasted a few more dates before he broke it off. He knew he had to get out after another trip to that playground, as he pushed Sheila on the swing while Doris went to get ice cream cones. The kid was just learning to talk, and here came one of her first words as she swung toward him, gripping the safety bar.

"Da-da."

That did it. Impending stepfather fears sent Becker running, even though Doris was a nice woman, a very nice woman. And now here he is all these years later, trying to nail her daughter, a young woman who once called him Da-da.

"Hey, Earth to Tom. Are you okay?"

Sheila is concerned. Becker has gone pale. He feels dizzy. He looks as if he's about to pass out, and while Sheila is eager for a quick bounce, she does not relish the idea of reviving him.

His mouth has gone dry. He finishes his cappuccino in a gulp and shuts his eyes. "This is wrong," he murmurs, more to himself than to Sheila.

She doesn't like hearing that. "Nothing is *wrong,* if it's okay with both of us."

Becker opens his eyes, forces a smile. "It's not okay with me."

"Did I do something wrong?"

"No, no."

"Too aggressive, right?"

"No, you're fine. This is how Tinder works, right? We both know what we're after."

"So what's wrong?"

She won't let it go. Becker sighs, which should be enough of an answer, but Sheila waits for more, unable to believe that a fat old man is turning her down.

"Guess I'm just too old for this," he says.

She chuckles. "Well, that's good to know, Grandpa."

He can't help laughing. Sheila stands and gives his shoulder a friendly farewell pat.

"You have a nice life, Tom."

That's one of the good things about Tinder - nobody gets angry when it doesn't work out, because you've only wasted an hour of your life. Nothing like the knock-down, drag-out scream-fests Becker has endured in his long history of break-ups.

He watches Sheila go. She even walks like her mother - the short, snappy, matter-of-fact strides of a person with somewhere to be. Sheila walks for a block down MacDougal Street before turning west, and dropping from sight.

Feeling raw, Becker sits alone at that table. He lights up a cigarette. It starts to rain, but he's safe and dry where he is, under the green Caffe Reggio awning, just a few feet from where Clare Owen stood and asked Carmine Rotolo for a job on that October evening in 1950.

CHAPTER TWENTY ONE

Hannah is lost. Her marriage, the reality show, the H & H brand...it's all going down the toilet. And why?

Because a stubborn old lady refuses to move out of the skylight room.

Normally when things go wrong even slightly in her life, she gets it out of her system by abusing one of her employees, but not this time. Instead, she walks slowly home through Central Park after that disastrous meeting with Fred Schotter. No shopping, no trip to the gym - none of the activities she so often savors to avoid irritating mothering tasks.

Her children look up from their iPhones, surprised to see Mommy, as Consuela, the latest nanny, quickly shuts off the Spanish daytime soap opera she's been watching on the wide-screen TV.

This would be a firing offense under normal circumstances, which no longer apply. Consuela hunches her shoulders, expecting the worst, and when it doesn't come, she sighs with relief.

"I make supper," she says as she scurries to the kitchen.

The kids's go right back to their iPhone games. Looking at them, Hannah feels ashamed all over again for having used half of the "N" word while ranting at Fred Schotter.

What if her children had heard her? How could she have done such a thing?

The whole selling point of their doomed reality show was to take the world in a love embrace, racial differences be damned, and show people how we can all live in harmony.

What a joke! Look at her children, locked in their iPhone trances! Do they even realize what's going on with Mom and Dad?

"How was school today?" Hannah asks.

"Fine," they reply tonelessly, still clicking away on their phones.

"Did you learn anything? Desmond?"

"No."

"Greta?"

The little girl's iPhone makes a beeping nose, signaling the end of a game. "Mom," she moans, "you distracted me."

"I'm sorry."

She stares at her mother. "When is Daddy coming home?"

What do you say to that? Greta's gaze is unbroken as she awaits an answer.

"Soon," Hannah says.

Desmond chuckles. "No, he ain't."

"Desmond."

"Don't bullshit us, Mom!"

"Young man, I don't like that kind of language."

The boy clicks away on his iPhone, then shows it to his mother with a sneer.

"Soon, huh?"

Desmond is holding up the Post story about Henry and the other woman, with the photo of them arm in arm. Hannah feels paralyzed.

"What's that?" Greta asks, but Desmond pulls his phone away before she can see, and then the two children are wrestling on the floor, Greta howling, Desmond laughing.

"Daddy's got a *girlfriend,* Daddy's got a *girlfriend!"* he shouts.

Hannah feels as if her head is about to explode. She pulls the kids apart and sends them to their rooms. Then she goes to the kitchen, tells Consuela to make sure the kids take baths after dinner and rushes off, without a destination in mind.

It's the wrong thing to do. She knows that, and guilt is eating her alive, but she has to get out of the house. She feels as if she's on the ledge of a burning building, twenty stories up.

You cannot go back inside the building. All you can do is jump.

Hannah's jump takes her to the river. When she feels stressed she likes being near water, and the pathway along the Hudson is a wonderful place to walk, except for those idiots on their Citibikes, refusing to yield the right of way to pedestrians.

Crossing the highway, she's nearly clipped by a fat guy coming toward her on a Citibike. She jerks her hip out of the way just in time and smacks him on the back of the head.

"Watch where you're going, fatso!" she screams.

He turns and calls her a shithead. She dares him to come back and say that again, but the man, truly frightened by her enraged face, keeps pedaling.

If only he knew who'd just hit him! He'd land a million dollar assault settlement, just like that! Hannah can't help chuckling. It's the first break she's caught all day.

She heads downtown, as if she's being pulled by a force beyond her control. Her feet are starting to hurt. There was that long walk through the park, and now this. She wishes she'd switched to her running shoes, but it's too late for that now.

She's really moving, past the Intrepid, past Chelsea Piers, past 14th Street and into Greenwich Village proper. The red brick house she's purchased is just a block to the east, but she doesn't even want to look at it.

She's being drawn to the end of the Christopher Street pier, and the golden sunset that's happening over Hoboken. Couples recline on blankets in the lush lawn down the middle, bounded on either side by wood plank walkways.

No bicycles, though the joggers can be almost as much of a nuisance. Except for walking, Hannah believes that indoor exercise is best - thirty minutes on a treadmill, or a stationary bike, to get that heart-rate up. Good for your cardiovascular system, and nobody's around to annoy you.

She walks all the way to the end of the pier and grips the top of the guard rail. The water swirls with the changing tides, and the early evening sun is warm on her face as it blazes a golden path across the river.

A guy in a canoe paddles past. A canoe! She shuts her eyes and imagines that's she's out at sea, far from her problems. Wouldn't that be great!

She senses someone standing next to her and opens her eyes to see a pair of wrinkled hands beside hers, gripping the guard rail. She turns to see that it's Clare Owen, smiling at the sunset.

"Pretty, isn't it?" the old lady asks. "Even now, this is a view I never get tired of."

It feels like a dream, and then it makes sense. Hannah remembers the Becker story, and the photograph of Clare lounging at the end of this pier. It's one of her spots. In a weird way, Hannah feels like a trespasser.

"I guess you were looking for me," Clare says.

"I swear I wasn't. I just took a walk and wound up here."

"Hmm."

"It's the truth."

"Are you making me another offer?"

"No. It doesn't matter anymore. My TV show is dead, my marriage is over and my kids barely know me. Otherwise, everything's just great."

Clare stares at Hannah before saying, "I read about your husband. I'm sorry. Why don't we sit?"

They move to a bench facing downtown, where the giant Freedom Tower looms over everything.

"I watched the twin towers fall from here," Clare says. "Were you in town when that happened?"

"Yes."

"Quite a day."

"Henry was actually down near the Trade Center, at a card show."

"What's a card show?"

"A bunch of retired ballplayers sit at a table and sign baseball cards for their fans. Henry was supposed to get twenty grand for the day, but of course the show was interrupted by the terrorist attacks."

"Twenty thousand dollars?"

Hannah shrugs. "Pretty much a standard card show fee."

"That's insane."

"Like I said, the show was cut short. Henry had to settle for five thousand."

"Aw, your poor husband."

"Don't make fun, Clare. He came home covered in that horrible dust."

"How was he?"

"Shaky for a few days, but he got over it."

"No. How *was* he?"

Hannah is puzzled. "What do you mean?"

"Your husband. You know. At night."

She winks at Hannah, who is stunned by this hairpin turn in the conversation. "Are you asking me what I *think* you're asking me?"

"Yes."

"Jesus!"

"Don't get upset! I've seen his picture in the papers, read about his big home runs. Big and strong, but that doesn't always mean they're any good in bed."

"My God, Clare, how can you say that to me?"

"Because he was a baseball star. That's not necessarily a good thing."

"Is that so?"

"You're under them, and you're not even *there*. They're not loving *you!* They're showing off, doing it for the crowd! 'Hey, everybody! Look how *great* I am at sex!' "

Hannah is shocked. Then she can't help laughing. It's the laughter of recognition, and Clare knows it.

"Yeah," she says, *"you* know what I'm talking about. 'Take me out to the ballgame' takes on a whole new meaning, doesn't it?"

Hannah does not even try to deny it. "How the hell do you know so much about baseball players?"

Clare shrugs. "To be fair, I only knew one."

"Would I know him?"

"Oh, he's dead now."

"I figured *that,* but who was he?"

"It doesn't matter, dear."

"Come on! Who was he?"

Clare sighs, shrugs. "I guess Joe wouldn't mind, at this point."

"Joe? Joe who?"

Clare rolls her eyes. "My dear, when it comes to baseball stars, I do believe there's only ever been one Joe." She smiles. "He played center field for the Yankees, long before your husband was born."

CHAPTER TWENTY TWO

It happens at the Beatrice Inn on West 12th Street, soon after Clare's photo shoot on the pier with Richard Avedon. He's thrilled with the way the pictures turned out, and wants to celebrate. He believes he's found the Next Big Thing, and to make sure Clare doesn't get the wrong idea he invites Francisco to join them, an unofficial chaperone.

It works. Clare is totally relaxed as the three of them clink glasses and sip red wine. Francisco does most of the talking, advising Clare to maintain her figure by staying away from cheese and sauces.

"But not tonight!" he says. "Tonight, we indulge."

And they do. Lasagne, chicken parmigiana, garlic bread...by the end of the meal they're all stuffed, and slightly buzzed from the wine. Avedon squares the tab, says he's got work to do back at his studio and asks Clare if she needs a ride anywhere.

"No," she says. "I live right on this street."

Off Avedon goes, leaving Francisco and Clare to finish the last of the wine. They are facing each other, and Francisco is delivering a juicy bit of gossip about a famous fashion model when suddenly a flush of blood reddens his face.

"Oh my God, Clare, oh my *God.*"

"Are you okay?"

He jerks his head forward. "Right over there, the corner table. Don't look, don't *look!*"

"How can I see if I don't look?"

"All right, take a quick look, but for God's sake don't stare."

Clare turns to look at the round table in the corner, where three well-dressed men are having dinner. They lean forward to speak and to listen, as if to thwart eavesdroppers. Two of them are middle-aged and thick-set but the third is slender, with ramrod-straight posture. His black double-breasted suit fits like a coat of paint, his white shirt seems to gleam and a perfectly knotted tie completes the picture.

He sips his drink with a delicacy that's almost dainty. You wouldn't call him handsome - his face is horsy, the nose long, with wide nostrils - but somehow, Clare can't take her eyes off him.

Until Francisco speaks up.

"I said don't *stare,* Clare!" he hisses. "Jesus!"

Clare breaks the stare and turns back to Francisco, whose face remains red.

"Who are they?" she asks.

"They? Well I have no idea who *they* are. But the drop-dead gorgeous one is Joe DiMaggio."

He pauses, raising his eyebrows for effect. Clare does not react. She whispers, "Who's he?"

"Oh my God, you little *hick!* How long have you lived in this city?"

"Calm down, Francisco!"

"He was only the *greatest* center fielder in the history of the New York Yankees!" Francisco purses his lips and cocks his head. "You have heard of the Yankees, I take it."

The wine brings out Francisco's bitchy side. Clare ignores it and replies, "The baseball team."

"Oh, very good. Go to the head of the class."

"He doesn't play anymore?"

"He's retired."

"What does he do now?"

"Whatever he pleases, I suppose. Oh my *God,* he's coming this way!"

Gliding like the Yankee Clipper he's known as, DiMaggio makes his way to their table. Francisco is trembling, bracing himself for a reprimand he expects to get for staring. He looks down at his hands while Clare stares frankly at DiMaggio's broad, toothy smile.

"Excuse me for intruding," he says. "I'm Joe DiMaggio, and I was just wondering if you'd care to join us for dessert."

His voice is higher than she expects it to be, reedy and tenor-like. He sounds like a teen on the brink of adolescence.

"Oh, Mr. DiMaggio," Francisco babbles, "that would be *such* an honor."

DiMaggio cocks an eyebrow at him and puts a consoling hand on his shoulder. "Not you," he says gently, like a sympathetic coach sending a player to the bench. "The lady."

Mumbling something or other, Francisco gets up and scurries off into the night. DiMaggio and Clare are staring at each other, the way you stare at a painting you just can't turn away from. Clare suddenly remembers that he's waiting for an answer, but what's the answer?

He's too old for her, he's not her type, and she's not crazy about the way he dresses - too somber, too serious, like a damn banker.

What's a man like this doing in Greenwich Village?

But she's transfixed by his eyes, big and brown, and the way he's standing there, hands behind his back, like a boy at the prom, hoping not to be embarrassed by the girl he's just asked for a dance.

"Sure," Clare says, rising from her chair, and when she looks at DiMaggio's table she sees that the two other men are gone.

DiMaggio pulls back a chair for Clare. So courtly! Nobody has ever done that for her before. They settle in and the waiter appears with dessert menus. It's all pastries, with sugary fillings and whipped cream.

"I don't usually eat dessert," Clare says.

"Neither do I. Goes right to my hips, these days."

Clare giggles. Such a funny thing for a man to say! DiMaggio realizes how he sounds and blushes.

"Since I retired, I mean. I ate like a bear when I was playing ball."

"Do you miss it?"

He seems surprised by the question. "Sometimes. Not really. When you know your skills aren't what they used to be..."

He doesn't finish the thought. He doesn't have to. Clare is sorry she brought it up. She can see he's feeling bad. She points at his left hand and says, "I really like your ring."

It works. DiMaggio's toothy smile is back. 'My first World Series," he says with quiet pride. "Nineteen thirty-six. Beat the Giants in six."

"May I see it?"

He takes it off and puts it in her hand. It's a bulky thing, like a college ring, with a glittering diamond in the middle. Clare slips it on her ring finger. It's as loose as a hula-hoop, and with sudden shame she realizes what she's done and rushes to take it off, dropping it under the table.

"Oh my God, I'm so *sorry!*"

She dives under the table to retrieve it and hands it to a laughing DiMaggio, who slips it back on his finger and rubs the diamond with his right thumb.

"Did I damage the stone?"

"Don't worry, it's fine."

"I shouldn't have done that."

"Well, honey, now you've worn my ring, and I *still* don't know your name. That's a first, I have to tell you."

"It's Clare."

"Well, it's nice to meet you, Clare."

The waiter returns to take the dessert orders. DiMaggio asks for black coffee and scans the menu one more time.

"Would it be possible to get a plate of fresh fruit slices?" he asks. It's not on the menu, but the waiter says "Of course, of course!" and dashes off, probably to the nearest fruit stand.

You can tell DiMaggio is used to people rushing around to get whatever he wants, but it doesn't seem to make him happy. He's embarrassed by the waiter's reaction.

"I shouldn't have asked for the fruit," he says. "But I really like it."

"Me too."

"Why don't you eat dessert, Clare? Don't tell me you're on a diet!"

"Well, I'm about to start modeling, and I don't want to get fat."

It feels funny to say it out loud. She hasn't told anyone at Reggio's about the photo shoot on the pier with Avedon. Except for Francisco, Joe DiMaggio is the first to know.

He leans back in his chair in bemused astonishment. "*Start* modeling! I would have sworn you've been doing it for years!"

"No, I just had some pictures taken. I'm a waitress."

"Not for long," DiMaggio predicts. "You've got what it takes, kid, take my word for it."

He smiles again, sadly this time. "I'm past my prime, and you're on the rise," he says softly. "Funny how that works. Appreciate it while it lasts, Clare."

She feels sorry for him. DiMaggio is the oldest young man she's ever met - not even forty, and bemoaning his lost youth!

"You're not past your prime," she says. "Lots of good years ahead for you."

"All I know is baseball."

"You'll learn other things."

A tickle of a smile. "Think so?"

Clare shrugs. "What choice do you have? You'll probably live another fifty years. Can't just sit around counting your money."

DiMaggio laughs out loud. "Clare, you're good for me, you know that? I hope you live another hundred years."

The waiter appears with the fruit plate, breathing hard. There's definitely been some scrambling to put this thing together, and it's a beautiful thing: slices of apple and pear in a star formation, encircled with costly out-of-season strawberries.

DiMaggio lifts the plate and offers it to Clare, a ladies-first man all the way. Clare takes a strawberry and bites into it, and it's the most perfect piece of fruit her tongue has ever met.

But when DiMaggio bites into a strawberry, the juice dribbles onto his shirt, a blood-red splash in the middle of his chest.

In a flash Clare dips a cloth napkin into a glass of water and goes to work on the stain.

"If I do this fast enough it'll come out," she says.

DiMaggio holds still while she rubs at the stain. She can feel his chest under the shirt. She's never felt a chest like this. It's as hard as a washboard. She keeps rubbing until it's a clean wet spot.

"Got it out, Mr. DiMaggio," she says. He reaches out and holds her wrist, gently but firmly, with a hand still rough from all those years of gripping and swinging baseball bats.

"For heaven's sake," he says, "call me Joe."

Hannah is slack-jawed. By now the sun is almost gone behind the train terminal in Hoboken, and seagulls are shrieking, as if to mourn its departure.

"You had an affair with Joe DiMaggio," Hannah says, sounding like a trial lawyer eager to nail down an elusive fact.

"It was hardly an affair, my dear. It was a one-nighter."

"In the skylight room?"

"Yes."

"You never saw him again?"

"Not that I recall."

"And you're saying he wasn't much good."

"Well, he had the best body I ever held, I can tell you that. And I suppose he was okay, technically speaking."

"*Technically* speaking?"

"He could do it, all right. Plenty of energy. But it's that star thing we were talking about. It was all about him. I was just there to make him look good. Plus, he was a little too fussy. Folding his clothes just so, and frantic because I didn't have any hangers for his suit. That's hardly appealing to a woman, is it?"

"I guess it didn't bother Marilyn Monroe."

"Oh, this happened before she came along. By the way, she was supposed to be a slob, wasn't she? No wonder it didn't work out for them."

Clare stands up. "It's past my bed time," she says. "Come on, walk me to the street."

They're just a few steps into the walk when a graying bearded hippie wearing a head band and a leather vest over his bare torso spots her, makes a fist and shouts, "Hang tough, Clare!"

Clare salutes him and turns to Hannah. "See that? You made me a star."

"I'm lucky he didn't recognize *me,*" Hannah says.

She's actually worried about Clare, and fights an urge to take her by the elbow. She seems tough and fragile at the same time, or maybe she's just tired. Tired of answering questions, too, but Hannah has a few more.

"What was Richard Avedon like?"

"Oh, an absolute gentleman, all the way."

"I met him once, and I could barely speak! He was a legend. And he must have been impressed, if he took pictures of you."

"I suppose I wasn't hard to look at, back then." Clare jerks a thumb over her shoulder. "Shot the pictures right on this pier, in fact. This was a crummy place before it was renovated, I can tell you that much."

"So what happened? Did you have a modeling career?"

Clare presses a hand to an aching hip, but does not break stride. "No."

"Why not?"

"Let's just say I got derailed."

They reach the street, the point where they will part. The sun is gone, and a crescent moon dangles from the sky like a silver earring.

"Derailed *how?*" Hannah asks.

Clare sighs and studies the moon, as if to draw wisdom from it. Then she turns to Hannah and abruptly asks, "What are you doing on Friday?"

She says it as if she and Hannah are longtime friends making girly-girly plans.

Hannah tells the truth. "Not a thing."

"Come with me to Staten Island."

"Staten Island? Really?"

"Have you ever been to Staten Island?"

"Never."

"Well, you've missed out. Join me on my annual voyage off

Manhattan Island. You might even enjoy the ferry ride! It's free, you know. When you're me, you've got to take advantage of things that are free."

"This Friday, the day after tomorrow?"

"Right."

That will work out perfectly. Henry is picking up the kids early on Friday morning, off to Bridgehampton for the weekend.

"Okay, I'm coming," Hannah says. "But come *on*, Clare! Are you going to tell me how you got derailed?"

"We'll get to that. It's kind of a long story. Meet me at the ferry terminal at ten."

"I can pick you up."

"No," Clare insists, "meet me there."

"May I walk you home?"

"I can get there on my own, thanks very much."

Hannah is just a few steps into her long uptown walk when she's startled to hear her name being yelled. She turns to face Clare, who stands where they parted with her legs apart, gnarled fists clenched.

"We can talk all you like," the old lady says, "but I'm *not* moving."

Hannah smiles. "See you Friday," she says. Then she begins the long walk home to her children, wondering what the hell she's going to tell them.

But when she gets there the kids don't want to talk about the story about their father in the Post. They don't want to talk about anything. All they want to do is hug their mother for a long, long time before they go to sleep.

CHAPTER TWENTY THREE

Tom Becker is in a fog he cannot shake. That foolish Tinder date has left him spooked. For the first time in his life he feels his age, and he doesn't like it. A career in tabloid journalism is as good a way as any to prolong your adolescence, and Becker has ridden the ride longer than most. Sixty-two years old, and still behaving as if life is one long panty raid!

He looks around the newsroom and wonders if these guys even know what a panty raid is. They're so serious, so educated, so...*well-behaved!*

Oh for the days of Post legends long gone! The cigar-smoking misogynists, the boozy police reporters, and that promiscuous secretary on the fifth floor who never met a cock she didn't like!

Imagine saying something like *that* in the newsroom now! The Politically Correct Police would put you in front of a firing squad!

Becker blames journalism school for the woes in the game today. It was better the way he came up, a hungry kid from The Bronx who took a copyboy job and worked his way up, learning this racket the way you should learn it, through your skin.

Journalism, Becker believes, cannot be taught. It must be *absorbed.*

Seems to Becker that the first thing they do in journalism school is make you undergo a humor-ectomy. Nothing is funny, because one person in a million might be offended, and we can't have that! And you know right away these days if something you've written is offensive, because the readers are all over it like rabid dogs with their instant online comments.

It was better in the old days, when an angry reader had to write an actual letter to the editor. That took work. You had to get a pen and paper, and dig up a stamp and an envelope, and once you had the letter written you had to leave the house to mail it, which meant putting on your shoes and walking to a mailbox.

Too much bother for most, and the few who made it to the mailbox were usually dismissed as lunatics, their letters rarely making it into print.

But now - Jesus! If some idiot is annoyed by something you write in the online edition all they have to do is sit there in their underwear, type out a rant and hit "send."

It's bad news for a reporter like Becker. He's in hot water now because his story about Henry Rivers and his new girlfriend has dozens of female readers riled up, for two reasons:

One, he refers to Hannah Schmitt as Henry's "estranged wife," and two, an anonymous "baseball source" claims Henry "has always had an eye for the babes."

Managing Editor Ken Wilson, twenty years Becker's junior, calls him into his office for a private pow-wow, as private as you can get when you're in a windowed cubicle in the middle of the newsroom. Wilson is very much one of the new breed, which is to say he wants minimal trouble from the readers, especially the women, who do all of the shopping and therefore matter most to the advertisers.

He lays the problem out to Becker like a kindly priest admonishing an altar boy for swiping the sacramental wine. It's an odd scenario, the black-haired young father of two lecturing the graying father of none, and a few reporters can't resist sneaking glances from the newsroom, though they can't hear anything.

"I know you're old school, Tom," Wilson says. "We've just got to be a little more careful with language these days."

Already Becker is pissed off. He knows that "old school" is code for "old," and out-of-date. He reaches for his cigarettes.

"Okay if I smoke in here, Ken?"

"I'd rather you didn't."

"Come on. I'll shut the door, so's not to poison the rest of the staff."

"I'd really rather you didn't."

Becker shoves the cigarettes back into his jacket pocket and points to the horseshoe, where four hunch-backed copy editors sit staring at their screens.

"You do realize that one of those bozos approved my story."

"I know. I'll be talking to them as well."

"Look up 'estranged,' Ken. It means Hannah is no longer living with Henry, which is completely accurate."

Wilson purses his lips in a not-so-fast gesture. "Thing is," he says, "it's a little hard to nail that down with the rich, what with all the homes they have. They might just be spending a little time apart."

"I'll bet my left nut that they are estranged."

Wilson erases the air with his soft hands. "That's not even the

119

point, here. It's the sound of the word that has women upset."

Becker can't believe what he's just heard. "What the fuck?"

"Read the comments, for Christ's sake! 'Estranged' sounds like something that happens to a helpless person, which Hannah Schmitt most certainly is not."

Becker's shoulders sag. "Jesus, Ken, is this conversation actually *happening?*"

"I know, I know. But this is the world, my friend. We're all afraid of the Me Too movement."

"I'm not."

"Tom, please. Play along."

"And what the hell am I supposed to do when a guy says 'babes' in a quote? I know things have changed, but I'm pretty sure we're still supposed to quote people accurately!"

"Of course, of course! But 'babes' is a red flag word. In a situation like this, it's best to lose the quote. Just say a source said Henry always enjoyed playing the field. Something like that."

"Playing the field. That's genius."

"Or something like that."

"You realize you've just gelded my story, don't you?"

"That's a little extreme, Tom. We've got to tread lightly these days. Especially when it's an anonymous source."

Becker feels a tingle at the back of his neck. He hopes he's not blushing. He really doesn't have a case here, because he made up that quote from the "baseball source," and suspects that Wilson knows this. Becker's anonymous quotes tend to sound like they all come from the same person, a person who sounds a lot like Becker.

It would be a bad idea to continue arguing. Wilson might ask him to produce his "baseball source," and Becker, who hasn't followed baseball since Mickey Mantle retired, would have a hard time bluffing his way out of trouble.

He sighs, pissed off and relieved at the same time. "Anything else, Ken?"

"That's it for now. Do we understand each other?"

"Yeah. From now on any time I find myself writing something exciting, I'll be sure and fix it."

"Excitement we want! Just don't piss off the ladies."

"Gotcha."

Wilson can't help chuckling. He likes Becker, even though he thinks of him as a relic. "Must have been a lot of fun around here, back in the day."

"You have no idea."

"Exciting times, huh?"

"We took the First Amendment out for joy rides every chance we had. Brought it back with bald tires and stripped gears."

Wilson laughs, but it's a polite sound. Becker hates being patronized. It's time for Ken Wilson to get a lesson, old school style.

"Let me tell you something," Becker begins, so softly that he's practically whispering. "Back then a broad was a broad, unless she was a chick. And after work, we hit the bars with those broads and those chicks, and then we hit the sack. That's how *we* worked up a sweat. You guys would rather do it at the gym, on treadmills. That pretty much sums it up."

Becker is breathing hard. Wilson looks at him in wonder.

"Thing is, Tom, with our online editions needing constant updates, there's no such thing as 'after work.' I only wish - "

"Oh, *bullshit!*"

Becker yells it loudly enough to draw stares from the other side of the glass walls. He stands, puts his hands on the edge of Wilson's desk and leans into his face.

"The truth is, you've to be a little crazy to do this job right, a little bit wild, and you need a little bit of a self-destructive streak, too. That's just the way it is, Kenny boy, and you kids will never understand that."

Wilson, a vegan who does Pilates during his lunch break, forces a smile as Becker gives him a mock-formal salute before returning to his desk.

He feels a lot of eyes on him and hears a few muffled giggles as he settles in. This is a new thing. Over the years Becker has been accused of being everything from a tightwad to a womanizer, and none of it ever bothered him. He actually liked it.

But now, suddenly, he's a laughingstock, and he doesn't like it. He doesn't like it at all.

CHAPTER TWENTY FOUR

Henry is late, picking up the kids. Hannah expected this. He's always a little late, and she's used to it, but she's a little frantic this morning because she doesn't want to leave Clare hanging at the Staten Island Ferry terminal.

The kids are dressed and ready to go when Henry finally shows up, greeting them with kisses on top of their heads.

"You're late, Henry."

"Sue me."

Hannah tells the kids to go down and wait for Daddy in the lobby. She waits for the elevator doors to close before turning to her husband.

"Henry," she says, "keep that girlfriend of yours away from my children."

"*Your* children, huh?"

"*Our* children."

"You got it."

"I'm serious, Henry. If I find out they've met her..."

She can't finish the thought, but Henry can. He presses the elevator button, then leans close to deliver the words.

"There's not a fuckin' thing you can do about it."

He says it softly, almost kindly, for greater impact. She clenches her fists, and they stay that way until the elevator returns and Henry boards it, blowing a kiss to Hannah as the doors close.

She feels sorry in advance for the Uber driver she knows she's going to harass, all the way downtown.

Clare gets to the Staten Island Ferry terminal a few minutes early, with the promptness of the elderly. She stands out front looking as if she's been fished out of the river, red-eyed and wet-haired, and when Hannah spots her she lets out a shriek.

"What happened?"

Clare is puzzled. "What do you mean?"

"Your hair is soaking wet!"

"I just came from my swim and my shower."

"You've been swimming *already?*"

"It's ten o'clock. What have *you* been doing all morning?

"Waiting for my late-as-always husband to pick up the kids. Why are your eyes red?"

"They use a lot of chlorine in that pool. It's a dirty world, you know? Come on, let's catch this ferry."

Clare leads the way. She's wearing her usual beat-up running shoes, gray sweatpants and a hooded gray sweatshirt with a kangaroo pouch. An old knapsack hangs from her back, sagging with its contents.

Hannah wears black jeans, a black blouse, a short black leather jacket and big-rimmed Chanel shades, the kind meant to hide a face but which often draw attention. Clare points at her ankle-high black boots.

"I do hope you can walk in those things."

"Will we be doing much walking?"

"Enough to give you blisters, if those shoes are as uncomfortable as they look."

"I'm used to them."

Clare chuckles. "Getting used to pain, when it's so easy to avoid it. I'll never understand that."

The ferry pulls into the dock, its sides making wet squeaking noises as it wedges between rows of mossy wooden poles. The gate opens, and everyone piles on board.

Caught in the middle of the crowd, Hannah momentarily freezes until Clare gets behind her, holds her shoulders and guides her to a bench on the outside deck.

"Are you all right?"

Hannah nods and shuts her eyes. "It's crowds," she says. "I get claustrophobic in crowds." When she opens her eyes a loud blast of the ferry's whistle makes her jump, and then they are on their way.

"Want to stand by the rail?" Clare asks. "You might feel better if you catch the breeze."

They go to the rail, and it works. Hannah starts to relax. It's not a rush-hour ferry, so there's plenty of room for the passengers to disperse. Hannah and Clare have the rail to themselves for twenty feet on either side. Anyone looking at them will think a stylish young woman is taking her mother out for the day, or maybe her grandmother.

"Nobody's looking," Clare says. Now's your chance."

"For what?"

"To toss me overboard. Then you'd have the skylight room without a battle."

"Tempting, but it wouldn't work. You're too good a swimmer.

You'd survive, and I'd go to prison."

Clare laughs. "Good point."

"Besides, I'd never hear about you and Avedon, and that's why I'm here."

Clare sighs, and it's a bittersweet sound. "Well, after he took those pictures he took me to a party," she begins. "An amazing party at the Plaza."

They are taken there in a shining yellow taxicab driven by a clean-shaven man wearing a jaunty billed cap. Avedon looks like he was born to wear his tuxedo, while Clare seems dazed, as if she's just entered the Witness Protection Program.

Which would make sense. It's already been a hell of a day. Everything she's wearing from the skin out is brand new, brought to the skylight room just three hours earlier by a Bergdorf Goodman's delivery man, a chubby fellow who had to stop to huff and puff for five minutes after ascending the stairs.

She feels giddy. All for free, courtesy of Harper's Bazaar Magazine, the company throwing this bash! Underwear, stockings, high-heeled shoes, a strapless bra, and the *piece de resistance*, a black silk dress with spaghetti straps.

She's amazed by two things - one, everything fits perfectly, and two, it's all so comfortable that she feels as if she's naked. Which she suspects is the way a model is supposed to feel, up on the runway.

The dress is a killer. It shows off her shoulders so beautifully that it looks as if angel wings might sprout behind them. Francisco has done her hair and makeup with a light hand, nothing major. Avedon just wants the right people to get a look at Clare and see her potential, the way he does.

The main thing is her face, especially the eyes. The eyes are the key.

Their cab glides to a halt in front of the Plaza, where a doorman wearing a gold-braided uniform opens the back door and offers a gloved hand to help Clare out. She accepts his help only because it's her first time in heels, and she's a little wobbly, a thoroughbred colt taking its first steps.

Avedon knows this. He appears at her side, links Clare's elbow in his and leads her up the red-carpeted stairs, ready to catch her if she falters.

They enter the hotel, and Clare has just three words:

"Oh, my God."

"Yes," says Avedon, "exactly."

Flowers, flowers everywhere, all shapes, sizes and colors! They looks as if they're exploding, a silent fireworks display in golden vases atop massive tables with legs ending in lion's-claw feet, and gleaming hard-polished terra cotta tiled floors, and a multi-tiered chandelier that twinkles in a way that's somehow like laughter, and Jesus, this is just the *lobby!*

"This way," Avedon whispers, because something about the grandeur of the Plaza makes you lower your voice, the way you do when you're in church.

They approach the sound of music, which turns out to be a string quartette, four white-haired musicians they see as they enter the Grand Ballroom, where hundreds of beautifully dressed people sip champagne, nibble canapes and laugh the laughter of those lucky, lucky people who know they are, without a doubt, God's favorites.

Clare suddenly feels dizzy and clutches Avedon's elbow for support.

"Are you okay?" he asks.

"What's today's date, Richard?"

He's surprised by the question. "The eighteenth, I believe. Why?"

The dizziness passes, replaced by a sense of wonder. It was a year ago today that she arrived in New York City on that bus from Pittsburgh, homeless and jobless. October 18th, 1950.

And now this.

"I came to this city one year ago today, Richard, and now look where I am. Crazy, huh?"

"Life is crazy, kiddo. Happy first anniversary." He gives her elbow a tug, a snap-out-of-it gesture. "Now listen. I'm going to introduce you to some people. Just say 'hello' and be polite. And be sure to look 'em in the eye."

"I shouldn't talk?"

"It's not really necessary, unless you feel like it. Tonight's your introduction. I want them to get a look at you, that's all."

Clare gets it. "Like walking a horse around the paddock before the race, right?"

Avedon smiles. "You got it, kid. And remember, this is the Kentucky Derby."

Off they go, working through the crowd. Quick hellos and

handshakes, and even a few hugs and double-cheek kisses. Avedon keeps them moving, and he's totally relaxed until they reach a severe-looking woman with a prominent nose and dark hair combed straight back.

"Clare Owen," Avedon says, "say hello to Diana Vreeland, our fashion editor."

Clare offers her hand. Vreeland has a grip like a man's and gazes into Clare's eyes as if they contain all the wonders of the universe.

"So this is the waitress," she says, maintaining the grip and the gaze.

"Yes," Clare says. "Never broke a glass. If they run short of help here tonight, I'm happy to pitch in."

Clare smiles. Vreeland's eyes widen.

"Richard," she says, the gaze and the grip unbroken, "you weren't kidding."

"I'd never kid you, Diana."

At last she blinks and lets go of Clare, who feels a tingle of blood return to her hand.

"Lovely meeting you," Vreeland says, and she is gone.

Avedon leads Clare to the champagne table. She expects to be scolded.

"I'm sorry, Richard, I don't know why I said that."

"Clare," he says, handing her a glass of champagne and taking one for himself, "that was *perfect*. Short and sweet. Diana will remember you now, believe me."

They clink and drink. It's the good stuff, Veuve Cliquot, and there are two dozen bottles of it on ice in silver buckets.

Avedon sets his empty glass down. "Ready to get out of here?"

Clare is disappointed. "We're *leaving?*"

He shrugs. "We did what we came to do."

Avedon doesn't like to hang out. He's like a homing pigeon. Wherever he goes, he always feels the pull of his work, his studio, his favorite place in the world.

"Richard," Clare says, "would it be okay if I stay?"

Avedon doesn't like the idea. "Why?"

"Well, I've never been here. Come on! It's the *Plaza,* for God's sake!"

He looks at her like a father trying to decide whether or not to lend the car to his daughter.

"Can you get home all right?"

She rolls her eyes. "Richard, *please*. I'm not a child."

"Okay. But listen to me." He gently holds her chin between thumb and forefinger. "Don't get drunk. Do you promise you won't get drunk?"

"Of course!"

"You've created an image tonight, a beautiful image. That's what you want to leave them with." He releases her chin. "It's as delicate as a Ming vase, Clare. Protect it."

She holds up a hand, like a Girl Scout taking a vow. "I swear I won't get drunk, but is it okay if I eat? I'm starving."

Avedon grins. "Eat all you want. If this goes the way I think it will, this is the last time you'll ever hear those words." He kisses her forehead. "Get ready to be hungry all the time, Clare. Rich, and hungry."

With those words he is gone.

Clare keeps her promise. She takes one more glass of champagne but she nurses it, taking tiny sips while grazing off trays of food carried by bow-tied waiters in red waistcoats.

What food! Succulent canapes, broiled shrimp on skewers, and the tiniest, reddest lamb chops she's ever seen, with none of that fatty taste you always get with lamb! She eats three lamb chops and wonders where to put the bones, sneaking them into a potted plant when she's sure nobody's looking.

Without Avedon at her side Clare is a wide-open target. Men find excuses to make small talk, chubby graying guys with ruddy complexions who look like coronaries waiting to happen. Their wives stand there glaring at this dazzling girl, unconsciously lifting their chins to flatten out the wattles on their necks.

I was young once, too, their glares seem to say, but deep down they know they never looked anything like this young woman.

Clare can sense trouble brewing. Now she knows why Avedon left early, and she realizes that Diana Vreeland is gone, too. The true professionals know that nothing good can happen by sticking around at a party like this. You make your point and you split, before things get messy.

So she slips out of the Grand Ballroom. Luckily it's an unseasonably warm night, so she didn't bring a jacket, which will make her exit even easier.

But that plan is thwarted when she reaches the lobby, where

there's a major hubbub over the arrival of Frank Sinatra and his new bride, Ava Gardner.

It's obvious they've both been drinking. There's a sloppiness to the way they're moving, bumping into each other with every step, and they are followed by a fat man in a too-tight suit, obviously someone who's prepared to shield them from the general public and, on occasion, each other. Clare realizes it's Rocco, the bulldog-faced bodyguard from that night at Zito's!

Sinatra looks as if he's gained some much-needed weight, and he's got a little moustache that looks ridiculous. Gardner is dazzling in a gas-blue evening gown she has to lift as she walks. It wreaks havoc with her balance, and she slips, nearly knocking Sinatra down.

"Will you watch where you're goin'?" he pleads, struggling to maintain his own balance.

"It's this fucking dress!" she shouts as she falls to the floor, and as Rocco rushes to pull her to her feet Sinatra turns and locks eyes with Clare. He stands absolutely still, taking her in, and then the first part of his body to regain motion is his arm, which he lifts to point at Clare, the way you'd point at a distant star. He is smiling, making that little moustache look even sillier.

"I *know* you," he says, his brow knotted in puzzlement. "How do I know you?"

Clare is too spooked to speak, or even move. She's hoping he gives up and turns back to his wife, but he doesn't. By this time Gardner is back on her feet, staring at this young beauty who's got her husband mystified.

"What's going on?" she asks, no longer sounding drunk.

Suddenly Sinatra's face brightens. "Zito's!" he cries. "Right? *Zito's!*"

He staggers toward Clare and embraces her. She keeps her arms at her sides as Sinatra breaks the embrace, holds her elbows and gives them an affectionate shake.

"How ya doin', kid?"

"I'm okay."

"Remember that night?"

"What night?" Gardner demands.

Sinatra turns to speak over his shoulder, without looking back. "Shut up already," he says, gazing at Clare. "She's a friend o' mine." Gardner breaks away from Rocco and gives Sinatra a shove from behind. He lets go of Clare and turns to face his wife, a finger in her face.

"Don't you ever push me," he says.

She shoves him again. "Did you screw this girl?"

"Watch your mouth."

"Did you screw her?"

Sinatra grabs Gardner's arm, but she pulls free and turns to Clare, who stands there quaking.

"You fucked my husband, didn't you?"

It would be less scary if she screamed the words, but she speaks them softly. The venomous hiss of a snake, coiled for the strike.

By this time a crowd has gathered in the lobby, some of it spillover from the Harper's Bazaar party. Rocco is busy waving his arms to keep them away, with little effect.

Clare could lie, but that's not who she is. Also, she hasn't done anything wrong, as far as she's concerned. So she pulls the trigger on the truth.

"He wasn't your husband at the time," she says, so softy that only Sinatra and Gardner can hear her.

Sinatra nods, the cartoonish way a drunk does when he thinks he's heard something profound.

"She's right," he says with a hiccup. "I was single back then. A free agent."

Gardner's lips are pursed, as if to suppress a gas building up inside her head. Suddenly she screams and lunges at Clare, but is caught in mid-air by Rocco, who carries her, still screaming, straight into an open elevator. Sinatra follows them, looks back at Clare and shouts "Night, Zito!" as the elevator doors close.

The crowd swarms around Clare, who is suddenly lifted to her feet from behind, then carried outside and down the Plaza steps. Only when she is set down on her feet near the famous outdoor fountain is she able to turn and see her savior, and it's an image that will never leave her.

He's handsome the way a tiger is handsome, with the same menacing aura that makes Clare wonder what would happen if she tried to touch him. Dark hair, even darker eyes, a broad nose that's tasted a punch or two and the muscular but slender build of a boxer. He's wearing a three-piece pinstripe suit but you can tell it wasn't his idea. You get the feeling he'd rather be running through a jungle in a loin cloth.

After he sets Clare down he dusts his hands clean of dirt that isn't there and says, "You okay, lady?"

She's jolted by the gentleness of his voice, which doesn't go with his body. It's like a tiger speaking in the voice of a deer.

"Who are you?" she asks.

"Security. Come on, we've got to get out of here, before the photographers show up."

We?

"Let's go," he says, holding out his hand for her to take. She's sitting on the edge of the fountain, feeling a damp spray of water when the wind shifts.

"Go where?" she asks.

"Out of here, for starters." He looks back at the hotel, where two men in fedoras enter the Plaza, carrying Speed Graphic cameras. He wiggles his fingers and says, "Please, lady, we gotta move."

She takes his hand and allows him to pull her to her feet. Clare suspects his smile will be a crooked one, the playful smile of a good-natured rascal, and she's right.

"By the way," he says, "I'm Johnny."

"Clare."

"Pleased to meet you, Clare."

They cross Central Park South and walk north on Fifth Avenue, toward Johnny's car. He explains how he and Rocco work security for Sinatra whenever he's in town, and that he was late getting to the hotel because he had to park two blocks away after dropping everybody off.

Clare says nothing about her encounter with Rocco and Sinatra, all those months ago. She's not sure why she's keeping it quiet. Just an instinct.

"Happens every time they're boozing," Johnny says. "Frank glances at a woman, she goes nuts. Same thing if she looks at a man. They're gonna kill each other, those two. Where am I droppin' you?"

"The Village."

"Ooh, the *Village*. What are you, a beatnik?"

"No. A waitress."

"What's a waitress doin' at the Plaza?"

"I was at the Harper's Bazaar party." She hesitates. "I'm trying to become a model."

Johnny looks at her and nods. "Yeah, I can see that. I can definitely see that."

He opens the car door for her. It's a long black Oldsmobile, newly polished, and as they glide down Fifth Avenue and pass the Plaza flashbulbs are popping outside the main entrance.

"Too late, guys," Johnny chuckles. He smiles that crooked smile again as he turns to Clare. "Listen," he says. "Am I takin' you home, or do you feel like goin' for a ride?"

And Clare, who's until now has been feeling exhausted and wants nothing more than to go home and sleep, turns to this total stranger and changes her mind.

"Where are we going, Johnny?"

The crooked smile widens. "It's a surprise."

CHAPTER TWENTY FIVE

It's too late to change her mind, and anyway, she doesn't want to. It's *exciting,* whatever happens next! Johnny hits the gas as if they've just knocked over a bank, roaring crosstown to the West Side Highway and then north to the 79th Street exit, where he pulls over and parks on Riverside Drive.

He gets out, opens the door for Clare and takes her by the hand as they make their way down the grassy slope to the Boat Basin on the Hudson River.

It's a hard walk for Clare, her heels stabbing into the dirt. "I thought we were going for a ride," she says.

"We are," he says. "In a boat."

Clare stops walking. Sudden gooseflesh, as if her skin is warning her that this could be the wrong move. She can handle herself on dry land, but does she want to be in the middle of the Hudson River if things go wrong?

"I'm not sure this is a good idea, Johnny."

She braces herself for outrage, and is surprised when he plays it cool with a shrug.

"Guess I'll go by myself, then. Nothing like being out on the water on a starry night. Nice meeting you, Clare."

He turns and continues walking toward the dock, and that's all it takes.

"Hey! Wait up!"

She runs after him, her heels poking holes in the turf at every step.

"Oh," he says with a chuckle, "changed your mind?"

Her left heel is stuck in the ground. She struggles to pull it free. "This better be good, Johnny."

"Oh, it's good, honey." He squats to pull her heel free. "You won't be sorry."

As they make their way down the dock Clare lets out a yelp when one of her heels gets wedged between the planks. Again, Johnny has to pull it free, and as he does he continues the upward motion by lifting Clare in his arms and carrying her the rest of the way.

"Johnny, where the hell are you taking me?"

"We have arrived, my lady."

He stops before a light blue yacht with a gleaming teak deck, surrounded by a shiny golden rail. It's a sleek craft, a thirty-footer, rocking gently with the river.

With Clare in his arms, Johnny steps aboard. He's got the strength of a bull and the balance of a cat, traits Clare finds appealing, and as he sets her on the deck he says, "Shoes off, please."

"With pleasure."

The heels that seemed so comfortable when the night began have turned on her. Her feet are on fire. She undoes the straps and takes them off. There are blisters on her big toes and raw red stripes across the tops of her feet.

How blissful it is to walk barefooted! Johnny has unmoored the boat, and she follows him into the cabin, where he starts the motor and heads for the middle of the river before turning north, toward the George Washington Bridge.

There are no other boats around, save for a lone tugboat chugging along the other way.

"Okay," Clare says, *"now* can you tell me where we're going?"

Johnny grins and points straight ahead. "That-a-way."

"What's that-a-way?"

"You'll see. Relax, stretch out if you like."

Johnny jerks his chin toward a daybed in the cabin. It sounds like a good idea. She's been riding on adrenaline all night, and now, suddenly, she's crashing. She stretches out, and soon the rumble of the motor and the rocking of the river put her to sleep.

She awakens to the touch of Johnny's hand, stroking her cheek. They are not moving, and the motor is silent. The whole world is silent, and dark as a tomb, so dark that when Clare opens her eyes, she fears she's gone blind.

"Johnny!"

"It's okay, it's okay. You conked out."

"Where are we?"

"About twenty miles up the river. I dropped anchor. C'mon outside, I want to show you something."

They go out on the deck and there's not a light in sight, on either shore. It's a moonless night, and the sky is ablaze with stars.

"This is my favorite spot," Johnny says. "Woods on both sides, no houses, no bullshit....it's like the world was just *born,* you know?"

Clare is touched by this perception. "Do you come here a lot?"

Johnny nods. "Yeah, whenever things get too crazy. Always alone, though, until tonight."

Clare smiles. "That's a pretty good line."

"Yeah, I thought so, too." He grins his crooked grin. "You okay?"

"My feet are killing me."

"It's those fucking shoes," Johnny says, picking the heels up off the deck. "They're inhuman."

And with that he casually flips the hundred dollar shoes over his shoulder, and they're gone with a splash.

"Johnny! I can't believe you *did* that!"

"Ahh, I'll get you some new ones. Flat ones. You were not meant to wear heels. Let's go inside, I can fix this."

Fix *what,* Clare wonders as Johnny points to the daybed and says, "Lie down."

She stretches out on her back. Johnny sits on the edge of the bed before taking her left foot in his surprisingly soft hands and beginning a gentle massage.

It's heaven. There's no other way to describe it. Clare is moaning with pleasure. Johnny switches to her right foot, giving it the same treatment. Then he works both feet at once, squeezing toes and heels, pressing his thumbs along her throbbing arches.

She's losing control. She doesn't like that. She thinks about asking Johnny to stop, but it would be like trying to stop a sneeze.

Her toes curl up. Johnny chuckles. He knows what's happening. He moves from her feet to her calves, working the muscles with both hands.

And from there he works ever northward, knees and thighs and waist. She sees he's holding something between his teeth, and it's a condom, still in its foil wrapper. Good, good, as her diaphragm is back at the skylight room. Clare sits up momentarily to pull the dress up over her head, at which point there is no doubt about where this is going, and it's a place she has never, ever been.

Hannah turns to Clare, just as the ferry is passing the Statue of Liberty, glowing green in the morning sunshine.

"Hang on," Hannah says. "What exactly are you saying, here?"

Clare clears her throat. "I'm saying that he hit the bulls-eye, if you know what I mean."

It can't be put any more plainly than that.

"Nobody ever did that before?"

Clare giggles. "My dear, until then, I wasn't aware I even *had* a

134

bulls-eye."

"So you didn't really enjoy sex, before that."

"Oh, of course I did! But this was different, the absolute limit. A perfect fit. Johnny knew my body, all right. Good God, how he knew it. I think he could have hit the bullseye by *staring* at me."

Clare speaks as if this amazing thing happened to her last night, not seven decades ago.

They both need a moment. They stare down at the foam in the ferry's wake, bubbly and white.

"Sounds like he swept you off your feet, Clare."

She cringes. "How I hate that expression!"

"But it fits, doesn't it? He carried you out of the Plaza, and he carried you to that yacht!"

Clare rolls her eyes. "You're being a bit literal. Think about the kind of men who sweep women off their feet. A bunch of loud-mouths and showboats, aren't they? Your husband, for instance."

Hannah snorts. "Henry swept me off my feet, all right. Swept away my summer house while he was at it. But he never once rubbed my feet, in nine years of marriage."

"Well, Johnny was different." Her eyebrows go up. "And he did carry me a few more times on that crazy, crazy date."

Johnny and Clare awaken on the boat at dawn, to the songs of innumerable seagulls and terns. They are stark naked when they step out on the deck, steaming cups of black coffee in hand, prepared by Johnny in the tiny kitchenette.

"Look at us," he says. "Adam and Eve."

He's right. Nothing but the two of them and all those birds, criss-crossing the sky. Johnny is beautiful, built more like a boy than a man. Slim hips and minimal chest hair, standing there without shame in the first light of day.

"Admit it, honey," he says. "You never had a date like this."

Clare giggles. "Is that what this is? A *date?*"

"What would *you* call it?"

She thinks about it. "An adventure with a rich man."

Johnny grins. "What makes you think I'm rich?"

"Any guy with a yacht is rich, in my book."

"Yeah? How many guys with yachts you been with?"

"Including you?"

"Yeah."

"One."

He laughs. "Damn, where'd you come from, girl?"

"The Plaza."

"I mean before last night."

"There *is* no before last night," she says, and in a way, it's true. Last night was a beginning for Clare, the start of a brand new life.

And maybe it was for Johnny, too. He hit the nail on the head, moments earlier. Adam and Eve, all right. The first man and the first woman, greeting the day.

But of course the Garden of Eden can't last, and it doesn't.

"Uh-oh." Johnny points at an approaching sailboat. "Civilization up ahead. Better get dressed, honey."

Johnny drives the yacht back to the Boat Basin, an arm around Clare, her head on his shoulder. He brings it to an expert stop at its slot, tying it up with the sure hands of an old sailor.

The wind picks up. Clare stands on the dock, shivering in her bare feet.

"No shoes for me, thanks to you," she says, and with that Johnny pats himself on the shoulder.

"Climb aboard."

She rides him piggy-back all the way to the car. It feels like years since they got here, but it's only been seven hours since he carried her out of the Plaza, seven of the craziest hours of her life. Johnny drives downtown on the West Side Highway, his left hand on the wheel, his right massaging the back of Clare's neck.

"I really like your yacht, Johnny."

He smiles. "It's not mine."

"Oh. Whose is it?"

Johnny shrugs. "You got me."

Clare sits up straight, shrugging his hand off her neck. "What do you mean?"

Johnny jerks his head back toward the Boat Basin. "Those rich assholes always hide the key in the same place, under the lid where they keep the life preservers. Friend o' mine told me that. He used to work there, cleanin' the boats."

Clare's blood is tingling. "So we stole that yacht."

"No, we *borrowed* it."

"My God!"

"Just a little joy ride, Clare! You had fun, no?"

"I wouldn't have had fun if I knew all this!"

"That's why I didn't tell you."

"Johnny, we could have been *arrested!*"

"Ahh, I didn't see any cops out there, did you?"

"What if we'd run out of gas?"

She can tell by Johnny's face that he feels insulted. "The tank was full. Don't you think I checked before we left? I'm not an idiot."

They look at each other, Johnny relaxed, Clare breathing hard. Then Johnny winks, a gesture Clare would normally hate, but this time it makes her laugh out loud.

What a night! A tickle in her belly tells her this guy is nothing but trouble, really bad news, but it's washed away by the glee that comes with a perfect crime.

They don't speak as they continue rolling downtown. Clare studies his hands on the steering wheel. His touch is strong but soft, so whatever he does when he's not driving people like Frank Sinatra around can't involve a pick or a shovel.

She shifts her gaze to his profile. He's pleased to catch her staring at him.

"Fuckin' fun, wasn't it?"

She breaks out laughing. "The best."

He returns his hand to the back of her neck and gives it an affectionate squeeze, keeping his hand there until they pull up in front of the rooming house, which he looks at in disbelief.

"Here? You live *here?*"

"Top floor."

"Rough neighborhood for a girl like you, no?"

"I like it."

Johnny gets out and opens the car door for Clare. He pats his shoulder and says, "Climb aboard."

"I can walk it, Johnny, the stairs are carpeted."

"Come on. Giddyap!"

And so with Clare aboard Johnny carries her all the way to the skylight room, where she slides off his back and flops on her mattress.

"Jesus," Johnny says, "no lock on the door?"

"Been meaning to get one."

He looks around in wonder. "This is all you got? This one lousy room?"

"It's not lousy, and besides, I'm only one person."

He stands with his hands on his hips, like a finicky inspector. "You get roaches up here? Mice?"

Clare shakes her head. "They can't climb this high."

"Jesus, you freaky Village types."

Clare giggles. She loves being thought of as a Village type. Johnny kneels to kiss her goodbye.

"It was fun," he says. "See you around."

And with those words he's out of there, taking the steps two at a time on his way down.

Clare can't believe it. She can't believe he didn't want to stay, or nail down a plan to see her again. Normally that would be a relief, a guy who just runs off, but this time it's different. Something's happening to her, and she hates to admit it.

She misses Johnny. He's only been gone for ten seconds, but already she misses him.

CHAPTER TWENTY SIX

They disembark with everyone else at the St. George terminal, and for the first time Hannah sets foot in a strange place called Staten Island. Clare leads the way on a short walk to the nearby train station.

"Wherever we're going, I'm happy to pay for a cab," Hannah says.

"Not necessary. It's a nice train ride."

Hannah doesn't push it. She realizes she's joined Clare on some kind of a ritual visit, and it's got to be done her way.

The train arrives within minutes, and then they are chugging along through the island's leafy interior.

"It's kind of pretty," Hannah says. "Hard to believe it's part of New York City."

Clare nods. "People used to have summer homes here, along the beaches. And until the water went bad the oyster beds were the finest in the world."

"What the hell, everything eventually goes bad."

Clare chuckles. "Spoken like a woman whose marriage just collapsed."

"Well, we can't all be like you and Johnny, can we?"

Clare puts her hands on her knees and squeezes them, as if to soothe a twinge of arthritis.

"It would have been perfect, if we'd just had that one time. But nobody ever leaves perfect alone, do they?"

Johnny Palermo, aspiring wise guy, part time security guard, full time pursuer of pleasure, is unlike any man Clare has ever known. He's exciting and impulsive, and you just know he's never going to let the world crush him, as so many men do by surrendering to the drudgery of their existences.

That's what's good about him. When he doesn't show up in the days after the yacht episode Clare figures she'll never see him again, and she's sorry about that, until he does actually show up.

Then she realizes she may never be rid of him.

Johnny pops up at the skylight room or at Reggio's whenever he wants to see her. He doesn't make plans. His life just happens to him, much the way Clare's life just happens to her, and when two people like that collide, one of them is going to become possessive.

In this case, it's Johnny, because suddenly Clare's life isn't just happening to her anymore. She's on the brink of a modeling career, a serious thing, a life-altering thing. If it works it could lead to bigger things, maybe even an acting career....who knows?

She's scheduled for a shoot at Avedon's studio, and the last thing she needs is for Johnny to be there, but he insists upon coming along.

"I gotta look out for you, babe," he says.

He's changed since that night at the Plaza. His clothes, for one thing. It turns out that the tasteful dark suit he wore on that night was his uniform for the evening. On his own time Johnny favors shiny suits, open collars and - worst of all - a gold chain around his neck, and a pinky ring.

The sex is still amazing, but Clare wonders if it's partly because she can no longer stand the sight of Johnny fully clothed.

While she's being prepared for the shoot, Johnny leans against the wall with his arms folded, the classic stance of a man with better places to be. Avedon ignores him, but it's obvious he doesn't want him around, especially when Johnny chuckles at the sight of the clothespins holding the back of Clare's dress snug.

"Been tellin' her she's gotta eat more," he informs the crew, to which they respond with nervous chuckles. Avedon's jaw is tight as he turns on a large upright fan and directs it at Clare.

"Hell's that for?" Johnny asks.

"A windblown look," Avedon says, without turning to look at him.

"Little blow job, huh?" Johnny chuckles.

Nobody laughs. Francisco rolls his eyes. Clare feels as if she's dying. She tries to focus on Avedon, and his softly whispered directions. She's already told Johnny he can't be talking during the shoot, and this is his way of showing her who's the boss. She shoots him a steely look and makes a zipping motion across her lips, to which he winks while twisting his pinky ring, a habit she finds maddening.

The shoot lasts a little more than an hour before Avedon calls it quits. He won't need to print a contact sheet to know how it went.

"We'll try it again soon," he whispers to Clare. "I'll call you."

He means he'll call her at Reggio's, as she has no phone.

"Richard, I'm so sorry."

"Next time, don't bring him."

It takes her two minutes to get dressed. She's too upset to say goodbye to anyone. They go outside to Johnny's car, parked directly in front of the studio. He takes the parking ticket from under the windshield wiper blade, crumples it without looking at it and tosses it to the curb.

"Get in already," he says.

Clare is changing. Before Johnny, any man who ever spoke to her that way would be history, on the spot. No second chances.

But she takes it from Johnny. He can still hit the spot as no other man could, but something has changed since that night on the yacht, and it's this:

Clare is afraid of him. For the first time in her life, she is afraid of a man.

So she gets in the car, and they ride in silence until they reach the entrance to the FDR Drive.

"So?" Johnny says. "Did it work out all right, or what?"

"No, it did *not.*"

"How come?"

She hesitates. "You shouldn't have been there, Johnny."

She feels her shoulders tighten in anticipation of his reaction, which surprises her.

He laughs.

"You serious, baby?"

"Yes."

"What the fuck did *I* do?"

"You were...distracting."

"Me? I didn't say ten fuckin' words."

"I was trying to focus."

"On *what?*"

They're on the highway, heading downtown. Johnny's knuckles are white. He's gripping the steering wheel as if he means to strangle it.

"Come on, tell me," he says. "What the hell were you tryin' to focus on?"

"It's hard to explain."

"Oh. And I ain't smart enough to understand."

Was his grammar this sloppy, that night at the Plaza, and was he this much of a...*baboon?* No! He was totally different! Was that all a performance, or is *this* the performance?

"Johnny," she says, "don't get mad. I just couldn't relax with you there staring at me, that's all."

He laughs again. "That's a good one! You couldn't focus, and you couldn't relax! That's two completely different things, Clare! You can't do 'em both at once!"

As his rage builds, so does the speed of the car.

"Slow down, Johnny, please."

"Were you tryin' to focus, or relax?"

"Johnny!"

"Answer me!"

"Both! *Both!* Slow down!"

"Anything the lady wants."

He jams on the brakes, skidding to a screeching stop in a matter of seconds. Johnny knows it's coming so he clenches the steering wheel, but Clare is thrown forward, instinctively grabbing the dashboard with her hands to keep from going through the windshield.

A howl of car horns behind them, which Johnny ignores. He has stopped on the inner lane, and it's a miracle they haven't been rear-ended.

Clare can't speak. She's quaking, not so much over what's just happened as by the sight of Johnny's face, and the way he's staring at her. The fury in his eyes wouldn't be so bad if it wasn't accompanied by his cunning smile. It looks like he wants to kiss her and kill her at the same time. He reaches over and strokes her hair.

"You relaxed *now*, honey?" he asks. "You *focused?*"

She bolts from the car and sprints across three lanes of traffic without looking, lucky to reach the other side alive. Johnny, still parked on the inner lane, still ignoring a chorus of car horns, gets out and stands shouting at Clare to come back, but all he can do is watch her run away without a backward glance.

Her forehead is throbbing. She touches it and feels a hot lump, like a golf ball coming up. It takes her a moment to realize that she's bashed her head against the windshield.

She's dizzy, and weaving like a drunk as she heads crosstown. Should she go to St.Vincent's Hospital and see if she's suffered a concussion? She thinks about it, decides against it. What could they do? Look into her eyes, tell her to ice the lump, and charge her twenty-five bucks for what she would have done in the first place? Forget that.

So she walks all the way home, gripping the banister on the climb to the skylight room. By this time each step feels like she's lifting her feet out of a tar pit. She gets inside and literally collapses on the mattress, fully clothed. She rolls onto her back, and the last thing she remembers before passing out is a fluffy cloud the shape of a swan, drifting past the skylight.

The next thing she remembers is a crescent moon glowing silver through the skylight, and the sense that she's dreaming in a garden of roses. But it's not a dream.

She sits up and sees that her bed is surrounded by vases filled with red and white roses, dozens and dozens of them. There's also a strange flickering light in the room, coming from half a dozen white candles in silver holders, burning away with the sweet fragrance of pure beeswax.

Then Johnny enters the room, a bag of takeout Chinese food in hand. He looks like a little boy who's been naughty, and is sorry.

"Look at you," he says. "You're alive."

Clare nods. "Barely."

"I got us some Chinks, plus some ice for your head. How can you live without a refrigerator?"

"I manage."

"Lemme tell you somethin', there's more to life than just managing."

He sets the bag down, wraps half a dozen ice cubes in a wet towel and holds it to her head. Clare sighs with the sudden, instant relief.

"I didn't know you bumped your head."

"Neither did I."

"How do you like the roses?"

"They're beautiful."

"How about the candles? They're the real deal, beeswax, like they got in church."

"Really nice."

She's holding back, gradually coming to the realization that this man she thought she knew is actually a stranger. A crazy, crazy stranger.

He holds up his hand, fingers spread wide. "Five trips I made, up and down the stairs. Six if you count the Chinks."

He's apologizing. He can't actually say the words, so this is the way he has to do it, with deeds.

Which Clare can't help but grudgingly admire. She's not much of an apologizer herself.

Johnny's touch is surprisingly delicate. He holds the ice to the bump with just the right pressure, wringing out the towel at just the right time, before it can drip down Clare's neck.

She can't help but be touched. He doesn't mean to hurt her, doesn't mean any of the wrong things he does.

But if she knows one thing, it's this: she cannot go on with this man, despite his miraculous ways in bed. She's going to miss that. Suddenly it hits her with a jolt.

"What time is it? I'm on the night shift, I'm due at Reggio's at six!"

"Ahh, forget about that."

"I can't forget about my job, Johnny."

"It ain't your job anymore."

She feels dizzy. Her mind is swimming. She pulls the ice away from her head.

"What do you mean?"

"I mean, your days at Reggio's are over." He says that last word in two separate syllables, like a couple of rocks dropping: "oh-*ver.*"

Her heart is pounding. "I don't understand, Johnny."

"Well, I told that bitch boss of yours that you quit."

His smile is one of the scariest things she's ever seen, a blend of madness and joy. It feels as if her heart is falling from a mile-high cliff.

"Please tell me you didn't do this."

"Hey, it was no big deal. She didn't even seem surprised. Said she knew you weren't gonna last."

"I don't believe this."

"What are you, upset? You should be *happy!* I can carry us from now on, no problem!"

Us. It feels as if a tarantula is making its way up Clare's spine.

"Us?"

"You and me, babe. I got a big promotion comin', gonna really get my thing goin'. You don't have to bother with this modeling shit, either." He gestures around the skylight room. "And I'll get you out of this box, once and for all."

She dreads to think about Johnny's promotion, and is too weak to object to the death of her budding career, or to the way he's just called her home a "box." She puts the ice back on her throbbing forehead and watches as Johnny removes cartons of Chinese food and paper plates from the bag.

"You hungry, honey? Wanna eat first, and then do it?"

"*Do* it?"

"You know." He pumps his fist twice, grins his crooked grin. "Unless your head hurts too much. Might do you good, though. Always makes me feel better."

CHAPTER TWENTY SEVEN

Clare and Hannah get off the train after a twenty minute ride and begin walking.

"*Now* can you tell me where we're going?" Hannah asks.

"Wouldn't you rather be surprised?"

"I've had all the suspense I can stand, hearing about Johnny Palermo. Did he actually expect you to have sex with him after what he'd done?"

"Yes. And we did, but we ate chicken lo mein first."

Hannah is staggered. "My *God,* Clare! How could you do that with a man who was so obviously dangerous?"

"Don't you see? That was the safest way to handle it. I wasn't at my full strength. The dangerous choice would have been to *deny* him."

"So basically, you let yourself be raped."

"Oh, I don't know. Can you call it rape if I enjoyed it?"

Hannah stops walking and catches Clare by her bony elbow. "You *enjoyed* it? How could you enjoy it?"

Clare shrugs, as if the answer is obvious. "Why do you enjoy a roller coaster ride? Because it feels dangerous. If it felt safe, what would be the point?"

"That's just great. Danger and pain, the keys to great sex!"

"No," Clare says, "not pain. Not with Johnny, not in bed. He was gentle, the gentlest of all. If we could have lived our entire lives in bed, there wouldn't have been any problem."

Clare pulls her elbow from Hannah's grasp, and they resume walking. "But that's the thing," Clare says. "Sooner or later, you have to put your clothes on. That's where I ran into trouble with Johnny Palermo, when he was fully clothed."

Johnny does not stay the night. He gets dressed, scoops up the empty Chinese food cartons and tells Clare he's got to be someplace.

"Tomorrow night," he says. "I'm gonna have big news for us tomorrow night, honey. Can you meet me at the end of the pier at seven o'clock?"

He's referring to the Christopher Street pier, knowing it's one of Clare's favorite spots. It's a strange enough request anyway, a plan from a man who never makes plans, but why would he want to meet there?

She doesn't ask. The main thing is, it gives her a full day to recover. By then she'll be strong, and ready to straighten everything out, so she promises to be there. Which delights Johnny.

"That's my girl!"

He plants a gentle kiss on the bump on her forehead and rushes out, the way he always does, as if the cops are hot on his heels.

Clare spends the whole of the next day in bed. She is literally wiped out, drifting in and out of naps. The lump on her forehead is still hot but of course the rest of the ice Johnny brought has melted, so she has to make do with cool wet cloths that don't bring much relief.

She really should get herself to Reggio's and let Gabriella know she is not quitting her job. What's more, Avedon may have left a message for her there regarding the re-shoot.

But she hasn't got the steam. She's going to need every bit of her strength for this meeting with Johnny. It isn't going to be easy, but at least it will be happening in a public place, which should make it harder for Johnny to make a scene.

So she heads to the pier at a quarter to seven, determined to dump Johnny Palermo as gently as she can, wish him well and head home. Or maybe she'll go to Reggio's to straighten everything out, if she's got the energy.

She'll have her life back. She's eager for the re-shoot. Without Johnny around she'll be able to breathe, be herself. She realizes she has not really relaxed for one minute since she met the man.

Is that what love is? A state of constant low-level anxiety, interspersed by spurts of high-level anxiety? If so, who the hell needs it?

She can hear the bells from St. Veronica's on Christopher Street tolling the hour. No sign of Johnny, and she's wondering if she's being stood up. That could be a good thing. It could start an argument the next time she sees him, the perfect trigger for a break-up, because who does he think he is, leaving her standing like a fool on the pier?

Seven-thirty, and still no sign of Johnny. She's ready to give up and go home, but suddenly people on the pier are pointing toward the river, where a long golden yacht is approaching, helmed by a burly man all in white, from his cap to his shoes. It looks as if it's going to slam head-on into the pier until he turns deftly at the last instant and pulls up alongside it, the rumble of the engine drowned out by a double-blast of the horn.

Johnny Palermo has arrived.

People are laughing with delight and then oohing and aahing as a tuxedoed Johnny appears on the deck, arms spread wide.

He is absolutely dazzling, waving and beaming a hundred-watt smile at the cheering crowd. A dumbfounded Clare can only stare, until Johnny spots her and beckons.

"Come on, baby!" he shouts. "We're not supposed to stop here, we gotta move!"

What can she do? Refuse? Her plan to break up with him on the pier is dead. She's got to go through with whatever Johnny has in mind.

And so Clare takes Johnny's hand and allows herself to be hoisted onto the yacht, in what the applauding strangers will long remember as the most romantic thing they've ever seen.

This yacht is bigger than the last one. The muscular man at the wheel, Gino, gives a courtly tip of his cap to Clare before pulling away from the pier.

Johnny takes Clare in an embrace she does not return. She is mortified, and trying not to show it.

"Jesus, Johnny, what's going on?"

"Like I told you, it's a special night." He sweeps his hand from her t-shirt to her sandals. "Nice of you to dress up."

"How was I supposed to know what you were doing?"

"I'm only kidding, honey. Come on, come inside, you're gonna love this."

"Whose yacht is this?"

"Belongs to a friend o' mine. Hey, don't worry, it's all legit, this time."

Johnny leads the way into the cabin, where a table for two has been set with fine china and crystal glasses. There's a bottle of champagne buried in ice in a silver bucket, and a small man in a white apron and a tall puffy chef's hat stands there smiling, hands behind his back.

"This is Enzo, our chef for the night," Johnny says. Enzo bows to Clare before rushing to the galley to work on the meal.

Clare's heart is hammering. She knows what's coming. All she can do is take it a step at a time, and try not to panic.

Johnny pops the champagne and fills two glasses.

"To us," he says. She manages a smile as they clink and drink. By this time they have cruised below the Brooklyn Bridge and are approaching the Statue of Liberty.

"I've got things to tell you," Johnny says, "but I think we should eat first."

That appears to be his rule: eating before talking, eating before sex, eating before anything else on the agenda.

On silent feet Enzo brings out two plates of salad, arugala and sliced tomatoes drizzled with vinaigrette dressing. Clare amazes herself by devouring the salad. She hasn't eaten all day, and she knows she'll need her strength to get through whatever's about to happen.

Enzo whisks away the salad plates and returns with two perfectly broiled sirloin steaks, with asparagus and potatoes au gratin on the side.

"I know you're not a big beef eater," Johnny says, "but I wanna get some meat on those bones."

To his delight, Clare digs into her steak. She can feel her strength building with each bite. Soon they've both polished off their meals, and Johnny tops up the champagne glasses.

"Okay," he says. "I told you this was a special night, and here it is - I got made today."

Clare is baffled. "Made?"

"Yeah. You know, *made?*" He touches the side of his nose and winks. "I'm in, honey. All the way in. A made man!"

It hits her like the night train. Johnny Palermo is now officially a soldier in one of the city's major crime families.

"Jesus," Clare says.

"Yeah," Johnny says, believing she is impressed and not appalled. "How 'bout that?"

He hoists his glass. Once again they clink and drink, and as Clare looks out the porthole she can see they have left the Hudson and reached the New York Bay.

There's no way she can jump overboard and swim to shore, though that is exactly what she wishes to do as Johnny produces a small velvet box from his pocket, which he opens to reveal an oval diamond ring.

"Whaddaya say, baby?" he asks, gently as can be. "Let me make an honest woman out of you."

The ring is dazzling, with a stone twice the size of the one poor Carmine offered her. Clare knows it must have cost more than she could make in a year, maybe two, working the tables at Reggio's. Unless it's hot, which is certainly a possibility.

She looks toward the galley and sees Enzo taking a peek, a huge grin on his face for the luckiest girl in the world. Then she looks at Johnny, and that crooked smile she once found so attractive.

"Jesus, Johnny."

"Gonna try it on, or what?"

"I take it this is a marriage proposal."

"Ayy, you catch on quick." Johnny wiggles the box, oh so temptingly. "Come on, Clare, see if it fits."

She feels dizzy. "I don't think so, Johnny."

He laughs. "Come on, don't fuck around, try it on."

"No."

He shuts the box. Enzo ducks back into the galley. "What the hell is this?" Johnny asks softly. "Am I movin' too fast for you?"

"No, that's not it."

He's humiliated. It's a feeling he's rarely known. He suddenly feels foolish in his tuxedo, a clown in a silly costume.

"What's wrong?"

"It's just not what I want."

His eyes widen. "You don't want *me?*"

"What I mean is, it's not what I want out of life."

She's getting too cosmic for Johnny. He wants specifics. "Hang on. You sayin' you don't want to get married?"

"That's right."

"Ever?"

"Right."

"Why not?"

"It's just not part of my plan."

Johnny snorts like a bull. "Oh, all of a sudden you have a *plan?*"

"That's right."

"And what *is* this plan, if I'm allowed to ask?"

She doesn't want to say it, but he leaves her no choice. She takes a deep breath and says, "I'm going to be a model."

Johnny actually rolls his eyes, like a man trying to get his point across to a slow-witted child. "Baby, I *told* you," he says, believing the crisis is past, "you don't have to bother with that any more."

"Bother with it? *Bother* with it? Thanks a lot, Johnny."

"Are you sayin' you *enjoy* posin' for pictures for those weird people?"

"They aren't weird."

"Come on, Clare. You gonna tell me that makeup guy ain't a queer?"

"What if he is? What's wrong with *that?*"

Johnny cannot believe his ears. He's reeling from the double-revelation that the girl of his dreams won't marry him, and she has no problem with homosexuals. He sinks down in his chair with the weight of it all.

"Don't you get it?" he says, his voice reduced to a croak. "I want you to be the mother of my kids."

This is his ace card. If this doesn't work, nothing will. Clare leans across the table and shakes her head.

"I don't want kids, either."

Johnny literally gasps. He's stunned. His head is down as he breathes through his mouth, staring at his shoes.

"So," he says, "no marriage and no kids for you, huh?"

"That's right."

He lifts his eyes to Clare, a studious look on his face. "What are you, a sicko?"

"No, Johnny. It's like you said, the night we met. I'm a freaky Greenwich Village type."

"And you're *proud* o' that?"

"No. But I'm not ashamed of it, either. It's just what I am."

She's rolling. The words are coming more easily, now. She might as well shake out the tablecloth, get it all out at once.

"See, I want to do what *I* want to do, when *I* want to do it. I need my freedom."

"So I guess you want to live the rest of your life in that stupid skylight room."

"I don't know, Johnny. That's my point. I don't *want* to know. I just want my life to happen."

He nods. "But not with me."

"Johnny. I'm sorry."

Deep down, she's not really sorry. She's annoyed at Johnny for pulling this crazy stunt, and she's sorry she's had to defend her life and her beliefs to this man.

She's also sorry that it's going to be a long, slow ride back to the Christopher Street pier. It is silent, save for the throbbing of the engine and a hissing sound from the galley, where Enzo is toasting the top of a Baked Alaska with a bottle-gas torch.

"Could you ask Gino to take me back?" she says.

"After dessert. That okay with you?"

"Sure," she says, glad to grant him this tiny victory.

Are they actually going to eat dessert, to top off this disastrous night? They stare at each other like a pair of poker players. Enzo comes and takes away the dinner dishes, ignored by both. When he's gone Johnny pockets the ring, folds his hands and smiles at Clare, like a man conceding victory to a worthy opponent.

But something isn't right. His face is actually changing. She notices nets of wrinkles around his eyes, and a few gray hairs at his slicked-back temples. It's like he's aged ten years in ten minutes.

He clears his throat. "What's Zito's?"

Clare's stomach drops. Somewhere in her soul she's been fearing this question from Johnny, but in no imaginary scenario did it ever come up in the middle of the deep, dark sea.

Her mouth is dry. She takes a sip of champagne, wishing it were water. "I don't know what you're talking about, Johnny."

She's no good at lying, never having had any practice. "That night at the Plaza, with Sinatra. He called you 'Zito's' when he got in the elevator."

"He was drunk, Johnny."

"Drunk, my ass. He *recognized* you. He knew you. What the hell was that all about?"

"Maybe he thought I was somebody else."

"Oh, no. Don't gimme that bullshit. Rocco recognized you, too, but he won't tell me nothin.' "

Clare's heart is pounding. Johnny leans close, breathing champagne into her face. "So don't fuck with me, Clare. Not tonight. You wanna break my heart, go ahead, but do *not* fuck with me."

Tears are rolling down his cheeks as Enzo, not noticing, sets a perfect Baked Alaska before him. When he turns for approval to serve it he sees the tears, sets down his knife and scoots back to the galley.

A weeping gangster in a tuxedo, dropping tears on his dazzling dessert. It may be the saddest, strangest thing Clare has ever seen. She shuts her eyes, working out her next move. Maybe the truth will help Johnny. The lame lies certainly haven't worked.

"Zito's," she says, her eyes still closed, "is a bakery."

She opens her eyes. Johnny stops crying. He sits up straight, his eyebrows raised in genuine surprise.

"A *bakery?*"

"In the Village."

"Why would he call you that?"

"I'm not sure you want to hear this, Johnny."

It's the wrong thing to say. He reaches across to hold her by the wrists, so tightly she can feel the pulse of her blood.

"Just tell me."

So she does. Maybe the truth, delivered as gently as possible, will be her ticket to liberty from this man. She tells the whole story, from Sinatra's arrival at Reggio's to her early morning departure from the Waldorf-Astoria.

By the time she's finished the sagging Baked Alaska has melted down both sides of the table, but Enzo has not dared come near to clean it up. Johnny looks as if he's just been told he has days to live. He releases Clare's wrists, and her hands tingle with a sudden rush of blood.

"That's what happened," she says, putting a ribbon on the story. "Long before I knew you."

That last sentence is a mistake, and Johnny pounces on it. "Oh, sure. That makes it all right, huh?"

"It certainly does, Johnny."

He studies her through slitted eyes. "How many guys have you fucked, anyway?"

"That is none of your business."

"How many?"

"I've had fewer guys than you've had women."

"It's different for a man, Clare."

"Ha! Who says?"

Johnny spreads his arms. "Everybody!"

"Not me, Johnny. Not me."

Clare gets to her feet as if to leave, though of course there's no place to go. Johnny gets up too, ready to block an exit that can't even happen.

"You hadda go and fuck Frank Sinatra."

She squares her shoulders. "Yeah, I fucked him. Okay? Are you happy, now? Can we each get on with our lives, with that out of the way?"

"Anything you say, sweetheart."

153

He turns toward the door to the deck and makes a sweeping gesture with his hand. "Right this way," he says, faking gallantry. "Get out on the deck for the rest of the ride. Tell Gino to take you back. You *disgust* me."

This suits Clare. She'll happily shiver out there, however long it takes. It'll be better than riding under Johnny's relentless glare, but as she moves toward the door he pounces from behind and throws her to the floor.

She lands on her back, and then Johnny is on top of her, holding her down by her shoulders.

"Fucking slut," he sobs, before grabbing her by the hair and slamming her head repeatedly against the floor. She hears Enzo scream, and by the third impact Clare is out cold, dead to the world.

CHAPTER TWENTY EIGHT

A quarter of a mile into the walk, Hannah's feet are killing her. They have to stop and sit on a roadside bench, facing a wooded hollow. She takes off her shoes and rubs her feet.

"Told you those shoes would be trouble," Clare says. "That's one thing Johnny Palermo was right about. Heels are ridiculous."

"Never mind that," Hannah says. "He beat the hell out of you on that boat! Then what happened?"

"I'm getting to it," she whispers. "Look!"

Clare points toward the woods, where a silver fox creeps out of the hollow, sniffing the ground. "Hard to believe this is actually part of the city, isn't it?"

"Yeah, it's amazing. Now what the hell *happened?*"

Hannah's booming voice sends the fox diving into the woods. Clare sighs, genuinely disappointed.

"Not exactly at one with nature, are you?"

"Clare, please. What happened next?"

"I'll tell you, but first, I have to show you something. Let me turn this way."

She tilts her face to the sun. It's a relief map of deep wrinkles and loose skin. She puts the fingertips of both hands on the folds of her left cheek.

"Okay," she says, "look closely, now."

She pulls the folds apart, revealing a white line deep in the crevice. It's like an ancient carving on a tree trunk where the bark has grown over. She does the same with her right cheek, then her forehead, and finally her chin, revealing deep white lines each time, all about three inches long.

Hannah has never seen anything like it. "What are they, scars?"

Clare nods, her eyes glistening with sudden tears.

"They," she says, "are Johnny Palermo's final farewell to me."

Clare is lying in a soft bed when she opens her eyes in a dim room with the curtains drawn, looking up at the face of a man sitting on a chair at the edge of the bed. He's been waiting for her to awaken. She sees him smile, a smile of relief for the fact that she's alive.

She's groggy, and her head hurts. She tries to sit up but is eased back down very gently by this mysterious man. She realizes she's wearing a nightgown. Whose nightgown? And where are her clothes?

"Who are you?" she asks. Her mouth is dry. The man takes a glass of water with a straw from the night table.

"You're dehydrated," he says. "Take a sip."

She sucks on the straw, swallowing half the water in one gulp.

"Good, good. You needed that."

Something about him inspires trust. He looks to be in his early thirties. His voice is gentle, and his thinning brown hair is perfectly barbered. His hands are large, and so is his nose. Not a classically handsome guy, but a man made attractive by the intelligence in his dark brown eyes, friendly behind tortoiseshell glasses.

Clare licks dry lips. "Who are you?" she asks again.

"You can call me Martin."

"Are you a doctor?"

He answers with a faint smile. Is that a 'yes?' Instead of answering the question, he asks one.

"How are you feeling?"

"My face hurts. Back of my head, too....where am I?"

"Hold still," Martin says as he beams a small flashlight into her eyes and takes a close look. His breath is as sweet as mint, and he hums approvingly at what he sees. He clicks off the flashlight and pockets it, then folds his arms across his chest and clears his throat.

"How much do you remember, Clare?"

He knows her name. She closes her eyes, as if to summon up a distant memory that's only six hours old.

"We were on the yacht," she says. "Johnny threw me down, then he slammed the back of my head on the floor."

"You don't remember anything after that?"

"No."

"You've got a bump on your forehead, too."

"That's an old injury," she says, not wanting to get into details. "Why does my face hurt?"

"Please don't get excited."

"Is this a hospital?"

"No. We're in a private house on Staten Island."

"Staten Island?!"

"Shhh, shhh."

"Is Johnny here?"

"No."

She touches her cheeks, feeling bandages. "What happened to

my face?"

Martin sighs, the kind of sound that always precedes bad news.

"Well, you suffered a few cuts."

A shiver chills her to the core. "Cuts?"

"Please calm down."

"I need a mirror."

"That's not a good idea."

"Get me a fucking mirror, Martin!"

He reluctantly hands her a pocket mirror. Clare does not hesitate, holding it up and not even gasping at the sight of thick white bandages across her chin, forehead and both cheeks.

"The good news is that they're straight, clean cuts," Martin says. "You didn't lose much blood, and the edges held my stitches well."

"Stitches? You stitched me?"

Martin nods. "Right here, in this room."

Her lips are quivering. "How many stitches?"

"A lot."

"How many?"

Martin shakes his head. "Tell you the truth, I lost count. I'm so sorry."

Clare hands the mirror back to Martin. "That fucking bastard carved up my face," she says matter-of-factly.

Martin purses his lips. "Yes. And your evaluation of him is absolutely correct. A fucking bastard, indeed."

"I need to know what happened, Martin."

He thinks it over. As a doctor he knows that some patients need to know, and some don't. He sees that this girl doesn't pull punches, and hates it when others do that.

So he decides to throw the punches that must be thrown, in the softest voice he can muster.

"You suffered a concussion," he says. "And while you were out cold..."

Martin needs a moment. He cleans his eyeglasses with a handkerchief and puts them back on. Then, like a child screwing up his courage to jump off the high dive, he races to the finish.

"While you were unconscious he took a steak knife and sliced your face in four places."

Clare sits bolt upright. "Oh my God."

"It happened before Gino could pull him away."

"Gino? The guy who was driving the yacht?"

"Correct. Johnny sliced his arm, during the struggle. It's a miracle he was able to get him off you."

"Oh yeah, Gino did a marvelous job! *Look* at me!"

Martin leans close to Clare. He's not sure he should tell her, and then he does.

"Do you remember Enzo, the waiter?"

"Of course. We wasted his beautiful Baked Alaska."

"Enzo said Johnny was screaming at Gino to let him go, because he wasn't finished. Said he wanted to..."

He can't finish the sentence. Clare nudges his shoulder.

"Come on. Wanted to what?"

Martin rubs his face with both hands. "He wanted to quote - 'cut your fucking nose off' - unquote."

At last Clare is crying. Martin seems glad to see the tears, as if they indicate a step toward healing. He eases her onto her back and pulls the blanket up to her throat.

"Do you need the bathroom?" He points to a door on the side of the room. "It's right there, if you need it."

"I want to get out of here."

"Of course you do, but sleep first, you're still full of anaesthetic." He forces a tiny smile. "If it's any consolation, he never went near your nose. It's perfect, probably the most perfect nose I've ever seen."

Martin leaves the room and closes the door. Clare gets out of bed, so dizzy that she nearly falls down, but there's something she needs to know. She staggers to the door and tries the knob.

It's locked, from the other side. Just as she expected it to be. She is a prisoner. She gets back in bed and passes out.

When she opens her eyes Martin is sitting by the bed, holding a bowl and a spoon.

"Minestrone," he says, stirring the soup. "Italian penicillin."

"It's not poisoned, is it?"

"No, I left the poison in my other medical bag. Come on, eat."

Clare sits up and allows Martin to feed her. Somehow, there's nothing awkward about it. The soup is delicious, and she's famished.

"How long did I sleep?"

"Almost twelve hours. You needed that."

"Where am I, Martin?"

"I told you. We're in a house on Staten Island. A very nice

house, right on the water, with a private dock."

"How come I'm not in a hospital?"

"Gino brought you to the dock, and that's when they called me. There wasn't time to get you to a hospital."

"Bullshit, Martin."

He sighs, sets the bowl down on the night table. "Okay. The family wanted to contain the situation, as I'm sure you can understand."

"So you risked my life to keep it all quiet."

Martin holds up his hand, like a man about to take a vow. "I assure you, the care you got from me is as good as anything a hospital could offer. I'm a doctor, the real deal." He gives her elbow a gentle squeeze. "Hey. We're *both* in this mess, Clare. If the medical board ever finds out about this, I can kiss my license to practice goodbye."

She believes him, and she knows what he's talking about when he refers to "the family." It's the crime family Johnny was bragging about being welcomed into as a "made man."

She reaches to feel her face, but Martin catches her by the wrist.

"Try not to touch your face. The stitches are delicate."

"You're here to guard me, aren't you?"

He forces a chuckle. *"Guard* you?"

"I tried the bedroom door after you left last night, but it was locked from the outside."

"Sure, I locked it. Didn't want you to wander off, in the state you were in."

"So I can leave now, if I want."

Martin sighs. "No."

"Can I at least make a phone call?"

"No."

"Can I see Johnny?"

Martin's eyes widen. "Why would you want to see Johnny?"

"I might have a few things to say to the man who mistook my face for a Thanksgiving turkey."

"He's not here, Clare."

"Is he under arrest?"

"The police were never called. That shouldn't surprise you."

"Where is he? On a tramp steamer to Sicily?"

"Ha! Not a bad idea. Trust me, the less you know, the better." He looks at his watch. "I'll be back," he says, getting up and heading for the door.

"Don't forget to lock me in, Marty."

He stops and turns to her, a serious look on his face.

"It's Martin. Nobody calls me 'Marty.' "

Days pass. Martin brings Clare books, magazines and newspapers. He brings meals, changes the sheets, keeps Clare supplied with fresh towels and nightgowns. She dozes off many times in the course of a day, and when she opens her eyes he is always there, reading a book or a medical journal. Her guardian angel, as well as her jailer.

"Do you ever sleep, Martin?"

"Not much. I close my eyes, the phone rings, and I'm off on another emergency."

"Lucky you."

He shrugs. "I'm not complaining."

She is totally relaxed with him. Martin's intelligence makes him appealing. She cannot imagine him ever losing his temper, or being unkind.

He's not a big man, and as her strength returns Clare feels confident that she could overpower him, get past him and down the stairs, but she doesn't do that. The people downstairs would be waiting for her, and she's not strong enough to get past them.

And besides, she realizes that she wouldn't want to get Martin in trouble. How crazy is *that?*

She hears muffled sounds of them speaking down there, often in the dead of night, maybe half a dozen gruff male voices and one shrill female voice. The woman occasionally shrieks at the others, a sound that makes Martin wince.

"Who is that woman, Martin?"

"Ahh, just a crazy old lady. Don't worry about her."

Martin allows her to keep the curtains open, night and day. She realizes this is not a regular house. It's more like a fortress. The bedroom window looks out on a walled-in lawn that leads to a dock jutting into the New York Bay, and beyond that, the Atlantic.

"That's the dock where they brought me," she says.

Martin nods. "Thank God Gino got you here fast, before you lost too much blood. Enzo put pressure on the wounds. That helped."

"Martin."

160

"I'm right here, Clare."

"How could Gino drive the yacht, if he had to keep Johnny from hacking my nose off? Especially if he had a wounded arm."

Martin shrugs, but it's not convincing. "Great question."

"So what's the answer?"

"Wish I had one." He looks at his watch. This has become his exit strategy, whenever Clare's questions get too tough.

"I'll be back soon. You'll be happy to hear the bandages are coming off tomorrow."

Martin is good to his word. The next day he carefully peels the bandages from Clare's face as she sits with her eyes shut.

"Nice," he says. *"Damn,* I do good work."

Clare opens her eyes. Martin's face is a bittersweet blend of pride for his work and sorrow for Clare's injuries.

"How bad is it?"

"See for yourself."

He tries to hand her the pocket mirror, but she wants to look in the bathroom mirror. She holds his elbow for support on the walk.

"Keep in mind, bathroom lighting is harsh. It'll look worse than it actually is."

"Don't bother sugar-coating it, Martin."

He snaps on the light, and Clare, who thought she was prepared for this, realizes she is wrong.

It's like four black zippers framing her face, each encrusted in dried blood, each as thick as a caterpillar, and what makes it worse is the neatness of each cut, as if Johnny had been working with a ruler.

He didn't just slash away like a madman. He went at Clare's face with the precision of an avenging surgeon.

She feels nauseous. "Holy shit, Martin."

"It's not as bad as it looks," he assures her. "The swelling will go down in a few days. Then I can remove the stitches, and you'll see a huge difference."

"Really?" She points at her reflection as she'd point at a stranger. "Back to normal?"

"Well, I wouldn't say normal."

"What am I going to look like a year from now, Martin?"

He forces a smile that would rather be a frown. "White lines. When all the healing is done you'll have white lines, as if somebody drew on your face with a piece of chalk. And they may be slightly raised."

She knows he is downplaying the damage. It's going to be worse than that.

"Makeup should help," Martin adds. 'You've got to think positive."

Clare lets it all sink in. "Thing of it is, I was going to be a fashion model. That's not likely now, is it?"

Martin sighs. "I wouldn't count on it, but you never know. It's such a beautiful face, and I swear to God, I've never seen eyes quite like yours."

She turns to hug him, sobbing her heart out.

Downstairs, the crazy woman is screaming and yelling at somebody in Italian.

Three days later Clare sits stone-still on a chair in the bathroom as Martin, seated on a chair facing hers, clips the stitches and pulls them out, one at a time.

"You're a good healer. They're coming out nice and clean."

"Martin."

"I'm right here."

"Ouch!"

"Sorry. I need stronger eyeglasses."

"Are you married?"

He can't help laughing. "That's what I call a question out of the blue!"

"Are you?"

"I have a wife and two girls, five and three."

"Don't they miss you?"

"They know I'll be home soon."

"But then you'll be off on another emergency."

He shrugs. "I never really know, until it happens. Been six months since the last...what did you call it?"

"Emergency."

"Right. Good way to put it. Anyway, the rest of the time I'm at the hospital, so either way, I'm pretty busy."

"Do you love your wife?"

Martin laughs. "What a question! Yes, I do."

"Why?"

"Maybe because she puts up with me."

"That doesn't sound very passionate."

"Oh, I don't know. Passion may be overrated, not to mention dangerous, as you well know."

"But you love her."

"Of course I do."

"How do you know?"

"Well, when I hear her key in the lock, my heart jumps. She makes good coffee. She's got good toes, nice and straight. You know, little stuff that adds up to big stuff. Makes me wish I was going home. Hold still, for God's sake!"

"Martin."

"I'm still here, Clare."

"Will *I* be going home?"

He pulls back to look at her. "Of course you will! We just want to make sure you're a hundred per cent, after what happened to you."

"Who's *we?*"

He sighs. "I think you've figured that out."

"But you're not like them! You're a doctor!"

Martin resumes cutting the stitches. "True. They call me the white sheep of the family. Funny, huh?"

"So why do you have anything to do with them?"

Martin looks at her as if he's baffled by the question. "These people are my blood. They helped put me through med school. When they call, I come. That's the deal." He spreads his hands. "They're my *family*. Doesn't family mean anything to you?"

"No."

"What do you mean, no?"

"I left my parents a year ago and haven't been in touch since."

Martin is truly astonished. "How could you do that?"

"We were strangers. They didn't know me."

"Of course they did. They brought you into this world."

"It was an accident. My father knocked up my mother, so they had to get married. I was their burden."

"You sure about that?"

"I can count to nine. I showed up six months after their wedding."

"They probably tried their best."

Clare forces a laugh. "You're defending people you've never even met!"

"I'm not defending anybody. All I'm saying is, family is family.

If you're not connected to a family, you're all alone out there."

"I like being alone."

"If you *really* liked it, you wouldn't have been on that boat with Johnny. That was the act of a desperate girl."

"I wasn't desperate! I was going to break up with Johnny. That's the only reason I got on the boat."

"Come on, Clare, you *must* have known how badly it would go, rejecting a wild card like Johnny out at sea! Why'd you do it? You're a smart girl."

She has to think about it. "I guess I had to see what would happen. Like, when you're watching a bad movie, but you just have to see how it ends."

Martin makes a snorting sound. "Life is not a movie."

"No kidding."

"You know what they say about curiosity, don't you, Clare?"

"Yeah. It got the cat's face sliced in four places."

Martin pulls back, takes off his glasses and rubs his eyes with the heels of his hands.

"Ooh, I've got to get those stronger eyeglasses." He puts his glasses back on and returns to work, with more than half the stitches to go. "I'm sorry, Clare."

"For what?"

"For the tough situation you had with your family."

"Look who's talking, Martin."

"Yeah," he chuckles. "Look who's talking."

"Martin."

"You keep saying my name, and I'm still right here."

"Do you like Johnny?"

Martin hesitates. "My favorite cousin, until I became afraid of him."

"Why were you afraid?"

"His temper, as he got older. He could be the sweetest guy in the world, but he could also go from laughter to rage in a heartbeat. But look who I'm telling. Who knows that better than you?"

"What's wrong with him?"

"I'm not a psychiatrist, but he was probably a psychopath. This family has its share of mental problems, as I'm sure you've guessed, but Italians don't believe in doctors for that kind of thing. You spend money on a doctor, you'd better be bleeding, or have a bone showing."

Silence, save for the clipping of the scissors. Clare waits until Martin is working the final wound before speaking.

"You said 'was,' Martin."

"Excuse me?"

"You said Johnny probably *was* a psychopath."

His hands hesitate. "Did I?"

"Is he dead?"

Martin sets down the scissors, takes off his glasses and polishes the lenses with his handkerchief.

"Oh boy," Clare says, "it's always bad news when you clean your glasses."

Martin does not deny it. He puts the glasses back on and looks her right in the eye. Once again, he gives it to her straight.

"After Gino pulled him away from you, Johnny put a gun under his chin and pulled the trigger. Guess he couldn't live with what he'd done."

"Oh my God."

"Yeah. Quite a mess to mop up on that yacht, between what Johnny did to you and what he did to himself."

Martin picks up the scissors and goes back to work. He seems relaxed as never before, with that secret out of the way. Clare is surprised to feel tears roll down her cheeks, tears for the man who mutilated her.

"Poor Johnny," she murmurs.

Martin's eyebrows go up. "Wow. It's quite a testament to your character that you can feel sorry for him, after what he did to you." He wipes her tears with a Kleenex. "You want to ask me anything else, Clare, now's the time. No more secrets."

"Who's that woman I hear downstairs?"

"Well, that's Johnny's mother. Her husband, rest his soul, left her this estate."

Martin makes a sweeping gesture with his scissor hand, to indicate the riches surrounding them. "He did very well in the family business, obviously, and Johnny was her only son. Her *prince!* He was dying to introduce you to her, the girl he was going to marry."

Clare feels sick to her stomach. "I've been here before," she whispers.

"What do you mean?"

"Italian mothers. Another Italian guy wanted to marry me, and I broke his heart. His mother looked at me like she wanted to kill me."

Martin can't help chuckling. "They're savages, Italian mothers. Everybody thinks the men are tough, but the mothers are the ones."

"Great."

"Ahh, don't worry. They threaten murder, but they rarely go through with it. Can't kill someone with a spaghetti strainer."

"Martin, I'm scared."

"Don't be. I've got her medicated, enough to tranquilize a horse."

"She makes a lot of noise, for a tranquilized horse."

"Shh. Hold still, I'm almost done."

Clare obeys. She's trembling with fear, and she's got another question, which she asks in a stammering voice.

"Are they going to kill me, Martin?"

He laughs out loud. "They'd better not, after all the work I put into this face. There. That's it." He holds up a thin bit of black thread. "The last of the stitches."

He moistens a cotton ball with alcohol and gently wipes the four wounds clean of dried blood before they get up together to look in the mirror. The scars are slightly less swollen, and with the stitches gone it looks like four earthworms are stuck to her face.

"Okay," Martin says. "That's a little better, wouldn't you say?"

"No."

"Come on now, Clare." Martin squeezes a thick yellow ointment onto his fingertip and dabs it on the scars. "A step at a time, one step at a time."

"Can I ask one more question, Martin?"

"Shoot. Sorry, I should have put that another way."

"Where's Johnny's body?"

Martin is truly stunned by the question. "His *body?*"

"Yes, his body. Was there a funeral?"

"No, of course not."

"So where is it?"

He stands and holds out his hand. "Come with me," he says, as if they are about to embark upon a long voyage, but when Clare takes his hand all he does is lead the way to the bedroom window.

It's a clear, chilly afternoon. The wind rattles the windowpanes, and whitecaps fleck the surface of the water. Martin points toward the horizon.

"He's out there, in a sealed steel barrel, filled with cement.

Probably a mile from shore, maybe two." He turns to Clare, shaking his head. "He had to disappear, Clare, like he was never born. I think you can understand why."

CHAPTER TWENTY NINE

The old lady is slowing down, which suits Hannah fine, as her feet are throbbing with each step. They're on a wide dirt path with lush trees on both sides, alive with squawking birds.

Clare won't answer any more questions about where they're going, which Hannah doesn't mind. She's blown away by the sights, like the pheasant that crosses right in front of them, followed by half a dozen chicks, and the corral with two black horses in a nearby field. What makes it even more amazing is the view behind it, just across the river. The top of the Freedom Tower, gleaming in the sunshine. The past and the future, close enough to collide. How amazing! And all within New York City limits!

But nothing is more amazing than the story Clare is sharing. Hannah points toward the sea.

"So your boyfriend is still out there in the deep, we assume?"

"Unless the barrel rusted away and the fish got to him."

"Jesus, what a family, Clare."

"Most families are dangerous, especially when they mean well."

"Is that so?"

A distant look comes to Clare's eyes, a surprise visit from an ugly memory. "My parents wrote me off as soon as they found my diaphragm. My father slapped me, called me a whore and locked me in my room. So I went out through my window and came to New York."

"Just like that?"

"Exactly like that." Clare's lips are trembling. "A righteous man, my father, which was actually kind of funny, considering the money he spent on hookers. My mother was worse, cursing me by day and lighting candles to save my soul by night. Never had the chance to tell her I just didn't want to wind up like her, letting an accident rule my life." She forces a smile. "The accident being me."

They walk in silence for a minute.

"They had diaphragms back then?" Hannah asks.

"Certainly. And we had fire and the wheel, too."

"I'm just asking."

"I'm not *that* old, my dear."

"What terrible parents!"

"Doesn't sound like your family was much better."

This is a bolt from the blue. Hannah stops walking.

"I got your book from the library last week. Sounds to me you did the same thing I did, when you fled Germany. Lying about your age, coming to America at fifteen to work as an au pair? Pretty brave of you."

Hannah struggles to stay calm. One of her major regrets is the time she talked into a tape recorder for two days so that a ghost writer could knock out quickie as-told-to autobiography called 'Model From Munich.' She should not have been drinking wine while talking into the recorder.

"I *left* Germany," Hannah insists. "I did not *flee.*"

"With your family's blessing?"

"Well, maybe they weren't happy about it, but they didn't stop me."

Clare smiles. "Nothing stops people like you and me. I think you know that."

"There *is* no you and me."

"Okay, okay. Let's keep walking."

But Hannah isn't ready to let it go. "I loved my parents," she says, "and you can't tell me otherwise."

"Are they still around?"

"Yes."

"When did you last see them?"

"Well, it's been a while, with everything that's happening."

"Do they like your husband?"

Hannah swallows hard. This is her answer.

"What about your first husband, the one who turned out to be gay?"

"They never met him. Tell you the truth, *I* barely met him."

"He hardly gets a mention in the book."

"I don't really count that marriage."

"Got you your green card, didn't it?"

Hannah struggles to remain calm. "I'm not the only foreigner who ever used that tactic."

"Well, good for you. But how about the second marriage, the one that's falling apart now?"

Hannah's eyes narrow to slits. "That was for real."

"I'll say! Big hootin'-shootin' wedding at the Plaza, my favorite place of all!" Clare cocks her head in mock puzzlement. "Were your parents there? Didn't notice them in any of the pictures in your book."

"They couldn't make it."

"Couldn't make it? Something more important than their only daughter's wedding came up?"

"It was a medical issue. My mother's hip."

"And you've been married how long?"

"Nine years."

"Hmm. Plenty of time for a hip to heal. Have they met their grandchildren?"

Hannah wipes away tears and shakes her head. She suddenly feels weak, and has to sit on a grassy patch by the side of the path, hands covering her face. Clare sits beside her.

"Are you okay?"

Hannah nods, her face still hidden. "We have more in common than you might imagine, Clare."

She strokes Hannah's back, to encourage the words. It works. The words come, a flood of them.

From the age of six, it's clear to everyone that little Hannah Schmitt is going to be a world-class swimmer. She cuts through the water like a blade, leaving opponents choking on her foam.

Her father, a chemical engineer and onetime Olympic alternate named Hans Schmitt, is her personal coach. He's determined that his daughter is going to reach the peak that eluded him.

She also happens to be beautiful, a characteristic not common among female swimmers.

Every morning at five they're at the local indoor pool in their Munich suburb, Hans with his whistle, Hannah in a Speedo and goggles.

The exercises! Back and forth she goes, clutching a kick board, scissor-kicking her way through endless laps, no arms allowed. Then arms only, her legs dragging behind, as if she's been paralyzed from the waist down, with a sharp tweet of the whistle from Dad at the slightest sign of a kick.

She loves winning, touching the wall at the end of a 100-meter race and looking left and right to make sure her competitors haven't gotten there yet.

The years go by, and the medals and trophies pile up. The Olympics are looking very real.

But by the time she's a teenager, she is gripped by something stronger than the need to out-swim everybody in Germany.

It's *boredom!* The sheer freaking boredom of those endless laps, back and forth, staring down at those painted lines at the bottom of the pool! Not to mention the endless stink of chlorine, the relentless red eyes (even with goggles), pruny fingers and toes...

There's got to be more to life than this, but *what?* And how can she even find out what it is, with swimming and school devouring every waking moment of her life?

She brings it up one night at the dinner table when she is fifteen, suddenly and abruptly as a belch.

"I'm getting tired of swimming."

Her father is a strong man, not a pound over his competitive swimming weight. He looks menacing in rimless glasses and a crewcut, and he freezes at Hannah's words.

"You don't mean that," he says.

He slaps a huge spoonful of mashed potatoes on her plate. She hates mashed potatoes, but all that swimming calls for a big carbohydrate intake.

"Eat," he says.

"Did you hear me, Papa?"

"Yes. Eat."

She turns to her mother, a nervous, bird-like woman named Marta.

"Mama, I'm tired of swimming. Don't look at him!"

Marta can't help it. She always looks to Hans before speaking, but now her daughter is telling her not to do that, so she looks down at her plate, like a woman praying for the salvation of her soul.

"I want to quit," Hannah wails to the ceiling.

Her mother shuts her eyes. Her father's eyes widen.

"No," he says.

"Yes."

"You're just nervous about tomorrow," Hans says, referring to an important swim meet the following night.

"No, Papa, I want to quit."

"And do what?"

"I don't know. Something else."

He points at the lump of mashed potatoes on her plate.

"You're a swimmer. Swimmers need fuel. *Eat.*"

She obeys. They all eat in silence.

But it's far from over for Hannah Schmitt. She's working out a plan, even as she chokes down those hated potatoes.

The following night she stands on the starting block in the middle lane, flanked by three girls on either side, all of them waving their arms and kicking their feet to loosen up before the hundred meter freestyle race - two lengths of an indoor pool, in freezing-cold water. Through her goggles she can see her father in the stands, looking stern and proud at the same time. He's getting his way.

Her mother isn't there. She's far too nervous to attend these events.

The starter raises his pistol, fires, and they are off.

Hannah as always takes a commanding lead, cutting through the water faster than the rest. She's fifteen meters ahead of her closest competitor at the end of the first lap, does a flip-turn off the wall and begins the second leg of her journey to certain victory.

But stroke by stroke, the others catch up as Hannah eases the pace. Hans gets to his feet in the stands, screaming at his daughter, who of course can't hear him, but knows exactly how he is reacting as she slows down more and more, stroke by stroke.

A heavy favorite to win, Hannah places fifth out of seven in an event she is known to own. The crowd can't believe it. Whistles and jeers as Hannah gets out of the water, takes off her goggles and stands there dripping, smiling at her father, who stares back with a blank face.

He says nothing on the way to the car. He gets behind the wheel and Hannah slides in beside him, and just like that he back-hands her across the face.

Her hands fly up to cover her nose, which is bleeding. Hans starts the car.

"Tell Mama you swam into the wall," he says calmly. "The water was cloudy, and you didn't see the wall."

"Yes, Papa."

"This mustn't happen again, Hannah."

"No, Papa."

"No swimming for you tomorrow."

"Okay, Papa."

She fights to keep from laughing out loud. He's just made it easy for her. She knows exactly what she has to do now, freed from her orbit.

Her mother weeps at the sight of her nose. The bleeding has stopped but the nose is swollen, and tender to the touch. She gives Hannah a plastic bag filled with ice cubes to bring down the swelling. Hannah goes to her room, but she doesn't go straight to bed.

She already has a passport, acquired in anticipation of the inevitable international competitions ahead. She's saved her birthday money and her allowance for the past few years, the equivalent of about seven hundred dollars. Her nose is throbbing as she packs a bag and leaves the house at dawn, while her father enjoys a rare late-morning sleep.

At Munich Airport she buys a ticket and boards a flight to Los Angeles, where she gets by on her remaining money until she wangles work as an illegal au pair, and meets people, and is noticed, and noticed some more, and finds an agent, and is photographed, and becomes, after a few tumultuous, amazingly lucky years, the Face of the New Millenium.

"Wow," Clare says. "I must say, that bit in the book about you swimming into that wall did not ring true. You're not the type who swims into walls." She grins. "You're the type who smashes *through* them."

Hannah, though still tearful, can't help giggling.

"I was going to ask you to join me for a swim at the Carmine Street pool," Clare says with a straight face. "Guess not, huh?"

"Please. I haven't gone near a pool since that race I lost on purpose."

"That was a good tactic."

They get to their feet and continue walking.

"Our fathers should have met," Hannah says. "They would have gotten along."

"Oh, don't be bitter, dear. Think of the time they saved us! You hopped that plane as soon as you could, and half an hour after my father slapped me, I was on a bus to New York. *Half an hour!*" She smiles. "Three hundred and seventy-eight miles. A nine hour ride."

"Did they come after you?"

"I doubt it. Never saw them again, and I was free to live my dream in Greenwich Village."

"So you don't know when they, you know...."

She can't bring herself to say the word, but Clare can.

"Died. No, I don't know. But in my mind, they died the night I left Pittsburgh."

Hannah fights an impulse to be mean, then gives in to it.

"Your dream turned into a nightmare on that boat, didn't it?"

"Guess you could say that."

"You should have left that party with Richard Avedon, instead of hanging around."

"Don't think that hasn't occurred to me, dear."

"Think about it! You don't bump into Frank Sinatra, Ava Gardner doesn't try to attack you, Johnny doesn't carry you out of the Plaza -"

"Yes, yes, I *get* it."

"You were *cheated!*"

"Think so?"

"You could have been a top model! You could have been rich! You could have been..."

She searches in vain for the right word, which Clare provides.

"*You,* dear. I could have been you." She fakes a shiver. "Thanks, but no thanks."

Hannah is momentarily stunned. Then she bursts out laughing, and so does Clare.

"Come on," Clare says, "let's step it up a little, we're not far now."

After twelve days at the Palermo house, Martin brings good news to Clare - she can go home. The clothes she arrived in have been washed, and the bloodstains on her sandals have been scrubbed off. In two minutes, she's dressed and ready to go.

"I'm driving you," Martin says, "but you have to wear this when we leave."

Embarrassed, he holds up a narrow length of black cloth. Clare gulps.

"A blindfold?"

"Just until we get away from the house. They don't want you to know where you've been."

"I don't want to know, either."

"Good."

Martin gently ties the blindfold around her eyes, then takes her elbow and leads her out of the room.

"Here come the stairs," he whispers. "One at a time, nice and slow."

She can hear breathing when they reach the ground floor, wheezy sounds, the kind that come from overweight people. There's also a muffled sound, like someone struggling to speak. She wonders how many are watching her, hating her. She wonders if Johnny's mother is among them, making that strange sound.

She wonders if this is a trick that will lead to her death.

A door opens, and a salty sea breeze fills her lungs as they step outside. How good it is to breathe fresh air! At least I have *this,* even if they kill me!

They step along more quickly, now. She senses that they have crossed a street, and then Martin stops, opens a car door and eases Clare into the passenger seat.

"They're still watching. Don't touch the blindfold."

The car starts, and after they're rolling for two minutes Martin tells her she can remove the blindfold.

And only at this point does Clare believe her life is being spared, as she pulls it off to see that they are riding along the Staten Island waterfront in a bottle-green Cadillac.

She looks at Martin, who pats her knee with true affection. "How are you feeling, kid?"

"I'm okay."

"You did great."

"Who watched me go?"

"You don't need to know."

"I thought I heard somebody trying to speak."

"What does it matter?"

"Was it Johnny's mother?"

"Clare. You do not need to know."

"Was it?"

"*Yes!* She insisted on seeing you, but they gagged her to keep her quiet. You were blindfolded and she was gagged, with two guys holding her by the elbows. Got the full picture, now?"

It's not really the full picture. Martin does not tell Clare about the murderous gleam in Johnny's mother's bulging eyes, or the way she strained to attack Clare, frantically kicking at the shins of the men who held her back. It's a sight that will haunt Martin for the

175

rest of his days.

Clare weeps silently as Martin takes a handkerchief and wipes his forehead, where sweat has broken out along his hairline.

"Sorry I got upset." He waves his hand back over his shoulder, to indicate the past. "It's all over, now. Put it behind you, Clare, and let's get you home."

Martin is exhausted. He hasn't had it easy, looking after her all this time. Now he can go home and collapse, but not before Clare composes herself to ask her toughest question yet.

"You talked them out of it, didn't you?"

Martin shrugs, faking puzzlement. "Talked them out of what?"

"Killing me."

His hands grip the steering wheel. "We don't have to get into that."

"They wanted to, didn't they? Johnny's mother certainly did, that's for sure."

"Her vote never counts."

"Well, lucky me. But I'm sure it would have been quicker to just get rid of me."

Martin nods. "Cheaper, too."

That surprises her. "Come on, Martin, I didn't eat *that* much."

"Reach back and take that bag from the back seat, would you?"

Clare does as she's told, bringing a bulging canvas knapsack up front.

"Open it."

She unzips the bag, and her jaw literally drops. It contains packet after packet of twenty dollar bills, rubber banded into small rectangular bricks.

"Holy shit, Martin!"

"Getting this was harder than begging for your life," he admits. "They love money, you know? But they got my point. A young innocent girl, her whole future as a fashion model ruined...I have to say, I made a good case for you."

Clare's mind is blown. "How much is this?"

"Count it when you get home."

She closes the zipper. "Don't drive me home, Martin. Take me to the ferry."

"Are you crazy? You can't ride the ferry with this cargo! I've got to take you to your door."

"I'll be fine. I really want to take the ferry."

"If you get mugged - "

"I won't. My face will keep the muggers at bay."

Martin gives her a funny look. "You don't want me to know where you live, do you?"

"I don't want *them* to know where I live."

Martin nods in understanding. "You're learning," he sighs. "The ferry it is."

Ten minutes later they reach the terminal. Martin offers to ride across with her, but Clare declines. He helps her get the knapsack on her back. She looks like a kid on the first day of school, even more so when Martin claps a New York Yankees baseball cap on her head.

"If people stare, you can pull the bill down."

"Thank you, Martin. Thank you for everything."

She takes him in a long, hard embrace, careful to keep her chin above his shoulder to protect the wounds. They are both weeping.

"I apologize," he says, his voice shaky with sorrow, "on behalf of my poor crazy cousin, God rest his soul."

Clare can't help smiling. "Do you believe in God, Martin?"

He breaks the embrace and wipes his eyes. "Ahh, I go back and forth on it. You?"

"Not since about twelve days ago, no."

The ferry arrives, and the gate slides open. Martin gives Clare the nickel fare.

"Good luck, Clare."

She's jolted by a sudden thought that should have occurred to her much, much sooner.

"I'm never going to see you again, am I, Martin?"

He shakes his head. "Can't happen. I'm sorry. Keep the cuts clean, and use the ointment until it runs out."

"Stop being a doctor for a minute and kiss me."

Before he can respond she kisses him on the mouth, in a gentle embrace he chooses not to break. When at last she pulls back his face is beet-red and his glasses are fogged.

"Well," he says, "I'll remember that for the rest of my life."

"Thank you, Martin."

"Can I give you one piece of advice?"

"I'm listening."

The redness has receded from his face. He takes his glasses off and wipes them with his handkerchief before saying, "Want less."

Clare doesn't understand. "Want less of *what?*"

"Thrills. Danger. Whatever drove you to be with someone like Johnny is going to kill you eventually. Stay away from extremes, you know? Live in the middle, like the rest of us. It's not so bad."

She lets it sink in, peering into his soft brown eyes. "Thought you said you weren't a psychiatrist, Martin."

"You're right. What the hell do I know?" He taps the knapsack. "Anyway, be smart with this money. And remember, none of this ever happened. Especially that kiss. Goodbye, Clare."

"I'll never forget you, Martin."

"You'll be hard to forget, too."

He turns and walks quickly away, as if he's just lit a fuse. He doesn't want her to see that he's sobbing. Clare boards the ferry and goes to the rail for a last look at Martin, thinking he'll be waving from the shore, but he is gone, now and forever.

With a bone-rattling toot of its horn the ferry gets moving. Clare moves to the prow, like a sea captain of old peering ahead at the new world. She's aware of people staring at her, wondering what in the world could have happened to such a pretty girl's face.

She realizes that this is a new way of being stared at. She was beauty, and now she is the beast. She wonders if the sight of her face is going to scare little children. She wonders if it would be best to jump off the ferry and let the current carry her past Hell's Gate and out to sea, weighted down by a soggy fortune on her back.

But that's just a momentary thought, a flash. This isn't the time to think like that. *Get back to the skylight room* - that's the main thing. Keep moving, and let people stare. It's what they do best.

She catches the subway from South Ferry and rides uptown in a nearly-empty car. She wonders if it's deserted because of the way she looks, and gets her answer when a young black man boards the train at Chambers Street, looks at her face and cries "Lawd Almighty!" before rushing to another car.

She gets off at Christopher Street and walks toward Bleecker, head down, watching her feet as she goes, all the way to Zito's Bakery, where Louie is stacking fresh loaves on sanitary white paper in the front window.

He's alerted by the bell that rings whenever someone opens the door and turns to Clare with his usual smile, which turns to a frown at the sight of her face.

"Yes ma'am?" he says, recovering quickly.

Her heart sinks. He doesn't recognize her.

"My usual, Louie."

His eyes narrow and then widen in sudden recognition. He puts a hand over his open mouth.

"Oh my God, what happened to you, sweetheart?"

She almost feels like laughing. *Well, Louie, it all started that night we had bread with Frank Sinatra in the basement....*

"I had an accident."

"Madonna mi, your face!"

She tugs the bill of her cap even lower. "I'll be okay, Louie."

"What was it, a car crash?"

Why not? "Yeah. My face hit the windshield."

"Who the hell was drivin'?"

"Nobody you know. Could I have my bread?"

"Anything, sweetheart, anything..."

Louie gives her two loaves instead of the usual one, slipping them into long paper sleeves.

"Need a ride home? I can getcha a cab."

"I'd rather walk."

"Okay, whatever's best, sweetheart."

It occurs to her that Louie doesn't know her name. He's always called her "sweetheart," and that's probably a good thing. He hands her the bread, his eyes moist with sympathy.

"C'mere, you."

He takes her in a fleshy embrace, careful not to push up against her face. She thanks him and leaves the shop, the fortune on her back, a loaf of bread under each arm.

Isn't that an expression to indicate good fortune, and luck, and abundance?

The climb to the skylight room isn't easy. She feels weak, and has to pause for breath halfway up. Once inside, she tosses the knapsack on the floor and begins nibbling on one of the loaves, the way a squirrel might. It's a wonderful taste, as good as it was on that night with Sinatra a lifetime ago, a beautiful face ago.

When she's devoured half the loaf she sets the rest aside, takes the knapsack and empties it out on the floor. The tightly bundled bills look like green building blocks, the kind a child would play with.

She counts the twenties in a single bundle, then multiplies that by the number of bundles. A shiver goes through her as she realizes she's sitting on a hundred thousand dollars, give or take.

The hush-up price for an aspiring model mutilated by a psychotic suicidal gangster, in 1951.

CHAPTER THIRTY

Clare is walking slowly, now. The sharing of her life story takes a toll on her steam. Hannah, on the other hand, feels more alive than ever.

"Jesus, Clare, they paid you off!"

"They sure did."

"You kept your mouth shut."

"Obviously."

"That was dirty money, you know. They made it selling drugs, and who knows what else."

"I think of it as blood money. *My* blood."

"You're right. You certainly earned it the hard way."

"And I never invested it, if that makes you think better of me."

"How long did it last?"

"Oh, I've still got a little."

Hannah is flabbergasted. "A hundred grand has lasted you *seventy years?* How the hell did you manage *that?*"

"I listened to Martin. I wanted less. Here we are."

They reach a pair of wrought iron gates that open into a large, rolling cemetery, the kind that goes on for acres and acres.

Hannah can't control her excitement. "Johnny's grave!" she cries. "We're here to visit Johnny's grave, right?"

Clare rolls her eyes. "How can he have a grave when he was buried at sea?"

"They could still build him a headstone. Italians love headstones."

"You're right about that."

"So that's where we're going, to visit the great love of your life."

"If you say so, dear. Let's have a snack first."

They sit on a wooden bench in the shade of an oak tree, where Clare takes two containers of strawberry yogurt and two small bottles of water from her battered knapsack.

"I didn't know you had all that," Hannah says. "I would have carried it for you."

Clare waves away the too-late offer. "I don't like yogurt much, but I know you're probably watching your figure."

"Not lately."

Clare gives Hannah a plastic spoon and a bottle of Evian.

"Bottled water is a scam, but there are no fountains out here."

"So," Hannah says, digging into her yogurt, "you learned to want less."

"I think so."

"I can see you never wanted new luggage."

"Oh, you mean this?" Clare pats the faded green knapsack. "Nothing wrong with it. Still holds up. It's what Martin packed all that money into, the day they set me free."

For three days Clare does not leave the skylight room, existing on tap water, crackers and Zito's bread. She naps, she reads, she puts ointment on her cuts and she lies on her back gazing through the skylight, alone up there with all that cash.

She could stay holed up even longer but she's dying for a shower, and that means a trip to the Carmine Street gym. She looks at her face in a pocket mirror. The scars are still sensitive, but not painful. The good doctor has kept infections at bay.

Clare applies the last of the ointment - a mild sting, but not too bad - and now she's ready to venture outside. She packs a change of clean clothes, puts the baseball cap on her head, turns up the collar of her lightest jacket and puts on a pair of big-rimmed sunglasses.

She pauses at the door and takes a deep breath before hurrying down the stairs. Luckily she doesn't bump into any of her neighbors, a collection of loners who keep to themselves, anyway.

It feels good to be out on the street, and she walks fast, head down, all the way to the gym. The woman at the desk barely glances at her ID card as she breezes inside, and the showers are empty. One good break after another.

The water feels wonderful on her body, and she's careful to keep her face and her hair dry. On her way home she buys fruit, vegetables, a pair of scissors and a bottle of red wine.

She's lost her taste for alcohol, but this one time she needs it to fortify herself for the task ahead. She drinks a glass of wine, picks up the pocket mirror in her left hand, takes the scissor in her right and cuts her hair, chopping away until it's the same two-inch length all around.

Clare Owen the model-to-be is officially gone forever.

Two days later she goes for a walk in the Village, the now-loose baseball cap on her head, sunglasses on her face. She heads to MacDougal and lingers across the street from Reggio's, worrying that she will be spotted, but it doesn't happen. It's a sunny day, and business is brisk, her former fellow waitresses rushing in and out to keep the customers happy. She wonders if she could go in and order a cappuccino without being recognized. She might get away with it, keeping the hat and the sunglasses on, and *oh,* how the waitresses would be clucking later about the poor girl with the carved-up face!

She's actually giggling as she walks away and heads to Sixth Avenue, where she sees a line of down-and-outers waiting to get into the soup kitchen at St. Joseph's Church.

She's curious. She's never noticed this place before, though she's walked past it many times. When the doors open she joins the line, shuffling along with the people, mostly men.

Inside, everyone behaves well - no pushing to get at the food, which is some kind of beef stew beside a pile of sliced white bread, and a huge coffee urn surrounded by dozens of chipped, much-used mugs.

Clare stands there staring when she feels a gentle hand on her shoulder, which belongs to an enormous black woman wearing overalls and a sanitary net over a fierce helmet of hair.

"What happened to your face, baby?" she asks in an irresistibly buttery voice.

Clare removes her sunglasses, to give her the full view. "Car accident."

"Hmm." The woman knows it's a lie, but she leaves it alone. "Want me to fix you a plate?"

"No, thanks."

"Cup o' coffee, maybe?"

She surprises herself by saying, "I was wondering if I could help."

The woman's big yellow eyes widen to saucers. She chuckles and says, "Well, shit, we ain't *never* got enough help 'round here."

"You don't have to pay me."

"Well, that's good, 'cause I got no money to give you."

"When do I start?"

"How's ten o'clock tomorrow morning? That's when we do the prep work."

"I'll be here."

They shake hands. "I'm Shoni."

"Clare."

Shoni maintains the clasp while gazing into Clare's face.

"Damn," she says, "ain't never seen eyes like those."

And so begins a new life for Clare Owen, one block west and a whole world away from her old one at Caffe Reggio.

The work suits her. She enjoys sitting in the big kitchen beside a mountain of potatoes, peeling them and dropping them into a giant stainless steel pot, to be boiled and mashed and spooned onto the plates of the daily dozens who get their only real meal of the day here.

And when the lunch crowd is gone and the dishes are done she's got the rest of the day to do as she pleases, for the first time in her life. No expectations of any kind.

Her only worry is the sack of cash in the skylight room. She knows she can't deposit it in a bank account without answering a lot of unanswerable questions, and then it hits her: a safe deposit box.

She carries the sack to a bank on Sheridan Square and is interviewed by a polite man in a dark suit who is satisfied when she says she needs to store a significant amount of "personal papers." She fills out a form, is issued a key and taken to a gloomy vault upstairs, where a uniformed guard brings her a long rectangular metal box and escorts her to a cubicle with an opaque glass door, where she can do her business in private.

There's plenty of room to stash her money, nearly five thousand twenty dollar bills. She pays for a year's rental in cash and leaves the bank, tingling with relief.

"Everything's going to be all right."

She says it out loud and laughs. Then she goes to the Jefferson Market Library at Sixth Avenue and Tenth Street to get herself a library card.

She's always wanted a library card, and now, without men devouring her time or a modeling career to worry about, she's got time to do what she's always wanted to do.

She wants to read. She wants to think. She wants to *be*.

Hannah sets down her empty yogurt cup, takes a swig of water and says, "I don't see it."

Clare eats slowly, with half her yogurt to go. "What don't you see?"

"You couldn't just disappear like that!"

"That's the beauty of New York City. You can disappear without leaving."

184

"Didn't people come looking for you?"

Clare chuckles. "Things moved fast in the Village, back then. I was gone nearly two weeks, more than enough time to be forgotten. The circus leaves town quickly, you know?"

"Avedon didn't come looking for you?"

Clare shrugs. "He didn't know where I lived. Maybe he tried at Reggio's, but they didn't know my address, either." She smiles. "Nothing is narrower than a window of opportunity, my dear. You probably knew that."

"So Johnny Palermo was the last man you had."

"Correct."

"I don't understand how you just...turned it off."

"Turned what off?"

"Your desire."

"My dear, it wasn't up to me. After that men were attracted by my eyes and repelled by my face. Jump ball, as they say."

"You can't even see the scars now."

"Well, that's only been for the last five years, when the wrinkles took over. Anyway, I was always able to pleasure myself, you know?" She winks. Hannah feels herself blush. "Come on, Clare. Didn't you ever miss being with a man?"

"Let's just say I had my fill, so to speak. More than my fill, that first year in New York."

"So you never, *ever* longed for a man?" Hannah hesitates. "Or a woman, maybe?"

"Oh, Lord, I never went *that* way! Pretty comical, don't you think, that whole lesbian culture? I mean, when two women fight, who gives in? How does it ever *end?*"

Hannah can't help laughing. "Good point."

Clare finishes her yogurt and crushes the carton. "Nobody enjoyed men more than I did, but I always went too far. If Johnny hadn't happened, something else would have happened to me. I pushed that man to the breaking point. I pushed them *all* to the breaking point. I was living dangerously."

"So you've played it safe, ever since."

Clare laughs out loud. "*Safe?* A woman alone, with no medical insurance, no job, no children to look after me in my old age?"

"I'm not sure my children will be looking after me."

"Well, you'll have money. *Somebody* will look after you, even if it's an employee. Sorry, my friend, but one of us played it safe, and it wasn't me."

"Funny, I don't feel safe."

Clare shrugs. "Neither do I. But I don't worry about it."

Hannah sighs in exasperation. "See, *that's* what I can't understand. How can you be so serene, and so happy, with the way you've had to live?"

She is practically shouting. Clare strokes her back to calm her and gestures at the surrounding headstones with her free hand.

"Quiet down, or you'll wake the dead."

"I'm sorry. I'm just trying to understand you."

"Look, I lived a lifetime in my first year in New York. I was lucky to be alive. Martin saw that. I knew that if I were to survive, I'd have to live my life at a distance from people. *Near* them, but not with them."

She stands up and spreads her hands. "What better place for that than Greenwich Village?"

It doesn't take long for young Clare Owen to establish her dock poles: the Carmine Street gym, the soup kitchen at St. Joseph's and the Jefferson Market Library.

She works each morning with Shoni, chopping or peeling whatever is needed for the day's meal. Clare has little to say at first, but Shoni is patient.

"Clare," she ventures during their second week together, "you wasn't in no car accident."

Shoni states it as a truth, like a lawyer who has his facts down cold. Clare continues chopping celery, refusing to respond.

"Cuts is too even," Shoni says. "Somebody done carved you up."

Clare looks up from her cutting board. "It wasn't really his fault. He had a problem."

Shoni can't help cackling. "Yeah, I guess he did." She cocks her head toward Clare. "You ain't even mad at him, girl!"

Clare, surprised by Shoni's perception, realizes she is right.

"Wouldn't be much point," she says. "He's dead."

Shoni's eyes widen. She looks around, making sure they are alone in the kitchen.

"Joo kill him?" she whispers.

"No! How could you ask me that?"

" 'Cause you're awful good with that knife, honey. I wouldn't want to piss you off."

Clare laughs out loud, for the first time since Johnny slashed her. It feels like healing, the start of healing.

Once a month she visits the bank to take out as many twenties as she'll need. She eats a banana for breakfast and then lunch is whatever she prepares at the soup kitchen, and dinner is as simple as bread and vegetables. The Salvation Army shop on Eighth Avenue becomes her source for clothing, including shoes.

Sturdy shoes, because she walks and walks and walks, all the way to Harlem and back on some afternoons. If it's sunny she stops to stretch out with a book on the grass in Washington Square Park, taking in the musicians, the magicians, and the crazies ranting about the end of the world.

And the fifties give way to the sixties, when she sees and hears a skinny musician who would appear to be just days from death performing under the arch, guitar and harmonica going at the same time, and who could have guessed that Bob Dylan would amount to anything?

The seventies bring a wave of S & M clubs to the Village riverfront, beefy leather-clad men with handlebar moustaches clearly proud of the menace they radiate, followed by the shock of the eighties when AIDS ravages the neighborhood, and the skeletal men shuffling through the soup kitchen are clearly marked for death.

In the nineties homelessness becomes another epidemic. Cars that stop for red lights on Hudson Street are under siege by half-crazed men who swab their windshields with filthy rags and turn violent if the driver refuses to tip them.

Then comes the new millenium, and a mayor with the cruelty to make it all go away.

Suddenly, the homeless and the crazies are gone, nobody knows where, and almost nobody cares. It's safe to walk the streets again!

But the Mom and Pop stores on Bleecker Street are also gone, chased away by suddenly skyrocketing rents. The artists can no longer afford to be here, so now Greenwich Village is more like a petting zoo for tourists, and what, if anything, remains from the old days, when Clare Owen first set foot here?

Not much.

But the lady in the skylight room is still there. She knows the wind by the speed of the clouds, knows the rain by the patter on the panes, knows winter has arrived when the glass is frosted, and her feeble radiator starts to whistle.

And no matter what's going on outside she feels safe up here, like a tiny bird in a nest in the tallest of trees.

Hannah stares at Clare's face, trying to get her head around this strange woman's life.

"It's hard to believe you could hide like that for all these years."

Clare is offended. "I wasn't hiding! I've been out and about, probably more than you." She grins. "But I was shunned, because of my face. That can be a real privilege, if you treasure your privacy. Then, when the wrinkles covered the scars, I was shunned just for being old. It's the great leveler, old age. You'll see."

Hannah shakes her head. "All those years in the Village, and none of your old friends spotted you. Unbelievable."

Clare holds up a bony finger. "Well, one person. Just one." She smiles, but it's not a happy smile. "Raymond. Oh, *Raymond.*"

CHAPTER THIRTY ONE

When she first sees him at Reggio's, she can't help thinking: *What an asshole!*

It's just two days after Avedon photographed her on the Christopher Street pier. He's holding court at one of Clare's tables with three other young guys, all of them loud, with the kind of boisterous laughter that drives the other customers crazy. Not the brooding, pensive clientele Reggio's is known for, but what can she do?

Blond and blue-eyed, he looks as if he's been plucked from a Nebraska cornfield. Clare figures he must be getting married in the morning. This table has bachelor party written all over it, and this looks to be their last stop. They arrived liquored up, and they've been downing coffee and pastries for more than an hour, so now they're drunk, caffeinated and sugared up, not a great combination for settling down.

"To Raymond!" one of the others shouts, and he clinks his coffee cup so hard against Raymond's that both cups break. The pieces fall to the table and they all laugh hysterically.

Clare comes to the table. "Maybe it's time to call it a night, guys."

A chorus of "oohs" from the guys, but not Raymond, who seems to notice Clare for the first time. His smile is dazzling.

"Sorry about the cups, ma'am," he says. "I'll pay for 'em."

He actually calls her "ma'am," and there's a midwestern twang to his voice. He seems to have sobered up, or maybe he wasn't all that drunk in the first place. He gets to his feet and squares the tab as his buddies stagger off into the night, offering drunken congratulations as they go.

"Sorry about my friends," he says. "They get carried away. See, I'm off to Hollywood tomorrow. Got a part in a picture."

An actor, behaving like a jerk. What a shock. "Good for you," Clare says, busily cleaning up the broken cups.

"Not a *big* part, just a few lines, but it's a start, you know?" He tries his smile on her again. It's a damn good smile, and he knows it. Clare can't help smiling back.

"You can bullshit with the best of them, can't you?"

He laughs, a genuine laugh. "I try my best, ma'am."

"That's twice you 'ma'am-ed' me. It's getting a little old."

"You're right, and I'm sorry. I'll just say good night now, gotta get back to my room and pack. Thanks for everything."

He offers his hand for a formal shake, pressing a folded bill into Clare's palm before turning to leave. He's out the door before she sees what it is.

A one hundred dollar bill.

Clare rushes outside and sees that he's already half a block away, his long strides carrying him down MacDougal Street. She runs to catch up, grabs him by the elbow and holds the bill up to his face.

"You made a mistake. This is a hundred."

"I know. It's for your splendid service."

"Are you crazy?"

"I told you, I got a part in a picture. Life is good! Just spreadin' the good luck around a little bit, you know?"

She drops the bill to the sidewalk. "Get over yourself," she says, turning to head back to Reggio's.

Now it's his turn to grab her by the elbow. "Whoa, *whoa!*" He picks up the bill. "Let's see, now, if this is legit." He actually bites the bill! "Uh-huh. Just as I thought, it's the real deal, all right. A hundred smackers, and the lady doesn't want it."

"Let go of my elbow, please."

"Yes, ma'am."

She rubs her elbow. "Jesus, if you *'ma'am'* me one more time - "

"Listen, I got an idea. When do you get off?"

The question stuns her. "Actually, my shift is just about over."

"What say you come with me on a little adventure?"

She doesn't normally go for a guy like this. He's glib, he's full of himself, he knows he's handsome and it's obvious he's used to girls falling into his arms.

On the other hand....*an adventure.*

"What'd you have in mind?"

"You'll see." He offers his hand for a shake. "I'm Raymond."

The hand is rough, a worker's hand. She likes that. "I'm Clare."

"Okay, Clare." He holds up the bill, smiling that smile. "First thing we gotta do is head back to Reg-gi-*oh's,* and break this sucker into singles. Can you do that?"

She can. She makes the exchange and hands Raymond a thick wad of dollar bills, which he doesn't bother to count.

"Now what, Raymond?"

"Now, we take a little walk in the park."

She's disappointed. "Doesn't sound like much of an adventure."
"Oh, ye of little faith." He offers his arm. "Come along, my dear."

She hooks elbows with Raymond, and off they go, into the shadows of Washington Square Park. He tells her about his life in New York, doing grunt work on construction sites between auditions, and after two years of struggle he's been spotted in an off-Broadway show by a director who likes his looks, supplying him with a plane ticket and expenses for the trip to Los Angeles.

"I'll be playing a juvenile delinquent," he says with a chuckle. "Funny, huh? Hope nobody notices I'm twenty-four years old. Gonna have to shave close. Oops, right there, Clare, our first stop."

He leads the way to a bench where an old man is asleep under a ratty green blanket. Raymond tucks two dollars under the old man's chin and covers it with the blanket as he continues snoring. Then he turns to Clare.

"I've slept on a few benches, in my time. Two bucks'll get him breakfast tomorrow, right?"

Before Clare can answer Raymond is off to catch up with a snaggle-toothed woman who's muttering to herself as she drags a crooked two-wheeled cart, brimming with the kind of junk that makes you itchy just to look at it. He hands her two dollars.

"Thanks!" she snarls, grabbing the bills without breaking stride to get wherever she's going.

Raymond turns to Clare. "Two down, forty-eight to go." He shakes the remaining bills. "What do you think?" He stretches his arms toward the sky. "Breakfast for fifty down-and-outers! Are you with me, Clare?"

She is.

The homeless are peppered throughout the park, some of them wandering, most of them sleeping on benches, or under shrubs, or snoring away as they sit upright against the base of the arch, arms wrapped around their worldly goods. Raymond and Clare distribute the money into the hands of those who are awake, inside the clothing of those who sleep. All the while they share their life stories, Raymond telling her all about the movie he's about to be in, with a director she's never heard of, but don't worry, he assures her, you will.

He grew up in Indianapolis and always dreamed of moving to the big city, and making it as an actor, and just as he was about to give up hope - *bam!* He's spotted in this forgettable Off-Broadway play, and Hollywood beckons!

"People like you and me, we're the *real* New Yorkers," he says. "The people who were born here don't even know what makes this town tick." He smiles. "Look at you, a waitress from Pittsburgh, and now you're gonna be on magazine covers."

"It hasn't happened yet."

"Oh, it will. Believe me. Now tell me the truth - what did you think of me when you first saw me?"

"I thought you were an asshole."

"Ha! I *knew* it. Knew the second I put that hundred in your hand it was a mistake."

"Then why'd you do it?"

"To make you come after me." He grins. "Worked, didn't it? So I guess it wasn't a mistake, after all."

"You *asshole.*"

He laughs, holding up two single dollars. "My last deuce. Oh, boy, look, over there, by the statue."

A white-haired woman in soiled pink tights and a ballerina skirt is dancing around the base of the Garibaldi statue, to whatever music is playing in her head. She's graceful and seems as weightless as a kite. She may be fifty, she may be ninety, and she is certainly crazy. She whirls and jumps, landing on filthy bare feet, concluding her dance right where Raymond and Clare stand, a wrinkled hand extended, palm up.

Into that palm go those last two dollars. She closes her hand on the money, bows, and begins a new dance.

Raymond turns to Clare. "So, now I'm tapped out. Am I still an asshole?"

"Maybe not."

"Would a kiss be out of the question?"

They kiss, then they kiss some more.

Raymond pulls back for air. "I'm leaving town tomorrow. My first time on a plane."

"Are you nervous?"

"Hell, no! Truth is, that's one of my dreams - learning to fly. Acting and flying! Get myself my own small plane, go wherever I want! Not a bad life, eh?"

"Sounds good to me."

Raymond sighs. "Thing is, I don't know when I'll be back."

Clare hides a smile. Poor Raymond! He's confessing in advance for his absence! He doesn't know that his appeal is increased by the fact that he'll soon be three thousand miles away. It's time to torment him a little.

"Thing is, if you're a hit, Raymond, you'll probably stay in Hollywood."

"Maybe." He swallows. "Does that mean we're saying goodbye?"

"No. I just hope you won't mind."

He's puzzled. "Mind what?"

"Climbing stairs. There are a lot of stairs to my place."

They kiss one more time, before she takes his hand and leads the way to the skylight room. It's an enjoyable night for both of them, a perfect one-night stand, and Raymond is gone before dawn.

Gone forever, Clare figures.

But not quite. Just thirty-three years, to be exact.

It happens on an October afternoon in 1984, as she's dishing beef goulash onto a plate at the soup kitchen.

"Clare?"

Like a voice from a tomb. Without looking up she knows that the trembling, yellow-nailed hand holding the plate must belong to someone from long ago. At last she looks into the quivering blue eyes of the man who treated fifty down-and-outers to breakfast before taking off to conquer Hollywood.

"Raymond. My God."

He smiles, a smile darkened by the loss of many teeth. He's bald on top, fringes of silver hair tickling his bony shoulders. A wispy beard completes the picture.

"Nice that you remember," he says.

He can't be more than fifty-five, but he could pass for eighty. Clare can't stop staring at him, and he stares right back. At fifty-three, Clare's scars are still visible, gone wiggly with time. Raymond points at her face.

"What happened to *you?*"

"Funny, I was going to ask you the same thing."

The people on line behind Raymond are grumbling and shuffling, like impatient cattle. Clare adds a spoonful of mashed potatoes to Raymond's plate and a slice of buttered bread.

"We'll meet after lunch," she says. "Keep moving, this crowd can turn ugly."

She watches Raymond shuffle off to a corner table. He's wearing a tattered denim jacket and filthy jeans that bunch up around his scuffed work shoes, the way pants hang after a dramatic weight loss, and in that moment Clare knows he hasn't got long.

It's a brisk but beautifully sunny day. Clare takes Raymond on a walk to the gardens at St. Luke's Church, at Hudson and Grove. It's one of those hidden gems that true Villagers know about, a peaceful place to sit with a book and a cup of coffee. Sparrows fill the trees and crooked brick paths wind around the gardens, tended by old lady volunteers pulling weeds and digging away with hand shovels.

At this time of year St. Luke's is especially beautiful, carpeted with golden leaves. Clare and Raymond sit on a bench beneath the boughs of a crabapple tree, sipping from paper cups of coffee. The short trip from the soup kitchen has exhausted Raymond. He's skinny, almost skeletal, and his breathing is labored as he tells his story.

The movie didn't work out - a fight with the director, his scenes landing on the cutting room floor, and just like that he was out. *Out!* The spiteful studio cancels the other half of his round-trip ticket, and there he is, stuck in the City of Angels.

He can't land a West Coast agent. He's lucky to find work of any kind - waiting tables, washing dishes, digging ditches. Now and then he attends open auditions, going in cold, and nothing happens. Everybody is after the same thing in Los Angeles, and blond, blue-eyed lifeguard types are hardly on the endangered species list. Whatever spark he once had is gone, and it's not coming back.

So he softens the blow with drink. He drifts from town to town, ever eastward. If you called him a hobo, you would not be wrong. The years go by, and not one at a time, like the calendar says. Raymond is 27 and then he's 33. He blinks, and he's 41. So it goes, a chaotic, hazy life, until at long last he's back in New York City, at 55.

Far from a triumphant return. It's more like the last of the bath water going down, and there Raymond sits on the drain, bottomed out at last, in the city that once gave him so much hope.

He sips his coffee. "Your turn," he says to Clare. "What happened to your face?"

"A night with the wrong guy."

"Jesus. So no modeling career."

"No. And I'm guessing you never got your pilot's license."

"Nope. Another dream that didn't come true. Gotta tell you, Clare, other than those scars, you look good. Strong."

"I get by."

"Angel o' mercy, feedin' guys like me."

"I'm no angel."

"Look at me. I just let go of the rope, you know? Gave up. But not you. How do you do it?"

She has to think about it. "By never depending on anyone."

"Really? You can do that?"

"Yes."

He looks at her in a new light. *"Damn,* you're a tough nut, aren't you?"

She can't help chuckling. "I guess so."

"Musta been all those stairs you climbed when you were young." His face brightens. "That little room you lived in, with the skylight. I remember that room."

He assumes she's moved on, and she's not about to correct him. She can't invite him to stay the night. She suspects he's lice-ridden, and even outdoors, seated at opposite sides of the bench, his odor is overpowering. Besides, he'd never make it up the stairs.

She dares to ask him where he's staying. He makes a sweeping gesture at the sky. "Oh, I'm camping out in Washington Square Park. Got a few more weeks before it turns cold." He chuckles. "Hey! Remember all those people we helped that night in the park, with my hundred bucks?"

"Sure do."

"What comes around goes around, eh?"

She takes a ten dollar bill from her pocket. "Take this. Buy yourself some dinner, and come back to St. Joseph's tomorrow for lunch."

"Yes, ma'am." He takes the bill.

"Food, Raymond. That money is for food."

"Absolutely. Hey! Remember how you got annoyed at me, for callin' you 'ma'am'? "

"I remember everything about that night."

"Great to be young in the Village back then, wasn't it?"

She nods, her eyes brimming with tears as she gets to her feet. "I have to get back to the kitchen. Make sure you come for lunch tomorrow, Raymond. We've got to fatten you up."

He arches his bony back, throws her a salute. "Yes, ma'am."

He doesn't buy himself a meal, and he doesn't sleep in the park. He spends the money on a bottle of Seagram's whiskey, which he drinks behind one of the pillars at St. Joseph's. That's where he's found by a janitor the next morning, his dead hands clutching the empty bottle.

By the time Clare arrives at the soup kitchen cops are on the scene, making notes, and a coroner is preparing to take the body away. Clare tells them he was at the soup kitchen for lunch the day before, but not that she knew him. What good would it do? She doesn't even know his last name!

They search his pockets for identification, but there isn't any. All they find is feathers. Pigeon feathers, dozens of them, crammed into all four pockets of Raymond's pants.

The cops are baffled. "Why the hell would anyone collect feathers?" one of them asks aloud.

Clare shrugs. "Maybe he wanted to fly."

The cop laughs. "That's a good one," he says. "Collectin' feathers, so he can fly. Gotta remember that one."

Raymond is zipped into a body bag and taken away, as Clare goes to the kitchen to begin the day's prep work.

CHAPTER THIRTY TWO

Hannah has to stop walking. This tale has literally sapped her strength.

"My God," she says, "are we going to Raymond's grave?"

"No, no. Heaven knows where *he* wound up. Potter's Field on Hart's Island, most likely."

"What did he die of?"

"Who knows? They wouldn't have bothered with an autopsy."

"That's about the saddest story I've ever heard."

"Well, you're still young. Plenty of sad stories yet to come, my dear. Come on, we're not far now."

They make their way up a tree-shaded hill when Clare suddenly comes to a stop and stands like a soldier at rest, feet apart, hands behind her back, before a polished gray marble headstone, humble beside the taller, gaudier headstones surrounding it.

"Hello, Martin," she says, in the friendly way you'd greet an old buddy in a bar.

Hannah reads the inscription: *Martin Bonaventura, 1917-1967. Beloved husband and father.*

"Holy shit," she says. "It's the doctor who stitched you!"

"*Saved* me," Clare says, in gentle correction. "Yes, it's him."

Beside it stands a slightly smaller stone: *Rosemary Bonaventura, 1920-2001, beloved wife and mother.*

"His wife lived a lot longer than he did," Hannah says.

Clare nods. "They usually do, don't they?"

"I thought you couldn't stay in touch with him."

"I didn't. Came across his obituary in the Daily News. The papers used to run obituaries for regular people, before celebrity deaths became the only thing that mattered." She turns to Hannah. "You, for instance. You'll probably get a pretty good spread, unless you live to be my age, and everybody who ever knew you is dead."

Clare sets her backpack on the grass, then sits in front of the headstone, a friend settling in for a visit.

"You thought we were going to see Johnny's stone."

"I was wrong."

"No, you weren't. You said we were going to see the 'love of my life.' Well, you were right about that." She gives Martin's headstone an affectionate pat. "This man, he really *got* me. If I ever loved anyone, I loved him." She smiles. "His name, Bonaventura. It means 'good adventure.' That's what we might have had together, under different circumstances. Marriage, maybe even children. He could have changed me. I believe that. I truly do. Oh well."

And with that she is crying, silently, as she does every year on this day when she comes to visit Martin. Hannah kneels beside her and reaches out to stroke her back.

The bones, the bones! It's like stroking a xylophone, and then Hannah is fighting back tears of her own, for a man she never knew.

Suddenly Clare stops crying and opens her backpack. She takes out a small chocolate cupcake, which she sets atop Martin's tombstone. She sticks a small candle in it and lights it with a match.

"What's the occasion, Clare?"

"I was born on this date, ninety years ago. See, I always visit Martin on my birthday."

Hannah doesn't know what to say. Wisely, she says nothing. Clare appreciates the silence.

"I need a few minutes alone with Martin," she says, as if it's the most natural thing in the world. Hannah walks off to give her the privacy she requires.

From twenty feet away she watches Clare sitting there, her hand stroking the face of the headstone, the way you'd stroke the head of a loyal, aging dog. She says nothing, and after a few minutes she gets to her feet and shoulders the backpack.

"Enough," she says. "Let's get out of here."

Off they go together, the candle still burning on the cupcake, which will be discovered and eaten by the cemetery gardener, unless the squirrels get to it first.

Hannah links a supportive arm with Clare's on the walk down the hill, and the old lady does not object.

"I'm calling an Uber," Hannah says.

"What's that?"

"A car to take us back."

"No."

"Yes."

"Only to the ferry," Clare allows.

She doesn't know about Ubers and marvels at the way a driver can track them through Clare's phone.

"My God," she says. "There's no place to hide any more, is there?"

The Uber glides to a halt, just as they reach the gates. They get in the back, side to side, thighs touching. They both have strong, slim legs, legs meant for the runway, the runway Clare never got to walk.

The driver has a beard and a turban. He makes sure their seat belts are fastened before he hits the gas.

"I'm trying to remember the last time I rode in a car," Clare says. "No fussing about seat belts back then."

"Alarms go off now if you're not wearing them."

"Don't you have to tell the driver where we're going?"

"He already knows. See the map on the dashboard monitor?"

Clare squints at the map, where a bright red line is leading from the cemetery to the ferry terminal.

"Incredible. Pretty soon people won't have to talk to each other at all."

And with those words she rests her head on Hannah's shoulder. A minute later she is fast asleep, snoring softly.

"Driver," Hannah whispers, "Change of destination, please. We're going to Greenwich Village, and from there to the Upper West Side."

Hannah gives him both addresses. He happily punches the far more expensive rides into his GPS, then looks back at his passengers with a smile.

"Your mother has fallen asleep," he says.

Hannah is about to correct him, but changes her mind. "Yes," she says, "she walked a little too far. She just turned ninety."

"Oh, God bless her," he says, swinging around to head for the Verranzano-Narrows Bridge and the long ride that will take them through Brooklyn on the way to Manhattan.

Half an hour later they reach the red brick building on West 12th Street. Hannah gives Clare a gentle shake. She opens her eyes before sitting bolt upright, startled.

"Whuh?"

"It's okay, it's okay! We're home, Clare."

She looks around, embarrassed to be so disoriented. "Conked out, didn't I?"

"Yes. Hope you don't mind missing the ferry."

"Oh, I'll get over it. Help me get this damn seat belt off, would you?"

Hannah gets out to run around and open Clare's door. She moves in a way Hannah has not seen, until now. She moves like a ninety year old.

Hannah beckons for the driver to wait, then turns back to Clare. "May I help you upstairs?"

Clare huffs. *"Help* me? I've been managing these stairs for nearly seventy years. I do believe I've got the hang of it, and I must say, the new carpet makes it a lot easier."

She turns to climb the stoop and is startled when Hannah grabs her elbow.

"Do you hate me?" Hannah dares to ask.

Clare is genuinely shocked by the question. "Why would I hate you? We're the same."

She gestures at the building. "Why, if I'd bought this place and an old lady was stuck in the skylight room, I probably would have had her killed."

Hannah stuns Clare by pulling her into an embrace.

"Let me build you a shower for your birthday, Clare! Please. Let me..." She has to think about it. "Let me make your life a little easier."

The old lady smiles. "Just let me be. That's all I've ever asked of anybody, and it's all I ask of you."

She eases herself out of the embrace and begins climbing the stoop, oh so slowly.

"Happy birthday, Clare!" Hannah calls out, as if to reach her ears from the other side of a lake.

Clare stops and turns on the top step. "I've been waiting for that. Thank you." She cocks her head. "Does your husband still have the children?"

What an odd question! "Yes, until Sunday night. Why?"

"Can you meet me at the Jefferson Market Library at noon? I have something I want to give you."

What can she possibly have to give? "I can come upstairs now and get it, if you like."

"No," Clare says, a bit impatiently. "Can you meet me there or not?"

"I will be there."

"Sixth Avenue and Tenth Street, twelve o'clock. Have you ever been there?"

"No."

"Got a feeling you'll like it."

And with those words, Clare goes inside.

Hannah rides in silence all the way to Central Park West, wondering what in the world Clare could have to give her. She notices the driver studying her in the rear view mirror.

"Excuse me," he says when they reach her destination, "but your face is quite familiar to me. Were you a model, perhaps? On the Sports Illustrated cover, many years ago?"

Many years ago. Hell, it wasn't *that* many years ago!

"No," she says, opening the door to get out. "A lot of people confuse me with that woman."

"Oh, I do beg your pardon. But I can see where your beauty comes from. Your mother's eyes, they are simply amazing."

CHAPTER THIRTY THREE

She knows her body. Oh, how well she knows her body.

Except for the occasional cold and the usual aches and pains that come with age, it has never let her down. Good food, daily exercise, little alcohol and no tobacco...it's all paid off, but she's always known it can't pay off forever. And ninety years is a pretty good roll of the dice.

Nothing hurts, but she can feel the strength leaving her body, like an outgoing tide. She was barely able to haul herself out of the swimming pool earlier in the day, and on top of that came the Staten Island expedition, and all that walking.

And on that last climb to the skylight room, she has to stop at each floor to catch her breath. That's a first.

She hates what's happening, but she's resigned to it. She's made the right decision, asking Hannah to meet her at the library.

She settles into bed, under her one and only quilt, staring through the skylight at Venus until sleep comes.

Which it does, in a matter of minutes. Now all she has to do is wake up one more time, and it'll all work out.

Just one more time.

Morning comes, and she does not go swimming, or to the soup kitchen. She lies there for an hour, watching the clouds as she sips her tea and nibbles on a banana. She's still tired, even after sleeping late. She washes her face, brushes her teeth, and gets dressed in the best of her clothing, which at this point is a pair of jeans and a red blouse she's never worn before. The blouse is a brighter color than anything she normally wears, an attention-getting color, but it was only a dollar at the Salvation Army store and she couldn't resist it.

She puts one thing into her knapsack and takes a slow walk to the bank on Sheridan Square, where she informs a cheerful young teller that she's here to close out her safe deposit box account.

The teller is sorry to hear that - any particular reason for the sudden termination, after so many years?

"I just don't need it anymore," Clare says. She is taken upstairs, where she opens the box and removes what's left of the cash that's been there since 1951, and two other items she's been keeping safe for almost as long.

She packs it all into her knapsack, slings it on her back, leaves the bank for the last time and heads straight to the library.

Hannah is already here. She is blown away by the beauty of the place - its majestic brick tower, the gothic windows, and the spiral staircase to the main room, where she sits at a table awaiting Clare. When she sees her she gets up and pulls out a chair for her, a gesture the old lady might normally resent, but not today.

"Sorry I'm late," Clare says.

"You're not. I'm early. What an amazing place!"

"It used to be a courthouse, with holding cells. Billie Holiday got locked up here on drug charges. They say she'd lean out the window, and people would toss her cigarettes from the street."

"Did you do that?"

"No, my dear. Some things *did* happen before my time, believe it or not."

Clare is breathing hard. She struggles to get the knapsack off her back and put it on the table.

"Are you all right?"

"Just tired."

"I'm worried about you."

She waves off Hannah's concern. "You'll see what it's like when you hit ninety."

"I doubt that's going to happen."

"Sure it will. You're tough, like me, and you're selfish, like me, so you'll be able to handle the loneliness."

"Gee, thanks, Clare, that was almost a compliment!"

"That's the hardest part, the loneliness." She shakes her head. "Everyone my age is dead, and most of the people who are alive just wander around, looking at their phones. Maybe that's why I kept working at the soup kitchen. The people who go there can't afford phones to stare at all day. They make eye contact, you know? There's a lot to be said for eye contact. Sometimes, it's all you need."

Clare's mind is all over the place. Hannah has never heard her so unfocused. She pats the back of her hand.

"Where are you going with this?"

Clare chuckles. "Well, crazy as it sounds, I feel like you're the only person I can trust, and I'd like to trust you with something pretty important."

She pats the knapsack with a bony hand and manages a smile.

"But first, I have to tell you a story about a party I went to, a long time ago."

"How long?"

"Well, let's see. It was after I got to the Village, but before Johnny Palermo. So I still had my original face." She squints one eye, struggling to remember. "That's the only thing I remember, for certain. I still had my original face."

The party is at a loft on Varick Street, not far from the Holland Tunnel. The loft was once a candy factory, and the rough brick walls are embedded here and there with brown and yellow chunks of a substance that turns out to be crystallized caramel, like amber on the bark of trees.

When Clare enters the first thing she sees is a bearded young man in a beret, hacking at one of those chunks with a knife. When it breaks loose he licks its underside and smiles.

"Edible *walls,* man!" he proclaims, chopping the chunk into chips and distributing them to a few brave souls who squeal with delight as they suck on them.

People eating the walls! What kind of a party is *this?* It's jam-packed, like a crowd on a subway platform, and they're all drinking cheap wine from gallon jugs and talking at the same time, their voices echoing off the vaulted ceiling.

There's nothing to eat, unless you count the wall candy. The men need shaves, the women need makeup and Clare needs a reason to stay at this strange, strange place.

Where's her friend, Lois the Potter, the one who told her about this shindig? That's the trend, lately - you call yourself by your first name, and your artistic occupation. Lois the Potter. Frank the Abstract Painter. Jimmy the Poet. Makes it hard to track people down in the phone book.

And they all feel free to invite people to a party they aren't even throwing! Hey, why not? We're all together in this crazy thing called *life!*

Clare paces the loft through a thick haze of cigarette smoke, punctuated here and there by whiffs of reefer. No sign of Lois. She decides to cut bait and leave, before things get even weirder.

Then she locks eyes with someone who's been staring at her. He's a clean-shaven, lanky man in a dark suit, white shirt and tie, sitting by a window facing Varick Street, right where it feeds into the tunnel to New Jersey.

He's alone. Maybe he's being avoided because he's older than most of this crowd, and looks as if he could be an undercover cop. A narc, even. He's in his early thirties, but his big black eyes burn with a forbidding intensity that's somehow both older than the pyramids and younger than tomorrow.

"You look lost," he says. The sound of his voice is another contradiction. It's both urgent and gentle, with a true-blue New York accent. Like so many at this party, he did not come from far away to chase his dreams in this city. He was born here. He continues staring at her, waiting for a response.

"I'm looking for a friend," Clare says.

"At least you have a friend to look for."

He's not complaining. He smiles, lights a cigarette and offers one to Clare, who declines. She's staring at him as hard as he's staring at her, but neither one feels embarrassed. Something is going on, a connection, and they both know it. It's as if they've known each other, but not from an earlier party. More like from a former lifetime.

"What are you doing here?" he asks, without humility. As if he has a right to know.

Clare shrugs. "What do you mean?"

"I mean, it's obvious you don't belong in this crowd."

Me? Clare thinks. *Look at you, with your jacket and tie, and your prep school haircut!*

"Well, you don't exactly blend in, either."

"Not sure I'd want to." He jerks his head toward the front door. "Not if it means eating the wall. Did you see those people eating the wall?"

"I sure did."

"What are they going to do for dessert? Lick the floor?"

Clare laughs. "This used to be a candy factory, according to my friend."

"Well, now it's a nut house."

She laughs again. "What are you, anyway? A chaperone?"

It's his turn to laugh. "A chaperone. I like that! You know, I *feel* like a chaperone." He takes a long drag on his cigarette. "But I'm not. I'm a writer."

How many times has she heard *that* one? Every man in the Village is a writer, or a painter, or a musician, in that endless quest to get laid.

205

But it sounds real when this guy says it. He makes it sound more like a burden than a profession, something he's stuck with.

Which means he's not saying it to get laid. That makes Clare want to know more.

"What do you write?"

"Stories, mostly. But I'm working on something longer right now."

"Is it any good?"

He smiles. "I hope so." He drops his cigarette butt on the cement floor and crushes it under his toe. "What about you? What are you?"

What a question! It's almost Zen-like. "What *am* I?"

"What do you do, when you're not attending ridiculous parties like this one?"

"I'm a waitress at Caffe Reggio's."

"Anything else? I can't imagine that would be enough for you."

Clare rolls her eyes. "You've known me for five minutes!"

"True. Feels like five years, though."

"Huh! Sorry it's been so boring for you."

"No, no, far from it! Most exciting five minutes I've had all year."

He gets to his feet, and he's like a carpenter's ruler opening up, all elbows and knees. He turns out to be a full head taller than Clare.

"I think we should take a walk," he says. "But first, I think you should tell me your name."

"It's Clare."

"Clare, I'm Jerry. One good thing about these loft parties, you never know who the host is, so you never have to say goodbye."

It feels good to be out in the fresh air. Jerry is chuckling as they walk north on Seventh Avenue.

"You're half my size," he says, "but you have a good long stride. Very few women can keep up with me."

"Do many try?"

"Not lately. And you still haven't told me what else you do."

Clare hesitates. "Well, some people say I should try to be a model."

Jerry shoots her a look, as if she's just said she's thinking of becoming a gangster. "Watch yourself. Lots of phonies in that racket."

"I'm aware of that."

"Don't lose that thing that makes you special."

"Oh, I'm *special,* am I?"

"Obviously."

"Well, we've known each other for twenty minutes, now, so I guess that's about twenty years, by your clock."

Jerry stops walking and catches her by the elbow. "I'm not making a pass. I'm looking out for you."

From anybody else, this would sound like bullshit, but something about this guy is different.

"Why would you look out for me?"

"Because you looked out for me, at that foolish party. You rescued me from the wall-eaters, Clare. You were the only one who even noticed I was there."

She gazes into his eyes. He's clearly not hiding anything. He means what he says, and he's looking at her protectively, as if she's his kid sister, a look she rarely gets from men.

She's relieved, and also disappointed, because she was thinking this could have gone another way. But maybe it's best if it doesn't. Sex is fun, but it also makes things messy, and this guy could turn out to be that rarest of things, a male friend.

She eases out of his gentle grasp. "Should we continue walking, Jerry?"

"Great idea."

They lope along, happy to be in motion again.

"Who invited you to that party, anyway?"

He blushes. "Well, you might say I crashed it."

"Really?"

"I was working, and I was stuck, so I went for a walk. Kept walking until I heard the party from the sidewalk, and when I saw a bunch of people going into the building I just tagged along."

"Do you do that sort of thing very often?"

"Only when I need a break. I've been working hard, lately, trying to finish this damn thing."

"What's it about?"

Jerry sighs. "A troubled teenage boy."

"Title, please?"

"I'd rather not say. It's kind of unusual."

Clare chuckles. "Jerry," she says, *"you're* kind of unusual."

Jerry walks Clare all the way home, stopping at the stoop. Clare asks him if he wants to come up.

He digs his hands into his pockets, as if gripped by sudden shyness. "Gotta get back to work."

"Now?"

"I work best in the middle of the night. Listen, are you busy tomorrow?"

"What do you have in mind?"

"I haven't been to Central Park in a long time. I practically grew up there. Do you like the park?"

She shrugs. "Never been there."

Jerry can't believe it. "Jesus, you Village types have to learn that there *is* life above Fourteenth Street! Meet me at Columbus Circle, one o'clock?"

Her shift at Reggio's doesn't start until six. "Sure."

Jerry extends his hand for a formal shake. She holds on for an extra second and asks, "How do I get there?"

"The Number One train to Fifty-Ninth Street. You do know where the subway is, don't you?"

"It's that big rumbly thing under the sidewalk, right?"

Jerry laughs, lets go of her hand and then he is gone, his impossibly long strides taking him east on Twelfth Street, his shoulders hunched in joyful anticipation of the day ahead. Clare has no idea of where he's going, or if he'll show up tomorrow. The whole thing feels like a dream.

But it isn't.

There he is at one o'clock the next day, waiting for her, seated on the edge of the Columbus Circle fountain. He's dressed much younger, this time - blue jeans, black sneakers and a gray sweatshirt. In daylight Clare can see a few gray hairs at his temples. He could pass for a lackadaisical graduate student, in no hurry to get that sheepskin.

"I cannot *believe* you've never been here," he says in greeting, and then he is up and leading the way into the park. "It's the lungs of the city, and I'm a lucky man, getting to show it to you."

Clare loves his voice, the deep, mellow New-Yorkiness of it, as if he's the love child of a male opera singer and a female cabbie. It's a beautiful day at the start of spring, all green leaves and buds and birds, and horse-drawn carriages clip-clopping along.

It's all familiar to him - the playgrounds where his mother took him, the fields where he played touch football.

"This park is what I missed most, when I was in the Army," he says. "Used to dream about it in my foxhole."

Clare is impressed. "You were in the war?"

"Yes, ma'am."

"What was it like?"

He suddenly looks pale. "You don't want to know."

So why did he bring it up? "Are you okay, Jerry?"

"Yeah, sure." He yawns, rubs his face with both hands. "Sorry. I was up late. I'm near the end of this thing I'm working on, but I can't quite get there. Endings are murder." He smiles. "Anyway, it's nice to be outside, away from the typewriter."

He's both open and mysterious with Clare. He tells her he's holing up in a midtown hotel while trying to finish his work, but he doesn't tell her which hotel, or where he actually lives.

"You obviously love the city," she says. "Why did you leave?"

"Too many distractions."

"I *love* distractions!"

"Of course you do. You're young."

"You're not exactly ancient. Maybe it's time you came back."

"I don't think so."

"I know I'll never live anywhere else."

Jerry chuckles. "Spoken like a true out-of-towner."

"Well, I can't be a model if I'm off somewhere in the woods, can I?"

Jerry frowns. "I warned you about that modeling racket. You be careful."

"Don't worry, Jerry. This is my town now. It looks after me."

"Famous last words."

"You're awfully pessimistic for a writer."

He nods. "I've found it makes disappointment more bearable."

Clare laughs out loud. What a character!

They walk past the zoo, which they're not interested in entering, but from outside they can see a man in rubber boots feeding the sea lions, tossing fish to those who clap their flippers.

"I hate that," Jerry says. "Making them perform for their suppers."

"I hate putting anything in a cage," Clare says.

Jerry seems amused. "Had a feeling you'd say something like that."

"I mean it. Freedom is everything, isn't it?"

"You may be right about that, Clare."

A hot dog vendor up ahead! Clare runs to the cart and orders a dog with mustard and sauerkraut. Jerry makes a face as the vendor, a mustachioed Italian with a baseball cap, slaps it together and passes it to Clare, who digs in while Jerry pays up, dropping the coins into the vendor's hand while being careful not to touch it.

"Aren't you having one?" Clare asks.

Jerry shudders. "Do you have any idea of what they put in hot dogs?"

"No, do you?"

"No, and neither does anyone else. That's my point. It can't be good for you."

"It sure tastes good."

"And that vendor's hands weren't exactly the cleanest I've ever seen."

Clare can't help laughing, and Jerry laughs along at his own expense, aware that he's probably a bit of a germophobe.

Which Clare secretly finds strange. A guy who survived World War II, worried about a hot dog? In a funny way, it's also kind of charming.

Clare has just about finished her hot dog when she hears carnival music in the distance.

"What's that, Jerry?"

His face lights up. "This, you're gonna love. Come on!"

He takes her by the hand all the way to the carousel, and she is enchanted by the candy-colored horses going 'round and 'round.

"It's beautiful, Jerry!"

"Pick a horse."

Clare laughs. "I'm a little too big for that, don't you think?"

"No, you're not. Go ahead, while I get you a ticket. Pick one on the outer rim, it makes for a wider ride. And make sure it goes up and down."

"Are you serious?"

"Get going, before all the good ones are taken!"

Clare does as she's told, climbing aboard a big black horse on the outer rim. Jerry comes back and hands her three tickets.

"Whoa! *Three?*"

"Just stay on the horse when the ride stops and give the guy another ticket."

"I don't need three rides, Jerry!"

"Yes you do, to get the feel of it. Trust me, this is my turf. It's no problem, as long as there isn't a line of kids waiting to get on."

She points at the suddenly cloudy sky. "There's no line because it's about to rain!"

"Don't worry, you're sheltered."

"*You're* not!" she says, as Jerry jogs off to sit on a nearby bench. The music swells, the carousel starts to rotate, and to Clare's delight the horse she's aboard pumps up and down with the ride.

She catches sight of Jerry each time they whirl around. He's alone on a bench, arms stretched across the back of it, legs crossed at the ankles, smiling like a proud dad. On her second time around it starts to rain, fat drops that splash loudly when they hit. The storm scatters everyone, save for the parents of the kids riding the carousel. They rush under the carousel roof to catch the bit of shelter it affords, but Jerry stays put on the bench, getting soaked.

Clare can't believe it. He seems oblivious to the rain. After two rides she's the only one left on the carousel. She shouts for him to come in out of the rain, but Jerry just laughs.

"I'm already as wet as I can get!" he says, and it's true. His hair is plastered to his skull, and his sweatshirt is stuck to his chest.

"Go on!" he shouts. "You've got one more ride coming!"

Clare turns to the operator, standing beside her horse. "Can you run it if I'm the only rider?"

He shrugs, taking her last ticket. "Lady, it's all the same to me. You pay for a ride, you get a ride."

The carousel starts for Clare's private ride. She studies Jerry's face on every turn. He's still sprawled on that bench, and it's still raining hard, but something is different.

He's crying. Not in a sad way, because the smile on his face is real, but there is no mistaking the fact that happy tears are rolling down his face.

The carousel glides to a halt. Clare gets off the horse and runs to Jerry, who embraces her tightly, as if he will never let go.

"Are you okay, Jerry?"

"Yes. But I have to go, Clare. I really do."

He breaks the embrace and kisses her cheek. "Thank you. Thank you so much."

"For what?" she asks, but she gets no answer as he turns and runs like a man who's late for a train, excited as a child hurrying downstairs on Christmas morning.

Clare stands there in the rain, wondering what the hell just happened.

She never sees J.D. Salinger again.

Hannah is slack-jawed by the end of Clare's story.

"Okay, now, 'The Catcher In The Rye' happens to be my favorite book," Hannah says. "If I've read it once, I've read it a dozen times."

"Yes, Jerry had a charming way with words, all right."

"So now you're telling me that you were the inspiration for the ending of 'Catcher', when Holden takes his sister to the carousel in the rain?"

"I didn't say that. I told you I had something to give you, and now I can give it to you."

She opens her knapsack, takes out a book and hands it to Hannah. It's a first edition of The Catcher In The Rye, complete with the dust jacket illustration of a carousel horse on the front and J.D. Salinger's face on the back.

"Jerry dropped it off for me at Reggio's soon after it was published. Wish I'd been working that day. Would have been nice to catch up."

Hannah turns the book over in her trembling hands. It is in mint condition.

"This is incredible," she breathes.

"It's the only book I own," Clare says. "Kept it in a drawer all these years."

"In the skylight room?"

"Where else?"

"Jesus, Clare, what if it had been stolen?"

"It wasn't. It's right there in your hands. Go on, read the inscription."

Hannah lifts the cover, and there it is, in ink that remains bold, protected from the ravages of sunlight by all those decades in the darkness of the drawer.

To Clare
Hope you like the carousel chapter
J.D. Salinger

She snaps the book closed, as if to keep the inscription from escaping, letting out a shriek that earns her a scowl and a "Shhh!" from the librarian.

"Oh my *God,* Clare!"

"Calm down, dear, it's just an inscription."

"He's acknowledging that you inspired the ending!"

"I wouldn't go that far."

Hannah cradles the book in her arms, oh so gently. "Do you realize what this is *worth?* A signed first edition of 'The Catcher In The Rye,' in perfect condition?"

"Well, I know collectors go crazy for things like this, especially from a guy like Jerry, who apparently hated signing his books."

"I'm guessing it's worth fifty grand. Maybe more!"

"You think?"

"Yes! This book should be in a climate-controlled room, in a Plexiglas box! Nobody should even touch it!"

Clare makes a cackling sound. "Wouldn't really be a book then, would it?"

Hannah feels dizzy. "Why are you giving it to me?"

"I want you to get whatever you can for it."

"I don't understand."

"You asked me if you could do anything to make my life easier. I thought of something, and this is it."

She reaches across the table to hold Hannah's wrist. "Take it to an auction house, or a rare book dealer, and get the best price you can, dear. Then donate half the money to the soup kitchen at St. Joseph's, and the other half to this library. Can you do that for me?"

Hannah's lips are trembling. "What's going on, Clare?"

"Answer me, please. Can you do that for me?"

"Why don't *you* do it?"

Clare moans. "It's too complicated, I'm too old, and I don't need any more attention in my life. Yes or no?"

Hannah removes a silk scarf from around her neck, wraps the book in it and slides it deep into her handbag.

"I'll guard it with my life."

Clare is smiling. "That's a load off my mind. I have to go now."

"Can't we grab lunch somewhere?"

Grab lunch! As if they've been friends for years!

"No time for that. But thank you, Hannah."

Hannah's neck tingles at the sound of her name, spoken by Clare for the first time. She watches her get to her feet and shoulder the back pack.

"I'll walk out with you," Hannah says.

"I wish you wouldn't."

But she does. The trip down the spiral staircase isn't easy. Clare grips the banister the whole way, moving like the old lady she finally has become. She doesn't want Hannah to see this.

"Clare," she says when they reach the sidewalk, "are you okay?"

Clare squares her shoulders and turns to cross Sixth Avenue. "I feel great," she says. "Never better."

It's the only time she's ever lied to Hannah Schmitt.

CHAPTER THIRTY FOUR

Henry is waiting for Hannah at the penthouse. He's gotten there just minutes before her arrival, sprawled on the couch in the exaggerated way a weekend father exhibits exhaustion after less than two days with his children.

"You were due back tomorrow," Hannah says, genuinely annoyed.

"They wanted to come back early."

"Where are they?"

Henry sits up. "No 'hello' or nothin'?"

"Are they okay?"

"Well, they argued most of the way back, but other than that..."

He trails off with a big yawn, stretches and flops on his back, as if unable to go on. "They're in their rooms, Hannah. Where the hell else would they be?"

"We have to talk, Henry."

"Yes, we do," he agrees. "It's about time."

This is one of his most annoying habits, the way he turns one of her ideas into one of his ideas. Hannah sits at the opposite end of the couch, with enough room between them for two lawyers. And before she can open her mouth, he opens his.

"I got the call. Didn't make it."

She doesn't know what he's talking about. "What call?"

He rolls his eyes. "The Hall of Fame vote. Didn't even get *half* the votes I needed. They'll announce it tomorrow."

"I'm sorry, Henry."

"Well, what the fuck."

"Maybe next year. Isn't that what baseball players always say?"

"Yeah. The losers."

"Life can be disappointing, Henry. I'm sure you've noticed that."

He punches a pillow. "They ain't never proved *nothin'!*"

His grammar falters when he's angry. Hannah struggles to stay patient.

"They don't have to. You know how it works. All they need is rumors."

"It ain't just that. They don't like me. Don't like my *attitude.*"

She can't go through the whole persecuted black man thing with Henry. He's probably right, but she just can't listen to it. Not today, not ever again. She's had enough of him, once and for all. It's time to clean up unfinished business.

"Let me ask you something, Henry," she says softly. "Were you juicing?"

He sighs. "A little. But only 'cause I kept gettin' injured. Hadda stay strong."

"Well, okay, then. You cheated."

"I still would've hit the damn home runs, Hannah, juice or no juice."

"That's not how they see it."

"Obviously."

"You swore under oath that you didn't do it. Maybe if you'd told the truth from the start - "

"Hey. We've all got secrets, Hannah, am I right? Ain't you got a secret or two?"

"Yes."

"Know what? I'd like to hear one of your secrets. Lay it on me, baby."

"Not now."

"Come on."

"Bad time, Henry."

"Come on, Hannah, amuse me."

He won't let it go. He's just lying there, so righteous, so smug, so totally self-absorbed.

What the hell. She touches her nose, right where it bends.

"I didn't swim into a wall when I was fifteen, Henry. My father broke my nose."

He sits up straight. "Holy shit."

"Yeah. He gave me a good, hard belt."

"Why?"

"It doesn't matter. It's why I fled from Germany, and came to this country, and wound up with you. Okay?"

Henry just stares at her, as Hannah realizes Clare picked the right verb, after all. She *did* flee from Germany.

"Oh, baby," Henry says. He rubs his face with both hands, as if to erase the ugliness between them and return to the beginning, when it was all so easy. "Look, I'm sorry I called you the c-word. I was out of line."

"No, you weren't."

This surprises him. "Jesus, who are you, and what have you done with my wife?"

"You were right, Henry. Chasing that reality show had me crazy.
I was out of line."

Now he's truly surprised. "Wow. Do you realize you almost
apologized? Never thought I'd see the day!"

"What do you want, Henry?"

"I want you and me together again." He gets to his feet. "And
if you *really* want that show, I'm with you. We'll get the old lady out
of there, make it happen. For her own good, right?"

Hannah folds her arms across her chest. "The show is dead."

"What?"

"That picture of you and your girlfriend in the Post killed it."

"She's *not* my girlfriend."

"Regardless, the show is dead. And the old lady is staying right
where she is, for as long as she wants. I'm trying to get her to let me
build her a shower."

Henry looks at her with the mock-astonished face he used on
umpires whenever they called him out on strikes.

Only this time, the face is real.

"What the fuck is goin' on, Hannah?"

"Well, let's see. You and I are getting divorced, and the kids and
I are moving downtown, whenever the house is finished, and you
and I will hurl a couple hundred grand at lawyers to straighten
everything out."

"Hang on, hang on!" Henry waves it all away, to be dealt with
later. "Suddenly you want the old lady to *stay?*"

"Yes. That's one thing you were right about, Henry. The skylight
room is her home."

Henry can't believe what he's hearing. "Jesus, woman, you
actually have compassion for her!"

Hannah fights a sob she feels brewing in her throat. "She's
probably the most amazing person I've ever known."

That staggers him. "What the hell did she do, change water into
wine?"

"She's taught me some things, I can tell you that. The things
she's seen, the things she's been through."

"Like what?"

"Henry, I'm exhausted. Say goodbye to the kids and go."

"Go where?"

"Back to the Hampton house. Back to your girlfriend.

Whatever."

"She's *not* my girlfriend."

"All right, then, your fuckbuddy."

"You *bitch.*"

"Oh, I'm a bitch, all right. But it's still time for you to go."

It's really over this time. They both know this could be their last conversation in the absence of lawyers.

"Well," Henry says, "you might as well know, I always hated the H & H brand thing."

"Not as much as I did."

This truly surprises him. "Then what the fuck was it all about?"

"Henry, I felt us drifting apart, long before you did. Guess I was trying to keep us together. Figured if I couldn't do it with love, I'd do it with business. Bad, bad idea."

All he can do is stand there and let it penetrate. "Almost worked," he says. "If that old lady hadn't been there - "

"Oh, thank *God* she's there, or this farce of a marriage would have dragged on for *years,* as long as the damn show lasted!"

Henry rubs his face with both hands, a man in turmoil, but that's not what gets Hannah's attention.

"Henry. Is that your World Series ring?"

He holds out his left hand. "Yeah, it turned up. Meant to tell you."

"Where did it turn up?"

"What's the difference?"

"So we fired Josephine for nothing."

"You fired her for nothing. That's your impulse, baby. Every time something goes wrong, a body must fall, right?"

Hannah lets it sink in. If not for the firing, Josephine would never have called Page Six, Tom Becker's crusade to save Clare Owen never would have happened, and who knows? With nobody watching, there might have been a sneaky way to get the old lady out of the skylight room, and the reality show would have happened.

Hannah does the only thing she can do, under the circumstances. She laughs out loud, grateful to the gods of fate.

Henry is baffled. "Gonna let me in on the joke?"

"I don't think so." Hannah gestures at the door. "Go now, Henry, I'm exhausted."

"My kids - "

"Come back and see them tomorrow. But get out now, *please,* before my head explodes. I mean that."

Henry reaches the door when Hannah frantically calls to him.

"Henry, *wait!*"

He turns to her, a tiny smile on his face, that of a victor who knows he had it in the bag all along. Hannah gets up and takes three steps toward him, arms spread, as if to offer a one-more-chance embrace. She wants him good and relaxed when she uncorks the big one, and before he can take her in his arms she uncorks it, right in his face.

"You were never *really* with me in bed, were you?"

Henry's eyes widen and his arms drop. "Ex*cuse* me?"

"You're a typical star. You do it for the crowd. Hey, everybody, look how *great* I'm fucking! It was all about *you,* wasn't it? Like running out a home run. I wasn't your lover. I was home plate, wasn't I?"

He does not answer. But for the first time since she's known this man, Hannah sees her husband, the smoothest of operators, do something she never dreamed he would do.

He gulps.

"Your girlfriend will catch on, sooner or later!" she shouts, as he leaves and slams the door. "Mark my words!"

She stands there for a few moments, breathing hard, before going to her bedroom to lock 'The Catcher In The Rye' in her wall safe. Then she goes to see her children, wondering how much of the fight they might have heard.

But they're both in iPhone trances, barely looking up when Mommy arrives.

CHAPTER THIRTY FIVE

Tom Becker can't believe his ears, but Ken Wilson isn't smiling. He's called Becker into his office to discuss the matter, and he's dead serious.

"Come on, Ken," Becker says. "What's the *real* problem, here?" Ken spreads his hands. "I just told you - you're spending too much time smoking. Every time you leave the building you're gone for twenty minutes."

"Somebody been *timing* me?"

"No, of course not! But you're getting hard to find around here, these days."

Becker stares at him. "Let me guess. You want me to take the buyout, right?"

The paper is offering early retirement buyouts to everyone over fifty. The idea is to trim the dead wood, take the money they're paying a guy like Becker and use it to hire three run-and-gun kids to replace him. Kids who'll dive on grenades to get the story, the way Becker once did...

"Tom," Ken says, "you're a great rewrite man, faster than anyone else. I don't want to lose you! I just want you to keep your ass in the chair, that's all."

Becker leans back and shuts his eyes, as if to make it all go away. "You never saw the old newsroom on South Street, did you?"

Ken rolls his eyes, a safe thing to do so as long as Becker's eyes remain closed. "Long before my time."

"Like a giant ashtray," Becker recalls, a wistful smile on his face. "So many cigarette butts on the floor, it was like walking on sponges."

"Sounds wonderful."

"Oh, you have no idea, kiddo. Big blue cloud over the horseshoe - cigarettes, cigars, even a pipe. Couldn't get two days out of a shirt back then, I can tell you that."

He sits up and opens his eyes, gone soft with memories. "What the hell was that pipe-smoker's name? Tall fucker, very gangly. The closer he got to deadline, the faster he puffed."

"Listen, Tom - "

"Leo something! Hell of a rewrite man. Never lost his cool."

Ken holds up two fingers to Becker's face, like a corner man trying to see if his dazed boxer can count. "Two smoking breaks per shift, okay? You go, and you come right back. And you let us know when you're going."

Becker lets it sink in. "Let you know? You mean, like, ask *permission?*"

Wilson sighs. "It's not like the old days, Tom. With the online paper, it's all deadlines, all the time. No gaps between editions. Can't play catch-up in this game anymore, you know?"

"How about trips to the toilet? Same deal, two per shift?"

Wilson forces a smile. "No restrictions there."

"There's got to be a better way to do this, Ken. Hang on, I've got it! How about if you stick me on a catheter with a piss bag, chewing nicotine gum?"

"Tom, please."

"Then I can just live at my desk! Shit, I won't really need an apartment anymore, will I?"

Wilson stares at Becker. "That about it, Tom?"

"Yeah, I'm done."

"Two smoking breaks per shift. Please."

"Anything for you, Ken. May I go back to work now, since I'm such a valued employee?"

"Yes. And I know you were kidding, but I heartily recommend that nicotine gum. It helped me quit smoking."

"I may just give it a shot."

Becker goes to his desk and periscopes the newsroom before sitting. Youngsters, wherever he looks, and nobody's bullshitting with anyone else. Locked in on their computer screens or on their iPhones, half the time tuned to Facebook and Instagram, clicking away.

This is how they communicate. It's time to shake things up.

He sits down, puts his feet up on the partition and shakes a Marlboro into his mouth. Then he lights up, just like that, and blows smoke toward the woman on the other side of the partition, a grim 21-year-old intern named Karen Morton, fresh from the Columbia School of Journalism.

She leaps to her feet with a scream and turns to Becker.

"What are you doing?" she shouts.

"Oh, pardon my manners," Becker says, offering his pack. "Smoke?"

She runs off. By this time everyone has moved to the edges of the newsroom, as if a suitcase bomb has gone off in the middle, with Becker at its epicenter. Nobody has asked him to stop smoking. That's someone else's job. Ken Wilson is on his phone, calling security.

Becker sits puffing smoke rings toward the ceiling. It's the happiest he's felt in a long time.

CHAPTER THIRTY SIX

Here's Clare Owen crossing Sixth Avenue and going to the Post Office, just off the corner at Tenth Street. How long has it been? The last time she was here the place had ink wells, where you could fill your fountain pen.

Does anybody bother with fountain pens anymore?

A young black clerk with a shaved head and a gold earring provides Clare with a large envelope and a sheet of stiff cardboard, the kind that keeps the envelope from bending in half. She takes these supplies to a tall table in the corner, addresses the package with a pen on a chain and returns to the clerk to pay for it.

"You want a return receipt with that, lady?" he asks. "It's good insurance."

"Thanks," she says, "but I don't believe in insurance."

He can't help cackling. "You go, girl! Roll them dice!"

It comes to $3.37 for everything, including first class postage. She pays with two singles and the rest in change.

She's tired. She feels like she could go back to the skylight room for a nap, but she's got a couple of missions left, and this is the day to complete them.

She takes a thick wad of bills from the knapsack, which leaves it empty. She discards the sack in a wire trash basket outside the Post Office and walks south on Sixth Avenue.

"Raymond, my old friend," she says to the sky, "this one's for you."

Three bearded homeless guys are squatting by the subway entrance a block past Eighth Street, hands out, palms up. They are ignored by everyone who passes until Clare arrives, pausing to place a bill in each hand.

Three $20 bills, each minted in 1950. She's gone before they can thank her, or think about going after her for more.

She continues walking south on Sixth, making a left on Washington Place. Two more beggars, two more twenties, boom-boom, and she's gone.

Washington Square Park beckons. She feels like she's floating as she makes her way under the arch, pausing to drop a twenty into the upended hat of a guitar player with little talent. Homeless people are sprawled all over the grass, and each of them gets a twenty. A woman who can't be much younger than Clare, deeply cocooned within three tattered blankets, looks in wonder at the bill that's been placed in her grimy fingers.

"It's a fake!" she shrieks.

"No, dear," Clare assures her, "it's the real thing. Just old."

She spends nearly an hour circling the park, distributing twenties to needy people and marginally talented performers. She can't keep doing it, because it's just a matter of time before word gets around about the crazy old lady giving away money, and somebody jumps her. She's in no shape to put up a fight.

She leaves the park, the wad of cash in her hand considerably lighter as she approaches her destination on MacDougal Street, a place she has avoided for nearly seventy years.

She walks into Caffe Reggio and does not wait to be seated, heading straight for an iron-backed chair at a marble-topped table in the corner. Little has changed here, and isn't that remarkable, the way everything else in the neighborhood has changed? Same tables, same chairs, same pictures on those walls. Same big chrome and bronze espresso machine, hissing away like an angry dragon.

A young dark-skinned waitress with her hair pulled back so severely that it gives her eyes an unnatural slant comes to Clare's table.

"Would you like a menu?"

"No, thank you."

"What can I getchoo?" She sounds a bit irritated, maybe because Clare went ahead and seated herself without waiting.

"Do you have herbal tea?"

"We got camomile and green tea."

"Camomile, please."

"That's it? Can't interest you in a pastry?"

"Okay, a pastry."

"What kind?"

"Surprise me."

The waitress is uneasy about the responsibility. "Well, we got a lotta pastries. You got any allergies? Gluten, and whatnot?"

"I'm a horse, dear. I can eat anything."

"You like chocolate?"

"Love it."

"Okay. Now we're in business."

Clare watches her go to the kitchen. She can't remember any

black or Puerto Rican waitresses back when she worked here. What a different city it was, men in suits and ties and fedoras, women in dresses and heels. Even the beatniks had a certain style, dressed in dark clothes to match those dark souls.

She looks around Reggio's. Everybody seems to be wearing warmup clothes, pinks and pastels, with Velcro-tabbed sneakers on their feet. Disney characters.

Oh for the days when men wore wing-tipped shoes, kept in shape by shoe trees when their feet weren't in them!

Do shoe trees even *exist* anymore?

The tea comes in a little silver pot, the camomile tag dangling down its side. The pastry is a chocolate croissant, shaped like a crescent moon.

"Lovely choice," Clare says.

"Want me to pour for you?"

"I'm perfectly capable, thank you."

The teapot feels as heavy as an anvil. The waitress stands by as she watches Clare pour tea into her cup, the spout chattering against the rim.

"You okay, lady?"

Clare sets the pot down, lifts the cup to her lips and takes a sip. "I have never felt better," she lies. She sets the cup on the saucer, leans back in her chair and smiles at the waitress.

"What's your name, dear?"

"Gloria."

"I'm Clare."

"You look familiar."

"Well, I used to work here, many years ago. Not that you could possibly recognize me! This was before you were born, and before your *parents* were born, for that matter."

Gloria's eyes widen. "Holy shit! You the lady in that, whaddayacallit, that room with the sky!"

Clare nods. "The skylight room."

"Read about you in the paper! Don't you be lettin' that bitch throw you out!"

"Actually, she's not so bad, Gloria. We're getting along quite well these days." She cocks her head, to alter the course of the conversation. "Do you like working here?"

"Ahh, it's okay, I guess."

"Got dreams?"

The questions stuns Gloria. "What kinda dreams?"

"About your life. What's coming next. This is a good place for dreams."

"Is that so?"

"Absolutely. I did my biggest dreaming right here."

She takes a bite from the chocolate croissant as Gloria, convinced Clare is a wacko, goes off to serve two people who've just walked in. She returns briefly to Clare's table to set down a leatherette folder containing her bill, and to tell her to have a nice day.

Turnover, turnover! This is something new. Customers never got rushed, back in the day. The tab comes to $8.65, with tax. Clare reaches into her pocket and takes out the rest of her cash, which comes to $360.00, and stuffs it inside the folder.

The very last of the money from the Johnny Palermo payoff, to which she adds seventy-two cents in change. She is now officially flat broke.

She feels a fluttering in her chest, like distant thunder. She stares at the shiny espresso machine, an old friend. An ocean of coffee has flowed through its pipes since her last time here, and an ocean of blood has flowed through her veins, and they're both still going.

It's a comforting sight. It's just what she needs to calm down, shut her eyes and fall asleep.

In this dream she's back at that Harper's Bazaar party at the Plaza with Richard Avedon, and when he tells her it's time to leave, she goes with him. They are safely in a taxicab and rolling downtown long before the drunken duo of Frank Sinatra and Ava Gardner reach the Plaza.

Avedon is pleased, telling her she handled herself just right.

"Mystique, Clare," he says. "How you look is just the half of it. Smile, and don't say too much. You keep them interested by keeping them wondering."

"I get it, Richard! And now they'll assume I'm stupid because I'm beautiful, which makes them feel good about themselves."

He's surprised by this perception. "Listen to you," he chuckles. "Looks *and* brains."

"I'm right, aren't I? If I'm stupid, they figure I'll be easy to work with."

"I guess that could be true."

"You know it is. They'd hate me if they thought I was as smart as they are. Might lead to conflict. They *hate* conflict."

Avedon sighs. "Clare, do me a favor. Keep these perceptions to yourself."

"No problem, Richard. It'll be our little secret."

He rides all the way to the Village with her, arranging the photo shoot at his studio for a day later that week. He is shocked when the cab comes to a stop in front of Clare's building.

"You live *here?* Christ, we've got to get you somewhere safe!"

"I love it. I've got the skylight room."

Avedon rolls his eyes. "Do you have any idea of how easy it is to break in through a skylight?"

She can't help giggling. "You worry too much, Richard. No wonder you're going gray already."

She kisses his cheek and jumps out, Avedon watching to make sure she makes it safely up the stoop and through the front door before telling the cabbie to head uptown.

Clare takes the steps two at a time, feeling as if she could fly. She strips down to her birthday suit and gets under a piecework quilt she picked up at a junk shop. It's a clear, starry night, the kind of night that makes her feel like she's camping out as she lies there, staring at the sky.

She's giddy, light-headed from the champagne. She didn't eat anything at the Plaza, and hasn't eaten since lunch, but she's not hungry.

Not hungry for food, but she really could use a man beside her on this glorious evening. Funny how that works - the biggest night of her life, and she winds up by herself! Maybe that's the deal. Maybe success is a solitary thing. My good news isn't anyone else's good news, is it?

Richard was right. He knew how a night like this could affect me. That's why he delivered me all the way home, to make sure I got here. Good luck makes people crazy. Best thing to do is end the night like this, alone in bed with your dream. *Protect that dream!*

That night is the key. She gets through it by playing it safe for once, and things start happening fast.

A few days later she's in Avedon's studio, being photographed in an array of gorgeous clothes. During wardrobe changes Francisco fusses with her hair and makeup, and she can sense from his glee that it couldn't be going any better.

The pictures are sent to Diana Vreeland, who loves what she sees.

Avedon helps Clare get a good agent, and it's goodbye to the job at Reggio's. Gabriella and the waitresses are not sorry to see her go. Envy has been eating them alive.

A beautician trims and tints Clare's hair. She debuts in the pages of Harper's less than a month after the party at the Plaza, and then she's flown to Paris for the annual Fashion Week.

Clare Owen is a sensation. Now her career is rolling. One of the New York fashion writers proclaims that the new girl is sure to be "The Face of the Fifties."

Suddenly she has a bank account and a financial manager, who urges her to plow some of that modeling money into an apartment, lest she lose half of it to taxes. He finds her a one-bedroom place in a brand-new doorman building on the Upper East Side. Safe, trendy and convenient.

She goes along with the plan. She makes a down payment on the place, even though she's not completely sold on the idea. It's as if she's being carried along by a strong current, and all she can do is ride with it. There's so little to pack! Her worldly goods, including the quilt, fit into four large cardboard boxes, taped tightly shut. She's leaving her battered mattress behind.

The moving guys take the boxes for her. Clare assures them she'll be down in a minute. She stands in the middle of the barren skylight room, staring up at the clouds. Gray clouds, brimming with rain. A sense of dread grips her like a sudden fever. She senses she is making a terrible mistake.

"What am I doing?…"

Her eyes close. She's going to faint. The strength leaves her legs, and she is falling backwards...

"Hey, Clare! *Clare!* Are you okay?"

She opens her eyes. She's at Reggio's, and Gloria the waitress is holding her by the shoulders, as if to keep her from collapsing.

"I'm fine, dear," she says. "So kind of you to ask."

Gloria takes her hands off Clare and holds up the leatherette folder, which looks like a fat sandwich made with cash.

"Why'd you give me all this money?" Gloria asks. "It's too much!"

Clare pats the back of Gloria's hand. The waitress is shocked by how chilly those fingers feel.

"Oh, I can afford it, my dear," Clare says, sinking low in her chair. "I'm the Face of the Fifties."

Her final words.

CHAPTER THIRTY SEVEN

The head of security at the New York Post is a retired cop named Barney O'Loughlin, who put in his "twenty" at the Police Department before taking the pension and accepting what had been a pretty cushy job, until today.

Barney, embarrassed as always by the uniform gray pants with the white stripes up the legs, stands at Becker's desk with his arms folded over his bulging belly, a walkie-talkie in hand.

"Kindly extinguish the cigarette," he says in a well-practiced cop-calm, last-chance-before-the-shit-hits-the-fan voice.

Becker, sitting back with his feet on the partition, takes a leisurely drag. "Barney, tell me something," he says, breathing smoke his way. "Back when you were chasing bad guys, would you ever have believed you'd be arresting a guy for enjoying a Marlboro?"

"I'm not arresting you, Mr. Becker. Just asking you to comply with the law."

"Call me Tom."

"Smoking is forbidden in this building, Tom. I'm sure you know that."

"I do, Barney, but see, we've got an issue, here. Seems I take too much time when I leave the building for a smoke, so I figure the best way to save time is to cook a butt right here. Time is money, you know, and money keeps everything rolling."

"I'm afraid you can't do that."

"Well, as you can see, I'm doing it." Another puff as he gestures at his colleagues, huddled in corners. "Nice of them to give me lots of room, don't you think?"

Barney sighs, brings the walkie-talkie to his mouth and mumbles into it. Moments later two young guards appear, both crew-cut, both with that chubby look of disappointed college football players who didn't get called to the pros, but continued eating as if they were still playing ball. They bookend Barney and stand at parade rest, hands behind their backs, feet spread.

"We're going to have to ask you to leave," Barney says.

"No problem. Soon's I finish my cigarette."

"*Now,*" Barney says, his long-dormant cop rage ignited at last. He nods to the crew cuts, but as they prepare to take Becker by the elbows Ken Wilson butts in.

"Tom," he says, "I'm sending you out on a story."

Becker is genuinely shocked. *"Out?"*

"Yes. I'm entitled to do that."

Becker shrugs. "Geez, I haven't been on the street in ten years."

"Same as it always was, Tom. Hard and flat."

Becker can't help chuckling. "Hey, duty calls." He turns to the guards. "I'm leaving now. You guys can go, I can manage it myself."

The guards turn to Wilson, who dismisses them with a nod. Becker squashes his cigarette butt on his desk top next to the first one he smoked and puts on his jacket.

"Where to, boss?"

"Get your ass to Caffe Reggio in the Village. You know it?"

"Of course I know it."

"That old lady from the skylight room just dropped dead there."

Becker swallows. "Clare Owen is *dead?*"

"Channel Five just reported it on the noontime news, and get this - she tipped the waitress a couple hundred bucks for a cup of tea and a muffin just before she croaked. Or maybe it was a croissant, the reporter wasn't sure. Get down there, find out what the fuck's going on."

Becker grabs a fresh notebook and leaves. Karen Morton returns to her desk, holding a handkerchief over her nose. She points over the partition at the two squashed cigarette butts on Becker's desk. The fresh one is still smoldering.

"Can we get someone from maintenance to clean this up?" she asks. "That stink is making me nauseous."

It's a classic media cluster-fuck at Reggio's by the time Becker gets there - two TV crews, half a dozen news photographers and dozens of citizens-turned-photographers with their iPhones jostling for position outside the cafe, while two cops keep everybody from going inside.

Becker's press card is on a chain. He hangs it around his neck, trying to remember the last time he wore it. Back in his street reporter days he always got a thrill from wearing the press card, secretly considering it his armor as he braced himself for journalistic battle.

"Is that you, Becker? Jeez, who let *you* out of the building?"

The voice belongs to a Daily News reporter named Salvatore Siriano, balder and fatter than the last time they saw each other.

Siriano is Becker's age, but he cannot write worth a damn, so he remains a leg man on legs that don't move as fast as they once did.

But he's good on the street, with rat-like instincts to sniff out what he needs, and he's still as annoying as ever.

"Been a while since you hit the bricks, huh Beck?" he asks. "Last time you covered a story you arrived on horseback, didn't you?"

"You wouldn't even be here if it wasn't for me, Sal. I'm the one who broke the original story about this woman."

"Well, on behalf of everybody who rushed to cover this stupid story, I'd like to say 'Go fuck yourself.' "

"You're welcome, pal."

Siriano jerks his chin toward a woman giving an on-camera interview to a local TV news crew across the street.

"That's the waitress who served her, Gloria something. Told me she tipped her, like, three hundred and something bucks and dropped dead. You're gonna want to talk to her."

"Thanks for the tip, Sal."

"Hey, I'm thinkin' you might be a little rusty, you know? Jesus Christ, look at her go."

Gloria is dabbing tears from her eyes as she speaks, taking deep breaths to hold back the sobs.

"That ain't an interview," Siriano says. "It's an *audition*. Oh, Christ, make way for the corpse."

The cameramen and photographers jostle for position at the doorway as cops clear the way for two Emergency Medical Service workers carrying a stretcher bearing Clare's body. A collective moan of disappointment fills the air because the tiny body is covered with a white sheet that shields her down to her ankles.

All anybody can see of Clare as she's loaded into the ambulance is her feet, in those well-worn Nikes. The driver hits the siren, the ambulance pulls away and she is gone.

"Oh well, that's show biz," Siriano says, quoting a line from Sweet Smell Of Success. He turns to Becker. "So what was she like, anyway?"

Becker thinks about it for a moment. "Unique."

"Bet you never even met her, did you?"

"Talked to her on the phone. She called me an asshole."

Siriano chuckles. "Perceptive old girl, eh?" He pats Becker's shoulder. "Great catchin' up with you, Tom."

"Where are you off to?"

Siriano smiles. "Wouldn't *you* like to know?" he says, before waddling away.

Becker's shoulders sag as he takes notebook and pen in hand and heads for Gloria the waitress, who's nearing the end of her performance for the local news crew.

But he's intercepted by Paul Frisch, who pulls up on his bicycle.

"Jesus, Tom, who let *you* out?"

"That's twice I've heard that today."

"Seriously, it'll do you good to get a little daylight. Vitamin D."

"What have you got, Paul?"

"Not much. Same shot everybody else has, the body on the stretcher. Big nothing. Plus I got the waitress holding up the folder with all that cash. Tried to get her to fan the bills out, like, you know, a poker hand, but she wouldn't do it." He smiles. "No complaints, man." He winks. "I'm makin' a killing on my pictures from that day I followed the old lady around."

Becker can't believe his ears. "You can't do that! They belong to the Post!"

"Afraid not. That was my day off. I was freelance that day."

"You're fucking me but good, Paul."

"Nothin' personal, buddy. Hey, I'll sell a few shots to the Post, if the price is right." Frisch smiles, rubbing thumb and forefinger together. "Ca-ching, ca-ching. God bless America, am I right, Tom?"

He does not wait for an answer before pedaling away.

Becker turns back to Gloria, whose TV interview is over. He has to hope she'll have something worthwhile for him. Sometimes, people shoot their wads so hard for TV reporters that there's little left for the print guys.

It's looking like this event is wrapping up. The police tape is removed from the doorway at Reggio's, the media is dispersing and customers are heading inside for coffee, as if none of this ever happened. Becker knows he'll be lucky to get two minutes with Gloria before her boss starts screaming for her to get back to work.

Then what? Where to go, who to interview?

The worries of the street reporter! No wonder Becker couldn't wait to get inside the cocoon of the newsroom.

At the entrance to Reggio's Gloria holds her hands up defensively at the sight of Becker with his notebook, as if she's a longtime celebrity under constant siege from a relentless media.

"One minute of your time," he begs.

"I really gotta get back to work, man."

"Hang on, hang on! I'm the one who broke the story about Clare and the skylight room in the first place. She was a friend of mine."

That last part is a lie, but he can live with it. He's lived with worse.

Gloria exhales, long and hard. "Come inside and order something. That way I won't get fired."

She takes Becker to a corner table. The rest of the media is gone. An old lady died, and left a huge tip. Cute, touching, but the real story is the heartless super model who wanted her out, and probably hastened her death.

It suddenly occurs to Becker - *that's* where everybody's heading, after getting their sound bites and quotes about the giant tip, and the shot of the old girl on the stretcher!

Becker isn't worried. Hannah Schmitt will have no comment, except for something a publicist might cook up for her. Let them all go up to Central Park West, and stake her out all night long. Smart ass Siriano is certainly on his way there, gloating about the overtime he'll be racking up.

Good, good. They're out of the way.

Becker is staying put. He'll drink as many expense account lattes as it takes to find out every little thing Gloria can tell him about Clare Owen's final moments, the stuff the others might have missed.

Gloria sets his first latte down with a dramatic flourish. "I hope you realize," she says, "that she died in that very chair you're sitting in."

"Wow." Becker's butt cheeks clench involuntarily. "Well. Life goes on, huh?"

"Yes, it does."

"Can you remember what she said to you? Her last words, so to speak?"

"Oh, man, she was *out* of it. I told her she was givin' me too much money, and she told me not to worry about it, 'cause she was the Face o' the Fifties. I mean, what the fuck was *that* all about?"

Becker sips his latte. "Face of the Fifties?"

"That's what she said."

Becker sets his cup down. "Anybody else ask you about those last words?"

Gloria shakes her head. "They just cared about the damn tip, and that bitch tryin' to throw her outta that building. I hate that shit, don'tchoo?"

"Yes I do, but you have to admit, Gloria, that was one hell of a tip." He hesitates, puts on his best shy-boy face. "Any chance I could get a look at that cash Clare gave you?"

Before she can answer they are distracted by a disturbance at the door, where a filthy homeless man is demanding to be seated. The manager is giving him the bum's rush when he holds up an ancient twenty dollar bill in his sooty fingers.

"I got money!" he shouts indignantly. "Old lady give it to me!"

CHAPTER THIRTY EIGHT

The media swarm moves to Central Park West, as Becker knew it would. Hannah Schmitt holes up in the penthouse, ignoring a blizzard of texts and voice messages. She does not issue a Twitter statement about the death of Clare Owen.

She is numb. She cannot believe what has happened, and at the same time, it makes perfect sense. Clare knew her own body as well as anyone who ever lived. When death approached, she could see it coming. She took care of her affairs and made that last trip to Reggio's, the way a dying elephant instinctively heads to the graveyard.

Hannah instructs the nanny to pick the children up from school and bring them straight home - no after-school activities, no talking to any of the media people outside the building. Then she tells the nanny to take the night off.

The kids are grumpy, so she decides to make cookies to cheer them up. She's never done it before, but she finds a roll of chocolate chip cookie dough in the refrigerator and follows the instructions on the wrapper.

Jesus, could it be any easier? Grease a tray, cut the dough into slices, lay them on the tray and stick it in the oven. All that fuss about stay-at-home mothers who bake! What's the big deal?

The kids watch with sullen faces as their mother gets it prepared and shoves the tray into the oven. They ask if it's okay to go on their iPhones, and Hannah permits it. She wants to go online and read the breaking news stories about Clare Owen.

The headlines are truly cringe-worthy. The Post goes with SKYLIGHT SAINT'S FINAL BLESSING - A HEAVENLY TIP!, while the Daily News favors A TIP TO DIE FOR, and the New York Times stays true to form with ELDERLY GREENWICH VILLAGE WOMAN, IN MIDST OF BATTLE TO KEEP APARTMENT, TIPS CAFE WAITRESS $360, THEN DIES.

Hannah comes off like the Wicked Witch of the West in every story, but there's nothing she can do about that, as everybody can say whatever the hell they want about her and then shield themselves by adding that Schmitt "could not be reached for comment."

The details, the *details!* She dies sitting up, chin to her chest! The waitress says she was the sweetest little old lady she ever served, and looked like she'd simply fallen asleep! Pending an autopsy, a doctor at Beth-Israel Hospital says there appears to have been nothing particularly wrong with Clare Owen.

"A little arthritis, some bone loss," he tells the Daily News. "Looks like she just wore out, basically."

A female columnist for Newsday writes a real hand-wringer about the plight of elderly women in New York City, and what the government must do to make their lives better.

But the city's Department of Social Services reports that they have absolutely nothing in their records about a woman named Clare Owen, so how could she have been helped?

"She existed under the radar," a spokesman says.

A fellow volunteer at the soup kitchen tells the Wall Street Journal that Clare was a devoted worker and an extremely private person.

"We wanted to honor her with a dinner for all her years of service," the volunteer says, "but she wouldn't hear of it."

It's the details of the Post story that interest Hannah the most. Only Tom Becker's report notes that the bills given to the waitress were minted during the late 40's and early 50's, as were the bills Clare distributed to a number of homeless people and street performers on her walk to Caffe Reggio.

And only Becker has the bit about Clare calling herself "The Face of the Fifties," just before she died.

That one chills Hannah to the core. Two decades ago, she was The Face Of The New Millenium.

A smoke alarm sounds. Desmond and Greta are shouting. Hannah runs to the kitchen, waves smoke away from her face and pulls out the pan of chocolate chip cookies, burned to cinders.

She bursts out crying, and not over the cookies.

She cries even harder on Monday morning, when the mail arrives.

Tom Becker is back at his desk, reading online comments for his story, still pouring in after the weekend. They're as predictable as he would expect, full of sorrowful rants and tearful Imogees for Clare, and nasty barbs directed at Hannah for the woes she caused the saintly old lady.

The one good thing about the comments page is the way it cuts down on phone calls from the general public. They vent their spleens online, and they go away.

Becker re-reads the story. It looks pretty good, considering it was written by Walter A. Larkin, who handled the rewrite duties in Becker's absence. Larkin fails to play up the wonder of the aged twenty dollar bills, and he refuses to speculate about how much money Clare might have given away in Washington Square Park.

It's a decent, non-litigious, tight-ass job you'd come to expect from a Columbia Journalism School graduate who uses his middle initial in his byline.

How different might my career have been, he wonders, if I'd written under Thomas J. Becker?

Becker's phone rings. He's actually in a playful mood, eager to mix it up with an irate reader or two.

"Becker here," he all but sings.

"Schmitt here."

A woman. He doesn't realize who it is at first, and then he does. He freezes. His scalp tingles. He craves a cigarette as he braces for the attack.

But it doesn't come. The suspense is killing him.

"What can I do for you, Miss Schmitt?"

"I need to meet with you."

He swallows. *"Meet* with me?"

"When can we meet? How about now? Does now work for you?"

"What's this about?"

"You'll find out when we meet."

"Where?"

"How about here, where I'm calling from? The skylight room. I'm guessing you know the address. Do *not* bring a photographer."

She hangs up without waiting for a reply. Becker's heart is hammering. He enters Ken Wilson's office without knocking.

"I've got to go out on a story," he says.

"Wow!" Wilson laughs. "Another day on the street! This could become habit-forming, Tom."

"Hannah Schmitt wants to see me. In the skylight room."

Wilson's mouth falls open. "You, personally?"

"Me, personally. She just phoned."

"Holy shit! Take a photographer."

"No photographer. That's the deal."

Wilson simmers for a few seconds. "Squeeze off a few shots on your phone."

"I'll try," Becker says, but it's a lie. His antiquated cell phone doesn't contain a camera.

As he climbs the stairs to the skylight room Becker, whose father was a carpenter, can imagine what must be done here. The walls to the left of the staircase will be knocked down to open up the house as a one-family dwelling, making the public staircase the interior staircase. Those giant holes will need joists and frames to make sure the building doesn't collapse, and if it's still standing they'll be ripping out old bathrooms and outdated wiring, and one floor will probably be designated as an eat-in kitchen, so everything on that floor will be ripped out.

He sees that the stairway carpet is brand-new, with that lingering chemical smell that makes your nose itch.

Why would they lay new carpet, beside walls that are about to be destroyed? The builder must be an idiot!

The architectural challenges are making his head bang by the time he reaches the top floor and taps on the door.

"Come in," says Hannah from inside, and with a turn of the loose doorknob he is in.

And there is she is, looking gaunt and haunted in a baggy navy blue warmup suit, sitting cross-legged on the bare wood plank floor. The skylight room is empty. The rug, along with Clare's bed and the rest of her measly possessions, have been carried downstairs and tossed into a dumpster.

Hannah wears no makeup and her hair is pulled back in a severe pony tail. Her eyes narrow at the sight of Becker.

"The man of the hour!" She spreads her arms. "Welcome to the room you made famous."

His heart is pounding. He needs a moment to settle down.

"Hello, Miss Schmitt," he says at last.

"Oh, call me Hannah."

Becker is truly shocked by her appearance. She doesn't look like a model. She looks like an overworked nurse at a home for the aged.

A flush of blood floods his cheeks as he remembers jerking off to her swimsuit photos in Sports Illustrated, all those years ago. Look at her now!

Gray storm clouds swirl above the skylight, and a rumble of thunder seems to tremble its panes. Hannah looks up at the sky, her cobalt-blue eyes rimmed in red. Then she turns her gaze to Becker, wide-eyed this time, and points at the door.

"No lock," she says. "She lived here without a lock on that door. Can you believe that? Anybody could have gotten in here."

"I guess she was lucky."

"She sure was, until her luck ran out." Hannah gestures at the floor. "Sit, please."

Becker settles down right in front of her, but he can't manage to cross his legs, so he sits with his hands on the tops of his knees. He'd love a smoke but doesn't dare ask if it's okay to light up.

"You're older than I imagined," Hannah says.

"Thanks. I guess that means I have a youthful writing style."

"I was going to say childish."

Becker ignores the insult, pointing at the skylight. "It's dusty."

"Yes. From the exterior renovations work."

"This room is much smaller than I imagined."

"True, but it grows on you."

"What are your plans for it?"

What a question, with Clare's body barely cold! Hannah responds with a glare familiar to the dozens of press agents she's hired and fired.

It actually makes Becker shiver. His voice fades to a whisper as he asks: "Are we trespassing, being here?"

"You tell me."

He shrugs. "Well, if she had a lifelong lease, and her life is over, and you own the building, I guess it's okay."

"So you won't be reporting me to the police for your next story?"

Becker doesn't take the bait. He looks around the barren room. "Where's her stuff?"

"I got rid of it. Junk. Even the Salvation Army wouldn't have wanted it."

He asks for permission to look in the bathroom and lets out a gasp.

"That's it? Just a toilet bowl?"

"I offered to build her a shower, but she said no."

Becker sits and leans toward Hannah. "Wait. Why would you do that, if you wanted her out?"

"Things changed. I wanted her to stay."

"But I thought - "

"What you *think* and what really *happens* are two different things,

Mr. Becker."

He can take the abuse. It's actually a relief, much milder than what he feared. He just has to hope there's more to this visit than a chance for a fading diva to rant in his face.

"Enlighten me, Hannah. Why am I here?"

"Well, this all started when my housekeeper called to tell you about the old lady I was tossing out the street, so it's only fitting that the story should wrap up with you."

"That's why you called me?"

"Actually, you're here at Clare's request, not mine."

"I don't get it."

Hannah takes a large envelope from her handbag. "This came in the mail today," she says, gently extracting a yellowed sheet of paper and passing it to Becker. It's Clare's copy of the lease she signed, kept in her safe deposit box all these years.

"She actually had quite a sense of humor," Hannah says. "Here's the note that came with it."

The blue ink is faint, as if the writer lacked the strength to press down hard on the pen:

To be torn to shreds upon my death.

"I don't think I'll do that," Hannah says, taking back the lease and the note. "I'd rather hang onto it. "Now, this other thing she sent is a real keeper."

She removes an eight-and-a-half-by-eleven photograph from the envelope and holds it out to Becker.

"Handle with care," she warns. "It's Clare, almost seventy years ago."

 It's the black-and-white shot Avedon took on the Christopher Street pier, moments after he told Clare to imagine herself back in Pittsburgh. It has Becker paralyzed. The look, the stance, the *attitude!*

"My God," Becker breathes. "Is that really *her?*"

"What do you think? Nobody else has eyes like that, man."

"She's an angel."

"Actually, she was more like a devil. But a good-natured devil. More interesting than any angel I ever knew."

"What a picture!"

"Richard Avedon took it. I assume you've heard of him."

"Jesus, are you shitting me?"

"She was on her way. That bit you had in your story about the Face of the Fifties? It could have been Clare, under different

241

circumstances."

"What were her circumstances?"

"In time, Becker, in time." She passes him another hand-written note.

"This came with the photograph. Read."

Hannah,

This is me, back in the day. Please give it to Tom Becker at the Post, to run with my obituary. Tell him I'm sorry I called him an asshole.

Yours,

Clare

Becker's hand is shaking as he returns the letter to Clare. "When did she write these notes?"

"Must have been yesterday, right after I last saw her. She knew what was coming."

"You're saying she knew she was dying?"

"Without a doubt. She tied up all her loose ends." She points at Becker like a prosecutor. "You were one of them."

He lets it all sink in. "She didn't have to apologize. She was right. I *was* an asshole."

Hannah nods. "I'd say she was right about most things. True wisdom. You don't come across it every day."

"Are you telling me you two became friends?"

Hannah nods. "Best friends, maybe."

"Come on."

She takes the photograph and slides it back into the envelope.

"Hang on," Becker says, "you're supposed to give the picture to me."

"I will, under certain circumstances."

"I'm listening."

"I want to tell Clare's story."

"Well, good, we're on the same page."

"In my own words. I'm no writer, so I'll talk it, and you write it."

"You mean, like, as told to?"

"Exactly. And I want copy approval."

Becker has to laugh. "The paper never gives anyone copy approval."

"No copy approval, no picture."

"Come *on,* Hannah."

She makes a fist and pounds the floor three times, jolting Becker. "Jesus Christ, take it easy!"

"I got burned once by the words in my own autobiography, because I was too damn lazy to proofread it! That will *not* happen again!"

It starts to rain. The drops patter the skylight, leaving clean streaks in the dust.

"What the fuck," Becker says, "it's worth a shot. I've got to pitch it to my boss. Best if I do it in person, show him the photo."

She cradles the envelope against her chest and twists to the side, as if to shield a baby from an attack dog.

"The photograph stays with me. I'm not letting it out of my sight."

"Well, then, you're coming with me, Hannah."

"Okay. In a few minutes."

She surprises Becker by lying on her back and gazing straight up. She almost looks young again.

"We'll go as soon as the rain stops," she says. "Don't you love being under a skylight in the rain?"

Becker makes a snorting sound. "Wouldn't know about that. My shithole apartment has one little window, looking out on a wall that's five feet away."

"Light is *everything*. More important than space. Clare knew that. It nourished her, kept her going. Don't be shy, lie down beside me. This is the way to enjoy it."

So Tom Becker, who has found himself in more than a few bizarre situations during his roller coaster career, stretches out on the hard floor beside the Face of the New Millenium, hands behind his head.

Hannah sniffs the air, detecting tobacco. "You smoke, don't you?"

"Yes, I do."

"Got a cigarette? I quit five years ago, but I really could use one now. There's a bowl in the sink the workmen forgot to take, the last trace of Clare. Grab it, would you, Becker? That'll be our ashtray. She wouldn't mind."

So they light up together, flicking ashes into the chipped bowl and puffing smoke toward the skylight, watching as the rain gradually washes it clean.

And deep in his belly Becker savors the street reporter's joy over the gold nugget that's landed in his lap, the one nobody else is going to get.

CHAPTER THIRTY NINE

Tom Becker and Hannah Schmitt walk through the newsroom together, triggering what would have been murmurs in the old days but which now result in texts and e-mails, shooting from desk to desk.

Who's that woman with Becker?
My God, I think it's Hannah Schmitt!
She looks like a bag lady! LOL!

They head straight into Ken Wilson's office without knocking, and as Wilson opens his mouth to object he is stunned into silence by the sight of Hannah, damp hair framing a face that seems almost wolf-like in its menace.

"Ken Wilson, Hannah Schmitt," Becker says, as if they are meeting at a cocktail party. "Hannah would like to tell her story about Clare Owen exclusively to the Post."

"Well, that's great," Wilson says.

"But we must do it *my* way," Hannah says.

They sit down to hash out the deal. Wilson is reluctant until he is shown the photograph of young Clare, and hears a few details about the life she was so close to having.

The photo blows him away. He agrees to Hannah's terms. She'll work the story with Becker, and have copy approval. This is a first in all his time at the Post, he proudly informs Hannah, and to be crystal-clear - is any other publication getting the Avedon photo?

Absolutely not, she assures him. Nobody, but *nobody,* has set eyes on this picture in seventy years. The readers of the Post will be the first.

"Go to it," Wilson says. "Bang it like a gong!"

But Becker and Hannah do not budge.

"We'll need your office," Becker says.

"What's wrong with *your* desk?"

Becker is going to answer, until Clare nudges him aside.

"We both smoke," she says to Wilson, the falsest of smiles on her face. "I understand there's no smoking in the newsroom." A catlike grin. "But we can smoke in here as long as the door is closed, right?"

All Wilson can do is grit his teeth and let them light up.

Here are Becker and Hannah in Ken Wilson's windowed cubicle, door closed, puffing away at such a frantic pace that from the outside it looks like a smoky aquarium.

They could be two Tin Pan Alley musicians from way back when, composing a song - Becker at the keyboard as Hannah paces the little room, waving her arms as she tells Clare's life story. He's clearly shocked by some of what he's hearing, amused by the rest, thrilled by it all. He types with a manic fury. She reads over his shoulder, pats his back when she's happy, shoves his shoulder when the words aren't right.

They're in there for two hours before they emerge, looking haggard, Becker carrying an aluminum pan that once held chicken lo mein noodles but now brims with cigarette butts.

"It's all yours, Ken," Becker says, referring to his cubicle.

Wilson peers into the smoky space. "Gonna give it a little time to clear. I'll read the story out here. Don't go far."

"Just for coffee," Becker says. "We'll be right back."

"How long is it?"

"I don't know. She's got enough stories for a ten-part series."

"This is a tabloid, Tom. After ten paragraphs my eyes get tired."

"Well, read ten paragraphs, take a nap and read the rest. You won't be sorry."

Wilson punches up the story on Becker's computer and starts reading. He's glad Becker isn't around to see his mouth fall open. When he gets to the last word he picks up the phone, calls the Post's legal department and asks the senior guy to please come to the newsroom.

At seventy-three Ralph Goldman is like a wise old owl, still capable of smothering a legal hot spot the way an owl pounces upon a fleeing mouse. He reads the story in Wilson's office, in the company of Wilson and Becker. It's still too smoky in there for Wilson's taste, but for this meeting privacy is a must, so he has to endure it.

Meanwhile Hannah sits at Becker's desk, holding the envelope containing the photograph to her chest and ignoring stares from all around.

Goldman's lips move as he reads. When he gets to the last word he takes his glasses off and rubs his eyes.

"Strange story," he says. "It's about the old lady, but it's also a

246

confession, isn't it?"

"We know what it is," Wilson says. "Can we go with it?"

"Well, it's pretty wild stuff, but the way I see it, it's libel-proof."

"Are you sure?" Wilson asks.

"Son, everybody in this story is dead, and the gangster isn't mentioned by name." He shrugs. "Who's around to deny anything?"

"What about the photo credit?"

Goldman turns to Becker. "May I have another look at the picture?"

Becker knocks on the glass to get Hannah's attention. She comes over and holds the picture flat to the glass so Goldman can have a second look, just like the first one she allowed. Nobody else can hold the picture until a deal is done. Goldman mouths "Thank you" and she returns to Becker's desk, shielding the photo from prying eyes.

"She really doesn't trust us, does she?" Goldman says. "I must say, I admire that."

Wilson rolls his eyes. "You know Avedon's work, Ralph. Does it look like one of his, or not?"

"It sure does."

"So we should credit him."

"I think you mean his estate. He died some years ago."

"I know he died some years ago. Don't you think we'd be calling him for an interview about this girl, if he was alive?"

"Calm yourself, Ken, calm yourself." Goldman holds up a wrinkled hand. "Legally, I must advise you to contact the Avedon estate, if such a thing exists, and get permission to publish the photo."

"What if they say 'no'?"

"That's why I'm giving you some non-legal advice, off the record - go ahead and use the photo without a credit. And I intend to forget that I gave you that advice by the time I reach the elevator."

"It's too bad," Becker says. "Avedon's name would give it that extra *oomph.*"

"You've got enough oomph here, Tom," Goldman says. "Sinatra, DiMaggio, Pollock, Salinger...oh! That's my only other question. Have either of you seen this alleged autographed copy of 'The Catcher In The Rye'?"

"It's at Hannah's apartment," Becker says.

"It better be," Wilson says. "If you can't produce it, the whole story falls apart and we look like idiots."

Goldman turns to Becker. "I'll ask you once again - have you actually seen it?"

"Yes," Becker lies. "She's keeping it in a safe. She refused to take it out in the rain."

Wilson stares at Becker. Goldman stares at both of them. Nobody caves.

"Okay, then," Goldman says, with a clap of his hands. "Let the presses roll, gentlemen, I'm really looking forward to this one."

Goldman leaves. They watch as he stops at Becker's desk, startling Hannah as he takes her hand and plants a kiss on the back of it.

"Bravo, Miss Schmitt, you truly have *class,*" he says, leaving her speechless as he departs.

Wilson turns to Becker, ears red with anger.

"You haven't been to her apartment, and you haven't seen the book."

"I know it's there, Ken. I'd bet my lungs on it."

"Your lungs wouldn't be worth much, the way you've treated them."

"Okay, then, I'd bet *your* lungs on it."

"You always have to gamble just a little bit, don't you, Tom? Even when you've already won."

"Oh, *bullshit,* man!"

"Make up a quote here, nudge the facts just a little bit there. Makes it more exciting for you, doesn't it?"

"Not this time. Every word holds up. And thanks a lot for the use of your office."

He goes to Hannah, who's both puzzled and tearful.

"Strangest thing happened, Tom. That lawyer just kissed my hand."

"He loves your story. We're good to go with it, Hannah."

She blinks to clear her eyes, which instantly turn steely. "My way?"

"Word for word. Well, we can't mention Richard Avedon, but that's the only hiccup. We'll say 'world famous photographer' instead. It's good to keep the readers guessing, anyway. Come on, let's get that picture to the photo lab, it's tomorrow's front page."

CHAPTER FORTY

The front page features a recent photo of Hannah, looking miserable on the red carpet, beside a Paul Frisch photo of Clare's face, under a screaming headline:

EXCLUSIVE! SUPER MODEL SHARES SKYLIGHT WOMAN'S AMAZING STORY!

The story jumps to page three, with Richard Avedon's photo of Clare below this headline:

A MODEL LIFE THAT NEVER WAS

By HANNAH SCHMITT
as told to Tom Becker

The stunning woman in this black-and-white photograph is Clare Owen, better known to New Yorkers as the Skylight Woman.

You know - the old lady I was trying to evict from the Greenwich Village building where she'd lived for nearly seventy years.

Look at that face. Has there ever been another face to compare with this one?

A world-famous photographer took this picture in 1951. Clare was well on her way to becoming a top fashion model - the Face of the Fifties, so to speak.

Why didn't it happen? I'll get to that. First, let me tell you about this remarkable woman who came to New York City with a burning desire to live life to the full - and by God, she did just that.

Clare started out as a waitress at the very place she died, Caffe Reggio's. She savored the free-wheeling ways of the true Greenwich Villager, with a robust love life that included flings with Frank Sinatra, Joe DiMaggio and Jackson Pollock.

But it was a love affair with a temperamental gangster that dashed Clare's dream. In a fit of rage he slashed that flawless face to ribbons when she turned down his marriage proposal,

then took his own life.

What did he want that she could not surrender? He wanted her freedom. And that was the one thing she could never, *ever* give up.

Much has been made of the huge tip Clare left for the waitress at Caffe Reggio's, the very last of her money. By giving it away, she literally died without a nickel to her name.

Where did those ancient twenty dollar bills come from? I can reveal that they were the last of a $100,000 hush-hush payoff from the gangster's family.

Clare could never tell anyone the source of that money, never tell anyone what happened to her. That was the deal she made, and she stuck to it. Incredibly, the money kept her going for almost seventy years, living as humbly as she did.

She had just one prized possession - an autographed first edition of The Catcher In The Rye, given to her by J.D. Salinger in appreciation for a magical afternoon they spent together shortly before his legendary book was published.

Just hours before she died, Clare gave me that precious book and asked me to auction it off and donate the proceeds to the soup kitchen where she worked for all those years, and to the library that meant so much to her.

Now, you may ask: Why would a woman I was trying to get rid of honor me with such a responsibility?

First of all, things had changed. We became friends, and I didn't want her to leave the skylight room. I even offered to build her the shower she never had.

But Clare didn't want the shower. All she ever wanted was what she already had.

And second, I think she felt sorry for me, and the way my life has been going.

Imagine that: a woman who lived on the very edge her whole life, taking pity on a woman who's been a totally spoiled brat for twenty years. A spoiled brat whose marriage is collapsing, whose children barely know her and whose every whim, however ridiculous, was satisfied at every turn.

The almost Face of the Fifties, looking out for the Face of the Millennium.

Funny thing is, Clare Owen was right. I am to be pitied, and she is to be mourned.

She was the bravest person I've ever known.

The story is surrounded by stock photographs of Sinatra, DiMaggio and Pollock, as well as Paul Frisch's shot of Clare on the Christopher Street pier, catching the last of the evening sun.

It's a sensation. Hannah is under siege by TV news producers, clamoring for a chance to sit her down and dig deeper into this juicy story that spills no actual juice.

Details, *details!* They all want the dirt about those famous flings, and especially about that crazy gangster who slashed that flawless face!

Everyone assumes this is Hannah's plan - to give the public a preview of what she's got to tell in the Post story, then ride the wave of publicity to her advantage. Kick-start her sagging career.

But she has nothing more to say, and she takes particular pleasure when Fred Schotter calls.

"Hannah! Wow! The woman of the hour!"

"Nice to hear from you, Fred."

"Well, the wheels are back on the car, so to speak."

"Excuse me?"

"Your show. The pulse is back. We want it."

"I'm getting divorced, Fred."

"Doesn't matter. Total re-think. We're thinking a modern-day single mom, living with her children in an old house with true history, you know? History's very *in* these days. That skylight room wants to talk to us, about all the things that happened up there with that amazing woman. Flashbacks galore, re-creations...look, I'm spitballing away here, and I hate doing that alone. Are you free for lunch?"

"Hang on, Fred, the skylight room is talking to me right now."

"Oh boy. See? This is what I'm talking about. What's it saying?"

"It's telling *me* to tell *you* to go fuck yourself."

All anyone can do is believe the story or dismiss it, the way the rival Daily News does in an editorial trashing it as "a tale of self-serving claptrap." The New York Times opts for a more cautious route, calling it "an interesting take on a long life, with no way to prove or disprove a single word of it."

The story gains legitimacy a week later, when J.D. Salinger's autograph in Clare's book is proclaimed legitimate by three handwriting experts. The book goes up for auction at Sotheby's and fetches $170,000 from an anonymous telephone bidder. In a sweet public relations coup the gallery waives its commission, noting that all the money is going to the soup kitchen and the library.

And way out in the village of Patchogue, Long Island, an 88-year-old man named Vito Positano - strong, short, wiry, with most of his marbles and very little of his hearing - is eager to have his say to a young blonde TV reporter from WLIW the day the story breaks.

The onetime night shift baker at Zito's wipes tears from his eyes as he recalls the night Frank Sinatra broke bread in the basement with Clare Owen.

"I can still see it," Vito says. "The two o' them sittin' there with my Uncle Louie, eatin' my bread, drinkin' that wine."

The reporter holds up the front page of The Post. "Are you sure it was the girl in this picture?"

He can't hear her. Vito's granddaughter, the one who arranged this interview, shouts the question into his ear.

He nods vigorously. "Yeah, that's her. For sure."

"How can you be so sure?" the reporter asks, attempting to put an edge on an edgeless story.

The granddaughter shouts the question into his ear. Vito's brow knots. He is insulted.

"It's her," Vito insists. "You don't forget eyes like that."

"Did you ever see her again?" the reporter shouts, to avoid repetition.

Vito shakes his head. Fresh tears trickle down his craggy cheeks. "No," he says. "I got drafted. They sent me to Korea. I thought about that face o' hers many times, in my foxholes. A face like that gets you through a war."

In the midst of the day's excitement Becker taps on Wilson's door and waits like a rookie to be beckoned inside.

Wilson spreads his hands. "Sensational," he says. "No other word for it, Tom. Truly."

"I'll take it."

Wilson is puzzled. "You'll take what?"

"The buyout."

Wilson is shocked. "Are you kidding?"

"No, Ken. I'll take the money and go."

"Why?"

"Ever heard of Ted Williams, Ken?"

"You mean the baseball player whose kids had his head cryogenically frozen after he died?"

Becker sighs. "Yeah, well, long before *that* happened, he was a hell of a ballplayer, and he hit a home run in his last time at bat. He went out on a good one, and that's what I want to do."

"You mean *now?*"

"They can send me the paperwork."

"Jesus, Tom, we wouldn't mind a little notice!"

"Sorry. Thanks for everything. Sign this, will you?"

Becker slides an expense sheet across Wilson's desk. It's for $18.75 - three lattes plus tip at Caffe Reggio's, with the printout receipt stapled to the sheet.

"Long time since I've filed an expense sheet. Let me tell you, Ken, these printed receipts make it hard to cheat."

"Is that right?"

"Oh, *please.* In the old days I'd have taken a hand-written receipt for this amount and made the one into a four, gotten myself an extra thirty bucks."

Becker winks. Wilson laughs, signs the sheet and puts it in his out box. They shake hands.

"Good luck, you son of a bitch," he says to Becker's departing back.

"Mail me what I got coming," Becker says over his shoulder. "And don't forget my expenses."

Everyone watches in silence as he tosses his stuff into a cardboard box. There isn't much. He hoists the box and heads for the elevator, pushes the 'down' button and waits until the doors open before turning to face the newsroom for the last time.

"So long, you fuckers!" Tom Becker shouts, and he is gone.

253

CHAPTER FORTY ONE

The work on the house kicks into full gear upon Clare's death. Sledge hammers swing, buzz saws whine, cement mixers spin, illegal alien laborers sweat. Dumpsters are filled with broken plaster and old appliances, endless delivery trucks screw up traffic, neighbors complain.

Six months and seven hundred thousand dollars later, the building is ready to be occupied. The ground floor is an eat-in kitchen. The floor above that is the living room, the one above that is Desmond's bedroom, the next one up is Greta's.

The skylight room is Hannah's.

The splintery floor has been sanded and lacquered, the crumbling putty surrounding the individual skylight panes scraped out and re-filled to fend off leaks, and the walls suck up a coat of primer and three coats of white paint to hide the years. A hole has been cut in the western wall to install an air conditioner, the sink in the skylight room has been taken away and the tiny refurbished bathroom now has a sink and a toilet - but still no shower.

Which is fine. There are two full bathrooms to choose from downstairs.

The radiator Clare used to dry her clothing in wintertime is gone, and not replaced. Hannah likes a chilly room, and anyway, the heat from the rooms below rises to warm her.

The furnishings are nearly as sparse as they were in Clare's time - a bed, an end table and a lamp. There are pictures of Hannah's kids on the walls, and in one corner hangs Avedon's photograph of Clare in a silver frame, above a small clay urn containing her ashes.

Hannah says good morning and good night to the urn, every day.

She is pretty much left alone on the street, maybe because she's not easily recognizable, as she has gained fifteen pounds. The extra weight takes away her cheekbones but greatly improves her temperament. Maybe part of the reason she was so bitchy all those years was because she was always hungry.

The divorce goes through, with plenty of money all around.

Hannah has more time and more patience for her children. They turn out to be interesting people. Desmond looks like his father, but he's a terrible athlete, though a gifted artist. Greta can't stand girly stuff, and she's a wonderful athlete. She's a star basketball player at the Carmine Street Recreational Center, the same place where Clare swam and showered all those years.

An artistic son, and a jock daughter. Funny how the wires can get crossed on a thing like that.

Becker has trouble with retirement. The push-pull of the newsroom is gone, that daily rugby game between nouns and verbs...he feels more like a retired athlete than a burned-out reporter.

He quits Tinder, and he doesn't miss it. He's not feeling terribly sexual these days.

He looks up a retired reporter or two, meets them for lunch at Wo Hop's in Chinatown, but all they want to talk about is their grandchildren and their blood pressure. The grandchildren talk sounds mandatory, but they're truly passionate about their blood pressure, especially if it's right on the edge of where it should be.

"This could put me in the ground," says an old timer named Herbie Fletcher, as his shaky hand struggles to keep a fried dumpling dripping with soy sauce from falling off the tips of his chopsticks.

Becker forces a smile. "More likely you'll go up the chimney than in the ground, Herbie."

"Whatever. Here goes." He shoves the dumpling in his mouth, clutches his chest, fakes a heart attack.

Becker's soul sinks. He signals to the waiter. "Could we get a check over here, please?"

He's shaken when Paul Frisch is killed, run over by a bus while cycling the wrong way down West 78th Street in pursuit of a popular TV news anchorman and his mistress en route to their love nest. Becker reads about it in the Post but chooses not to attend the funeral. He's never been good at funerals, and he never really liked Frisch.

He smokes as much as he ever did, sometimes a little more. He thinks about moving to Florida or the Carolinas, with all that more-for-your-money bullshit they throw at you, but what would be the point? To extend a life that already feels too long?

Then one day, the cough arrives. Not the usual hack-up-a-morning-bouillion-cube cough Becker has known for years. This one begins deep in his chest, as if he's been shot in the back with an arrow.

He hates hospitals, but he goes for a checkup. The doctor is young, grave and handsome. He listens to Becker's chest, thumps his back, makes a few notes.

"How long have you been smoking, and how much?"

"Pack a day, since forever."

The doctor actually whistles. "Filters?"

"Yes."

"Well, that's something, at least."

"You're not much of a cheerleader, are you, Doc?"

The doctor folds his arms. "Smoking is like a roulette wheel, Mr. Becker. The wheel spins fast when you're young, but eventually it slows down, and then one day, it lands on your number."

"Great."

"Look, we're getting ahead of ourselves, here. Let's get some X-rays, see what we're dealing with."

"What year were you born, Doc?"

He's jolted by the question, hesitating before saying, "Nineteen eighty-six."

Becker's eyes widen. "The year the Space Shuttle blew up!"

He grins at the memory, the same wistful way some parents grin when they think of their children who've grown and moved away. "January, it was, so it was probably before you were born. Seven people died on the Challenger, including a schoolteacher they took on board. Can't remember her name."

"Mr. Becker - "

"McAuliffe! Christa McAuliffe! It blew up right after take-off, on live TV. *Christ!* Al Ellenberg was on the desk. Points at me and Mel Juffe and says, 'Divide 'em up.' I wrote four obits, Mel took the other three. We're typing away while the wreckage is still falling into the ocean. Talk about a deadline, baby..."

He stops talking. His eyes brim with tears.

"Are you all right, sir?" the doctor asks.

Becker wipes his eyes. "They never knew what hit 'em. And that poor schoolteacher! A mother, with young kids! What the hell was *she* doing on the fucking Space Shuttle?"

"I really don't know," the doctor says. "But we're facing a deadline of our own, here."

"Ooh, nice segue, Doc."

256

"The sooner we get those X-rays, the better." He consults a schedule on his computer screen. "We're jammed up today. Tomorrow morning, ten o'clock?"

With a quivering hand Becker fills out the paperwork for a series of X-rays to be taken the next day, and leaves the hospital.

He steps outside and starts walking downtown. It's a beautiful day. The sky is as blue as he's ever seen it, the clouds are fluffy puffs of cotton, and he's about to die of lung cancer.

His phone rings. No caller ID. Usually he ignores these calls, but he takes this one. Maybe it's the hospital, saying forget the X-rays, you're probably fine, just quit smoking, you *idiot!*

"Hello there Becker," the caller says, and his scalp tingles. It's been a year since he heard this urgent voice, but there is no mistaking it for anyone else's.

"Hannah. How the hell are you? How's the house?"

"Can you meet me at the end of the Christopher Street pier?"

He can't help laughing. She's all business. But this is just what he needs to get out of his head, however briefly.

"I'm not a reporter any more, you know."

"I know. Doesn't matter. Can you meet me?"

"Sure. When?"

"Half an hour."

"It'll take me that long to walk there," he says, but by then he's talking to a dead line.

Hannah is already there when Becker arrives, leaning back on the rail that faces Hoboken. He tries not to look shocked by her appearance. She's downright dowdy in a gray sweat suit, her hair pulled back in a ponytail that makes those chubby cheeks look even chubbier. Before he can speak, she does.

"Yes, I gained some weight."

"I didn't notice."

"The hell you didn't. How are you, Becker?"

"A little worried about this virus in China."

"I'm sure it's nothing. Just a way to scare people and sell newspapers."

"I wouldn't bet on that."

"Mr. Doom and Gloom.. So what are you doing these days?"

"Enjoying retirement."

"The hell you are."

"It sucks, actually. Heard your divorce went through. Are you dating?"

"No, but I'm mothering, which is nice. You?"

"No, I'm not mothering."

"Always the wise guy. Are you dating?"

Becker shakes his head. "I'm not much of a catch. Social Security and a pathetic pension."

"Some girls might jump at that."

"You wouldn't."

"Not in a million years."

They both burst out laughing.

It's a weird, weird scene. They have not hugged, or even shaken hands. Becker doesn't seem to know what to do with his hands. He'd love to light a cigarette, but he resists the impulse. Does it make sense to quit, at this point? He shoves his hands in his pockets, like a child who's been told he cannot have a lollipop.

Hannah stares out at the water, in a daydream. Has she forgotten he's there, that she actually summoned him? He's losing patience. He doesn't have all the time in the world anymore, but he's not about to tell this woman about his medical woes. That would make them all too real.

"What the hell are we doing here, Hannah?" he asks at last.

Hannah snaps out of the daydream and gestures at the area around them. "This pier was Clare's favorite place. She came here to read. It's where Avedon took that picture of her."

"Really?"

"I think it's as good a resting place as any, don't you?"

She slips a small knapsack off her back and removes the clay urn, cradling it like a bowling ball.

"Holy shit," Becker says.

"I kept her in the skylight room, but I could feel her getting antsy. She would have been ninety-one today, so for her birthday, I'm setting her free. Thought you'd like to be here."

"Got a feeling this isn't legal."

"Wouldn't be any fun if it was, would it, Tom?"

Becker looks around. A stiff, steady wind has kept a lot of people away, but there are a few here and there, reading on benches and napping on blankets they've spread on the grassy lawn that splits the pier.

She hands him the urn. "You dump the ashes. I'll be the

lookout."

It's heavier than it looks. Becker kneels on the edge of the pier, takes the lid off the urn and faces New Jersey. Seconds go by, then a full minute before Hannah hisses: *"Now!"*

He dumps the ashes, which swirl in a ghostly gray cloud before falling like a long ribbon on the waters of the Hudson.

"The urn and the lid, too....*now!"*

The lid sinks instantly. The urn bobs around as it fills slowly with water, sinking from sight a hundred yards out.

Becker stands up. "We're lucky the wind was blowing out, or we'd both be wearing her."

Hannah stares at the spot where the urn went down, as if to preserve it in memory. "Happy birthday, my friend," she whispers.

Becker touches her shoulder. "Heading back?"

"Not yet," she says, maintaining the stare. "You take care, now. Thanks for coming."

It's a dismissal. Once a diva, always a diva. Becker gives her shoulder an affectionate squeeze and leaves the pier.

But when he reaches the West Side Highway, he does not head for home. He crosses the highway, walks to Hannah's house and stands in front of it for a good long look.

It is stunning. Freshly pointed bricks, brand-new rectangular stone window sills, a refurbished front stoop, shining windows, a front door that's been scraped and sanded and painted in a glossy lipstick red.....no corners cut here. It's all perfect. He crosses to the other side of the street, but even from here, he can only make out the edge of the skylight room as he looks up.

Some day she'll invite me in to see what she's done with it, he thinks.

If I'm still alive.

He's still not ready to head home, so he keeps walking. Maybe he just doesn't want to think about tomorrow, and the X-rays, and information that just cannot be good. He needs distractions.

Anyway, it's a perfect day for a stroll around Greenwich Village, and he soon find himself on Bleecker Street, where things have really changed. Gone are the Mom-and-Pop shops he remembers, replaced by flagship stores, Ralph Lauren and Marc Jacobs. And the charming Parrot Jungle on the corner of West Eleventh Street is now Magnolia's Bakery, where people line up to buy costly cupcakes.

Do they ever find feathers in the icing?

But the Abingdon Square playground is still intact, and as Becker watches toddlers being pushed on the swings a memory pierces his heart like a dagger. A single word comes to mind, and it's not even really a word, but boy, it nearly knocks him on his ass.

Da-da.

And suddenly, this seemingly aimless walk has a destination.

Look! It's a bodega fronted by buckets of flowers, mostly roses and carnations, red and white and pink.

When was the last time he bought flowers? He can't remember. Whenever it was, the price has sure gone up - nine bucks for a small cone of carnations! He pays the Korean shop keeper and continues down Bleecker with the paper-wrapped flowers, his heart pounding. He reaches Bank Street and stops.

He recognizes the building, the way an old dog remembers that spot where he buried a bone. He lifts the latch on the wrought iron gate, walks three steps down to the basement door and knocks.

The sound of a rusty lock turning, and then the door opens. Wild-haired Sheila Greene stands there looking at him, momentarily dumbfounded by the sight of this man and his flowers.

Then it hits her, and she's even more disturbed to realize it's that old guy from that long-ago disastrous Tinder date at Caffe Reggio's. Does he want a second chance? It takes her a moment before the name comes to her as well.

"Tom, right?" she says. "Jesus, how did you *find* me?"

He ignores the question, clears his throat and squares his shoulders, for the first time in years.

"Is your mother home?" he asks.

THE END

Printed in Great Britain
by Amazon

68008665R00153